WILDCAT
PLAY

WILDCAT PLAY

A MYSTERY

HELEN KNODE

HOUGHTON MIFFLIN HARCOURT · BOSTON · NEW YORK
2012

For information about permission to reproduce selections from this book, write to Permissions, Houghton Mifflin Harcourt Publishing Company, 215 Park Avenue South, New York, New York 10003.

www.hmhbooks.com

Library of Congress Cataloging-in-Publication Data
Knode, Helen.
Wildcat play : a crime adventure / Helen Knode.
p. cm.
ISBN 978-0-15-100429-4
I. Title.
PS3611.N63W55 2012
813'.6—dc23
2011044598

Book design by Brian Moore

Printed in the United States of America

DOC 10 9 8 7 6 5 4 3 2 1

To the Knodes

WILDCAT
PLAY

1

I STOOD AT THE window of the Kwik Gas and suddenly laughed out loud. The only people on the streets of Wilson at two A.M. were drunks leaving the bar, meth addicts, and cops. I watched a patrol car glide into the curb across the way. A policeman got out to check on a guy who'd collapsed in front of the newspaper office.

What on *earth* was I doing here?

I'd left L.A. to come live with an old family friend in Wilson, an oil town in the San Joaquin Valley over the mountains to the north. But for weeks I couldn't find a job. I'd discovered that being an ex-journalist and –movie critic qualified me for nothing. In fact, it made people suspicious. It made them even more suspicious that I'd settle for any crumb-bum gig when my only reference was Joe Balch, Wilson's leading citizen and largest local employer. Then yesterday the manager at the Kwik Gas hired me for nights – and tonight was my first shift on.

I watched a battered sedan pull up and park outside. There was a kid asleep in the car seat in back.

The woman driving wore a parka over her nightgown. She came in to buy five dollars' worth of gas and a pack of cigarettes. Not bothering anymore with hello or a smile, I took her money and switched on the pump she asked for. I'd been making some version of that sale for hours – gas and cigarettes, beer and/or candy. Occasionally a quart of motor oil or milk. People who used the Kwik Gas, I'd learned, did not smile or want to chat, especially after midnight.

The woman left and I turned back to the window. Smiling, I tapped my reflection in the glass.

Ann Whitehead.

Of Calgary and Paris and L.A.

I was barely thirty-five and my life was a smoking ruin.

A year ago I'd found a woman murdered in the guesthouse where I lived behind a mansion in the Hollywood Hills. I pushed my way into the LAPD investigation and, in the process, fell in love with Detective Douglas Lockwood. The investigation led to near death for me, bloody death for three people – which I witnessed up close – and a political scandal. I'd quit my hip, happening newspaper job because movies and hip tasted like dust. With no idea what to do next, I spent my savings and sold my laptop and car to eat. I was living out of a suitcase, sleeping on a girlfriend's couch, and resisting Doug's invitation to move in when Joe Balch said come to Wilson. Joe and his wife, Alice, were old friends of my grandparents. I'd known the Balches since before I was born.

Leaning closer to the glass I checked my face. It was tough to see with the lights of the store behind me.

I'd deserved every minute of the apocalypse, though, and felt like a better person for it. Dire experience had also improved my looks.

Not physically. Physically I was about the same as a year ago. I was still attractive, without being pretty, in a small, athletic way – and still had too much unrestrained personality around the jaw line, although my brown hair seemed wavier and my blue eyes were sparkling again after being so dead and harrowed. The big thing was, I was finally over the worst. I was feeling coherent inside, more stuck together, and my humor was back. That's really what improved me, I thought: the return of my normal sense of fun.

Engine rumble caught my ear and I looked outside. A tractor-trailer hauling drillpipe went screaming by headed east, probably to Bakersfield.

I watched the semi disappear and flashed on a scene from one of my favorite movies — *Sunset Boulevard.*

It's New Year's Eve, the night Joe Gillis realizes Norma Desmond's in love with him. He and Norma are lounging on a divan in her private ballroom and she's bought him a gold cigarette case he doesn't want to accept. He says she's bought him too much already. Norma doesn't get what his problem is: she has tons of money. The way Gloria Swanson says it, she lolls her head back, flaps her wrists inward, and goes, "I'm *rrrich.*" She describes how rich she is, listing her various investments and ending with "I've got oil in Bakersfield *pump*ing, *pump*ing, *pump*ing." Her wrists flap in a bored way with each *pump* in *pumping.* She even sticks one leg up and flaps a bored foot.

Lifting my foot, I flapped it in rhythm and said out loud, "Pumping, pumping, pump —"

"Open the cash register and give me the money."

I froze.

The guy was standing behind me pointing a gun at my back. He had on dark glasses and his hair looked like a wig in the reflection.

"Now."

Anger boiled up so fast I almost choked. This was *not* going to happen my first shift.

"No — I — won't!"

Yelling, I twirled and slapped the gun right out of the guy's hand. It went flying down an aisle as I raced around the counter:

"Get out of here! Get out of here! Get out of here! Get out of here!"

Caught off-guard, the guy started to back away. I shoved him towards the entrance.

"Go get a job, you freaking loser! There's a boom on in the oil fields! The price of crude oil is at record highs!"

He caught his sleeve on a rack and spun around. I kicked his leg, snatched the door open, and shoved him out to the parking lot.

"Drilling companies are hiring! Service companies are hiring! Western Well is hiring! Halliburton is hiring! Balch is hiring!"

The guy tripped over the sidewalk, losing his glasses, stumbling for balance. He didn't see and I didn't see the cops who'd pulled in for gas. I was yelling and the guy was running and out of the dark two cops were there. Shouting, "Stop!," they blocked the guy, knocked him down, and had him spread-eagled and cuffed in four seconds flat. The guy was too surprised to resist.

I yelled, "He tried to rob the store!"

The cops looked over as my knees gave way and I sat down abruptly on the concrete.

One cop hurried up to me. "Are you okay?"

I managed to nod, then burst out laughing. I was shaking from the adrenaline, panting for breath, and I could feel sweat dripping down my face. But still, I had to laugh.

The armed robber was a sign. It was time to take my own advice.

2

"WHAT AM I GOING to tell your grandmother, Ann?"

Alice looked up from reading as she heard me cross the foyer. It was her cocktail hour. She was sitting on the sectional sofa in the living room, a glass of red wine in one hand and a letter in the other. A fire was burning in the fireplace and she had a string quartet on the stereo. I walked in and flopped down on the carpet beside the coffee table. A decanter stood on the table with a wineglass for me, and Luz had put out a plate of deep-fried flautitas and hot sauce.

Alice repeated, "What am I going to tell Evelyn?"

"You could tell her that fall in the San Joaquin Valley is beautiful and they've started harvesting the cotton." I grabbed a flautita.

Alice made a face of distaste and studied me over her reading glasses. I chewed the flautita and reached to pour myself some wine.

I'd never figured out how to like Alice.

She and Joe had lived apart for ages, and she'd moved to L.A. where she turned herself into a Beverly Hills snob in the old-money style. A youthful sixty, icy blond, tight-faced, and too thin, she was perpetually in classic Chanel and perfectly groomed. I'd never seen Alice not looking perfect — not her hair or makeup, not her gold and pearl necklaces, not her cream silks and wools. She was my grandmother's best friend and she acted and thought so exactly like Evelyn it was weird. But those were only two of the reasons I had a hard time liking her.

Alice sipped her wine. "I'm very serious, Ann. Your grandmother would be horrified to know you were working at a gas station. She would blame me."

I reached for another flautita and dipped it in hot sauce. Alice didn't like me, either. She just didn't realize it.

"Hey, Evelyn should be proud—"

Interrupting, Alice pointed the letter she was holding at the flautitas. "We cannot eat these—they're much too greasy." She raised her voice. "Luz!"

Luz appeared from the kitchen wiping her hands on her apron. She was a short, plump older woman who wore baggy men's shirts over stretchy pants and kept her bun up with a ribbon.

Alice pointed at the plate. "Take this away, Luz, and would you please not serve it to Mr. Balch, thank you? We must be careful of his heart now."

"*Sí, señora.*"

I gave Luz a low-lid look that she returned as she walked in to remove the flautitas. Joe'd had a mild heart attack after I moved up to Wilson and Alice was using his health as an excuse for this visit. Frowning, she watched Luz until she left the room. I continued my sentence.

"Evelyn should be proud—the cops say I stopped a one-man crime wave. That guy was wanted for armed robbery all over the county." I smiled. "They've asked me to join Wilson PD. I have to put on a hundred pounds but they'll waive the height requirement—"

Alice clipped, "You will not. Under no circumstances. The sensible idea, don't you think, is to come back to Los Angeles? There is clearly nothing for you here, and with my charity work and social calendar I'm in need of a personal assistant. It would make your grandmother happy. She and I have already discussed it."

I quit smiling and took a slow drink of wine, buying time as I contemplated evasions.

Alice tapped the letter on her knee. "Well, Ann? Shall we say L.A.?"

"Alice, I don't—"

Joe's den was kitty-corner from us, at the far end of the foyer. His door swung open and saved me.

Joe walked out with two men, everybody trailing cigar smoke and talking. They had the country twang of the area and their voices were loud from liquor. The pear-shaped man was CFO of Balch Corporation—Joe's money guy. He was also running the oil company since Joe's heart attack. The bowlegged man in denim work clothes ran Joe's drilling business. They didn't give a hoot about me so I liked to torment them by being friendly.

"Hi, Mr. Mahin. Mr. Bray." I wiggled my fingers. "How are you this evening?"

That got lukewarm nods. But they gave Alice a distinct nod and an "Alice" as Joe herded them outside to their trucks. When he came back in I said:

"I have to talk to you, Joe."

"Not before I talk to you, young lady." He shut the front door. "Is this story about the Kwik Gas true?"

I drank a fast mouthful of wine and jumped up. "I was going to tell you but you were sleeping, then I was sleeping—"

Joe gestured in the direction of his suite. Alice said, "Joseph, you know you're not supposed to smoke."

Deadpanning her, Joe started across the foyer. He motioned for me to follow him with his cigar.

Alice set her glass down and stood, smoothing her necklaces. "I would like to speak with you first, dear. It's important. It concerns Junior."

She showed him the letter she'd had with her this whole time. Joe waved his cigar for her to come along also.

The house had two wings, off the right and left of the foyer. We turned right and trooped down the hall. Me in the rear, breathing expensive perfume, I thought again how mismatched the Balches

7

were. Alice was a low-voltage Doheny and Joe looked like a work-ing rancher – tall and spare, gray and weathered, with a crook in his back from roughnecking that made him slant. He was ten years older than her too, and looked older than that because of his hard, outdoor life.

Alice followed Joe into his sitting room and tried to close the door on me. Joe said, "Let her come in."

"But, Joseph. Junior –"

"She's family. She can hear."

Alice stepped aside and I went in. I was living across the hall and Joe's main room was similar to mine, in the same tans and browns, like the whole house – and it ran to the same oil theme in the books and pictures. But Joe had a drill bit, polished and mounted, by the fireplace, and his furniture was arranged to make space for a wet bar and a desk with two computers on it. One screen was showing that day's oil prices from the Bakersfield paper. The other showed an international oil newsletter with an ad for a conference in Dubai, and headlines from Calgary, Houston, China, and Norway.

Alice said bluntly, "Ray Junior is dead."

Joe was silent. He walked over to the sliding glass doors on the far side of the room.

Ray Parkerworth Junior was Alice's younger half brother. He'd run away as a teenager and was a painful subject for Joe. I only knew that because Joe never talked about anything painful to his feelings, and he and I had never talked about Junior beyond brief mentions of his name.

"This arrived today from Louisiana." Alice held the letter up. "I hope you don't mind – I opened it."

Turning his back on us, Joe gazed out the doors. "How did it happen?"

"I don't know. The letter doesn't say. It was written by a friend of Junior's from a welding shop and the man is barely literate. I don't know why he didn't just call you if he found your address among Junior's things. It has already been a week."

Alice waited for a response. Joe just puffed on his cigar.

"I am flying to New Orleans tomorrow morning. They're holding the body in a small town on the gulf."

Joe half turned, but didn't look at Alice. "You? Why you, for Christ's sake?"

"Please, Joseph – your language."

Joe turned away again as Alice said, "Because there is nobody else. The doctor won't let you travel and Luz can't be trusted –"

Joe cut in. "His mother."

"I have called down there and left a message. Who knows where she is – she might be anywhere."

"You'll bring Junior back to Wilson. We'll bury him on the Westside with his father."

"He may have had other wishes. He's been gone for such a long –"

Joe cut in again. "Ray Parkerworth's son belongs *here*."

Alice's mouth tightened slightly. "You're right, of course, dear. I would be very surprised if Junior left any formal instructions. I'll take care of it."

Scrunching the letter in her hand, Alice looked at me. "We will continue our discussion at dinner."

She walked out, perfume wafting, necklaces jingling. I started to go also, thinking Joe might want to be alone –

"What discussion is that, miss?"

Joe signaled me to come join him so I crossed the room and stood on his right as he pressed a latch and opened the glass door. A cold wind blew in through the screen and we heard a squalling noise in the distance. Joe was drilling a wildcat north of the house – that noise was the brake on the drawworks of the rig. It sounded like the trumpet of an elephant combined with the screechy sound of metal on metal.

"Isn't it pretty?" Joe tapped the mesh of the screen.

I cupped my hands around my eyes to look out. There was a windbreak of eucalyptus behind the house, but the country was flatter than flat and you could see the lights of the derrick through a gap in the trees.

Dropping my hands, I said, "It always reminds me of an elephant."

"Not a white elephant, I pray to a merciful God."

"I saw heavy crude broke seventy." I pointed behind us at the computer screens on the desk.

"Natural gas is up too."

"Alice and Evelyn want me to move back to L.A. and become Alice's pet poodle . . . I mean personal assistant."

Joe flicked a glance over. Deadpan was an art form in the oil fields and Joe was a grand master. No matter the provocation, he rarely changed his expression and his gestures were never big.

"She may also want me to lecture her movie group. From Billy Wilder to Bollywood."

"But you're finally coming to roughneck for me."

I smiled. I don't remember saying it, but according to Whitehead family legend, I was three years old on a trip to Wilson when I uttered the immortal line "Joe, me wuffneck."

"High time. I wasn't going to ask you again."

"I resigned at the Kwik Gas after the cops took their prisoner away."

"Let me see what I can do." Joe patted my shoulder. "Some of these crews I wouldn't want you within a mile of."

Which was precisely why, although he was desperate for rig hands, I'd hesitated about his offer before. When I was a child, roughnecking seemed all romance and glamour. I knew better as an adult.

"Thanks, Joe. Thank you."

He nodded and took a puff of his cigar. Turning to leave, I heard him say quietly, "Junior—poor kid."

I thought he was talking to me and glanced back. But he was talking to the screen, and the wind had carried his voice into the room.

3

NEXT AFTERNOON I WAS jolted out of a deep sleep by two thuds on the hall door. My eyes jerked open and I rolled over in bed, disoriented. I could never get to sleep anymore until the sun came up.

The door creaked as someone opened it. Joe called, "You awake?"

"I am now!"

"Sloth is a deadly sin. Meet me out front in fifteen minutes."

I kicked off the covers, jumped in the shower, threw on some clothes, grabbed a jacket and my Balch Oil baseball cap, and ran outside, stopping to button buttons when I felt how cold the day was. Joe was waiting in the passenger seat of the white pickup that said BALCH WEST VALLEY OIL & GAS.

He said, "*Vamanos.* You're driving."

I ran around and climbed in the truck. It was a new Chevy with bucket seats and no fancy extras. Joe was wearing a Stetson and a blue Balch Oil windbreaker with a derrick stenciled on it in white. I pulled the bill of my cap down against the sun and reached for the ignition.

I said, "The key's not here."

Joe glanced at the empty ignition slot and hit the catch on the glove compartment. "Check under the floor mat."

11

I tried under the floor mat and behind the visor while Joe rummaged through the console between the seats.

I said, "I bet Alice hid it. You're not supposed to be working."

"Look in the other truck. Should be a spare key and some cigarettes in the glove box."

The other truck had BALCH WEST VALLEY DRILLING on the driver's door and was parked farther around the circle drive. Jumping out, I ran and ran back, getting in behind the wheel and passing him the pack and lighter I'd found with the key.

"I'm smoking. No arguments." Joe tapped out a cigarette.

I started the engine and rolled down both windows for air. Putting the truck in gear, I pulled around the circle to the highway.

Joe's house was a large, ugly ranch in tan stucco with scraggly shade trees and a front yard full of gravel and cactus. It sat in open country between the east edge of Wilson and Interstate 5, miles from other houses and surrounded by orchards, cotton fields, and desert floor covered with tumbleweed and sage. A two-lane highway ran in front – the main road off the interstate to Wilson and the Belridge oil fields to the west.

I said, "Where to?"

"Minerva."

Hitting the turn signal, I watched traffic both ways. Booms were a busy time. Trucks of every size, weight, and use barreled by, most of them with company names – big names like Halliburton and Chevron, and smaller local companies for well services and equipment rental. California was the fourth-largest oil producer after Texas, Louisiana, and Alaska, and Kern County, where Wilson was, pumped 62 percent of California's oil. More oil every day than Oklahoma, Joe once told me.

Joe said, "You waiting for an invitation?"

I smiled and pressed the gas, turning left onto the highway, then making an immediate left onto the blacktop road at the east end of his property. To our right was a field of recently harvested cotton, rows and rows of bare black stalks, and white fluff blowing in the ditches. Minerva, the wildcat Joe was drilling, was off to our left.

The rig stood by itself in the middle of the fields, visible for miles in every direction.

I made another left at another blacktop road running west, parallel to Joe's back fence and the line of eucalyptus trees.

Up ahead at the intersection with the lease road there were two white metal signs. The small one was propped against the corner fence post and chained. It said OZARK DRILLING – RIG #184. The large one stood in the ground on metal legs. It said MINERVA NO.1-27 – BALCH-MIN LLC – BALCH FEE, and there were section numbers at the bottom. There was also a big POSTED NO TRESPASSING sign and a big PRIVATE PROPERTY – KEEP OUT sign.

I slowed down and made the right. The rig was straight ahead, and exactly due north of the house. In three minutes we'd driven in a sort of square – east, north, west, north again.

I said, "Remind me how much oil Oklahoma produces every day."

The lease road was gravel and I took it slow because it was washboardy from heavy trucks. With the our windows down, the rig engines were getting louder and louder.

Joe sucked on his cigarette and blew smoke out the window. "A hundred seventy thousand barrels, give or take. Stop for this youngster here."

He meant the stumpy old guy who appeared at the trailer that guarded the lease entrance. The lease was surrounded by barbwire and the entrance had a barrier gate. Right of the gate was another metal sign from Ozark Drilling: ALCOHOL, DRUGS, AND FIREARMS NOT PERMITTED ON LEASE.

The stumpy old guy walked up to my window. Ignoring me, he saw who I was driving and said, "Joe!"

"Afternoon, Tommy. Are you going to let me on or do I have to show two forms of ID?"

"I'll get the gate right now. Nobody told me you were coming."

Tommy cranked the barrier arm up and I pulled onto the lease, which was graded and graveled like the road. I'd driven Joe to the Minerva lease several times since his heart attack. Per ritual,

I swung around and parked, and he climbed out and disappeared into his trailer. He reappeared wearing a Balch Oil hardhat instead of his Stetson and carrying a pair of safety glasses.

He walked to the next trailer – a long portable like his – with a dirty green pickup in front. Stepping up on the metal stoop, he pounded on the door and then opened it without waiting. A few minutes later he emerged with Emmet. Joe was a fair-sized man but Emmet was a massive hulking bear: he made Joe look almost frail. Emmet wore overalls and a padded jean jacket, and he shouted into Joe's ear as they crossed the open yard between the trailers and the rig.

On this side of the rig there were two ways up to the floor – an open-cage elevator at one corner and a steep set of stairs at the other. Joe and Emmet got into the elevator and rode it up. I had to crane my neck to watch. This was the biggest land rig I'd ever been around. From where I was, I could only see the doghouse and lower part of the derrick.

When I lost sight of the two men, I took off my sunglasses, leaned back, and shut my eyes. A faint smell of diesel exhaust blew in the open windows and the steady roar of the engines lulled me to sleep before I knew it.

For the second time that day I was jolted awake by two thuds on a door. Sitting up, I rubbed my eyes and saw Emmet looming beside the truck. He crooked a finger at me, and I climbed out and followed him to his trailer. The sun had set and I realized I was freezing.

Joe was sitting on a threadbare couch reading papers, his face and hands red from the cold. Emmet was red from the cold too. He took off his hardhat and jean jacket, and sat down in a rolling chair at the desk. I removed my cap, rubbed my hands together, and glanced around for a place to sit. Emmet obviously used the couch to nap – there was a bed pillow on the far armrest – so I chose the desk. I bent my leg and perched one hip on the corner.

Joe said, "Be with you in a minute."

Nodding, I looked around. Emmet was an old friend of Joe's

from Wilson. His people were Dust Bowl Okies. At some point he'd gone out to Oklahoma to work and, at Joe's request, came back with this rig. I only knew him to say hey and had never seen his inner sanctum.

The trailer was narrow and too warm and too bright with overhead fluorescents. A wide window faced the rig, and Emmet had a long desk underneath it. Besides a computer there was stuff all over the desk, and stuff tacked all over the walls — pictures, papers, diagrams, charts, graphs, clipboards, a swimsuit calendar from a wellhead company. A TV at the end of the desk was playing rodeo with the volume off. And the place smelled like spaghetti sauce. There was a little kitchen opposite the door and two pots on the little electric stove. Steam was rising from the taller pot, and dried spices sat on the counter with a cutting board and part of an onion.

Joe remarked, "Smells good."

Emmet had his finger on something on the computer screen. He reached for the telephone and punched three numbers as he said:

"I is refinin the recipe. I brown my onions and garlic first afore I put my tomato paste."

Inside the trailer the engine noise was just a rumble. Sometimes the engines revved higher and the windowpanes rattled, but you could talk and hear normally with the rumble.

Emmet said into the phone, "See it draggin there, Von?"

Joe leaned sideways to check the computer. Emmet swiveled the screen for him and pointed at something.

Emmet nodded. "Yep . . . Nope, come on out thirty-five stands like we planned and fix it runnin back in . . . That'll work."

He hung up, glancing at Joe. "Spend more time wipin than drillin — bastard shales."

Emmet looked past me briefly. "Excuse my language."

His accent was very familiar from the American expatriates of my childhood. *I* and *my* sounded like "Ah" and "mah." *You* was "yew," and there were no *g*'s on *-ing* words.

Joe said, "You can't shock Ann. Her family's been in the business four generations."

Making a murmph noise, Emmet got up, brushing past me to

15

get to the kitchen. There wasn't much room between the desk and couch and I'd put him at well over six feet, close to three hundred pounds. He was also somewhere around Joe's age – late sixties, early seventies. Like Joe, he had a lot of hard miles on him too.

Emmet got two packages of pasta out of a cupboard. "Stayin for supper, Joe?"

"Thank you, sir – not tonight."

Emmet put one package back in the cupboard, and emptied the other one into the steaming pot as he glanced at a clock on the wall. Picking up a wooden spoon, he stirred the smaller pot and added a few shakes of salt.

Joe finished the papers he was reading and looked at me. "Emmet needs a lease hand."

I stared at him, and stared at Emmet as he brushed by to sit down again. I blurted, *"Me* – work on *Minerva?"*

I leaped off the desk and did a twinkle-toe dance, sticking my palms up and out like an Egyptian on a pyramid.

Joe deadpanned, "We take it you accept."

I was smiling, doing my dance. "Remember Alice and Evelyn, Joe? You know my father and Granpap agreed. The oil fields are no place for women. A woman on a drilling rig is bad luck."

Rocking his chair back, Emmet hooked his thumbs in the bib of his overalls. "Ran a all-female crew on a well out west of Reydon last year. Driller was a big ole gal, my lands. Knew her job, though – knew her job."

Joe said, "You'll go on morning tour starting Sunday."

Morning tour was six o'clock at night to six in the morning – perfect for my sleep schedule. And they pronounced *tour* like "tower" in the oil fields.

"Mornings are great." I stopped my silly dance and stood still. "The only question is, am I strong enough for heavy work?"

Emmet said, "Lease hand don't need no special strength. It's just a bucket of soap and a scrub brush."

Leaning forward, he fished some papers out of a messy tray and passed them to me.

16

"Fill these out and fax 'em to Elk City by end of the week. Call Payroll to make certain they get 'em."

I skimmed the blank employment forms. Ozark Drilling U.S.A. Inc. was based in Elk City, Oklahoma. Minerva was Joe's well but he didn't own the rig, so technically I wouldn't be working for him or Balch Drilling.

Emmet said, "I got two rules, little sister."

"My name is Ann."

"I'll make a pencil note of it. Two rules is—work hard and no vampin my boys. I run you off elsewise, hear?"

I wanted to say, *I'll make a pencil note of it.* But Emmet was way too intimidating.

"Same'll be for the hands. I won't tolerate no funny business on my rig. They cain't work beside a girl, they answer to their toolpusher."

Joe flicked a glance at the trailer door. Taking the hint, I thanked them both, folded my papers, and went. Out on the stoop I surveyed the lease, letting the cold wind and engine noise wash over me.

The Whiteheads were nomads of the oil-patch diaspora. They'd followed the booms from Pennsylvania and West Virginia to Mexico and Venezuela, to Oklahoma, to Texas—to Calgary, Alberta, where I was born and raised. But Whitehead men had monopolized all the danger and adventure, oil knowledge and expertise. When I finally figured that out, I'd resented it strongly.

So the summer I was sixteen, a girlfriend and I ran away to work on the rigs in northern Alberta. My friend's father was a drilling contractor and boys we knew rigpigged, and we wanted to try it too. What Americans called roughnecking, Canadians called rigpigging. Evelyn screwed the story out of my mother and sent the Mounties after me. I was found at the bus station in Edmonton and dragged home, and Evelyn signed me up for charm school. Instead of rigpigging, I learned how to apply lipstick and get in and out of sports cars in a tight skirt.

Both skills came in handy later—

But I'd done a violent flip-flop and began hating the oil business. I'd hated it for a long time, because I hated my alcoholic father, and because hate was required in liberal circles. We'd had some tough years, Joe and I, until endless, hilarious debates with Hollywood people restored my perspective. They were so ignorant and self-righteous about the oil business – and consumed so much refined crude oil to make stinky movies and build third homes in Aspen. Not to mention cosmetic implants.

"Ha!"

Doing my twinkle-toe dance, I jumped off Emmet's stoop and ran for the truck.

4

HE WAS A BIG, good-looking country boy with freckles on his cheeks and raspberry-colored Ozark Drilling coveralls unzipped at the neck. Raspberry red was Ozark's color. Their hardhats were raspberry, and the crown of the derrick was painted raspberry.

He said, "I'm Richie – I'm driller. This here's Kyle and Bobby. Kyle's in the derrick and Bobby's our motorman."

With his thumb he indicated the two guys beside him. Kyle and Bobby were beefy and fresh-faced, part of the Oklahoma crew like Richie.

We were standing in the top doghouse at the start of morning tour for safety meeting. Nobody was greeting anybody and nobody met anybody's eyes. I looked around the circle; the guys were deliberately *not* looking at me. My face was blank but I could barely contain myself, I was so stoked to be there. The intense maleness was an added perk. Richie, Kyle, and Bobby were about my age and looked like every woman's fantasy firemen.

Richie indicated me and the guy next to me. "Ann. Trey. They just hired on with us."

Trey was the oldest and tallest of everybody and no one's idea of a fireman, erotic or not. He looked more like a badass biker dude with his graying ponytail and beard, bulky muscles, silver tooth,

19

and gut sticking out. Snake tattoos showed at both his wrists and there were multiple pierces in his ears for earrings.

Bobby and Kyle said a vague "Hey" in Trey's direction. Trey didn't nod or talk back.

Richie said, "We're making a bit run. Daylight crew started out of the hole but we have a short ways to go yet."

Bit run meant they were pulling all the drillpipe out of the ground to replace the old bit with a new one.

Kyle joke-groaned and Bobby elbowed him. Richie didn't change expression as he said, "Derrick'll be cold tonight, poor peach."

I sympathized.

I had on two layers of clothes and a faded Balch Drilling coverall borrowed from Luz's son. I was holding the earplugs, safety gloves, and safety glasses Richie'd given me, and even though the doghouse was heated, my bare hands were already getting cold. And I was supposed to spend the next twelve hours outside.

Richie said, "We'll make up a new bit, then the mechanic's coming to change out the cathead. Trey, Ann – you'll clean the floor while the mechanic's working, then we'll run back in the hole. I want us on bottom and rotating by end of tour. Questions?"

Bobby and Kyle buttoned up and zipped up, and each pulled out chewing tobacco and stuck a wad in his cheek. Trey tucked his ponytail down his collar and took off his hardhat to put on a knit cap. Everyone had different clothing for the cold – only the fluorescent green safety gloves were standard. Kyle slid a steel door open and it suddenly got very loud in the doghouse. He, Bobby, and Trey filed out to the rig floor, putting their earplugs in as they went.

I said, "What do I do until it's time to clean the floor?"

Richie pointed at the steel bench running along the outside wall of the doghouse. "Stay put. Emmet'll come orient you soon as he's free."

Zipping his coverall, Richie stuck earplugs in, pulled on his green gloves, and walked out to the rig floor, clanging the door shut behind him.

I realized my hardhat was pinching and took it off. I put my hands in my pockets to warm them while I wandered.

We were forty feet off the ground and, like the rest of the rig, the doghouse was painted white steel. It had three doors and two windows, one that faced the rig floor and one that faced out. Kneeling on the bench, I checked the out view. It was miles of dark country, and the distant lights of Wilson and the Belridge oil fields. Down below was the line of trailers along the west side of the lease. Joe's trailer and Emmet's; a smaller steel hut where the hands changed their clothes; then a third trailer, pipe racks, and porta-potties.

The diesels revved. I felt the bench start to shake and went to the inside window to watch.

A stand of drillpipe was being lifted out of the ground. Trey hosed the mud off as Bobby stepped back, eyes up, his neck bending to watch the pipe rise.

I bent my neck too. The derrick towered another hundred feet over our heads. At night the floor was floodlit and strings of bright lights ran vertically, horizontally, and crisscross up the derrick to the crown. The noise of the diesel engines penetrated everywhere and you felt vibration all the time, in the steel and in your bones. But when Richie hit the throttle to lift tons of iron pipe, the whole rig shook with the strain. It was exciting and scary – and powerful and downright sexy.

Bobby and Trey had finished breaking out and racking the fifth stand of pipe when the doghouse door slid open and Emmet stepped inside.

First thing he said was "Put your hardhat on."

I put my hardhat back on.

The rig shuddered as Richie let the traveling blocks fall from the crown and braked them to a screaming halt a few feet from the floor. Grinning, Bobby showed Richie the distance with his hands.

Emmet turned and barked, *"Teach! Quit hotdoggin it!"*

Richie hunched his shoulders and Bobby got busy latching the elevators on to the next stand of drillpipe. Trey wasn't part of the fun. He dug out a cigarette and stuck it in his mouth without lighting it. There were NO SMOKING signs everywhere.

Emmet gave me a slitty-eye as he shut the sliding door. "They's showin off for you."

"I'm not vamping! I'm not vamping!"

"He's a fine-lookin young man, Richard. Got him a sweet little woman and two pretty daughters back in Sayre."

"I'm not vamping."

Emmet seated himself on the bench down from me, and I could see him giving Richie the slitty-eye even though the doghouse wall blocked Richie from view. Brushing a candy wrapper onto the floor, Emmet grumbled, "JD's crew gettin sloppy."

He stuck his legs out and leaned back. I reached over to grab the wrapper but Emmet said, "Ain't your job to pick up after the hands. You ain't their mama and you ain't their wives."

I sat back up. Emmet crossed his ankles and watched the action on the rig floor. That continued for a while until he said:

"Think you's up to this work, little sister?"

I looked at him. He was still watching out the window. I said, "I'm sure I'm up to it. But I also think I'm grossly underqualified and out of my depth."

"Talk louder – I cain't hear in both ears."

I raised my voice. "I'm grossly underqualified and out of my depth!"

"Well now, it ain't always a bad thing sometimes bein out of your depth."

I gave that a few seconds' thought and realized I agreed with him. Emmet went on, "There's plenty of folks, includin in the oil business, thinks they's better than us in the fields."

In his mouth it was "ohl bizniss."

He pointed out the window where the guys were sweating in the cold and already streaked with drilling mud and water.

"This is how you find the oil in the ground, see. It's a nasty, rough ole job but us here's got to find the oil's supposed to be in the ground, else where's your oil business at?"

"And gas. Oil and gas."

Emmet responded with a murmph. It was a sort of percussive hiccup in his throat.

"Don't go thinkin these boys is dumb Okies, neither. They's smart as whips every one of 'em."

Seeing a move he didn't like, Emmet got up heavily, walked to the window, and rapped on it. Bobby looked over and Emmet shook his head with emphasis. I got up to go stand at the window beside him. One of Emmet would've made three of me. All these guys made me feel like a shrimp.

"Here's what I tell new hands." Emmet folded his arms and spoke in profile. "Don't forget for one minute this is dangerous work. Don't daydream. Don't be comin to the rig moonin about your girlfriend's –"

He remembered who he was talking to, broke off, and coughed into his far shoulder.

"Take care of yourself. Don't be afraid to ask if you don't know. Stay alert and listen to your driller. Pay attention to normal rig noises so's you know if things ain't soundin right. This here's a fine, faithful rig but she's old and Ozark's been runnin her flat out since the boom started goin in '99."

Emmet watched the guys. "Hardest part of this job is the monotony of it – it's the hardest thing to learn. Mistakes get made from monotony and the boredom. I tell my hands it's the three Ps – patience, pride, patience. You got to accept the habit of doin the same thing over and over every day. Your only breaks is trips – trippin pipe like they's doin now."

I said, "Which is also repetitive."

"Yep." Emmet didn't nod.

That was it for my orientation. He left the doghouse without another word, stopping at the driller's console to shout something into Richie's ear.

I sat back down on the bench.

Bobby and Trey wrestled the last stand of drillpipe into the rack and Bobby chalked the number *123* on it.

After the drillpipe came the bottom-hole assembly – heavy pipe, drill collars, and corkscrewy gizmos that kept weight on the bit and helped drill a clean, straight hole. The crew tripped hundreds more feet of BHA and then the bit, only slowing down when Kyle flubbed something in the derrick.

Flexing my hands to keep them warm, I did the math.

A stand was made up of three joints of pipe – each joint was thirty feet long. By my calculation they were roughly two and a half miles into the ground. Minerva no.1 was a huge, important deal. Joe was wildcatting for natural gas and he'd shown me the drilling program and geology on the well. His projected zones of interest were somewhere between nineteen and twenty-one thousand feet – almost four miles down. Drilling to those depths was super-risky, super-challenging, and extremely rare for California where most of the oil and gas production was shallow.

And I was smack in the middle of the action, right where I *loved* to be.

By December I was a bona fide lease hand and I was in a groove.

I'd become best friends with a scrub brush and bucket of soapy water, and best friends with the powerwasher – a motorized, pressurized version of a scrub brush and bucket of soapy water.

The powerwasher looked like a big metal box on skids. It was gray and sat in the yard, and had long hoses that reached as high as the rig floor and as far as the mud pumps and pits. Over the weeks I must've cleaned every inch of the lease twice – some parts, like the rig floor and high-traffic walkways, ten or fifteen times. I didn't touch the trailers and wasn't allowed in the derrick, although I bugged Richie to let me click on the derrickman's harness and climb up to the platform where Kyle stood to work with drillpipe.

I mopped muddy boot prints until I was plenty bored, and came to appreciate a product called Floor-Dry that looked like coarse sand and absorbed oily water. I used Floor-Dry by the sack full because the steel surfaces were slick even when they weren't wet. I even washed the blowout preventers, the blackest, grimiest, most infernally daunting piece of equipment we had. They sat in the substructure under the rig floor – the reason the floor was forty feet off the ground – a gigantic, bulbous stack of iron with a series of rams that could be closed if pressures downhole got too intense. I stood way up high in the basket of the skylift, it took more than one tour, and the BOPs *still* weren't clean when I was done.

It was hard physical labor but I was having a total blast.

The crews worked a week-on/week-off schedule. For seven days, starting every other Sunday, I worked from six in the evening until six the next morning. Weeks on tour were like a grueling pajama party – awake all night, giddy towards dawn, where I always felt cold, hungry, thirsty, sore, tired, filthy, sweaty, smelly, and damp. Also impaired by bulky clothes and clunky steel-toed boots. And my hardhat never stopped pinching no matter how I adjusted it.

Socially, though, the rig was no pajama party.

I got some respect for the Kwik Gas incident but the crew was still guarded with me, partly because of Joe and partly because of my gender. I was never going to be one of the guys. My consolation was that even the guys on the crew weren't all the same guy.

There was Trey, the surly biker dude, who orbited a dark sun off in a galaxy of his own. He was perpetually chewing an unlit cigarette and giving everyone the thousand-yard stare. Then I had the Oklahomans – the band of brothers – part of Emmet's crack troops who'd follow their toolpusher "to hell or California," as Richie put it to bait me. Those three guys were amazing. Rig-smart and tireless, they'd known one another forever and Emmet had them trained to where they seemed to communicate by telepathy.

Richie was the leader, a worrier and pedagogue, who the Oklahomans called "Teach." He was the cutest, I thought, with his dark hair and dark freckles, and I had the most contact with him because he'd always stop what he was doing to answer any question at length.

Bobby the motorman was nicknamed "Carrot" for his coloring. He treated me like a bug splat on the doghouse window but I didn't mind because he seemed angry in general. Kyle was a goofy blond hayseed the guys called "Bale." He decided first tour that I needed hazing and tried to send me looking for the aluminum magnet. But I knew aluminum didn't magnetize so a few tours later he asked me to check on his pet lizard. He'd explained in a superb deadpan that the Oklahoma stick lizard was known for the stick it carried in hot weather to plant in the ground and climb on so its sensitive feet wouldn't fry. I was actually in the changing hut searching for Kyle's poor, possibly frozen lizard when I heard laughter outside the door and knew I'd been had.

That was a high point of hilarity and togetherness though. Whole tours went by where the only human voice I heard was Richie's, lining us out at safety meeting.

Off the rig, the voice I was hearing too often belonged to Alice.

She'd spent several weeks in Louisiana wrangling with the authorities over her half brother's body. Selfishly I was glad because I knew she'd start on me the split second she got back . . . and she did. Her problem was she had no leverage. She threatened to tell my father I was roughnecking. As if I cared what he thought – *yawn*. She cited Granpap, my Whitehead grandfather, and his well-known opposition to women in the oil fields. That had stopped my aunts but I'd never even met the legendary Jim Whitehead; he died the year I was born. Her worst threats involved my grandmother. Unlike Alice, however, I didn't fear Evelyn's wrath.

Finally Alice rolled out the big gun.

She said the Balches and Whiteheads were family. Since my mother was dead, she felt responsible: someone had to protect and watch out for me. I just laughed. My mother died when I was in college. She was a conventional, not brave woman, completely crushed by marriage to my father. But her family was oil patch and she was there for "Joe, me wuffneck." She'd encouraged my rigpig exploit and made me promise to try every wild thing I dreamed of. Which I'd done, sometimes to the point of recklessness and unreason. She would've been thrilled I was working as a lease hand and I told Alice that.

Alice still thought she'd win because the Whiteheads went to Hawaii every Christmas to get out of the Canadian winter. This year Alice was invited and she refused to believe I'd give up a free trip to Honolulu. To convince her, I had to show her. I phoned Evelyn, declined with thanks, wished her a happy holiday, and hung up before she could argue.

Anyway, Doug and I had planned to spend Christmas together until we realized how my work weeks fell. We talked almost every day but between his schedule and mine, we'd only seen each other once since I hired on with Ozark.

5

I WAS WALKING TO work Christmas Eve on the blacktop road east of the house. Normally I went to the rig by going out the back gate and cutting across the field, but I'd decided that wouldn't be prudent. Winter tule fogs in the valley were no joke, and fog had set in ten days before. Tule fog started at ground level and went up. Tonight it was *thick* thick and higher than my head.

Trey blew past in his old junker car as I walked along the edge of the asphalt. There was zero visibility but he didn't seem to care. The next vehicle was Richie, going slooow. I waved my flashlight and he stopped to give me a lift. He was alone in his truck. Usually he drove with Bobby and Kyle, although I'd noticed that Bobby had started riding in the flatbed.

"Thanks." I threw my duffle bag and cooler in back and climbed in the passenger side. "Where are Kyle and Bobby?"

Easing off the brake, Richie stuck his head out the window to see better. His windshield sparkled with fog damp and he had the wipers on intermittent.

"JD went home to take care of personal business—Emmet put Bale to drilling in his place. Carrot's driving JD's truck until he gets back."

"It must be serious if Emmet let JD go. He can't spare anyone."

Richie didn't respond. We were creeping along at five miles an hour and he was focused on the road.

JD was driller on daylight crew, Richie's opposite number. He was a mean little guy. I saw him at shift changes and he always made a point of sneering or walking a wide circle around me. But I hoped the Kyle switch wasn't permanent, or else how would I pay him back for the stick lizard? I was still percolating my revenge.

I said, "So we're short-handed?"

"It don't matter much. They're running logs."

"Didn't we run logs a month ago?"

Electric wireline logs told the exact profile of the rock we'd drilled through – vital information, especially on a wildcat.

Richie nodded. "This is different. Burger Boys are doing us a new survey."

He was talking about Schlumberger, the big service company. Their trucks had rolled onto the lease the previous night.

"What's a new survey mean?"

"You seem to know how to keep your mouth shut." Richie took his eyes off the road long enough to glance at me.

"For a girl" is what he meant. I just smiled at him. Richie said, "We think we're lost."

"Holy cow! How can we be *lost?*"

Richie shook his head and wouldn't elaborate.

Tommy waved us through the guard gate and Richie pulled up in front of the changing hut. For me, Emmet had rigged a lean-to out of welded pipe and tarpaulin behind the changing hut so I had a place to undress and keep extra clothes. I dropped my duffle of clean clothes and pulled on a coverall. Grabbing my cooler and safety accessories, I made my way slowly across the yard to the rig stairs. It took two tries to find them.

Looking up at the derrick, I couldn't tell how high the fog went. Joe said he'd been in tule fogs where the crown was in the clear but the derrickman couldn't see the rig floor – or the floor and derrick were free, but the rest of the lease was socked in. I'd noticed the fog also messed with acoustics. It distorted the sound of the engines and skewed your sense of distance and space. The bright lights made things worse, diffusing through the fog, turning it milky and opaque. It gave the rig an eerie, polar feel.

I slid the doghouse door open and there was a new guy standing inside. He had his hardhat off and he was tucking his scraggly hair inside the collar of his stained red coverall. When he saw me he did a comic double take.

I said "Hey" as I put my cooler on the bench and sat down. He stammered, "You're a g-girl . . . a, a woman . . . lady."

I just dug in my pocket for fresh earplugs. Because of the labor shortage, Emmet moved his experienced hands around and we'd had several strangers cycle on and off the crew. Every new guy made me feel like a grizzled veteran, although this one was older and positively ravaged. His chest was concave and his teeth were rotten. A meth addict, past or present – had to be.

He finished hiding his hair, zipped his coverall, and sat down close. Leaning closer, he said confidentially, "How's the driller? Good guy?"

I nodded.

"Word in town is this well's in trouble."

I shrugged and shook my head, sliding away from him. The guy let it drop but I watched him out of the corner of my eye. His gaze jittered and he had a nervous twitch. He put his hardhat on, and took it off again, and kept putting it on and taking it off until Bobby, Trey, and Richie showed up. Richie snapped at him to keep his hardhat on, then introduced him as Kenny and lined us out. I got the job of cleaning and organizing the other doghouse, the offside doghouse.

It was a pit. The crews used it as an all-purpose dump, and JD's crew – now Kyle's – were the slobs of the universe. I grabbed some couplings that belonged in the parts house and made my way off the floor by the back stairs. The fog slowed every movement down and turned the steel clammy and super-slick – but toughest was crossing the open yards. I'd learned to navigate by the glow of the derrick and the muted roar of the diesels.

I almost tripped over them before I saw or heard them.

30

Two guys were wrestling in the gravel. It was Richie and Bobby. Bobby was straddling Richie and had him pinned — Richie was trying to knee Bobby and heave him off. They had each other by the collars with their fists jammed in each other's throats.

I dropped the couplings and grabbed Bobby's jacket, yelling, *"Stop it, you guys! Stop it!"*

My voice went nowhere in the fog. Digging my heels in, I yanked Bobby as hard as I could. He let go one hand, swung his arm around, and knocked me sideways. I stumbled and fell on my knees. Jumping back up, I started running in the direction I thought Emmet's trailer was, and collided with a body in the fog.

"What the — ?!"

It was Trey. He pushed me back roughly.

I panted, "Richie and Bobby are fighting! I'm going for Emmet!"

Trey grabbed me. "No! Where are they?!"

I pointed in the direction I thought I'd seen them. Trey took off, and I turned and followed him. I *thought* I followed him. I zigzagged wildly in the fog and couldn't find anyone. Hearing a muffled shout, I twirled around and almost stepped on Richie's legs. Bobby still had him pinned. I fell on Bobby's neck, hooked one arm around, and threw myself to one side. Bobby flailed but I did enough for Richie to roll out from underneath him. Richie scrambled to his feet as Bobby tried to pry my arm off. I let go of him and he leaped up, elbowing me in the stomach. He growled and charged Richie with both fists swinging —

Trey materialized out of the fog and acted fast.

Grabbing Bobby from behind, he picked him up bodily, swung him around, dropped him, planted one boot on his rear, and gave him a vicious push. Bobby flew forward and disappeared from sight.

The three of us waited. Richie bent over, bracing his hands on his knees, breathing hard. I was panting too, hugging my stomach, and trying to hear over the noise of the engines. Trey faced the direction Bobby had gone, stock-still, his fists up like he expected a counterattack.

When the counterattack didn't come, we all moved. I reached

down and picked my hardhat off the ground, feeling nauseated from Bobby's elbow. Richie blew his nose with his fingers and realized his mouth was bleeding. Trey lowered his hands and started to leave. On his way he stopped and jabbed me in the shoulder, turning his back to Richie. He shouted in my ear:

"No squealing to the toolpush! Stupid fucking Okies!"

He swam back into the fog and I looked around for Richie but he'd vanished. I located the couplings I'd dropped, reset my compass by the rig glow, and headed for the parts house.

Walking inside I found Kenny asleep on the floor with his hardhat in his lap. When the overhead light went on he stirred but didn't wake up. I banged around looking for paint thinner, a spatula, and a wire brush: he still didn't wake up. Finally I grabbed a handful of bolts and chucked them on the floor. The floor was steel and the bolts made a racket in the enclosed space.

Kenny jerked up to sitting, wide awake and instantly nervous. He blinked his eyes and saw it was nobody important – only me.

He went, "Shush!" and settled back against the dope buckets. Retrieving the bolts, I threw them on the floor again, and Kenny sat up and opened his mouth to complain –

I said, "Don't you work here?"

He tried to stare me down but I just stared back. Shaking his head, he got to his feet, grabbing his hardhat as it slipped off his lap. I stepped aside to let him pass. He muttered "Bitch" under his breath so I couldn't miss it and slammed the door behind him.

Hours later I was in the offside doghouse scraping paint off a rolling metal box when I heard shouting from the rig floor. My first thought was that Richie and Bobby were at it again. Dropping the scraper, I ran to the door and saw two darkish shadows out on the floor. A blue shape was standing waving its arms. A reddish shape was sprawled out absolutely still.

I ducked and ran to the standing shape. It was one of the Schlumberger loggers, a young kid, panicky and pointing at the body. His voice wobbled:

"Get the toolpusher! This guy's dead! He's dead!"

Swaying, the kid sat down hard. The body was on its face, but the hardhat had rolled away and I could tell from the dark hair who it was. I raced to the top doghouse – I'd seen Richie call Emmet from the telephone in there. Tearing off one glove, I grabbed the receiver, and punched the numbers, praying that Emmet was in his trailer. My heart was pounding to where I was almost faint.

Emmet answered after two rings, his voice sleepy. "Yep?"

"There's a man down on the floor!"

"Where's Richie?" Emmet was suddenly sharp.

"It *is* Richie!"

Emmet barked, "Blow the air horn! Call the hands!" and hung up.

I ran out to the driller's console and pulled the lever. Up in the derrick the air horn started to blare.

Emmet arrived first. He appeared out of the fog right beside me and I pointed at the two shapes across the floor. Reaching them in long steps, he grabbed the logger kid and hauled him up by one arm, shouting:

"Pull your tools out the hole fast as you can! Lay 'em down on the catwalk and don't you boys go nowhere!"

The kid seemed stunned. Emmet bellowed, *"Quick now, damn it!"*

He gave the kid a push and the kid started for the front stairs. Emmet got down stiffly on his knees and felt for a pulse in Richie's neck. Meanwhile shapes were materializing on the rig floor. Trey appeared from the direction of the back stairs, Bobby a few seconds behind him. Richie popped up suddenly from somewhere and slapped my hand off the air-horn lever.

He shouted in my ear, "You don't blow it continuous like that! It's off, on, off, on!"

I saw who it was and blurted, "Jesus!"

He frowned. "What's up?!"

"It must be the new guy!"

I pointed to the group across the floor and Richie turned to look. Trey and Bobby had beelined for Emmet, who was still on his knees. Emmet threw his arms wide to keep everybody back. Richie's eyes got big and he took off.

Emmet was speaking loud and fast. "We's supposed to stop work minute a accident happens but I ain't settin here with nothin in the hole waitin to get my ass kicked."

Richie joined the circle. Emmet saw him but barely paused a beat. "Authorities's been notified. Christmas mornin, figure least two hours afore they get here—more, with this fog. We got to rig them loggers down and run some iron in the hole afore they do."

The guys were all nodding. Everyone except me was looking at Kenny's unmoving body.

Emmet pointed at Trey. "You, watch the flow line." He pointed at Bobby. "You, in the derrick." He pointed at Richie. "You, on the floor." He pointed at me. "Run light a fire under them loggers—tell 'em close them calipers and yank them tools. I'll take the brake myself."

Emmet held out his arms and Richie and Bobby helped him to his feet. He slapped Richie on the back and we scattered.

As I ran for the front stairs, I spotted a hammer lying beside the doghouse door. It hadn't been there last time I looked.

I ran down to the yard, pounded on the door of the logging truck, and pulled it open. Repeating Emmet's order, I twirled my finger to mean reverse the line. The head logger, a cute Dutchman sitting at a bank of monitors, dials, and readouts, started with the scientific spiel. I cut him off and stood in the doorway making the chop-chop sign until they reversed the drum to reel in their line—then I ran back up to the floor.

Emmet was still standing over the body. I told him how long the loggers would take. It wasn't fast enough so Emmet sent Richie down to talk to them in more muscular terms.

I said, "Is he dead?"

Emmet murmphed.

"What from?"

"Cain't say for certain—my guess, heart. Crystal-meth boogers that old, their heart goes." Emmet tapped his own chest.

I looked down at the new guy. I'd mistaken him for Richie because of the dark hair, and his red coverall had dampened to raspberry in the fog.

I said, "I found him asleep in the parts house."

"Probly lookin for my startin fluid. Them guys like to steal the startin fluid to make their drug – got so's I keep it in the bunkhouse by me."

Checking his watch he looked in the derrick, where the loggers' sheave was now revolving backwards. He yelled, *"Damn it, move your sorry behinds!"*

Joe appeared out of the fog, walking towards us in a hardhat and Balch Oil jacket. He deadpanned, "This sorry behind can't move any faster," taking in the body as he nodded at me.

I gave him a loose salute and said to Emmet, "What else can I do?"

Emmet pointed at the top doghouse. I went, pausing on the way to retrieve the hammer. I was bending down when an instinct told me to leave the hammer exactly where it was. The same instinct made me turn around to show the hammer to Emmet. But he and Joe were deep in conference so I postponed that and walked on into the doghouse.

It took almost three hours for the sheriffs and coroner's people to arrive from Bakersfield.

Emmet and Joe met the first cops on the floor and showed them the body. My crew and I were in the top doghouse not talking, pretending like we'd stopped work hours ago. The bro meter was below zero: Richie sat at one end of the doghouse, Bobby at the extreme other, as far apart as they could get. I stood up and went to the window.

A sheriff's deputy was assigned to guard us, and one started patrolling the rig floor. One guy set up to take flash photographs as the coroner squatted to examine the body. He picked the head up carefully, tested the motion of the neck, and felt around the skull. Judging by his reaction, he found a wound. Emmet meanwhile had noticed the hammer. Pointing, he called a detective over and then bent his neck back to squint into the derrick. I pressed against the glass and looked up too, although you couldn't see very high in the fog.

The doghouse door slid open and the second detective stepped inside to tell us they wanted statements. They proceeded to interview everyone on the lease, separately and alone. With me the detectives concentrated on the hammer. Where was it kept? When had I seen it last? What was it used for? They asked who was working derrick that tour. Had I seen Bobby go up or come down from the derrick? I realized they were thinking the hammer fell out of the derrick and killed the new guy, whose last name was Mills. Kenny Mills.

When the cops were through they stuck Richie, Bobby, Trey, and me back in the top doghouse under guard. They wouldn't let us leave, even though it was past six A.M. and daylight crew was down in the yard waiting to come on.

I stood at the inside window, drowsing on my feet. Trey was sound asleep with his jacket over his face. Bobby was slumped at the end of the bench sulking, and Richie sat on a stool up by the computer screen. He had a split lip from the fight and sat touching it as he stared into space.

The doghouse door slid wide and Emmet barked, "Carrot! You's wanted!"

My eyes flew open as Bobby flushed and stood up. He spat tobacco juice into the trash barrel and went out to the floor, buttoning his jacket and dragging his feet.

Emmet said to us, "We's shuttin the well in."

Richie said, "Right now?"

"Till OSHA comes out later. I's thankful we ain't locked down. They'll be wantin to talk to everybody – you, Carrot, Trey, little sister here."

Richie said, "Safety'll want to talk to Dean."

"They'll want to talk to daylight crew, yep – derrickman first. My bet is we's back to runnin logs this afternoon. Simple accident don't merit more lost time than that, even in California with they's nonsense regulations and eco-boogers up my ass."

Emmet looked at me but didn't excuse his language. I just wanted to laugh at *eco-boogers*. Ducking out, he started to slide the door shut. Richie called, "Emmet, sir!"

Emmet ducked his head back in as Richie got up off the stool.

"I haven't been doing what you told me. On a long hole, take a half-hour from time to time to make sure everything's secure in the derrick. I haven't been doing that."

Emmet eyeballed Richie with meaning. The blood on Richie's lip had coagulated to a dark clot and his face was scraped from rolling in the gravel of the yard.

"This ain't your fault, Teach, if that's what you's thinkin. It were a *accident*. We got us a tough hole and this damn fog, and you boys's seemin agitated and not doin your work like I taught you. I reckon y'all been gone from home too long."

Richie started to say something, then changed his mind.

Emmet modified his voice. He had a trick, I'd noticed, of talking more softly and still making himself heard over the engines. Looking straight at Richie's lip he said, "Somethin you want to tell me, son?"

Richie shook his head. Emmet lifted his eyebrows a millimeter of an inch, raising his hardhat up his forehead.

"Nothin?"

"No, sir."

Richie wouldn't look at Emmet and Emmet didn't believe him, but he dropped the subject. He said, louder, "Y'all go on now, get you some sleep. Send Bale and them up for me."

The doghouse door clanged shut. There was a pause, then Richie ripped off his hardhat and threw it at the trash barrel. Trey rolled over. Covering my ears, I jumped to avoid the rebound and stare as Richie stomped a Coke can that was lying there, then hauled off and started kicking the steel bench, swearing deliberately and savagely.

"Damn! God damn! Shit *damn* God damn!"

I said, "Hey!" and reached to grab him and stop him —

Then it hit me:

Bobby — Richie — their fight — the derrick — the hammer. My first thought that the dead Kenny was the dead Richie.

I looked at Richie's face and knew that's exactly what he was thinking. He was thinking Bobby had tried to kill him and got the wrong guy.

6

THE PROBLEM WAS, was it my problem? Should I get involved or pretend I didn't know what I knew and never saw what I'd seen?

I debated it as I staggered home in the fog at seven o'clock Christmas morning. I was still debating as I lay on the bathroom rug after a hot shower, too wiped out to even crawl into the bedroom. And I debated again after Joe's call came that the safety people wanted me back at the lease at eleven A.M. for questions. I couldn't decide no or yes — I kept getting a circular no *and* yes — so I called Doug in L.A. He had a family gig but was happy to drive up after, and we agreed to meet halfway between him and me at the Buttonwillow truck stop on the interstate.

The safety investigation took way longer than I expected. Joe had loaned his trailer for it and we waited around in the cold, gray damp, taking our turns with the OSHA inspector.

The atmosphere was super-grim. Richie stood stiff and still, his face blank, loosening up only when Kyle dropped by to gossip on his break. It was probably dumb but I edged closer, looking for signs of guilty knowledge between Richie and Kyle or signs that Kyle suspected the accident wasn't one. The two of them ignored Bobby, who paced in the gravel acting pissed off — not much different than usual. Trey was skulking around the corner, out of sight

38

between Joe and Emmet's trailer. He emerged after a while to go sit in his car. I imagined that's where he went, anyway: I heard a car door slam somewhere in the fog. He gave me the signature stare as he passed and looked bored beyond bored.

I found out what was taking so long when my turn came to be interviewed. The woman didn't know how drilling operations or drilling rigs worked.

While she consulted her notes I clarified the relationship between Balch-Min LLC and Ozark Drilling, using the parallel of building construction: Joe owned the well – Ozark was the contractor he was paying to drill it. I had to re-explain the hierarchy of the crew from Richie down to me. I explained what I was doing in the parts house where I'd found the new guy snoozing, why I wasn't allowed in the derrick, and why I couldn't possibly keep track of every hammer on the lease. I described Mills's twitch with his hardhat, and the moment Richie ordered him to put it on and keep it on. The inspector also wanted to discuss drug use. Was Mills cranked at safety meeting? If so, why did Richie let him start tour? I almost told the woman she was slowing Emmet down with stupid questions, but I controlled myself.

She finally released us when the homicide team showed up from Bakersfield to compare notes. I sped the whole way to Buttonwillow and pulled into the McDonald's early. The restaurant was empty except for the kids behind the counter but I decided not to wait inside. The tule fog had cleared south of Wilson and it was sunny and warm. I hadn't seen the sun in ages. Picking a spot against one wall, I sat down on a strip of grass to soak it in.

I smiled. Doug.

LAPD Detective Douglas Lockwood, Homicide, Northeast Division.

I'd met him because a woman died in my bathtub – and gotten to know him because, over his objections, I made the murder my problem. If I hadn't stuck my nose in, I'd still be blasting around L.A., a shallow hard case of a hipster, reviewing movies, sleeping with skunk men, unhappy and resenting it. Instead of that I'd chased killers and witnessed bloody death and done things I hadn't known I was capable of, some of them really bad. My life had burned to the ground and, over *my* objections, I'd fallen in love with Doug.

Checking the time again, I crossed my legs, leaned back, and tilted my face up to the sun.

Doug.

A muddy Jeep pulled into the McDonald's and parked alongside my truck. Doug got out wearing his off-duty uniform of jeans and a turtleneck fleece, and a pair of sneakers that had survived a lot of salt water and sand. He was carrying an oddly shaped object wrapped in gold tissue paper.

I said, "Dang! I didn't—"

He walked over and sat down on the grass, handing me the object. It had long, skinny ends and a thick, bulgy middle. I couldn't see his eyes because of his sunglasses, but one corner of his mouth was twisted a little.

"Open it." He nudged me.

"Can I look at you first? It's been weeks and weeks."

Taking off the dark glasses, Doug shaded his eyes as he struck a heroic pose in fun.

Back at the beginning I hadn't noticed how handsome he was. I only saw the stone-faced cop with the controversial reputation—more seasoned and square than me, and blocking my way. When I eventually had noticed, it didn't matter because Doug wasn't my type. He was too old, and a policeman, and, I thought, an inflexible jerk. But events had closed the age and experience gap between us. They'd also revealed the guy underneath the official function and the joke was, he turned out to be a way better person than me.

Tall and lean, in his forties, he was lean and loose all over, with the shoulders and hips of a swimmer, because his second job was surfing. I'd persuaded him to buzz his hair to a stubble, and the gray at his temples matched the gray-green of his eyes, which were almost crystal from decades of watching patterns in the waves.

Doug relaxed the heroic pose and, smiling, poked the object

in my lap. I tore the tissue paper and rolled the object out of its wrapping.

It was dark green with black toenails and red eyes. I held the thing up by its tail and head, mystified.

"A plastic dinosaur?"

Doug reached into the back pocket of his jeans and pulled out a longish twig. I said, "A twig?"

He stuck the twig sideways in the dinosaur's open jaws. It fit exactly between the pointy teeth and stayed there. Then I got it. I burst out laughing and threw my arms around him.

"A stick lizard! The mythical Oklahoma stick lizard!"

Doug held me close, laughing too, and we started to kiss. He pulled back to glance at the motel next door.

Reluctantly I let go of him, shaking my head. "We can't. I'm on tour at six."

"I never thought I'd be sleeping with a rig hand." He looked at his watch. "Then you better tell me what happened."

I started with walking to the rig, how thick the tule fog was, Kyle's switch to daylight driller, and Richie and Bobby's sudden, mysterious estrangement. I described Mills, described how I found him asleep in the parts house, then skipped to the logger finding Mills prone on the rig floor and my thinking it was Richie –

Doug frowned, interrupting me. "You don't know if Mills was alive or not. Emmet shouldn't take it on himself to pronounce him dead. I don't care if the rig's in county territory – he should've called the closest medics."

I just shrugged because I had no idea.

Doug continued to frown as I told how the crew worked around Mills's body before the cops arrived. But Doug was born and raised in the suburbs south of L.A., where there was a ton of oil. He'd worked on the rigs to pay for college, understood the basics of drilling, and had to see Emmet's point of view. Preserving a possible crime scene wouldn't be the toolpusher's first concern. His first concern would be a rank blowout with seventeen thousand feet of open hole, especially if they were lost in unknown rock.

Doug did repeat, "Emmet takes too much on himself."

Giving him as close to every detail of the sheriffs' activities and questions as I could remember, I wound up with that morning outside Joe's trailer and retold my interview with the dumb safety woman, word for word.

Doug's comment was "They send whoever's on call Christmas Day. She might be an expert in farm machinery."

He could never just be mean about people. Sometimes his large-mindedness was irritating.

I finished with:

"The verdict isn't in yet so who knows what they'll decide. I do know that nobody's mentioned the Richie/Bobby thing, and the only person who'd conceivably mention it is—" I tapped my own chin. "But I really hope Mills died by accident. I hate the idea of another murder because I'd have to start thinking murder follows me around and that's just plain creepy."

Doug squeezed my hand he was holding. I winced, "Ouch."

"What's the matter?" He turned my hand over and made me open it up. I shrugged. "It's just sore, an advanced case of scrub-brush cramp."

He ran his finger along the chapped skin of my palm—cracked in places because I spent so much time with wet hands. Kissing the palm and folding my hand in both of his, Doug leaned back against the restaurant wall and proceeded to think. I didn't expect him to come up with answers fast: it was a lot of information in one chunk. Watching, I imagined him sifting through the facts and impressions, organizing them in chronologies, spatial diagrams, and relationships, with linking arrows, and names double underlined. That's how he did it in his notebook.

He frowned, lost in concentration, kneading my hand gently between his. A while went by before he looked over and said:

"Sorry, baby, no—that hammer didn't fall out of the derrick. It's the least likely of your choices. Not that it would fall—but that it would fall, hit someone, and kill them."

He counted off the three steps by lifting one, two, three fingers. We'd argued crime theories before and counting off alternatives was a familiar gesture of his.

42

"It's not totally impossible, Doug. There are a jillion ways to die by accident on a drilling rig."

I counted off. "You can get run over by a delivery truck, mangled in the drawworks, crushed by rolling drill collars, sucked down and drowned by the agitators in the mud pits, sliced in two by a snapped line, hit by a pressure-driven projectile, fall from a height. Or objects can drop on you from a height, and they don't have to be big – gravity does the damage. The hammer is not impossible."

Clenching my free hand into a fist, I made a *grrhh* noise: "I *need* this to be an accident!"

Doug just shook his head.

I said, "Emmet thinks it was an accident. It looked like the sheriffs were buying the idea."

"There are reasons why the cops would."

"Which are?"

Doug squeezed my hand, lightly this time. "Do you know what we call industrial accidents?"

I said that I didn't.

"We call them trash runs."

"Nice. Not so the victim's loved ones hear, I hope."

"It isn't nice, but the fact is job-site deaths aren't investigated very hard unless something's hinky. It's also Christmas, remember. These guys have families and I know they're overworked because I've had cases bring me up to Kern County. The sheriffs have a six-man team plus a lieutenant working fifty to a hundred homicides a year – it's too much. They don't have motive unless you or someone else talks, and you're right, your crew isn't going to."

I sat forward and burst out:

"Dang it! I'm happy out here, Doug, except Alice is a drip and I miss you. This is a big, fat pain!"

Doug smiled. "'Dang it'? You've been around that Okie crew too long. You used to use stronger language."

"I'm trying to reform." I looked him in the face. "You think someone dropped the hammer out of the derrick on purpose? Bobby, you think, gunning for Richie?"

"You're not listening, Ann – or I'm not being clear. Granted, tools do fall out of derricks. I'm saying that hammer didn't fall out of your derrick by accident or premeditation."

I corrected him. "Emmet's derrick."

"The hammer didn't come from the derrick. You couldn't plant a hammer on a girt or the monkeyboard, say, hoping it would fall on the guy you wanted, and there's no way to aim it with any kind of accuracy in a fog like you describe. Mills could've been on the floor without his hardhat and happened to get nailed by accident – but that chance is too slim to bother with. Myself, if it were my case, I'd consider it only after I eliminated every other possibility."

Finally, finally, I realized what he was getting at. I wasn't normally so slow, but I had the clear image of Emmet seeing the hammer and, with no hesitation, squinting up into the derrick.

I growled, "I hate this!"

Doug patted my hand: "You don't hate it, come on – don't lie. You love it."

"What do you mean?"

"I mean I hope I know something about you by now. You love adventure – you love the chase and don't give a damn what it costs. I saw you go balls-to-the-wall for a murdered woman, a stranger, and it wasn't just for a story about Hollywood –"

"Okay, stop –"

"You care about the truth, baby. You have a strong sense of right and wrong, even if it isn't cool to admit it, and you don't listen to it as often as –"

"Stop! Stop!" I pulled my hand out of his and covered both ears. "No more character analysis! *Stop!*"

Laughing, Doug tried to pull my hands away. "You shouldn't be ashamed of –"

"No!" I snatched my hands back. *"Are you done, Detective Lockwood?"*

Doug just kept laughing and tugged at me. I let him take my hands down but hung on to his wrist.

"How did I know not to touch the hammer?"

"Sound instincts. You also have a great teacher." One corner of his mouth twisted. "It wouldn't matter if you had touched it, I

44

don't think. It's a short distance from A to B in this case—head injury, blunt instrument. If you'd put the hammer back in the tool locker you would've told the sheriffs. For forensic purposes, blood traces or hair would be obvious, and as for prints—the crews wear work gloves, correct?"

"*And,* except for the Oklahoma guys, and me and Trey that I know of, we've had a lot of turnover."

Doug shook his head. "Yeah, no—the hammer won't do you any good. I'd be surprised if they even took it on the off chance of prints. They didn't fingerprint you."

He bent his legs and pushed himself up to standing, pulling me with him. Brushing the grass off his jeans he checked the time.

"Come on—let's wrap this up in the Jeep. We still have an hour before you have to go and I brought something else for you."

I reached down and grabbed my stick lizard and the crumpled tissue paper. Doug had started across the parking lot ahead of me, putting on his sunglasses. I called, "There really is a Santa Claus!" and he turned back around.

"I love this!" I held up the lizard. "You're the best!"

"Wait until the other half of your present."

"You think Mills had his hardhat off when he got hit?"

Doug waved me forward with his arm:

"Hurry!"

7

EMMET HAD BET RIGHT. When I arrived at the lease Christmas night, the loggers were rigged up again with their survey tools deep in the hole.

The sheriffs ruled Kenny Mills's death an accident. State safety let us continue drilling because the accident wasn't due to broken rules or company negligence. I found this out by asking Richie before safety meeting – asking partly to gauge his state of mind. I was looking for signs of relief or lingering suspicion but he didn't vibe either, like his tantrum in the doghouse hadn't happened. He relayed the good news deadpan, his tone implying only that it's a miracle when bureaucrats make the right decision because they almost never do.

I especially wanted to see Richie's reaction to Bobby, but Bobby didn't show up for work. He was gone and Kyle was back in derrick, even though he'd worked daylight tour that day. Our new motorman was an Oklahoman Richie introduced as Lynn. Lynn wasn't a fantasy firefighter. He was just another big, strong farm boy in a raspberry coverall, with the roundest moon face, a round middle, shaggy hair, and obviously false teeth.

Kenny Mills wasn't mentioned at safety meeting, and neither was Bobby's absence.

Richie lined me out to finish the job I'd started the night before. I walked into the offside doghouse smiling about my hour with Doug in the back of his Jeep. He'd curtained it for privacy and brought cushions and candles in special holders for atmosphere – tricks from the days when he and his buddies camped along the coast waiting for the surf at dawn. I thought he'd given up the motel idea too easily: I'd found out why. The other half of my Christmas present was *him*.

Grabbing a rag and soaking it with paint thinner, I knelt on the floor and went back to scraping dried paint off the remote choke.

I was going to make Kenny Mills my problem. But it wasn't for love of truth or adventure. It was for Joe. What did I not owe Joe Balch? He was a profound friend and a better father to me than my own. Trouble on Minerva was trouble for him, and I had to help any way I could –

Richie stuck his head in the doghouse door. I'd left it open for the fumes, although it also let in the clammy damp. The fog was still bad.

"You okay?"

I pulled off a safety glove and showed him my chapped palm. "Do you think Ozark might spring for rubber gloves? I'm getting dishpan hands."

Nodding, Richie left, and I resumed.

Doug knew Joe and wanted to help too. But he had a heavy caseload, and besides, it was a politically delicate time: the department was deciding whether to reinstate his detective 3 status and reassign him to Robbery-Homicide downtown. After demotion and exile, a long slump where he lost his belief in police work, and the protracted mess of our shootings, that was a big deal. He could share what he knew, advise me unofficially, maybe finesse some useful information. Past that, he had to be careful.

Meanwhile he had an 82 percent solve rate – which was spectacular – and I'd learned the hard way to take his opinion seriously. His first assumption was that someone meant Kenny Mills to die. He'd challenged me to reason it through and prove him wrong. So driving back from Buttonwillow, I'd tried to visualize the murder using logical common sense.

Between engine noise and tule fog, anyone could've snuck up on anyone anywhere on the lease. To be absolutely safe the killer'd have to know where the crew was on their chores, where the mud logger was, where the Schlumberger guys were, and be sure that Emmet wasn't making a round. Emmet had a habit of popping up out of thin air: his vigilance was supernatural. But, given the conditions, you wouldn't have to be *absolutely* safe to get Mills without being caught.

The weapon wouldn't be difficult either. The crews left tools lying around all the time, so you didn't have to risk the top doghouse to grab a hammer. Locating your victim might be tough, but picking the rig floor as the place to kill him, in my opinion, wasn't the smartest idea. Bright lights; loggers; potential traffic; me slaving in the offside doghouse. There were so many dark, isolated parts of the lease where you could kill in peace and have the body go unnoticed – nobody missing the guy until end of tour when the crew clocked out.

In that case, though: How would your murder fool the experts and pass as an accident? *Duh*, Ann.

Emmet loomed in the doorway. I stopped scraping and watched him dart his eyes around – right, left, right, left. Last night, before and after Mills was found, I'd scrubbed layers of oil and grime off the walls and steel workbench, neatened the hanging hoses, racked the wrenches by size, and mopped the floor.

Emmet rumbled, "Doin good work, little sister." Walking inside for a closer look, he stooped to inspect the wall and floor underneath the workbench.

"This ain't been clean since the Black Flood of 1913."

I pointed my finger at the muddy boot prints he'd tracked in. Emmet glanced behind himself, then glanced at the mop and said, "It ain't been put away yet."

I said, "Can I have a raise?"

"Raise's automatic every six months."

"How much is it?"

"Fifty cents."

"Oh, one of those get-rich-quick deals." I went back to scraping.

Emmet said, "Got you some leftovers saved. Come see me at break," and he was gone just as Trey clanged into the doghouse through the far door.

He said, "Where's the stepladder?"

The stepladder was leaning against the workbench; he could see it as well as I could. I pointed and Trey picked it up and left. It was a regular parade tonight: I'd never had that much company on tour. It occurred to me maybe the crew was upset. Maybe dropping by was their hieroglyphic male way of worrying about me and how I was taking Mills's death. Very sweet, I thought, smiling – if that's what it was.

Rolling the remote choke away from the wall, I crawled on my knees to get behind it.

In the milky fog, against the basic brown-white of the rig floor, colors stood out clearly. Only three people were wearing red last night. I had on my faded Balch blues, and Schlumberger's color was crisp blue. The mud logger had made a rare appearance up with us to speak to the sheriffs; he'd worn a blue-and-white letter jacket. The guard at the lease entrance, Tommy, always wore a Balch windbreaker, and Emmet was perpetually in denim – overalls and a padded jean jacket. Trey worked in a filthy orange coverall with *Steve* stitched on the left breast. Which left Richie and Bobby in raspberry, and Kenny Mills in ragged red. Their hardhats weren't the same, though. Richie and Bobby wore raspberry Ozark hardhats where Mills had worn a beat-up white one with no stickers or company name.

I sat back on my heels, waved the fumes of the paint thinner away, and coughed.

It hit me that the problem was simpler than I thought. Driving in from Buttonwillow I'd gotten tangled up in Doug's assumptions about hardhats and hammer blows – matters of physical and medical fact he was in the process of checking. It hit me that the mechanics of Mills's death didn't matter. *If* accident was our last choice, *and* only three guys wore red, *and* hair color would be visible in the fog if you were close enough to swing a hammer – given the ifs and ands, the essential point boiled down to:

Bobby would be stupid to try to kill Richie right after they were caught wrestling by Trey and me. Bobby was pissed off and charmless, but I trusted Emmet on the intelligence of his boys: smart as whips every one of 'em. I also didn't believe Bobby would sink that low on the bro meter. Maybe Richie had realized it too, once the adrenaline stopped pumping.

On an impulse I dropped the spatula, jumped to my feet, and ran out across to the other doghouse. I slid the door open and caught Emmet and Joe in conversation.

Joe was saying, "Ron thinks we should go to top drive."

Opening the tool locker, I squatted down.

"Ron Bray don't know shit from apple butter, Joe. He's just spendin your money and mindin *my* business."

I rummaged through the hammers but didn't see the one that killed Mills. Emmet raised his voice. "Lose somethin, little sister?"

I stood up and turned around. "The four-pound shop hammer. Did the sheriffs take it?"

"Why would they do that now?" Emmet narrowed his eyes.

I squeaked, "Never mind," and left the doghouse in a hurry. What a dumbhead! I had to learn to think through my impulses before I acted on them. What was I going to *do* with the hammer if I'd found it?

The offside doghouse was done until the crews garbaged it again. I rolled the remote choke back into place, grabbed my implements, and headed down the back stairs for the engine house – what Emmet called the motor shed. Three thousand-horsepower diesels generated all the power for the lease and the noise inside the engine house was so loud it wasn't noise anymore: it was a painful thumping in every cell of your body. I put on extra ear protection and, grabbing the carburetor cleaner and a fresh rag, I sprayed the first engine.

Even if I'd been the cops – even if Doug could've used official connections and resources – certain standard lines of investigation were hopeless.

Fingerprints and footprints were hopeless. Tracking movements in the fog was hopeless. Alibis and time frames were hopeless. I'd have to start with motive, which meant I'd have to find out about Kenny Mills. He was local, I was guessing, based on his "Word in town is this well's in trouble" remark. I'd have to find out which town. He had a crystal-meth jones but still worked a job so he wasn't that far gone. He might've been a dealer or had a lab; he might've been part of a combine with enemies of its own. I could imagine the conspiracy going wide if drugs or warring gangs were involved. My crew I didn't suspect because they were all foreigners—the Oklahomans, and Trey from Wyoming. But I'd definitely have to check the local hands on the other crews, the mud logger, Tommy at the gate, the three Schlumberger dudes—

I stopped as a horrible thought hit me: *Almost anyone could've slipped on and off the lease in the fog.*

Richie appeared suddenly. The engine noise was like a cocoon and I hadn't heard him come in. Startled, I dropped my rag, and Richie bent and picked it up. I was standing on the steel platform with the diesel engine and we were eye to eye.

Handing me the rag, Richie shouted at my ear, "How you doing?!"

This was getting ridiculous. He'd never just asked how I was doing. I shouted at his ear, "I've seen dead people before, Richie!"

He stuck his hands in his coveralls and looked sheepish, like I'd caught him being girlie. I shouted, "Haven't you?!"

He shouted, "Saw a good buddy die once!"

"How?!"

"Coring! Left the pickup sub in the elevators and ran them up to the crown, and we were using winches to work with the core barrel on the floor! Winch lines got caught in the elevator latches—latches opened and the pickup sub came down! Ninety pounds—landed square on him before we knew what happened! Never made a sound!"

I started to shout, "I'm sorry—"

But Richie wasn't waiting for sympathy. He turned and walked out the back of the engine house. I watched him round the corner towards the mud pumps.

I liked Richie, and not just for his freckled fantasy-fireman looks. He was solid and all guy . . .

. . . and he'd just given me a tremendous idea.

Emmet had warmed up turkey and gravy and made an open-faced sandwich, with mashed potatoes and green beans on the side. I sat on his couch at break practically shoveling the food into my mouth – debating how to approach him because I knew I couldn't do what I wanted to without his sanction and help.

I said, "This is the best turkey I ever ate."

"Thank you kindly – it's a secret recipe."

I sopped up the last of the gravy with the last of the potato, stood, and walked my plate over to him. He had a stockpot full of water on the stove that he'd put the turkey carcass in, and he was chopping onion for a broth. With his knife he indicated where to set my plate. I would've offered to wash it except there was only room for Emmet in the kitchen, and barely him.

I said, "Where'd you learn how to cook?"

"Taught myself. Cain't be runnin to the café all the time, specially when you's pushin with no relief."

He pronounced *café* like "ke-*fay*." It reminded me of stories I'd heard as a kid: best meals in the oil fields. My father would talk about the pancakes here and the chicken-fried steak there. He could name every decent barbecue joint between the Canadian and Mexican borders, if there was oil within driving distance.

I stood and watched Emmet slice. He said, "What's my four-pound shop hammer to you?"

The big bear missed nothing. I decided just to tell him straight out. "I don't think Kenny Mills died by accident."

Emmet rolled his eyes. "Lordy me – a'course it weren't no *accident*. Some bastard sneaked up and bashed the poor sumbitch on the head."

I stared. "But . . . but . . ."

"But what now?"

"But you . . ."

52

Emmet stopped slicing and pointed his knife at me. "Listen, little sister. I been pushin tools more years than you been drawin breath and I learned me a thing or two along the way. One is, a pretty lie saves a world of trouble if the truth don't do nobody no good."

Lowering the knife, he threw the onion into the pot and reached for some celery. I was having a rare speechless moment.

"I got views on this here deal." Emmet started chopping the celery. "Looks like the perfect crime to my mind – bad tule fog – bastard knows rigs and the psychology of it. Nobody wants to slow drillin down with the police. We been standin over this hole three months and we might be three months more if I get unwelcome news from them fellas."

He dipped his head sideways in the direction of the Schlumberger trucks out in the yard.

I said, "But the cops ruled it an accident . . ."

"And now see, that weren't my doin. I only herded 'em at the chute – they ran on inside their own self."

He kept chopping.

I said, "You don't think murderers should be caught and punished?"

"Oh, I most assuredly *do* think."

"Only not while you're drilling this well."

"Not till we's TD – you got it." He nodded.

TD meant "total depth." I said, "Does my crew know it wasn't an accident? Does Joe?"

"Joe does. Smart hands too, I reckon. We ain't discussed it and we ain't goin to."

He threw the celery in the pot and turned the dial up on the heat. I looked at the clock: break was over. Buttoning my shirt at the neck, I zipped my coverall and, going to the couch, grabbed my hardhat, earmuffs, safety glasses, and gloves.

"This can't wait until TD. We have to start *now*."

Emmet raised his eyebrows at my tone, but I didn't back off.

"I'm not trying to catch the guy – I just want to get enough evidence to make the sheriffs take a second look. I was hoping you'd help and let Richie help, because we should work together. I don't want to do anything either that will slow you up or hurt Minerva."

"Leavin well enough alone won't slow us up none a'tall."

"In the short term. But if a guy's been murdered, there's something going on we need to pay attention to. It could hurt us later."

That idea seemed to strike Emmet, as far as I could read shades of deadpan. Like Joe, Emmet was a master. He hooked his thumbs in his overalls and leaned against the kitchen counter. Putting on my hardhat, I waited. Finally Emmet murmphed and came out with:

"We was drillin down around Santa Paula one time. Hellacious hole – bad runnin shales and boulders stickin the drillpipe, I cain't remember what all – shallow gas. Nasty hole, my goodness. They was truckin our water in and one mornin this water hauler gets him the bright idea to steal from my hands. Boys's on the floor and seen this guy go in the changin room – catch him comin out with their billfolds and wristwatches. They take that booger, tie him upside down in the elevators, run him up to the crown block and let go the brake."

I gasped, "Whoa! Did he die?"

"Passed out by the time he hit the floor. Sorry booger never drives onto a Balch lease nor any lease with a Balch rig never again."

"And I'm not talking vigilante justice – only justice justice. Whoever the killer is, he shouldn't get away with it."

Emmet rubbed his cheek. It made a scratchy noise because he didn't shave very often.

"Also – Joe's important to me and Minerva's important to him."

"All right, little sister, all right. Let me think on it."

"Great." I reached for the door handle. "The turkey really was delicious, thanks."

Emmet nodded one smidge of an inch.

I left the trailer, putting on my safety gear and flipping my collars up as I crossed the yard. The first blast of cold night air was always the hardest. Out of habit I looked up at the rig. The fog had thinned and you could actually see the rig floor and derrick. I also saw the new guy, Lynn, coming out of the engine house. When he saw me walking towards him, he changed direction.

I walked up and shouted, "Are you looking for me?!"

Lynn shouted, "Where's the left-handed crescent wrench at?! Run fetch it for us, will you?!"

I broke into a smile. "You tell Kyle there's no such thing as a left-handed crescent wrench!"

Lynn just grinned with his fake teeth and took off, headed for the hopper house where Kyle was mixing mud that tour. Adjusting my ear protection I headed into the engine house to clean the third and last diesel.

It was past midnight in California. In Hawaii my relatives would be finishing their meal at the hotel on Waikiki Beach where we stayed every year. I could just picture them – my grandmother, my father, my aunts and uncles and cousins and their kids. Sunburned and stuffed, they'd be complaining about prices and the tacky crowds in Honolulu. Father would be bombed, and Evelyn would be blitzed on gin and tonics. She'd reminisce about her early married life in Texas, then get maudlin about my grandfather and her glory days when they were king and queen of Calgary's American colony, glamour pair of the oil-biz cocktail circuit. I pictured Alice seated next to her, tipsy on champagne and nodding along because she thought Jim and Evelyn Whitehead were the cat's meow.

I grabbed a rag and glanced around the engine house, thinking I wouldn't trade that scene for this scene for anything in the world.

Except the dang murder part.

8

THE DOGLEG ROADHOUSE & Grill was a Wilson landmark. When Richie agreed to meet me on our week off he said the Dogleg was the Oklahoma crew's favorite hangout, followed by the Oasis in Taft and the Penny Bar in McKittrick. Those guys had done their homework on Westside bar life. They took their leisure as seriously as they took roughnecking for Emmet.

The Dogleg sat at a ninety-degree crook in the highway into Wilson — a place where the speed limit dropped and the road jogged to avoid some pumpjacks. It dated from the 1940s and was done like a Wild West saloon, with raised wooden sidewalks shaded by a deep overhang. They'd used salvaged rig timber to construct it, which gave the building a rough, recycled look. A frontier-fort look too: the street windows had been boarded up, leaving narrow slits like slits for the cavalry to shoot through. Because of the bend, half the building was set back from the other half, and each half had a thick wooden door.

I pulled open the right-side door and walked in. The tule fog had lifted, but at five P.M. in January it was already dusk. My eyes didn't have to adjust to the bar's dim interior lights.

So far I'd gotten nowhere on Kenny Mills. I was hoping that would change soon with Richie's help and muscle. Doug had made an official call about a witness wanted in an L.A. case who vaguely resembled Mills. Kern sheriffs told him that Mills was a Wilson native with a Wilson address. He'd died from a single blow to his bare skull – and had no jail or prison record, bench warrants outstanding, or known drug affiliations. They'd found evidence of methamphetamine use, however, in Mills's pickup truck.

Over the years I'd come to the Dogleg a bunch. The two halves of the building represented the social divide in the oil business.

I was in the right side, called the front room. It catered to the white-collar class – engineers, geologists, land men, salesmen, consultants, producers, executives, and management of every description. That side had younger waitresses, no pool tables or jukebox, and a more refined menu. Richie warned me not to go in the front room but he didn't know I knew the couple who owned the Dogleg. The flat-screen was playing CNN with the sound low, and the tables were empty except for two guys drinking whiskey and snacking on peanuts. Their jackets said BAKER HUGHES.

The guy behind the bar flapped his towel at me. It was Gerry, Joe's good friend, one of the owners. I'd come early because I knew Gerry would be an excellent source for local gossip. He was a wiry, tough old dude with crinkly eyes and sun-crinkled skin who always wore the same thing Joe always wore: a cowboy shirt and jeans. I walked over and Gerry stuck out his hand.

"Where've you been, young woman? Emmet working you too hard to come see your buddies? Your granddad would be tickled pink, you know, you being a worm on Joe's wildcat."

He was wrong but I didn't enlighten him. Smiling, I just shook his hand. "You're not supposed to say *worm* anymore, Gerry."

"Excuse me, I forgot – it isn't politically correct. Did you hear Yokuts had a toolpush call some new hand a worm? It hurt the kid's feelings and they sent that old toolpush to sensitivity class." Gerry motioned me to sit. "Roughnecks with hurt feelings. The oil fields aren't what they were once, I'll tell you that for free."

"Well, worms eat dirt and that's about what my job is." Climbing on a stool, I unbuttoned my jacket.

"What'll you have, dear? I'm buying."

"A Corona with a slice of lime would be good, thanks."

Gerry got a beer, stuck a lime in the neck of the bottle, and set it down on a napkin in front of me.

"How's it going out there? I hear you're lost."

"Very funny." I sipped my drink. "For your information, Minerva no.1 is a confidential well—AKA a tight hole. Top freaking secret. I'm not authorized to discuss the progress of drilling."

Of course Gerry knew that. He wiped the bar, even though it was clean and dry, and threw the towel over his shoulder.

"Anyway, I'm just the worm. Ask me if the mud pumps were painted lately or if we have a current count of all tubulars on the lease. And *anyway,* how can you possibly get lost? I've never heard of that."

Gerry lifted his eyebrows. "Who's responsible for your education? You've never heard of getting lost?"

He laid his hands on the bar side by side with his index fingers touching. His left thumb didn't bend and a lumpy scar ran from it to his wrist. You rarely met an ex-roughneck with ten healthy fingers.

"California is some of the toughest land drilling there is. We're sitting on top of the San Andreas, what they call a strike-slip fault, where the North American and Pacific plates come together."

He pushed one hand forward and pulled the other hand back. Gerry loooved to give lectures.

"The plates are moving like this and what the pressures do to our young rock, why, I have stories that would uncurl your pretty hair. You might drill the same formation three, four times on one well, or find the Monterey outcropped or at ten thousand feet. You hit a fracture your seismic didn't show you, it carries the bit away and you're lost. I've heard tell of drillstrings hanging in space, just hanging there, no idea where the rock is. Mud motor won't get you back to drilling straight. You have to set a plug and kick off or punch a new hole—"

The soundproof door at the end of the bar opened.

Richie stuck his head in, glanced around, caught my eye briefly, and ducked back out. Grabbing my drink and jacket, I slid off the stool:

"Sorry, Gerry, I have to go. But I need to talk to you some more."
I held up the beer bottle. "Thanks for this."

"You're very welcome – come back soon. Here, allow me."

Opening the padded door, he shooed me through, and I was in
the back room. This was where the workingmen drank – roust-
abouts and pumpers, construction guys, service guys, truck driv-
ers, well-pullers, and rig crews from driller on down. Townies and
non-oilies drank there too.

The place was cleaner than you'd expect and bigger than it
looked from the street. It had room for three pool tables, a jukebox, and a stage for a live band. The décor was more Budweiser
than the front room's, but the timber walls were covered with the
same profusion of oil-field memorabilia – signs and framed photographs – and western artifacts, from kitschy paintings to old bri-
dles and ropes. The flat-screen was showing a football game and
there was country music coming out of the jukebox.

Richie was playing pool with Kyle, Lynn, and Dean, the derrickman on daylight crew opposite us. I waved and Richie acknowledged it as I chose a high table for the view.

One guy was drinking at a high table nearby and a few more
guys were scattered at the low tables around the dance floor. Carrot Bobby was among them, his back turned to the pool game,
hunched over a hamburger and fries. I'd found out Emmet had
switched him to the other morning crew, so he was headed to the
rig. The only woman in the room besides me was standing behind the bar. That was Jan, Gerry's wife, a good-sized woman past
middle age. Another guy I recognized from daylight crew sat on a
barstool talking to her. I'd already decided he was local based on
what I'd seen at shift change. I gave him a long look but couldn't
tell much except that crystal meth wasn't his vice – or not yet.

A collective shout came from the pool tables. I glanced over
and Richie was walking towards me swinging his cue. He looked
so different when he relaxed, and all the guys looked more civi-
lized and less subterranean out of rig clothes. I knew I looked different too. Per Emmet's "no vampin" rule, though, I wasn't bombing around in the groover gear I'd normally wear in L.A. I had on

a flannel shirt and jeans and beat-up paddock boots I used to use for horses.

Richie tapped the table with the butt of his cue. "Going to a tie-break. I'll be a few more minutes."

I said, "No problem," and sipped my beer, reviewing the deal I'd made with Emmet.

He'd agreed to help on one condition: I leave his crews alone. Cain't pick and choose in a boom, Emmet said. Some of the rough-necks had criminal pasts; some were probably working under false names or Social Security numbers. If I started to pry, he'd have even more labor trouble. It added a kink that there were known criminals at the lease, but I had to accept Emmet's condition. I did wonder out loud if Trey had a record: Emmet's lips were sealed. I didn't dare ask about his precious Oklahoma boys, and I refused to wonder about Emmet. Doug told me I should because Emmet was a Wilson native and we knew nothing about his personal history except that he was friends with Joe. But I categorically refused to suspect Emmet of murder or conspiring to murder.

Checking the time, I saw Richie racking his cue. He grabbed his glass of beer, pounded Kyle on the back, and threaded through the tables to come sit with me. To cover us, Emmet said he'd spread the story that he might promote me to floor hand and Richie was schooling me in our weeks off.

Richie settled himself at a conservative distance, then, hunkering slightly, spoke in a low voice:

"Don't turn around. There's a guy sitting at the table behind you." Richie pointed with his eyes – dart, dart, left, right. He'd gotten the darty-eye from Emmet.

I spoke in a low voice too. "You mean the chubby loser in the gray sweatshirt and work boots wearing a Dodgers cap and a stud in his ear, in his early forties, maybe? Hard to tell with the beer bloat."

I thought the detail was funny but Richie ignored it. He darted another glance, speaking even more quietly. "That asshole's a *scout* – a lowdown piece-of-shit snake of a *spy*."

Richie bit out the separate insults. He used to excuse his language around me but not anymore.

I said, "I know what a—"

"Somebody's paying that asshole to spy on us and steal information about the well."

I twisted around for a peek, pretending to brush lint off my sleeve, wondering why Joe hadn't told me.

On a tight hole—which wildcats always were—they took precautions to protect information and access. Minerva had a guard at the entrance to monitor traffic and sat in a dead zone for cell reception. In the top doghouse the computer screen was covered and locked. Normally the crew washed samples, the rock cuttings coming out of the hole. But our crews were just bagging them for the mud logger to look at because a good hand would recognize types of rock.

The scout was lighting a cigarette. He had a mug and pitcher of beer beside him, and looked like he'd been rooted there for hours.

I whispered, "Does the scout have a name?"

"Mark Bridges. He's from in town here."

"Who's the somebody paying him?"

"We don't know." Richie indicated the room with a tilt of his head. "A bar close to the rig is the worst. Get a hand liquored up and get him to talking. That's why Emmet ran the other toolpusher off—for talking to some old boy from Oxy."

Oxy was short for Occidental of Elk Hills. They owned most of the natural gas production in the area.

I started to say, "What other toolpusher—"

Breaking in, Richie darted his eyes. "Guy doesn't think we know, but we sure as hell do. Emmet's put us to watching *him*."

I flashed on Kenny Mills. In the doghouse Christmas Eve he'd said: "Word in town is this well's in trouble." I thought he was just a gossip. What if he was trying to solicit information? What if he was part of the spying? A motive for his death had suddenly appeared—

I snapped back into focus at something Richie said.

61

"They may could have us bugged. We don't talk important business inside the trailers or by landline."

Realizing he'd forgotten about his drink, Richie picked his glass up and chugged the beer that was left.

"But anyone can count stands of pipe and know how deep we are."

"Yes, ma'am – they can and they do." Richie set his empty beer down. "I've seen the bastards set a mile off and count through field glasses. When we're making trips, Emmet sends Tommy out to patrol the roads – sometimes it's Mr. Balch that goes. Country's so flat you can see a fair piece but that works as much against us as for us. It's like Emmet says, there's cracks in the dike and we don't have fingers enough to plug them all."

Richie's eyes stopped darting and started tracking. Mark Bridges had gotten up with his beer mug and was crossing the room over to the bar.

I watched him too and knew who his target was – the local hand from daylight crew, the guy talking to Jan when I came in. He'd been drinking steadily on the same stool and now had a hamburger in front of him.

I checked the time: 6:15 P.M. by the Budweiser clock.

The scout's reasoning was clear. The back room was filling up and getting noisier and smokier. He'd waited for more cover to make a move.

Kyle, Lynn, and Dean were on their ninety hundredth game of pool, but they must've been keeping tabs on Bridges because they watched him cross the floor. Richie and I were sitting up higher, and I saw Richie and Kyle exchange a look over people's heads. At the bar Bridges took the stool next to the local hand, pulling his baseball cap around so the bill faced back. We all saw him say something to the local guy. Kyle started forward at that and Richie stood up.

I put a hand on his arm. "Let Kyle do it, Richie. I have an idea."

Richie was tensed to move; he wasn't going to take any order from me. Then Lynn nudged Kyle and they headed for the bar together. I felt Richie untense, but he didn't take his eyes off his homeboys.

They waded through the crowd and Kyle grabbed a stool on the local hand's left. Lynn sat down on the scout's right. Both he and Kyle looked like they had a buzz on. I realized violence would be stupid, though, because Bridges didn't know *they* knew. He also hadn't noticed their coordinated approach. Kyle smiled and joked with the local hand while Lynn started talking to Bridges. I was sure Bridges recognized Emmet's guys. There he was, flanked by two of them, and he had to know he wasn't getting any top-secret well information tonight. After ten minutes with Lynn he plunked money on the bar, twirled off his stool, and headed for the exit.

I pushed my beer away and stood up, grabbing my jacket. "Let's go."

Richie said, "Where to?"

"I don't know. We're going to follow the scout." I tugged his sleeve. "Come on."

Richie wouldn't let me drive so we jumped in his truck and took off after Mark Bridges.

Bridges pulled out from the Dogleg headed east, driving a red pickup with one of those cartoony lift kits that stuck him high in the air. I made a note of the license number and make of his truck as we tailed him past Joe's house to I-5, where he got on the south ramp for L.A. There was plenty of traffic on the interstate but Bridges was driving under the speed limit, the way someone who's been drinking does. Between that, the straight, flat highway, and the high-up truck, it was easy to keep his taillights in view.

I used the time driving to pitch Richie in earnest: let's help the cops get whoever murdered Kenny Mills.

Richie hadn't committed when I first mentioned my plan. Now he said he'd thought it over and didn't want any part of it. Mills was a worthless druggie – taking up other people's oxygen and no damn use to the world. I tried to sway him with my hot new theory: Mills's death was related to the tight hole and spying. Richie just said I was wasting my time and wouldn't listen to any argument, from abstract justice to the integrity of our drilling operation. He didn't even care that Emmet backed me, which I thought he would.

Was he refusing to help because he still thought Bobby swung that hammer?

I couldn't tell.

Bridges peeled off the interstate at Highway 58 and turned east again. Richie bet we were going to Bakersfield. He obviously enjoyed the game of tailing, and he was right about our destination.

Bakersfield reminded me of my hometown when I was growing up. Calgary had changed incredibly since the 1980s: it looked more like Houston now, with its glittering skyscrapers, green, and sprawl. But when I was a kid it looked like Bakersfield – a cow town on a bald patch of land with mountains close by. In Bakersfield's case, the southern Sierras. There was even snow on the peaks, although you couldn't see it in the dark.

The narrow highway ran for miles through agricultural and industrial outskirts, then new subdivisions, then it hit the city limits and turned into a wide commercial strip with lots of stoplights and traffic. That was trickier driving. We tailed the high red truck past malls, chain hotels, and chain restaurants, through a freeway interchange, past Buck Owens Boulevard, into a residential area.

Bridges made a right and a fast left, and I told Richie to drop back, which he resented without saying so.

Braking and hanging back at the corner, we watched the scout pull into the driveway of a big shingled house with a manicured lawn. He parked beside a white SUV, climbed out of his truck, steadied himself, and went up and rang the doorbell. I felt conspicuous in a dirty pickup with Oklahoma plates but Bridges had tunnel vision: he never looked around. We watched as an executive-type older man answered the door. Not shaking hands, he just stepped back and motioned Bridges inside. I asked Richie if he recognized the executive. He didn't. When the front door closed, Richie took the corner and pulled past the house into the shadow cast by a tree near a streetlight. He turned off the engine, I twisted around in my seat, and we proceeded to wait.

Richie wasn't cut out for the waiting part.

He fidgeted while I got out my cell and typed the make and license of the SUV, then Googled the address. Wireless reception was sporadic in the valley but, luckily, not in the middle of Bakersfield. Bopping around the Internet, I got MSN White Pages to give me a name: Daniel Fox. I Googled *Fox* and, skipping down, found an article from the business section of the *Bakersfield Californian*.

Dan Fox was vice president of acquisitions for West Coast Energy.

There was a headshot: it was the guy. West Coast was a large independent oil company headquartered, according to its website, about two miles from where Richie and I were sitting.

Joe needed to know about this. I dialed his number –

The front door of the house opened and Mark Bridges walked out alone. Richie started the engine. I turned around to face forward, grabbing my seat belt as I left Joe a message and then put the phone down. Bridges climbed into his truck, backed out of the driveway, and took off the way he'd come. Cranking a U-turn, Richie followed him. Richie'd lost patience for this game and barely spoke on the trip home.

I thought Bridges would drop by the Dogleg for a nightcap but he zoomed on past and kept going into Wilson. Richie braked in front of the Dogleg. Caught up in the chase, I snapped:

"Keep driving! We can't lose him now!"

Richie stepped on the gas again but that ended conversation for good. He went stony, his eyes fixed on the high taillights ahead.

We followed Bridges through the center of town, past the big intersection with the Kwik Gas, into a working-class neighborhood with old wooden bungalows and chainlink fences.

Bridges turned a corner, stopped, and reversed into a driveway to park beside a fishing boat on a hitch. Richie pulled in at the curb and cut his headlights, breaking the silence to make a snide remark about the smallness of the boat. We watched Bridges sit a few minutes, then swing down and walk slowly across a dirt yard into a house. I asked Richie to pull forward. He did, without enthusiasm.

Through the front window, we could see Bridges talking to his wife. She was in a fluffy bathrobe and as we watched she started to wave her arms. Bridges flung his arms up and it looked like the beginning of a you're-late-and-you're-drunk argument. Laying his head back, Richie shut his eyes. Gestures got bigger, the yelling started, and Bridges stormed out of the living room with his wife yelling behind him. The front window went dark.

I sat thinking.

What I needed was someone who knew Wilson and didn't have a big mouth. As Doug had pointed out, key to this investigation was not to appear to be investigating. It would alert the sheriffs before we were ready, and alert the killer . . . if he was still around.

I said, "Gyah!" out loud without meaning to.

Richie opened his eyes. "Did he hit her?"

"No, no. Hey, Richie – would you take me over to see Jean?"

Straightening up in his seat, Richie turned the key in the ignition.

9

WE PULLED INTO the alley behind a split-level house in Wilson's best neighborhood. The Oklahoma crews were billeted with families around town, and Richie, Kyle, and Lynn were staying with Jean Garcia. Because of Joe, I'd known Jean a long time and liked her tremendously. I'd also been a fan of her husband, Manuel – Manny – who died in an oil-field accident years ago.

It was after eleven P.M. and lights were still on all over the house. Jean kept late hours; she always said it was the Mexican influence. I followed Richie across the backyard and up the porch stairs to the kitchen door. He checked through the curtained window, rapping on the glass before he opened the door:

"It's me, Miz Garcia. I brought someone."

I walked inside behind him. The kitchen was purple and green and had an old-fashioned feel, from the frilly curtains to the patterned linoleum. A woman of sixty, Jean was standing at the sink rinsing dishes and taking puffs off a cigarette in an ashtray. She wore work clothes – a sweater set and skirt – with bedroom slippers and an apron, and she was listening at a green telephone on an extra-long cord. The receiver was wedged between her ear and shoulder.

Seeing Richie and me, she covered the mouthpiece, whispering, "Oklahoma – Arielle. Ann! How nice!"

I flapped my hand. Richie scowled *No!* without a sound. Jean shook her head and uncovered the mouthpiece.

". . . Richie isn't here, Arielle . . . He didn't say what his plans were for tonight . . . I don't know why he doesn't answer his cell phone . . ."

Richie was making the cutoff sign, drawing his thumb across his throat. Jean mouthed, *Have you eaten?*

I mouthed that we hadn't. She pointed at the refrigerator and whispered, "There's cold beer and tuna casserole left over. Will you serve our guest, Richie, please?"

Richie beelined for the fridge and Jean indicated a seat at the kitchen table, which was covered with papers. Waving cigarette smoke away, I sat down while Richie first grabbed a beer, twisted the cap off, and took a long chug, then got plates for us and spooned out casserole.

". . . I'll tell him you called . . . I'm sorry you're sad, honey . . . I understand – I'll be sure and tell him . . . Well, thank you. I'm always here if you want to talk . . . Good night . . . Yes, good night."

Jean hung up the telephone and sighed, giving Richie a worried look. She had a plain, very kind face and talked in an uneffusive country way. Richie's lips were pressed thin and he refused to look at her as he handed me a fork and a plate of food. Jean got busy straightening papers to clear space on the table.

"I apologize for the clutter. I'll get you a napkin –"

Richie preempted her. "Rest yourself, Miz Garcia. I can do it."

There was no argument from Jean. Sitting down across from me, she put her feet up on the third chair. Richie brought me a napkin and Jean her ashtray and picked up his plate of food and his beer.

"You ladies will excuse me. I'm going to see what's on the television."

He walked out as, smiling at Jean, I said, "Excuse me too. I'm starved," and dug into the tuna casserole.

Jean was the reason Joe should've divorced Alice – and probably also the reason he hadn't bothered to.

Wilson people didn't gossip to me about the Balches, and Joe was a clam. So I had no idea how long he'd loved Jean or how long she'd loved him. I didn't know if that situation had anything to do with Alice's move to L.A. I *did* know Joe was great friends with Manny Garcia, his right hand at Balch Drilling until he got hit by a frac truck out at Lost Hills. I knew that Minerva was Jean's middle name. And I also knew Jean was a pillar of the community. She ran the petroleum studies program at Wilson High School and was rumored to be in line for principal. My vibe was she thought Joe's divorce would cause talk that would hurt her reputation and reflect on Manny's memory.

While I was eating, Jean had been smoking. She took a last drag on her cigarette, stubbed it out, and leaned back. "Did you want something to drink, honey? Beer or soda?"

"I'm fine, but thanks."

"The students and I were talking about you today. We're rooting for you at the rig, my girls especially. Emmet says you have the makings of an excellent hand. The crew's given you a nickname, you know."

Now that, I was afraid to ask. I jumped over to "I came because I want to talk about Kenny –"

The telephone rang on the wall behind Jean's head. "Hold that thought." She reached up and lifted the receiver.

"Hi, Cath. Guess who's here. Ann Whitehead . . . Sure, I'll be up late. I have these applications to read . . . See you in a minute."

Saying, "My sister," she hung up the telephone and I started again. "I wanted to ask you about Kenny –"

Richie interrupted this time. He came into the kitchen with his empty plate, and Jean pointed at a glass-domed platter. "There's cake for dessert, Richie, and the coffee's fresh."

Richie dived for the counter. Grabbing my plate, I got up too. He cut two slices of cake, one for me, a giant one for him, and left again.

I said, "Cake, Jean?"

"Thank you, no — just coffee. I'm so glad to see you, Ann. What a treat."

"Me too, you. I feel like all I do these days is work and sleep. I can't get the sound of the diesels out of my head — it's wild."

I poured the coffee, then juggled mugs and cake to the table. "I wanted to ask you about the hand who died, Kenny Mills. He was from Wilson."

"I know he was — poor Kenny. I had him in my chemistry class many years ago." Jean made a sympathetic face and drank.

"I was wondering about his life, his friends — anything you can tell me."

Pausing her mug, Jean gave me a suddenly suspicious look over the rim. "Why do you —"

But the doorbell rang before she could finish the question. A familiar voice came from the other room — a booming, busybody voice. It belonged to Jean's sister, Cathy, the private nurse who'd been in and out of the house checking on Joe's health after his heart attack.

She boomed, "Jeannie! Where do you want this junk?"

Jean called, "Put it in the garage! Richie, would you help my sister, please?"

"Yes, ma'am!"

There was conversation in the living room, then Cathy's voice boomed, "Why you bother with this silly jumble sale is beyond me, Jean. Make Joe Moneybags write a check —"

Jean swiftly cut her off. "We're having cake and coffee in here. Come and join us."

Cathy appeared in the kitchen doorway and I thought to myself how much the two sisters looked like sisters. They were both large and thick through the middle, with plain, kind faces — and probably went to the same hairdresser for the same bad dye job and perm. Cathy was fifty, maybe — younger and more officious. She was wearing her white nurse's pants with a saggy cardigan sweater.

I waved hello and she waved back as she helped herself to coffee. She said, "How're you liking it at the rig, Ann?"

"I love it – but I'm a little freaked about the accident."

"What accident?" Cathy came to the table with her cup. Jean moved her feet for her sister to sit down.

I said, "The guy who died, Kenny Mills. He was on morning tour with us." I pointed at the living room to mean Richie. We could hear the TV set.

Cathy said, "It wasn't an accident. Kenny was murdered."

"Catherine Rintoul!"

Jean shot up rigid, slapping Cathy's leg and practically shouting. Her normal tone was subdued.

Cathy was unrepentant. "The whole town knows, Jeannie. You're such a Pollyanna."

"The whole town – fiddlesticks! It was an *accident*."

Cathy smiled in good humor but Jean shook her head, not pleased. A door banged in the front room. We heard Richie's raised voice – then Kyle and Lynn came trampling into the kitchen with Richie close behind. The two guys seemed pretty plastered but they were behaving themselves. Crossing his arms, Richie leaned in the kitchen doorway to baby-sit.

Kyle greeted the sisters with "Evening to you, Miz Garcia, Miz Rintoul," tipping his head like he was tipping a hat. The Oklahomans did the southern thing of turning *Mrs.* into *Miz*. They didn't mean *Ms.*

Lynn greeted them but not me, and I thought I heard Kyle say, "Evening, Pup." It was talked over by Jean.

"Help yourselves to cake, boys. You'll have to make another pot of coffee."

Richie walked over to take care of the coffee. Those three moose filled the kitchen to capacity. They were all in the six-foot, two-hundred-pound range, although weight was distributed differently on Lynn. He jostled Kyle aside to get at the cake, and Kyle jostled back. A jokey pushing match started.

Richie barked, "Stop it, y'all!"

They stopped instantly. Lynn said, "Yeah, Bale." Kyle said, "Yeah, Lynnie," and reached for the cake knife. Lynn said, "What happened with the scout, Teach? Where'd you and Pup go?"

I saw Cathy's antennae start to twitch. "Scout? What scout?"

Cathy was a *demented* gossip. Luz was a Garcia and when Cathy was watching Joe, she and Luz would sit in the kitchen for hours ripping people to shreds. Alice's arrival had put an end to that.

Cathy repeated, "Is someone scouting Minerva?"

Jean passed a look to Richie that Richie passed back. Cathy caught both looks. "What is it, Jeannie? Who's scouting Minerva?"

"I've asked you not to call it that, sister."

Kyle went, "This guy Mark—"

Cathy leaped. "Mark *who?*"

Abruptly, Jean stood. "It's late, Cath, and I still have these applications to read. I'll call you tomorrow, all right?"

Cathy looked at Jean, then at Richie, who'd shouldered Kyle into the stove to distract him. She knew she was being shunted out. Setting her coffee cup down, smiling ironically, she wished everyone a good night and let her sister escort her to the front door. I looked at Richie and wasn't surprised when he made the duck-quack sign with one hand and said, "Big old flapping mouth."

Kyle giggled. "Who, me?"

"Bale, Lynnie—get your cake. Let's check out the television."

Richie pushed Kyle ahead of him into the living room and Lynn followed. Jean reappeared and sat down again, rubbing her eyes with fatigue. She put her feet back on the chair seat and I cleared my throat to bring up Kenny Mills one more time—

The telephone rang.

I groaned inside. This place was a circus—but I already knew that. Jean was very popular. She felt for the receiver behind her head automatically.

"Hello? . . . It's not too late . . . Yes, do come ahead. I made Abuela's lemon cake . . . I'll see you soon."

She hung up. "That was Joe. He's on his way over and I know he'll want to hear about the scout."

Leaning forward, Jean untied her apron, took it off, and draped it over the back of her chair. Then she reached in her purse for lipstick.

It was the time of night that, on my reversed schedule, I really started to click. The three of us were sitting at the kitchen table. Jean'd had a slice of cake waiting at Joe's place and poured him coffee the second she heard his voice at the door.

I told them how we tailed Mark Bridges to Bakersfield and back, showing Joe my phone where I'd typed the address of the Bakersfield house and the specs on the SUV in the drive while I described the executive type who'd answered the door.

"His name's Dan Fox—you probably know him. He's head of acquisitions for West Coast Energy."

Adjusting his trifocals, Joe took the phone and skimmed the information on the screen.

"It could be something or it could be nothing." I shrugged. "Maybe Fox hired Bridges to spy—maybe they're planning a bar mitzvah. Richie and I just followed him from the Dogleg on an impulse."

Joe deadpanned, "It's something. You've got my attention."

"How come you didn't tell me Minerva was being scouted?"

"Didn't see the point. What were you going to do—shoot somebody?"

Besides Doug and the relevant police authorities, Joe was the only person who knew the whole story of what happened in L.A. Jean's expression said she thought Joe was making a joke. I smiled at her and curled my lip at him.

He handed my phone to Jean and reached into his shirt pocket for his Camels and lighter. Getting up, I walked to the sink to open the window. The kitchen was already stuffy with cigarette smoke. Joe hadn't been thrilled when I told him what I was planning about Kenny Mills. We'd gone around and around like Emmet and I had done, but I finally persuaded him too. He also liked Doug and trusted his judgment.

Joe inhaled then exhaled. "She thinks smoking causes lung cancer." Gently, Jean said, "You *have* been sick, Joe."

He just blew smoke rings at the ceiling and watched the draft from the window disperse them. I leaned back against the sink. "Richie can tell you what Mark Bridges was doing before five o'clock."

Joe raised his voice. "Richie!"

"Mr. Balch, sir?"

"Come here a minute, son."

Coughing into one fist, Joe pointed a finger at me. "You passed an important test this afternoon."

"Yes, sir?" Richie appeared in the doorway as I answered, "If you mean Gerry, you can't be serious. He'd have to stick bamboo splints under my nails to get a drilling secret. And besides, I don't know what Schlumberger said. *Are* we lost?"

Joe laughed, a noise like a short yip.

"Are we ever. Ah, hell – the whole county knows we're lost by now. Might as well hang a sign off the derrick."

He looked at Richie. "Tell me, son – who'd that turd Bridges talk to? By God I'd like to kick his fat behind."

Richie was standing stiffly: Joe made him uncomfortable. Joe made all the hands uncomfortable, although he was basically a plain workingman. Minerva was projected to cost between ten and fifteen million dollars to drill. If they found gas, the price would double to complete it. Joe wasn't paying the entire bill – he had some minority investors, including Balch Oil. You never forgot he was running the show but he acted like the mechanic they'd called in to replace the cathead.

Richie said, speaking stiffly, "Saw him talking to Jan, sir – he always does spend time with her. Tried to engage one of the daylight crew in conversation but Bale, I mean to say Kyle, and Lynn headed him off –"

Richie's cell phone rang and interrupted him. I hadn't noticed he was holding it in his hand.

"Pardon me, Mr. Balch. I have to get this." Turning fast, he left fast. It was rude by Richie's polite southern standards.

Joe flicked a glance at Jean, his signal for more coffee. For once

Jean wasn't paying attention. She seemed interested, or worried, by something I'd written on my phone.

I said, "What is it, Jean?"

Covering nicely she smiled, holding the phone out. "Nothing, honey. I'm . . . just always amazed by these fancy gadgets."

I walked over to get it as she and Joe exchanged a look. I could read the meaning easy: they knew something they weren't telling me.

What we hadn't discussed was the truck parked in Dan Fox's driveway. It was a white Suburban with a USC decal prominent in the back window. It could've belonged to Dan or Mrs. Fox, or another Fox. But I was getting the strong sense it didn't, and that Jean and Joe knew who it *did* belong to. And I wasn't supposed to know.

"More coffee anyone?" Jean stood up. "Joe?"

I said chirpily, "Well, it's late and you kids have things to talk about." I pointed at the living room. "I'll just get Richie. He needs to drive me back to the Dogleg for my pickup."

I walked into the living room. Nobody was there and the TV was off. Downstairs it was dark; that's where Kyle and Lynn slept – or passed out. Up a half flight of stairs to the upper level, Richie was talking. There were silences so he was still on the phone.

I heard Joe say, "I'm moving to the lease, Jeannie. Here's –"

I went to the front window to get out of earshot.

Jean's living room was done in her signature purples and greens, with frilly slipcovers and knickknacks and family photos on every wall and table. Above the couch in the place of honor was a large photograph of a pleasantly pie-faced Latino man, hardhat tucked under his arm, standing beside a Balch Drilling pickup. The late Manny Garcia. Jean kept a smaller picture of him in the kitchen.

The street was deserted and it was drizzling, and I was very glad I wasn't on tour. It had rained in December and working in the wet was a drag. Rain somehow always found a way to trickle in and turn to ice on your skin. It was much more fun to eat cake in Jean's smoky kitchen, even if I'd learned almost nothing I could use. The mystery around the Suburban might or might not be pertinent. It might just be something Joe wouldn't tell me because I'd shoot someone.

But I had to get going.

Crossing the room, I took the stairs and found Richie sitting on the floor in the upstairs hallway. He was hunched over his cell phone talking very low and intent – and defensively.

"Don't you believe JD, babe . . . Bobby's a damn liar . . . I never did say that! I never did! Arielle's a lying little whore!"

Richie was too engrossed to see me. I knocked on a doorjamb to get his attention and he looked up. His face was unhappy but I pretended not to notice. I tapped my wrist to mean the time, pointed in the direction of the Dogleg, and mimed a steering wheel, mouthing, *My truck?*

Richie turned his back on me. He cupped his hand over his free ear and said unhappily, "I know I promised not to, babe. I know I did . . ."

I shrugged. The Dogleg was only four or five miles – I'd walk it.

As I headed down the stairs, hearing the murmur from the kitchen, I knew Jean was a dead end. Cathy'd called her a Pollyanna and she was sort of right: Jean did tend to see and hope for the best. If she didn't believe Kenny Mills was murdered, she wouldn't help me.

I also knew why mean little JD had flown back to Oklahoma and what had come between Richie and Bobby. It was a woman named Arielle who wasn't Richie's wife.

10

I WENT OUT TO the lease the next morning to squeeze Emmet for information. Somewhere around dawn I'd realized that he *had* to know a whole bunch more than he was telling me. It was a bright, sunny, crisp January day – a beautiful day in the desert. But I wasn't enjoying it as I crossed the back field because I was sleep deprived, frustrated, and mildly mad at myself.

It'd been a week and a half since Kenny Mills died and I was making no discernible progress.

One big snag was my work schedule. I'd get home from the rig, shower, eat, and collapse for eight or ten hours because I was so toasted. That left only a few hours every afternoon before I was due back on tour. Once I'd tried setting the alarm to get up earlier: Richie caught me that night dozing in the compressor house beside a bucket of spilled water. But this was my week off and, even though sleep was a mess, I was determined to make things happen.

I also cursed Doug's ethics.

In theory he could've run the license plate on the Suburban. But LAPD had clamped down on requests unrelated to open cases and – despite my whining – Doug wouldn't consider a bogus story to get the information. He certainly couldn't go to Kern sheriffs for it. But he had made several helpful suggestions. He'd also given me Mills's address up front and that's what I'd been doing every day:

cruising Mills's mobile home or sitting and watching it. I figured I'd see a neighbor to talk to, or someone might come by to collect Mills's stuff. But his place seemed abandoned and the area was crummy to the point of menace.

Jogging up the lease road, waving at Tommy, I ducked under the barrier gate, jogged to Emmet's trailer, and banged on the door.

He was sitting at the desk in his sock feet, totaling invoices with a calculator. "What you stirrin up now, little sister?"

Not looking at me, he thumbed his papers. He had drugstore reading glasses way down his nose, an open can of 7Up beside him, and the country music channel on TV.

"Could I speak to you in the yard?"

Emmet shifted his tobacco to the other cheek and, turning his head, fixed me with the squinty-eye.

By this point I could've written an instructional pamphlet on Emmet's various eyes and what they meant. He had the slitty-eye, the squinty-eye, the darty-eye, the bland-eye, the eagle-eye, the x-ray-eye, the steely deadpan, and the Eyeball. A granite mountain emoted more than the rest of him: his eyes did the work. The squinty-eye was his speculating look – he was weighing my question and the possible motives behind it. It didn't take him long to decide. Rolling back his chair, he leaned over heavily and reached for his boots.

"Mind if I put my teeth in?"

"I'll wait outside."

The yard between Emmet's and the rig had four new trailers in it – six-wheel travel trailers parked in a tight row. Emmet found me snooping around them.

"What you bein so dang secretish for?!"

It was impossible to have a private conversation shouting over the rig engines. I motioned him across to the open yard in front of Joe's trailer, and, standing on tiptoe, I spoke into his less-deaf ear.

"I heard yesterday we're being spied on! Richie told me the trailers are bugged and the landlines are tapped!"

Without a word Emmet turned and tramped back across the gravel so that I was forced to follow him. When we got inside his trailer he sat down, pried his boots off, and propped his sock feet back up on the desk.

He said, "I'll speak to Teach. Joe had a outfit come sweep us here last week – we's clean."

"Okay, good." Draping one leg over the end of his desk, I half sat and said, "Are we on the same team?"

"Do what now?" Emmet cocked his head a centimeter.

"Are we on the same team? Are we trying to catch a killer or not? I'm asking because I don't think you've told me everything. I want *everything* you know about Kenny Mills. I want to know what you know about the scout, Mark Bridges, and who he's reporting to. I want to know about this toolpusher who was fired for talking to a guy from Occidental Petroleum. I want to know why you switched Bobby to a different crew, and who Arielle is. I want to know why Kyle and Lynn are calling me Pup. And I'm sitting right here until you answer me."

As I finished, I settled in, crossing my arms and giving him a kindergarten version of the Eyeball.

Emmet rumbled, "Want an egg in your beer too?"

I just widened my lids and intensified the Eyeball. Sometimes I couldn't believe myself: Emmet was my *boss*.

"All that there has a bearin on matters, you say?"

"Except for Pup, yes, and Arielle, maybe – I think all of it might have a potential bearing."

Emmet rocked back in his chair, tucking both hands inside the bib of his overalls. After a moment of cogitation he said:

"I pay no heed to gossip, mind, but I hear tell Kenny's girlfriend, name of Suzette, got him hooked on the crystal meth and now she's skedaddled – gone, supposably scared."

"Scared of what?"

Emmet just murmphed. Sometimes *murmph* meant "yes," sometimes "no" – sometimes "I don't know," or "I'm not telling." I interpreted in context: he didn't know.

"Bridges is a bone-lazy good-for-nothin livin off stripper wells his good-for-nothin daddy left him when he died. Never did a lick of honest work, neither of them sorry bastards."

A stripper well made ten barrels a day or less on a pump. And I realized that, like Richie, Emmet had stopped excusing his language.

"Joe shipped that yappy toolpush –"

"Hold it, stop. Is Bridges scouting for someone besides West Coast Energy? Is Dan Fox tied to someone we know?"

Emmet murmphed again. I interpreted in context.

"You know what Richie and I found out last night – you've talked to Joe." I tapped a fist on his desk. "You *have* to tell me. It may be that Mills's murder is related to the spying."

"Cain't do it, little sister. Cain't even if I wanted. We's checkin on it and if it is what we thinks it is, it's a bad deal – baaad deal."

I just looked at Emmet, going, *Yow,* inside. He went on. "Joe sent that toolpush up north to a rig drillin around San Ardo. Booger weren't worth a damn anyhow."

"There was another toolpusher besides you?"

Emmet nodded a non-nod.

"How did I miss that?"

"Happened right after spud – Joe was in the hospital. Usually speakin, we'd of had two toolpushers workin seven on/seven off like the crews but Joe ain't replaced that booger 'cause of security reasons. I like pushin with no relief. Reminds me of my younger days when we wasn't up to our ass in labor laws and damn sorry bureaucracy."

"Got it. What about Bobby?"

"Carrot asked to be moved – didn't say how come. If a boy asks I try to accommodate 'em. Don't know no Arielle."

"You're not telling the truth."

Emmet didn't bother to deny it. "They's callin you Pup 'cause the shortest hand's always Pup. A pup joint, see, is shorter than your standard thirty-foot joint of drillpipe. Anythin else now?"

Shaking my head, I stood up. "Richie's refused to help with this. He thinks the world's a better place without Kenny Mills."

"Somethin to ponder may be."

Emmet leaned forward and moved his stack of invoices, looking for a specific piece of paper. "Where you headed from here?"

"Back to the house for my truck, then around. Why?"

Emmet found the paper he was looking for and handed it to me. It was a grocery list.

"Mind doin my shoppin? I don't want to go nowhere whilest them directional boys's riggin up."

"Tell me why Bobby switched to the other morning tour." I fluttered the list back and forth like a flag.

Pulling his sock feet off the desk, Emmet rolled his chair forward, grabbed his reading glasses, and got busy with the invoices again. I waited. He took a swallow of 7Up and started punching numbers into the calculator.

If you kick a mountain, I thought, you just mash your toe. I stuck the grocery list in my pocket and left.

Kenny Mills had lived in a broken-down mobile home on a patch of sand fronted and backed by dead bushes. It was just off the state highway west of Wilson in a rural slum called Antelope Acres — twelve or so blocks in the middle of empty desert, built around a gas station in ruins.

I'd found it by a process of elimination because there was no mailbox or number anywhere on the property. The other houses on his street — and *house* was an overstatement for some of those dwellings — were in the same general shape as Mills's place. Sun-fried; trashed-out; rusting hulks up on blocks; rusting propane tanks; rusting air conditioners in boarded windows; junk all over the greenless yards. I'd seen a few people from a distance, but the only other signs of life were cars and trucks that moved between my visits and satellite dishes on roofs.

Pulling in front of Mills's place, I parked and turned off the engine.

I'd read up on the local crank scene and one statistic gave me serious pause: 85 percent of county homicides were related to methamphetamines. Long-term use produced volatility, anxiety, paranoia, and spur-of-the-moment killing, sometimes between strangers. The weapon of choice wasn't guns or knives or rig hammers: it was the nearest vehicle. Two doors up from Mills's was a weather-beaten house with psycho, hand-printed KEEP OUT! placards on the fence and garage. Crank did destroy entire neighborhoods – but it wasn't what destroyed this one. Judging by the age of the gas station, I figured the heyday of Antelope Acres was the 1950s.

I looked everywhere and didn't see any action inside the mobile home or any at the neighbors'. There were no dogs chained to stakes, even. That's how grim this area was. The only thing that moved was a rickety windmill in the KEEP OUT! yard.

Climbing down from the truck, I pocketed my keys and walked up the crumbled asphalt of Mills's driveway.

I circled his place looking especially for signs he was making crank himself. Chances were he hadn't been. The DEA had cracked down so hard that most of the methamphetamine used in the States was now manufactured in Mexico. I did a complete circuit of the trailer, back around to the driveway. All I saw was dead vegetation, and garbage and junk dumped on the ground and left to rot or rust. None of it was stuff you found with meth labs.

Continuing to check for neighbors, I walked right up to the mobile home. It had turquoise aluminum sides, faded and pitted by decades of sun and blowing sand. I cupped my hands and tried looking through a window. The glass was filthy. Licking my finger, I rubbed a spot clean and still could only see silhouettes of furniture and a kitchen counter. I knocked on the blistered door and tried the handle. The door was locked.

I circled the trailer one more time to see if any windows were open. Torn screens, yes – cracked glass, yes – no open windows. I wasn't going to break and enter. Those days were over, and besides, Doug would flip if I did.

Across the street was the best-kept house in sight, an old clapboard place with a cactus garden and a troll.

I walked over and rang the doorbell. A dog barked inside. I rang the doorbell a few times but nobody came and the dog barked more frantically. Backing down the walk, I shaded my eyes and checked windows. The curtains didn't move – nobody was peeking out. An enormously fat woman saw me, though, because she emerged from the dilapidated shotgun shack next door. Her arms were splotched with bruises and there was a baby crying somewhere behind her. I called hello and asked if she knew Kenny Mills. The woman turned right around and slammed her door in my face.

That did it. I decided Antelope Acres was more depressing than dangerous. I'd try every house on the street except the crazy KEEP OUT! place.

It was early afternoon and a lot of people weren't home. One neighbor only spoke Spanish, and at least one other neighbor refused to answer the door. I did find the old lady who owned Mills's trailer. She lived in a crappy house at the corner and told me Mills had lived with his girlfriend, Suzette. The couple were months behind on rent, she said, because Mills couldn't keep a job, and Suzette lost her beautician gig because of drug use. The landlady dropped one other interesting morsel: Mills hadn't roughnecked in years. But she couldn't give me Suzette's last name or last place of employment, or anything more about Mills.

I also talked to an ancient old guy – or he talked to me – who slipped off the topic into the twilight zone where immigration met fluoridation as part of a conspiracy to undermine the American way of life. I walked away in mid-rant, but not before I learned that Mills had repaired the old guy's pumping unit in Maricopa for a fair price. I grew up calling them pumpjacks, which must've been a Texas-ism. Around here they were called beam pumps or pumping units. The cost of services had shot sky-high in the boom, the old guy said, and well-pullers were so busy with the big producers like Chevron and Aera that you couldn't get them to come out for a little mom-and-pop like him. He may have linked it to the conspiracy. I didn't stick around to find out.

I was very glad to drive away from Antelope Acres and left a message on Doug's cell phone to tell him so.

Next stop: Balch Drilling in Wilson.

Boom or not, the Westside oil business didn't spend on frills or flash. The office of the Balch companies was in the center of town in an old brick building that had been retrofitted for earthquakes. If you didn't know what to look for, you'd drive right by it because the only signage was tiny: BALCH in blue letters on the glass door. I slowed down to stop in front of the building – and suddenly had a better idea. I knew exactly who to ask about Kenny Mills's employment history.

I drove out to the Dogleg and parked next to Richie's pickup. Taking off my sunglasses, I walked into the back room and could've sworn it was yesterday. Richie, Kyle, Lynn, and Dean were playing eight-ball at the same pool table. Bobby was gobbling a hamburger with his back turned to them. Jan stood behind the bar talking to the local hand on daylight crew – Richie'd said his name was Greg – who was sitting on the same stool drinking beer. The only character missing was Mark Bridges. I checked around. The scout wasn't at a high table or the bar today.

Richie acknowledged my presence with a dip of his cue. Kyle gave me a goofy grin and slapped the air to say come over. I smiled and shook my head, pointing to the front room –

"Ann!"

It was Jan calling from behind the bar. Still smiling, I veered in her direction to say hello. Jan wasn't one of my favorite people. She didn't like women and put on a phony maternal act with the male customers that made me urp.

"Take a seat. What'll you have – a Corona with lime?"

Wiping her hand on a towel, Jan put it out for me to shake. I noticed she wasn't smiling so I stopped smiling as I took her hand and shook it. She had a firm, almost painful grip. Greg glanced over and I nodded hey.

He nodded back.

I said to Jan, "Thanks, I can't. I'm running errands."

"I wanted to ask you a question, Ann." Jan spread her arms and propped herself against the bar. She was a hard, red-faced woman – wider and meatier than Gerry. Staring pointedly at my left hand she said:

"Why aren't you married?"

The question caught me sideways. My views on marriage were none of her business; it was enough that Doug and I argued about it. I wanted to kick her, but I kept my tone light.

"Why do you ask, Jan?"

She leaned in at me. "I ask because girls your age should be home raising children, not working in the oil fields, *that's* why."

Setting her jaw, she eyed me aggressively and waited for an answer. I couldn't think of one except *I'll make a pencil note of it,* so I turned to go.

Jan snorted "Hmph!" as I walked away, then threw at my back:

"That's where you should be! At home with a husband!"

Ignoring Kyle's shout, I headed for the street door. I started laughing the second I got outside and, turning left on the raised sidewalk, walked down to the entrance to the front room.

The room was deserted and Gerry wasn't behind the bar. I sat on a stool to wait. The flat-screen was playing ESPN today and I watched the latest sports news until Gerry came in through the door from the kitchen. He smiled when he saw me, a smile with no teeth.

"Sorry to keep you waiting—I had to run to the bank before it closed. What can I get for you?"

He bent down to the cold place where he kept the bottled beer, but I held up my hand. "Nothing to drink, Gerry. I'm back with my questions."

Shrugging, Gerry switched the TV over to CNN, then took a towel and started wiping the top of the bar.

I said, "I just heard Kenny Mills hadn't roughnecked in a long time. Do we know how he ended up with Ozark?"

"That's Ron's doing. He's sending Emmet his dregs."

"Would that be Ron *Bray?*"

Gerry nodded, still wiping. Bray was Joe's VP of operations at Balch Drilling, Manny Garcia's successor. He ran the company day to day, had bowlegs, always dressed in denim, and I liked to bug him by being friendly at the house.

I said, "Why's Mr. Bray messing with Emmet?"

"It's not for me to say. Ask Emmet, if he'll tell you."

"But you have a theory on the subject — or positive knowledge."

"I do."

I waited but he wasn't going to expand. "You big geek, come on! Is it theory or fact? Why can't *I* know?"

Gerry just winked at me. I took a guess:

"Mr. Bray is jealous of Emmet. He wishes he were the contractor on Minerva."

I'd nailed it.

"Smarty-pants. That is correct." Gerry finished wiping, threw the towel over his shoulder, and propped himself against the bar.

"Ron begged Joe to buy a triple to drill this wildcat. Joe didn't tell you? He said wait and see what they found with this hole first."

I started to ask, "What's a triple —"

Cost. The last word was *cost*. But Professor Gerry didn't let me finish.

"A triple's a big brute like Ozark's got out there on Minerva. Derrick's tall enough for a stand of pipe and the rig's rated to eight hundred tons so they can handle the weight of drilling and casing deep. Joe doesn't need a rig that size around here and he's damn lucky he got that one, excuse my French. You can't find free triples for love or money in this boom. Hell . . . excuse me, heck . . . you can't find free *rigs*. Joe booked with Ozark a year out, before he had his drilling program or permits —"

"Gerry!"

Jan startled us both. She was practically on my neck and we hadn't heard the door from the back room open or shut. I leaned away from her as Gerry unpropped himself and straightened up.

Glaring at me, Jan said, "*You* don't belong in here." Switching the glare to Gerry, she repeated, "*She* doesn't belong in here."

Jan stalked around the bar, clamped on to Gerry's arm, and dragged him towards the kitchen. Gerry let himself be dragged, not sure what was happening. Jan caught my eye on the way out to make sure I felt her disapproval again. I just winked at her, which got an offended snort.

As they disappeared I checked the clock over the bar, remembering I hadn't done Emmet's grocery shopping yet. I slid off the stool and pulled out his list. He was planning to cook beef chili, it looked like – but it had to be another secret formula because there was one item there I'd never heard of in chili.

11

PACKED A LOT of driving and talking into Friday, Saturday, and Sunday day before I went back on tour at six.

First off, Doug and I argued the safety question. He thought I was too cavalier about danger and finally made me see I couldn't just blast around asking questions about Kenny Mills. He suggested I pose as my former self, a journalist, and say I'm researching a feature on the life and death of a California rig hand. I thought that could make things weird at work: my crew might think I was only roughnecking for material. Doug said to run the idea by Emmet. Emmet said not to perturb myself – if it got back to the guys he'd handle it. So I broke out the groovy clothes, put on some makeup, bought a spiral notebook, and waded in. My sleep schedule was getting hopelessly screwed up but I dealt with fatigue by drinking coffee or napping in the truck when my eyes wouldn't stay open any longer.

Doug had originally said that the place to start with Kenny Mills would be his obituary and funeral service.

I'd read the obit in the *Gusher* but when I'd called the funeral home after Christmas to find out when the funeral was, the woman told me there'd be no formal service or public viewing of the body. I'd gathered there wasn't money to bury Mills right and didn't pursue the issue.

When I visited the funeral home Friday, though, billing myself as Mills's former coworker, I discovered that a wake had been held the previous weekend. I acted upset to've missed it and said I wanted to see the guest book. There hadn't been a guest book, the funeral director said, and his code of discretion wouldn't allow him to say who or how many had come. I wormed it out of him that Joe paid Mills's burial expenses, which led to the news that Joe and Emmet sat with the casket the day before the wake. Nervous that he'd said too much, the director suggested I go see so-and-so, who sent me to someone else, who sent me to two more people. In that way, I spoke to a self-selecting smorgasbord of gossips who were happy to drop what they were doing to talk about Mills and didn't care why I wanted to know.

Here's what I learned.

Kenny Mills was only forty when he died and had lived his whole life in Wilson. His immediate family were scattered, and he'd always been a boozer-stoner-doofus who'd always hung out with boozer-stoner-doofi. Since high school he'd roughnecked for Balch Drilling and other area contractors. Drug-testing had put a crimp in his job options because he was banned from oil-field work for six months every time he failed one. He'd had run-ins with the cops, *x* number of DUIs, and a common-law wife who'd left him for a plumber. Taken together, it sounded like Mills was no danger to anyone except himself. People couldn't explain it, though, when I pointed out the contradiction. They were positive Mills was murdered, and yet he seemed harmless. Who'd kill him and why?

The *why* was methamphetamines. But it was all gossip and speculation, or accusations that vibed of old grudges. I couldn't get one concrete lead.

Crank was epidemic on the Westside. You could walk into any bar or club in Wilson and buy it from the third person you talked to. There'd been a million local meth labs before the DEA landed. Now crank came up I-5 from L.A. and Mexico and was sold and used by too many people to count. I'd asked about Mills's and Suzette's dealer or if they'd been dealing themselves. I'd asked who the big dealers were. Nobody could, or would, say. Maybe this guy who sleazed around Taft—maybe some field mechanic who ped-dled dope out of the company truck. After enough of those conver-sations and making a swing through the main bars, I didn't believe Mills had died in a turf war or for money owed.

Some of the gossips were familiar to me so I didn't believe half of what they said.

But I did learn things about Wilson I never knew—and one per-son who cropped up in connection with crank was Jan. Boy, the town didn't like Jan. She styled herself local class because she'd come from the big city, Fresno, and married Gerry, whose family had owned the Dogleg since it opened. Jan considered the Dog-leg her personal property and acted all la-de-da—as if the Dogleg weren't just an oil-field honky-tonk like every other low den on the Westside. Drugs weren't bought, sold, or used in Jan's back room, no sirree: her you-know-what didn't stink. The truth was the ex-act opposite, I was told, especially on live-music nights. How could poor Gerry wake up every morning next to that shrew? The gos-sips loved to debate the question and didn't mind doing it in front of me.

Other people had no interest in Kenny Mills or his death. They were older, or involved in the oil business, and knew me as Joe's surrogate daughter and Jim Whitehead's granddaughter. Those people wanted to talk about Minerva no.1. They were hoping very hard that Joe's wildcat would hit pay and reverse Wilson's decline . . . again. Wilson had been dying when the young Joe drilled Lucy Boyd no.1 for Alice's father, Ray Parkerworth Senior, and proved up the Wilson Flats field. That was in the late 1950s and the Park-erworth, Balch, and town fortunes all rose together. Now, despite the boom, Wilson was dying again, and Joe was taking a much big-ger gamble on deep gas. But the cognoscenti put absolute faith in him and his guesses.

Going around, I was reminded just how Oklahoma the county was. You heard it in the twang and felt it in the oil culture and con-servative sensibility.

One old guy reeled off an amazing statistic: between 1930 and 1950, nine hundred *thousand* Okies came to California. Hadn't I heard that joke? he said. What were the first three words an Okie baby learned? Answer: *Mama, Dada, Bakersfield*. He and his cronies at the diner cackled over that and a famous Will Rogers line: when the Okies migrated to California, the IQ of both states went up. The old guys would've chewed my ear off about Kern crude and the Westside's golden age if I'd let them. I did say I kept a stick lizard on my coffee table at home and they cackled like fiends.

It wasn't hard to find women who knew Mills's girlfriend, Suzette. She'd worked at and been fired from every hair and nail place in town. She hadn't left any fans behind, either. By all accounts she had a bad temper, a princess complex, and a drinking problem that had turned into a raging meth problem. At her most recent salon, which I walked into during the Saturday rush, the owner said Suzette had tried crystal meth to lose weight and went to hell fast. She'd been fired for throwing a hairbrush at someone – and, frankly, Suzette had lost so much weight she looked like death on a cracker.

By the way, the owner added, where did I get my coat?

I'd thought a groovy look would help with the beauty professionals and it did. It also got the attention of customers who either loved or hated L.A. and jumped into the Suzette conversation with glee. In that particular salon, in the early afternoon, all the chairs were full and the owner invited general conversation by talking loud enough for everyone to hear. Imitating her, I asked my questions loud. Did Suzette have friends or family on the Westside? Was her relationship with Kenny Mills volatile? Did she attend his wake? Did she have any friends on the Minerva crews? Did she disappear after Mills's death because of a real fear or a drug delusion? What kind of car did she drive? Where might she be now?

I stood at the reception desk listening to crosstalk and heard one surprising item. Suzette was the daughter of Hilary Mahin – "Boots" Mahin – Joe's very old, close friend, the second most powerful man at the Balch companies and the second richest man in Wilson.

As I pondered that I was scanning the salon's appointment book. A name stopped my eye: Cindy Bridges. It had to be the wife of the scout because Mark and Cynthia Bridges were listed at the same address in the phone directory. She was due for a cut in half an hour. Suddenly I realized I needed a manicure and asked the owner if she could fit me in.

Ten minutes later, Mrs. Mark Bridges walked into the place. I recognized her even without the fluffy bathrobe. In person she looked like a disappointed and furious forty. She was in a lousy mood too, which she announced to the room as she took a seat and plunked her purse in her lap. The owner explained my errand to her and it unleashed a tirade I was grateful to hear.

Put *this* in your article, Cindy said.

Mark Bridges and Kenny Mills had been best buddies since Wilson High. *High* was the operative word — the two guys had boozed and smoked dope together for twenty-five years. Cindy had never liked Kenny or his influence on her husband. But when Kenny hooked up with Suzette Mahin, well, she didn't care *who* the Mahins were, she'd banned Kenny and Suzette from the house. Suzette was horrible and Cindy couldn't have tweakers — meth addicts — around her kids.

She'd tried to ban Mark from seeing Kenny period and from giving him money, but Mark had stopped listening to her. He was acting like Mr. John D. Rockefeller with the price of oil rising every day. West Coast Energy had made an offer on his leases, he *claimed,* and everyone knew West Coast was flush with cash and throwing it around, overpaying for producing properties and companies. But Mark was such a bullshitter she couldn't *believe* the amount he said West Coast was talking about. Meanwhile he was gone all the time — at meetings in Bakersfield, he *claimed,* or servicing his pumps. She hadn't slept a wink last night because he hadn't come home. He showed up at eight A.M. saying he'd fallen asleep in his truck and trying to placate her with money she had no idea where it came from. She was sure he was having an affair and she was going to kill the woman —

Checking my nails, I decided I didn't need a manicure after all.

I tried to tell the salon owner I'd changed my mind but she was busy with a client who announced she'd kicked two husbands out for philandering.

Emmet wasn't being fair when he called Mark Bridges bone-lazy. Bridges had a pretty demanding schedule. Besides spying on our wildcat, drinking at the Dogleg, neglecting his family, driving to Bakersfield for suspicious meetings, and maintaining his stripper wells, he was hanging around the Oasis in Taft for hours at a pop.

From the salon I drove over to watch his house, betting he'd be home baby-sitting the kids and also betting he'd take off the minute his wife got back from her haircut. He was and he did. Following the red cartoon truck to Highway 33 and south, I felt comfortable tailing Bridges even though it was daylight because the pickup Joe'd loaned me was a generic Chevrolet. It had no Balch markings and it was white, the most common color for pickups in hot country.

Taft was older than Wilson. It was also set more into the hills that formed the west boundary of the south valley, and had a whole bunch more oil. Midway-Sunset was California's largest oil field based on cumulative production—over a billion barrels of heavy crude since its discovery in 1901. But Taft had the same blend of prosperous and derelict as Wilson, with about the same population. And every last Taftite seemed to be out Saturday afternoon deliberately getting between Mark Bridges and me.

The highway turned into the main street and, trapped at a yellow light, I almost lost Bridges when he took a corner up ahead. I gunned it at the green, took the same corner, and at the next intersection saw he'd taken another right and was parking down the block. I braked and pulled into the parking lot of the post office. Slumping in my seat, I watched Bridges disappear into the Oasis across the way. It was a blue building with sun-faded OASIS signs, striped awnings over the doors, and a red tile roof. I remembered Richie mentioning the Oasis as a favorite hang and checked around for his truck or any truck with Oklahoma plates.

Four hours I sat there.

The sun set; it got dark and cold. More and more people went into the Oasis. I made up my mind to leave a dozen times and dozed off a dozen times. But Bridges eventually reappeared and I followed him back to Wilson – slightly under the speed limit, his drinking speed.

He didn't go home. At the Kwik Gas he curved onto the highway east but didn't stop at the Dogleg like I anticipated. We were headed for the interstate when he braked suddenly and took the first left past Joe's house. He was going to the rig.

I slowed down and made the left behind him. Pulling off the blacktop, cutting my lights, I jounced over bare ground until I was hidden under the eucalyptus trees at the back fence. I didn't want to get out in my good boots but I did, ducking through the drooping branches to see across the fields.

Bridges had turned off his headlights and kept going north up the blacktop road. There was no cover except the pitch-dark of the country. He passed the left turn to the lease, then pulled off the road to the right and parked in a field. He was level with the rig, due east of it – and almost invisible in the red pickup.

I looked over at the rig.

Drillpipe in the rack blocked my view of what was happening inside the derrick. It wouldn't block Bridges's view, though, and he probably had binoculars. I pulled out my phone and checked the reception: no bars. The temptation was to run in the house and call Emmet. But I didn't want to risk losing Bridges. So I watched from under the trees, straining my eyes in the darkness. After thirty minutes he came barreling past on the blacktop and turned right at the highway, back into town. I bombed after him and caught up where the highway jogged to avoid the pumpjacks. Bridges had slowed way, way down.

Now we were going to the Dogleg.

Cars and trucks lined the street on both sides and I could hear the band as I drove up. People dashed across traffic – people were crowding in and out of the back room and standing around on the raised sidewalk. When I opened the street door, the wall of hot air, loud voices, cigarette smoke, and country music was a shock after the cold vigil in Taft and the freezing, dark fields.

Taking off my coat, I elbowed and slinked my way through the bodies. I saw Richie playing pool with Kyle and some other guys; they weren't acting like they'd seen Bridges come in. The high and low tables were full of couples and stag and mixed groups in a range of ages. The dance floor was also packed and the band was deafening. Spotting a backwards Dodgers cap at the bar, I pushed my way over and found Bridges already with a glass of draft beer. A stool two down from him was miraculously free so I grabbed it and sat.

Jan and Gerry were both tending bar. Jan came over, wiping the bar top as she shouted, "Welcome to the Dogleg! What can I get for you?!"

I shouted, "A Corona with a lime, please! And a dinner menu!"

Her head jerked up—she hadn't recognized me in groover-journalist disguise. Slapping the bar with her towel, she glared and walked off. I half stood to flag Gerry, who'd stopped to talk to Bridges. I saw him lean over so he wouldn't have to shout so loud.

"Cindy called! She's looking for you!"

"Screw Cindy!"

Gerry barked, "Finish your drink and get out! You can't leave her by herself on Saturday night!"

"Damn it, Gerry, she's turned into a total bitch! There's no living with her!"

"Go home to your wife, Mark!"

Bridges flushed, and, slamming his glass down, twirled off his stool and left, shoving people out of his path. I swiveled on my stool and craned to look over at the pool tables. Kyle was lining up a shot. Richie stood with a cue in one hand and his other arm around a teenage girl who had both arms wrapped around his waist.

I decided to bag the dinner idea. Grabbing my coat, I stood, wedged my way around the dance floor, and came up on Richie's non-woman side. I shouted over the music:

"Richie!"

Richie glanced down and didn't recognize me, but I could tell he'd also had plenty to drink.

I said, "Ann! Your lease hand! I combed my hair!"

I laughed at the stupid look that came over Richie's face. He let go of his girlfriend, then wondered why he'd done it. She peered around him to give me a jealous stare. Standing on tiptoe, I pressed against him to speak into his ear.

"Bridges spies on Minerva from a field due east of the rig, twenty or thirty yards off the blacktop! He spent half an hour there tonight!"

The girlfriend pouted, "Richie!" and tried to separate us by pulling on him.

"Hush now!" Richie squeezed her shoulder.

Kyle came over saying, "We're playing the winners of –" and did a double take. Whistling, he tried to put his arm around me. He was full of beer too. "Pup! You clean up real nice!"

I batted his arm down. "Emmet will run me off if you start that, Kyle!"

Richie leaned in drunkenly to tell Kyle what I'd just told him, crushing me between them. I struggled to push them apart and discovered Richie's girlfriend had her nails out and was trying to scratch me. Grabbing her fingers, I crunched them hard and she yanked her hand back and yelped.

That broke the guys apart. The girlfriend started to whine as I leaned up to Richie's ear. "I'll tell Emmet about Bridges!" Turning to Kyle, I held his sleeve and stood on tiptoe, shouting, "Is that Arielle?!"

Kyle gave me a goofy grin as I waved and ducked off through the crowd. The salon owner had shown me a picture of Suzette Mahin. I hadn't seen her so far, but I wanted to check one more place before I left.

The back hallway was jammed with people waiting in line for the washrooms. I kept repeating that I was just looking for someone as I elbowed, excused myself, pushed, and wiggled through the crush. I didn't see Suzette, but drugs were definitely being consumed in large quantities. There were glassy-eyed, zonked-out, speedy people everywhere. When I squeezed into the wash-room I saw married women exchanging pills and cowgirls doing lines of white powder. I'd never been around crank but there was a nasty smell coming from the stalls. I nudged a door to see in. Two women were holding a lighter to tinfoil and inhaling the smoke off a nugget of pink crystal.

The Dogleg had a back entrance and I took it to get out.

Breathing deep for fresh air, I ran to my truck and drove to the gas station. While I was filling up I called Emmet in his trailer and couldn't reach him. Then I tried Joe at home, at the lease, and on his cell, and couldn't reach him either. But I knew where he'd be on Saturday night.

12

JOE'S TRUCK WAS parked in Jean's driveway. And the white Suburban with the USC decal was parked on the street in front of her house.

I tiptoed quietly up Jean's front stairs and peeked in the picture window. Joe was lying on the living room couch with his boots off and his eyes closed. I could see Jean's back through the lit doorway of the kitchen. She was sitting at the table wearing a purple sweatshirt.

Jean lived on a corner. I trotted around the house and up the alley, across her backyard, and tiptoed up the porch stairs to peek in the kitchen door.

Caroline Mahin was sitting at the kitchen table crying. She was Hilary Mahin's wife, a dainty and sort of silly woman who I'd met over the years in social situations. I couldn't distinguish words but she had a box of tissues and she was wiping her cheeks as she said something to Jean.

I rapped on the glass with one knuckle. "Jean? It's Ann!"

Normally I would've invited myself in but I stood and waited for Jean to come answer. I saw her push her chair back and stand, and Mrs. Mahin turn her face away to blow her nose.

I opened the screen as Jean opened the kitchen door, quickly stepped outside, and shut both doors behind her. Her forehead was crumpled and she was looking distressed.

I whispered, "What's wrong with Mrs. Mahin?"

Jean just shook her head.

I whispered, "I'm looking for Suzette. You wouldn't happen to know where I could find her."

"It's not a good time, honey." She glanced through the screen into the kitchen.

"Is it a good time to tell me what a Mahin vehicle was doing at Dan Fox's house in Bakersfield?"

Taking my arm, Jean turned me to face the porch steps. "Did you have a date? You're all dressed up."

I shook my head and whispered my Emmet imitation, which was getting better. "'No vampin mah boys, little sister. I run you off elsewise, hear?'"

Jean smiled faintly. I said, "I need to speak to Joe, though. I followed Mark Bridges around today."

"Joe's resting."

"Is he all right?"

Jean just squeezed my arm. "I'll tell him you're looking for him." She steered me towards the steps. "Good night, dear."

Starting to object, I changed my mind. Actually, it was fine. I was starving and exhausted and hadn't checked in with Doug for too long.

I bombed home to a dark house. Luz went to dances Saturday night and Alice wasn't back from Hawaii: Luz and I were hoping she never would be. I raided the fridge, left Joe a note, then spent a while writing Doug the revelations of the past two days. I called Emmet, reached him, and told him about Bridges's spying post. I called Doug several times but couldn't reach him and, even though it was nowhere near dawn, decided to try to sleep. If I could be rested for tour Sunday evening, it would be great.

I set the alarm for four P.M. and passed out instantly. A call from Kern sheriffs woke me up at nine A.M. The trial for the Kwik Gas loser was scheduled to start Monday and the robbery detectives wanted to check in and go over my testimony. I was one of their star witnesses.

That meant driving to Bakersfield.

I hauled myself out of bed, barely awake, and dragged myself over to sheriffs' headquarters. It had taken months for them to put their case together because this guy had been pulling armed robberies for years. He worked alone – that was the key to his success. Once the cops nailed him, though, he'd been identified by so many witnesses – there was so much surveillance tape, and so much evidence found when they searched his place in Oildale – that the prosecutors' problem was deciding which and how many robberies to try him for, and in whose jurisdiction.

While the detectives massaged me, working my story into the shape they needed for the judge, I was massaging them. I wanted to know if they knew anything I didn't about the Kenny Mills case. One detective did. He was buddies with the homicide guys called out on Mills, and he let it drop that the detectives weren't completely happy with the autopsy results. They weren't convinced a falling hammer would've produced that head injury: it didn't fit with the angle and the type of damage to Mills's skull. But they'd let the question slide in the absence of any motive or signs of premeditation.

I took this news casually – I was brilliant.

Back at home, after a short nap, I zoomed off an e-mail to update Doug and left early for work because I wanted to talk to Emmet about Hilary "Boots" Mahin.

The chainlink fence at the back of Joe's property was less than ten feet from the line of eucalyptus trees. The trees were old and Joe never had them pruned. Their drooping branches brushed the chainlink, and the ground all around was slick and spongy with shed bark, fallen leaves, and seedpods. Under the branches, it was always darker and colder than the falling dusk.

I paid no attention to the rustle as I closed the chainlink gate. Even without a wind, the eucalyptus rustled.

Suddenly someone had an iron grip on the back of my neck.

He slammed me full force into the twisted wire at the top of the fence. It happened so fast I couldn't yell – I could just turn my head to save my throat. I dropped my duffle bag and cooler and grabbed the fence, pushing backwards with all my might. The guy was too strong. He pressed my neck harder and harder against the chainlink. I struggled and flailed and tried to kick behind. But I was already lightheaded – I couldn't get air. Pinned to the fence, blacking out fast, I saw red streaks and white starbursts and my last thought was:

That's it. No more me.

13

ROLLED SLOWLY ONTO my side and lay there.

The night was still. I cracked my eyes open. I was looking at total darkness but I could smell the earth and the trees hanging over me, and hear the diesel engines at the rig.

My body was stiff from cold. From the shoulders up I felt numb, except for the piercing pain in my neck. I lay there a while longer, orienting myself, then pushed slowly onto my hands and knees. I tried to groan but the groan stuck in my throat and hurt like heck. Crawling to a tree trunk, I used it to pull myself up to standing. I leaned against the tree and adjusted to vertical, waiting for the nauseated, dizzy feeling to pass.

Doug is going to kill me.

The thought made me want to laugh – but the laugh stuck in my throat too.

Pushing off the tree, I started walking – slooowly – groping for the fence as a prop. My foot hit a soft object and I stumbled: my bag of work clothes. I left it there and continued along the fence line using the eucalyptus trees for a screen. When the trees ended, I struck out into the open, trudging a big, slow loop through the fields to approach the lease from the west. Light from the lease spilled over the boundary fences and I moved as fast as I could to the barbwire, in shadow behind the line of trailers. I was hoping for a back door into Emmet's . . . there wasn't one. Climbing slowly through barbwire, I snuck around the north end of his trailer. The gravel crunched, but I knew it was only loud to me. The diesels drowned out everything.

To get to Emmet's end door I had to pass in front of the changing hut and step into the lights of the yard. I crept to the corner, looked left, right, and up at the doghouse, then slid around fast and climbed up inside, opening and closing the door fast. The effort made me dizzy again. I was in Emmet's small, overheated storage room filled with paperwork and cans of starter fluid and—

"Put your hands up!"

Joe.

Putting my hands up, I teetered. My legs gave way and I collapsed on the floor, head spinning.

"Come out of there!"

I threw one arm wide, grabbed the corner of a filing cabinet, dragged myself up to the threshold, and lay still. Joe stood at the far end of the couch with Emmet's 12-gauge trained on the doorway.

When he saw who it was, he immediately lowered the shotgun. "What's wrong with you?"

I'd opened my collars to ease the pressure on my neck. Tilting my chin, I showed him and whispered, "A guy attacked me at our back gate."

"Good God in heaven." He set the shotgun down and started for the telephone on the desk. "I'll have Cathy take a look."

Cathy the nurse—Jean's loudmouth sister.

"No, Joe!"

I shook my head making the yak-yak sign with my thumb and fingers. My neck would barely turn but Joe got the gist and didn't dispute it. Changing direction, he went into the kitchen, opened the fridge, and reached in the freezer for ice.

The clock on the wall said 12:48 A.M. I'd left the house at 5:33 P.M.

I wanted to sit up, and tried to, using the file cabinet for a brace. Suddenly I felt just gruesome—in pain and burning hot and sick to

103

my stomach. Before I could catch myself or make a noise, I blacked out again.

I came to stretched on Emmet's couch with a bag of ice on my throat. Joe was gone and Emmet was sitting in his chair, sock feet on the desk, checking the computer screen. The graphics were bright blues, greens, and reds, and I could read the secret numbers on the grid clearly from where I lay. Across the top of the screen the columns read: Hole Depth, Bit Depth, Hook Load, Weight on Bit, Rotary, Torque. Down the side of the screen: Strokes #1, Strokes #2, Total Mud, Flow, Pressure, ROP.

The words and colors were vividly clear – hallucinogenically clear. It was funny how almost dying made everything more intense –

Emmet heard me stir and turned his head. "Teach didn't want to say you missed tour else we'd a'come huntin for you. He don't think sometimes, that boy don't."

Swinging my legs around, I sat up slowly, taking the ice bag with me and pressing it under my right ear where it really hurt. My head was still woozy but I smiled.

"Too much fornicatin, not enough thinkin." It came out a raspy whisper and only elicited an Emmet deadpan.

Ice was probably best for the swelling and pain but I craved a hot drink. I whispered, "Tea?"

"Don't keep no tea. Coffee do?"

Emmet pulled his feet off the desk and stood up. I shook my head. "Hot water . . . lemon . . . honey?"

"Got both." He went into the kitchen. "Bastard jumped you on the way to work, that right?"

"Right." I cleared my throat and said louder, "Right."

Emmet murmphed.

While I waited for the hot drink, I probed my neck, thinking the guy could've easily killed me and didn't: it looked like just a warning. Emmet came with a mug, then brought extra lemon and honey on a second trip, setting the plate on the arm of the couch. I nodded my thanks and took a test drink.

Emmet went to sit, but his telephone stopped him. He picked it up without a hello.

". . . Yep, I seen it . . ." He pointed at the pressure reading on his computer screen. "Went from twenty-three eighty to forty-one hundred . . . Don't you do it, Teach – I'll have a polite word with the young man myself."

Hanging up, Emmet bent over to put his boots on. I said, "Where are we?"

"World of pain is where we's at – been tryin for days to kick off that damn cement plug. You set right there."

He grabbed his jacket and hardhat and slammed out. According to the computer screen, the bit and the hole were at 12,932 feet and the rate of penetration was less than a foot an hour.

I sipped my drink, noticing that Emmet had closed the blind on the window over his desk. That blind was *always* up. Emmet and I were thinking along the same lines: I shouldn't be seen or our collaboration generally known – not now. I stretched my neck gingerly and pressed it with the bag of ice until Emmet got back ten minutes later.

Sitting down in his chair, prying his boots off, he swiveled around to face me. "You good for water?"

"I am." I started to add, "You're still –"

Emmet started to say, "Ain't we better –"

We both stopped and I raised my hand. "Me first." Emmet blinked for a nod.

I said, "You're still withholding important information. When did you move to Oklahoma?"

"Hired on with Ozark in 2002 to drill that deep gas out there. Wanted to try me some of them twenty-, twenty-five-thousand-foot boogers."

"Okay, so you lived in Wilson from 1902 until 2002, survived the Black Flood of 1913 –"

"Black Flood was Coalinga."

I smiled. "And Wilson's a small town. Everybody knows everybody, and everybody's business –"

"You cain't count on that, little sister. It ain't necessarily so."

"Maybe, but don't pretend you didn't know Kenny Mills hung out with our spy Mark Bridges. Don't pretend you didn't know that Mills's last girlfriend, Suzette, is Suzette *Mahin,* daughter of Hilary Mahin, Joe's money guy and lieutenant at Balch Oil, who you've probably known for decades like you've known Joe."

Emmet was doing a granite deadpan.

I said, "You realize if deadpan were an Olympic sport, you and Joe would be retired with all the gold medals."

Emmet waited a beat then deadpanned, "What's your point?"

"The point is . . ." I indicated my neck. "This proves Kenny Mills was murdered, if we had any lingering doubts. I can't think of another reason I'd be attacked unless you can. I've flushed the guy, who now knows *we* know Mills's death wasn't an accident. Meanwhile, the only traction I have so far is the conspiracy constellating around Mark Bridges. He and Mills were pals from way back. Richie and I caught him at Dan Fox's house, possibly negotiating to sell his leases except it was after business hours and Caroline Mahin's truck was also in the driveway. Caroline might be friends with Mrs. Fox from Petroleum Wives. *Or* – Hilary Mahin borrowed her vehicle for the evening."

I stopped to sip water and rest my throat. My head and neck were throbbing, and I said a quiet "ouch."

"Ain't we better call the sheriffs?"

I shook my head, barely moving it right and left.

"Remember you said nobody wants to slow drilling down with the police and asked me not to bug your crews because there are guys with criminal pasts? If we report this, the cops will swarm all over us. I'd end up telling the truth – that *any* local on your crews and the lease could've murdered Mills and attacked me. And what's looking most probable at this moment is Mills's death is connected to a conspiracy to scout Minerva, which brings in Bridges, Fox, and Mr. Mahin as suspects. That would be a baaad deal, to quote you, and it would go public."

Emmet stood up heavily, signaling for my mug, and walked to the kitchen to pour more hot water. On his way back he glanced up at the rig through the curtained window in his door.

"Joe ain't pleased this happenin to you – you know that." As he handed me the mug, I nodded, saying, "And then there's Bobby."

I got busy with honey and lemon and took a drink. Emmet sat down. "My Bobby? Carrot?"

"Carrot Bobby. Christmas Eve before Mills died I found Bobby and Richie wrestling in the yard. Trey and I had to break them up."

Emmet said darkly, "I suspicioned somethin of that nature."

"What if Bobby killed Mills by mistake? Richie believed it Christmas morning – ask him. He pitched a fit in the top dog-house. In the fog his coveralls were almost the same red as Mills's. They're close in size, they both have brown hair, and Mills had his stuck down his collar so it looked short. *I* made the mistake at first. Why couldn't Bobby?"

Suddenly Emmet slapped the arm of his chair. "It's a damn *soap opry* I got on my hands here! I swear to *God* I'll shut this booger in and bring a headshrinker out for one of them group-counselin deals!"

He slapped the chair arm again.

The idea of Emmet's crews in group therapy struck me as so funny that I burst out laughing – on the inside. The laughter bubbled up and stuck in my throat and I could only heave and gasp for air.

Emmet got that I was laughing and cracked a smile. He wasn't wearing his false teeth. Catching my breath, I said, "What happened to your teeth?"

"Nothin I know of. They's on the shelf where I keep 'em, should be."

That struck me as even funnier than group therapy, and I leaned on the couch arm, making weird gasping noises and holding my neck, whispering, "Ouch, ouch, ouch." I realized I must be hysterical.

Emmet swiveled to tap the tin of Copenhagen that always sat on his desk. "Been chewin since I's a kid and swallowin since I broke out in the oil fields – goin on fifty years now. You ain't got much left in the way of stomach nor teeth after that."

I thought of Lynn's obviously false teeth and realized Richie's might be false – Kyle's too. For some reason the idea sobered me up. Wiping my eyes, I looked around for the ice bag, took a drink of hot water, and went on.

"Richie and Bobby are fighting over some woman named Arielle. The driller opposite us, JD, is involved – that's why you let him go back to Oklahoma when you're short-handed."

Rocking back in his chair, Emmet hooked his thumbs in his overalls. After a cogitative silence he said:

"Arielle and JD's engaged to be married. Leastways they was – where the deal stands I don't know and I don't want to know. Arielle is Carrot's baby sister, see – nineteen, and a whole gondola of boys's had the use of her, which it ain't like Carrot don't know it. Teach is the smartest of my bunch and I aim to see that boy in a front office one day, but he cain't keep it in his damn pants. Here Arielle lands up pregnant and it ain't JD's 'cause her and him was feudin afore them all come out to California. Fur hits the fan right around Christmastime."

"Like I said, more fornicating than thinking." I sipped my drink. "Does Bobby have a history of violence?"

"Don't know what you mean by *history*. Nothin close to killin a man, but he's got a temper on him though and poor judgment when he's drinkin. He ain't about to take a hammer to Teach – those boys's knowed each other since they was little-bitty fellas."

"JD went home before Christmas so you must've known about the soap opera then. Didn't you suspicion Mills's death might be related?"

"Not a bit, not a bit. Only is I took Carrot aside for a talk 'cause his attitude was sourin."

"It didn't work – he's still sour. I see him at the Dogleg and he's ignoring Richie and the other guys."

"He don't have no leg to stand on neither, bein as he's sleepin with a married woman hisself back home."

I smiled. "Richie's wife?"

"You cease now –" Emmet crooked an index finger.

The desk phone rang. Automatically checking his computer screen, Emmet swiveled and grabbed the receiver.

"Mud motor's stallin . . . Yep, it burns out, we make a trip and he collects overtime in his sleep . . . Screw him, pick it up. I's comin . . . You and me both, son."

Emmet clunked the phone down. Leaning over for his boots he said, "What we goin to do with you? Want to cut and run?"

I just gave him the slitty-eye. "We also need to talk about Ron Bray. He sent Mills out here and Gerry says Bray is jealous of you. I don't know the guy's character at all. Could he be involved with Mahin and the spying?"

"Hold on." Emmet stood up, grabbing his jean jacket and hard-hat. "Got to whup me a directional hand first."

He stomped out and the trailer door slammed shut on a cold blast of air.

I needed aspirin.

I set my mug on the floor and very carefully levered myself to standing. Very slowly I tottered into Emmet's bathroom using the desk, fridge, and walls for support. Bracing on the sink, I looked at myself in the mirror. My head was aching. My neck hurt, and the pain was spreading to my jaw and face. I turned my head. Under my right ear it was a red, blue, pale, contused, abraded mess, only just starting to swell because of the ice. The outline of the chain-link was etched on my skin. Where the twisted metal ends dug in, there were dark points of bruise and blood.

Suddenly I wanted to fall down and sleep until next month –

The phone on the desk rang. I wasn't going to answer, but it kept ringing and ringing and ringing and ringing. Finally I moved to pick it up.

"Little sister?"

Emmet sounded vexed. He said, "Go home get you some rest – take the week off if you need it. I'll tell the boys you quit. Let the bastard think he scared you clean away."

"Would you mind driving me back to Joe's?"

"Cain't – cain't spare Teach now neither. I's sendin Lynn."

"But we need to talk about –"

Emmet had already hung up.

14

DIDN'T SLEEP UNTIL next month. But I did sleep thirty hours straight and would've gladly slept more except Luz came into my bedroom Tuesday at noon.

She switched on the light and shook me awake, saying she'd knocked and knocked and gotten no answer. I had a phone call. I'd left a note on the kitchen counter asking her not to disturb me for any reason, including meals, so I figured the call must be important.

Luz stooped to plug in the bedside telephone. Groggy, sitting up carefully, I turned my neck to test it and Luz saw the bruises.

"¡Madre de Dios! ¿Qué te pasó?"

I'd prepared a lie in advance. "It's no big deal, compañera – calm down. I ran into this iron thing at the rig." I mimed a chop at my neck, which made me realize how stiff and sore my shoulders were. "Who's on the phone?"

"Es la señora."

That's why she'd woken me up. We shared a meaningful and sardonic moment before I said, "Tell Alice I was sleeping. I'll call her back in an hour."

Nodding, Luz picked up the receiver. "¿Señora? . . . Missy Ann not feeling good. She have accident –"

110

I hissed, "Don't say that! Don't tell her!"

Luz broke off, winked at me like a conspirator, and listened. ". . . *No sé* . . . She say she call you in one hour . . . *Sí, sí, entiendo* . . . *Sí.*" Luz put the receiver down. "*La señora* say she call you back, okay?"

Carefully I pushed the covers aside. "Would you put the kettle on, please? I'll be out in a minute."

"*Sí, querida.*"

Luz had worked for Joe for forty years. She and I'd had a break-through the day she realized I wasn't Alice or Evelyn and didn't aspire to be: I could clean and fetch for myself. I'd evolved a theory about Luz since then. Alice treated her like a donkey, and she lived to get Alice back. She was mildly insubordinate, grumbling mono-logues in Spanish while she carried out some Alice request, and wore sloppy clothes and made extra-fatty Mexican food to drive Alice nuts. When Alice was gone, Luz let way up on the south-of-the-border act.

The house phone rang exactly an hour later. I'd done everything conceivable for my neck — hot tea, ice, aspirin, stretching, arnica cream. Plus I'd eaten a plate of huevos rancheros, and I felt pretty good. The damage wasn't as severe as I'd thought: it was just pres-sure on the carotid artery that made me black out. I took the call in the kitchen.

"Ann, it's Alice."

"Hey, Alice. How was Christmas?"

"We had a lovely time — you know how much I enjoy your fam-ily. I'm calling because I am still in Honolulu. Evelyn and I fly to Los Angeles tomorrow and we would like you to meet us there."

"Pick you up at the airport?" I was kidding.

"Of course not — my car service will come. We want you to meet us at the house."

"I can't do it, but thanks for the invitation."

"Your grandmother wants to see you."

I repeated, "I can't."

"What's wrong with your voice?"

"Nothing. I slipped at the rig and hurt my neck."

"Well, you can't work if you're injured. You can easily drive down on Thursday. That will give Evelyn and I time to unpack and settle in."

"No, Alice, I'm not going to. No." I could've softened the no with a joke or an apology but I wasn't in the mood.

Silence, then I heard Alice muffled. She'd covered the mouthpiece and was talking to someone in the room. She came back on the line. "Evelyn would like to speak to—"

My grandmother steamrolled over her: "Ann?"

It was her—peevish and imperial. She'd just turned eighty-two and wasn't improving with age.

"Hey, Evelyn." I was unenthusiastic. "Happy New Year."

"Alice says you're roughnecking for Joe out there."

"Not technically. I'm a lease hand on his wildcat but I work for Ozark—"

She pushed in. "No granddaughter of Jim—"

I pushed back. "—Ozark Drilling U.S.A. Inc. of Elk City, Oklahoma. Do you know them?"

I only asked that to needle her. My grandmother liked to hide the fact that her parents had run a greasy spoon in Duncan, Oklahoma, headquarters of Erle Halliburton's cementing business. She was waiting tables when my much older grandfather met her in the 1940s.

There was a breath while Evelyn ignored my question, then she snapped, "You quit that job this instant! Do you hear me? Joe Balch was nothing before your grandfather came along and made him rich. I'm sure it's a great joke to have a Whitehead rigpigging for him. I've always said Joe had no class—"

"Goodbye, Evelyn. I'm hanging up."

"—no class or—"

Cradling the receiver, I reached for my tea. I was debating between a hot bath and a warm bed when Luz passed through the kitchen and pointed to a note she'd stuck to the fridge. It said Doug had called the house several times since yesterday. He *never* called the house to reach me. I knew I should've called him before I crashed Monday morning. I was in deep doo-doo.

112

Dialing his cell, I caught him on lunch break at the courthouse. He was in the middle of a long, frustrating trial. Joe *and* Emmet had told him about the attack; he'd been communicating with both of them behind my back. Before he could start a lecture I told him my first thought after waking up under the eucalyptus trees: *Doug is going to kill me.* He didn't find it as funny as I had, but he laughed. *Then* he delivered the lecture.

I listened meekly because I knew he was right. I should stop what I was doing, report the attack, and let Kern sheriffs take over from here.

But I didn't want to stop—and furthermore, I wasn't going to. So I brought up the question of trust. After the attack, who should I trust?

I'd talked to dozens of people already, and those dozens had no doubt gossiped with dozens more. Doug didn't want me to trust anyone: we had no idea yet what was happening. Then investigation would be impossible, I said, and it didn't make intuitive sense besides. There were people I trusted absolutely. I trusted Joe and I trusted Emmet. I trusted Jean and Gerry. I also trusted Emmet's Oklahoma boys. Not with information necessarily, but with action—when and if action was needed. I trusted them to be loyal to Emmet.

I said, "I have to follow my instincts, Doug—you taught me that. If I'm wrong, I'm sure I'll pay for it."

His final advice was advice I'd heard from him before. "Be sensible, baby. Promise you'll be careful."

I promised.

As I drove to McKittrick that afternoon to talk to Cathy Rintoul, I was thinking about guns.

It was a Whitehead family tradition to carry guns in the oil fields. The tradition dated from the nineteenth century, to my great-grandfather who worked as a torpedoman in Pennsylvania and West Virginia back when they used liquid nitroglycerine to complete wells. In the 1930s my grandfather bought a brace of Colt .41 revolvers to protect himself from Bonnie and Clyde. He was also involved in the "hot oil" wars of the thirties, where operators in the East Texas field fought the railroad commission on production controls and the state declared martial law for a time. Whitehead lore had it that Granpap shot and killed a bit thief once – drill bits being the most valuable portable item on a lease – but never went to jail for it. And my geologist father had been held up on remote locations in Alberta for well logs and money.

I hated guns.

I was also afraid of guns because I wasn't afraid to use one. Doug knew it, which was one reason he worried: he'd seen me in action with my grandfather's Colt .41. After the dust settled and the blood dried, I'd mailed the Colt back to my father and vowed never to touch another gun as long as I lived. But I was seriously thinking about protection now, in case the jerk who'd tried to impale me on the chainlink fence tried something again.

Checking my rearview mirrors, I went over the attack, searching my memory for some feature that might identify the guy.

Was there any hint about height or weight that suggested anyone on my list of suspects or ruled anyone out? Uh-uh – not a single hint. It happened so fast I didn't even know if he stood to my right or left, or used his right or left hand to grab my neck. Even smell couldn't help. The eucalyptus overpowered everything else – cigarettes, beer, body odor, aftershave, the oily smell of the rig. The guy was bigger than me and his hand was strong and cold: that's all I could say for certain. *And* he knew I was on tour Sunday night – *and* that I walked to work across the back field when there was no tule fog.

How hard would it be to find out my schedule and habits? Not hard – especially if you worked at the lease or had connections there.

When I hung up from Doug, I'd gone out to the back gate to retrieve the gear I dropped and look for footprints or traces of any kind. I was still wondering why the guy hadn't just killed me; it would've been super-easy given my size and his strength. I wondered if maybe the starbursts before I blacked out had been headlights on a vehicle going to the rig. That might've scared him away.

Or: the attack had just been a warning.

A cushy carpet of tree sheddings covered the ground and I'd seen no signs of the struggle, or the imprint from where I'd lain unconscious for hours. I figured the guy parked and walked, and also figured the west end of the house was safer than the east end, since the blacktop to the lease ran up the east side. I'd walked west along the fence line, turned south at the corner, and walked behind the garage. The ground was too dry and hard-packed to show anything. I'd kept walking to the edge of the highway and looked into the almond orchard across the way. A square had been cut in it to accommodate a pumpjack and gathering tank. If the guy parked behind the gathering tank, you'd never see him at night. Dashing across the lanes, I'd checked for tire tracks in the shallow ditch, then circled the pumpjack and wandered into the rows of leafless trees. It had rained a little the previous week but the ground was too dry to tell a thing.

Checking my mirrors again, seeing nobody behind me, I cracked a slightly painful smile. One place I felt totally safe was speeding down a highway in open country on a cold, sunny day.

McKittrick was the next town south of Wilson, partway between Wilson and Taft. Luz had told me Cathy Rintoul was nursing an old man there. I'd led Luz to believe I was going to consult Cathy about my neck.

I knew I was taking a chance with Cathy. But I'd realized I trusted those two women too—Luz and Cathy—within limits. They had runaway mouths but their loyalty to Joe was fierce.

There wasn't much to downtown McKittrick except a couple of convenience stores and a Depression-era hotel with the famous Penny Bar. The old man lived on his oil lease in a doublewide trailer about a mile off the main intersection. Luz said to look for one small and one larger pumpjack, and his turn was right there. I found the property no problem and, as I bumped over the cattle guard, spotted Cathy. She was bundled into a shapeless brown coat, smoking a cigarette on a swing in the trailer's front yard, which was desert floor.

Stubbing out her cigarette, Cathy stood up and waved. Under

the coat she had on her nurse's uniform and I was struck again by her physical resemblance to Jean: a large, plain woman with the same kind face, only hers had a more assertive expression. I waved back as I parked and she hurried to the truck with a big smile of welcome.

"Ann! I was just thinking I couldn't take another crossword puzzle and then Luz called!"

Backing away so I could open the door and jump down, she frowned. "What happened to your face?"

I was wearing work clothes and I'd turned my jacket and shirt collars up, but the bruising had spread past my jaw line.

"Show me."

Cathy reached for my collars in her bossy professional manner. I preempted her by unzipping my jacket, folding my own collars down, and turning my head.

"Why . . . it looks like chainlink!" She peered up close and palpated under my ear with her fingertips. I winced as she said, "This happened at the rig? That can't be—there's no chainlink on the lease."

Pulling away, I stood my collars back up and zipped my jacket. Cathy eyed me. "I don't believe it. How did this happen really?"

"It's not serious. I'll be fine."

Cathy put her hands on her hips, looking like she was about to exert some authority. "Have you tasted or coughed blood? You should see the doctor."

I shook my head. "Cathy, I'm desperate. I need to ask questions and I need you to keep this conversation to yourself."

Leaning on the Oklahoma accent I made the yak-yak sign with one hand. "I'm sorry but you're notorious for your 'big ole flappin mouth,' and I mean you can't share this with Luz—you can't share this with *anybody*."

Cathy wasn't the least bit embarrassed by her reputation. She laughed and, forgetting about the doctor, hugged her coat around herself. It was a brisk day.

"My big sister won't talk, will she? I bet she won't. Life is always rosy at Jeannie-Jean's house—she was just born that way. People

116

don't murder other people. She's never said a bad word about that drunk driver who killed Manny. She even visited him in prison—"

I couldn't let Cathy get rolling; she'd be unstoppable. Breaking in, I pointed at the canopied swing. "Do you have some time?"

"Time is all I have—the patient's asleep. This is so exciting!"

She plucked at my jacket and hurried to the swing. I followed and sat down beside her. The swing was long enough to lie on and its green upholstery was bleached ragged from the sun. I drew a rectangle above our heads.

"We are underneath the Canopy of Silence here. If you repeat anything we say—anything to anybody—if you even *hint* at what's been said, bad s-h-i-t will happen, most likely to me. Treat this as a medical secret and swear."

Cathy went solemn and put a hand over her heart. "I swear."

"I know where to find you. My ghost will haunt you when I'm gone." I fixed her with a granite eyeball à la Emmet.

"I swear! Medical secret! Not a word to another soul, including my husband and kids!"

"You're on record." I resumed my normal eyeball. "I've been looking into Kenny Mills's death—"

Cathy interrupted gleefully, bouncing in her seat. "I heard! We heard! Didn't I say it was murder? The whole town's buzzing!"

Not stopping to think, I touched the cloth at my neck. Cathy was loud but she wasn't dumb: she caught the significance of the gesture and the glee evaporated. Her mouth dropped open.

"Oh-ho, so that's how . . . someone tried to choke . . ." She trailed off to stare at my bruised jaw.

I said, "You swore."

Chastened, Cathy put her hand over her heart like she actually meant it this time. I continued:

"Kenny Mills. Crystal meth, low-rent life—or *no*-rent life, since he owed on his place in Antelope Acres. But I can't find a decent motive for his death. I'm looking for Suzette Mahin, and I'm trying to figure out if Mills had business with a Wilson guy named Mark Bridges who you've probably heard of. I know they were friends—"

"Listen, Ann, listen, listen."

Cathy scooted closer and glanced around even though we were outside in wide-open country. There were no people or houses in sight, and the only sounds were the creak of the old man's pump-jacks and the wind. But I felt a tingle because I knew I was about to hear something.

Tapping my arm, Cathy said in a confidential voice, "I have my own idea about what happened to Kenny."

I nodded.

"Kenny was killed within a couple of months of Ray Junior, and Junior died while Joe was convalescing with his heart. If Joe had died and Junior was already dead, well then . . ."

She tapped my arm again, looked tremendously knowing, and left the implications to me. But I couldn't imagine what she was getting at.

I said, "What would've happened?"

Cathy opened her mouth to answer. Hesitating suddenly, she shut it, as if something had occurred to her.

I said, "What?"

Avoiding my eyes, she reached in her pocket for her cigarettes. "No, I shouldn't . . ."

It must involve Joe if Cathy realized she shouldn't say it.

"It's about Joe, isn't it? If it's secret, Cathy, you know Joe never talks about personal stuff. There's a ton he hasn't told me like, for instance, what possessed him to marry Alice. But if you think there's something relevant to Kenny Mills, you need to say."

Cathy lit up and blew smoke out for the wind to carry off. I nudged her with my boot, putting a hand over my heart.

"I swear I'll never tell him who I heard it from." I added, "Come on—you're dying to talk. Spill it."

Cathy started smiling. "You don't know why Joe married Alice?"

"I get the impression he married the boss's daughter—"

"What busybody told you that?"

"I—"

"It's the other way around! The boss's daughter married *Joe!* Alice set her cap for him and she *trapped* him. She wouldn't have two

118

nickels to rub together if it weren't for Joe Balch. *Joe* convinced Ray Senior to drill at Wilson Flats when Senior had never drilled his own well and everybody said the flats were a wildcatter's graveyard. Without Lucy Boyd there would've been no Parkerworth Oil and *that's* where all the money comes from — *not* from the drilling side of the business."

"Okay, okay, I believe you. But it's got nothing to do with Kenny Mills."

"Oh, yes, it does, Annie-Ann — yes, it darn well *does*." Cathy tapped me. "The whole town knows Ray Junior was next in line to inherit the companies. Senior died and left them to Joe when Junior was just a baby. The understanding was that the companies would belong to Junior when Joe retired or passed away."

"I didn't know that. I don't know much about Ray Junior. How old was he when he died again? Forty?"

"Only forty — *young*." Nodding, Cathy folded her arms on *young*, as if his age were proof of suspicious circumstances.

"Who gets the companies after Joe now?"

"That is a *very* good question. I don't know. But *I* think Kenny knew something and that's why he's *dead*. He and Junior ran together in high school and they were always in trouble for drinking or fighting. Most of it wasn't serious — the kinds of things teenage boys get into. Then they were caught with a stolen car trying to rob the Dogleg and the judge sent them to jail to straighten them out. Kenny did straighten out but Junior never came home again and —"

I stopped the roll. "You're saying Ray Junior was a lowlife like Mills."

I'd suspected as much. Unlike Alice, I didn't assume all welders were lowlifes. But she was supposed to wake me up for Junior's memorial service back in November and hadn't. It was clear she was ashamed of her half brother and didn't want me — and through me, Evelyn — to know anything about him.

Lowlife was too bald a term, though. It put Cathy off. Uncrossing her arms, she kept her cigarette away as she leaned closer to make her own point, speaking distinctly and emphasizing more and more:

"I'd trust Joe with my *life*. The whole *town* trusts Joe. They *love* Joe. Junior was his only logical *heir*. Joe would *never* in a thousand *years* try and steal the companies from him."

She glanced around us again. "It's *Alice* we need to worry about."

I already knew that Cathy disliked Alice. It was screamingly obvious on her nursing visits to the house.

I said, "How did Ray Junior die?"

Cathy poked me with her elbow. It hurt, even through the padding of her coat, because my upper body was sore.

"That's *it*, Ann — that's exactly *it!* We don't *know!* It happened in a little place called Galliano and that's all *anyone* knows! There wasn't any *body*. He was cremated down there and all we saw was the *urn* with the *ashes*. Alice *hated* Junior — *hay*-ted him. She *hated* him from the *minute* he was born. She didn't even want a *memorial* but Joe put his foot down. Junior *was* a Parkerworth, after all, although, I will admit, there wasn't much our poor minister could say. Nobody had even *seen* Junior in twenty-five years and he wasn't a model citizen before *that* —"

I finally cupped my hand over my ribs. "Quit it, holy cow! You have a sharp elbow!" She was poking me every time she emphasized a word.

Lowering her arm, Cathy smiled. "Sorry. Get me started on Joe and Alice and I just . . ."

"Alice has to know how her brother died —"

Cathy cut in. "Did you say Mark Bridges?"

"I did."

"Mark ran with Junior back in high school too. He and Kenny came to Junior's memorial, and Luz reminded me Mark was there for that dumb trick at the Dogleg. Can you imagine? They were drunk as skunks and didn't realize the Dogleg was still *open*. Mark crawled into the weeds to upchuck and wasn't with Kenny and Junior when they broke in through the kitchen. Gerry had those two boys by the scruff before they knew what hit them —"

Something hit *me*.

120

When Alice told Joe about Ray Junior's death, she said she'd left a message to notify his mother. I'd heard of the mother, Celeste, but had never met her because she only came to Wilson for the annual Balch Corporation board meeting. Joe was always busy then, and my father sat on the board: two good reasons to stay away.

I said, "Where's Celeste in all this? She must've come up for the memorial — she has to know the circumstances of her own son's death."

Cathy had leaned down to stub out her cigarette in the dirt. Looking at me over her shoulder, she smiled with juicy delight.

"Ooohhh . . . *Celeste*."

15

I WAS SUDDENLY REMEMBERING something from my previous experience with murder.

Names piled up. One name led to another name, and another, and another, multiplying and proliferating until you thought your head would explode trying to keep the stories and personalities straight. You'd zigzag from lead to lead not knowing for a long time who or what was relevant, but doing the work because you had to pursue every credible theory and cover every base. At some point you'd think you'd nailed motive and players. Then new information would come out, new facts converge that suggested a whole different angle on your conspiracy, as believable and compelling as your first idea that you'd thought was so groovy and right on.

I'd liked the idea of the spying plot. It was neat – it was contained – it was totally plausible. Now Cathy had forced me to consider a second serious possibility: that Kenny Mills's death was related to the fate of Joe's two companies, which, Cathy said, were valued somewhere in the hundreds of millions of dollars in the boom market. Or maybe that was Joe's estimated net worth: Cathy was hazy about business and high finance. Either way, I grasped the essential. Ownership of a giant pile of money was at stake.

Plenty of liars and gossiping fantasists had fooled me in the past. I'd learned my lesson, I hoped, so it wasn't like I completely trusted Cathy as a source.

But the fact remained that Kenny Mills and Ray Parkerworth Junior *had* been friends and *had* died within a few months of each other. What was the statistical chance of that, or of the fact they were both friends of Mark Bridges? It all definitely rated as a coincidence – and, as Doug once told me, when it came to murder, he never believed in coincidence.

I'd also been forced to put Alice on the suspicious list. It gave me a teeny-weeny twinge of conscience but I had to.

She didn't kill Kenny Mills with a hammer or try to strangle me. The idea of Alice in Chanel, with her gold and pearl necklaces and perfect hair, on a drilling rig or in a dirt field was preposterous. Anyway, she had an alibi: Hawaii. I also didn't consider Cathy's dislike, or mine, important. However, there were two points against her.

One. I had no idea what the financial arrangements were, but Joe's money was Alice's money to some degree or another. She had a stake in the inheritance.

Two. If it developed that money *was* the issue, the fact that Alice's half brother – heir to the Balch companies – died prematurely and mysteriously made Alice extreeemely interesting. If she'd hated Ray Junior, like Cathy said, I'd add a few more *e*'s to *extreeemely*. Why had she flown to Louisiana herself to fight red tape and claim the body? She'd said it was because Joe couldn't fly, Luz couldn't be trusted, and Celeste couldn't be found. That seemed believable. But still, no wonder Joe was surprised she'd go.

I hit the south edge of Wilson debating my next move after hot tea from the diner and another dose of pain cream.

I couldn't talk to Gerry about the drunken robbery attempt; Jan would shut me down. I couldn't get started on the former Celeste Parkerworth because Cathy couldn't remember her latest married name and Celeste hadn't bothered to attend her son's memorial service. She'd married some wealthy dude with an Italian name who Cathy thought must be Mafia. *Tramp, rotten mother, gold digger,* and *flake* were the nicest things Cathy had to say about her.

Calling Joe, I asked if he had time to meet. He proposed dinner so I spent the rest of the afternoon trying to locate Suzette Mahin. I checked back at Antelope Acres and her last beauty salon. I also swung by the Spud Inn, a sleazy bar close to the Kwik Gas where she'd been spotted over the weekend. Nobody could tell me where she might be.

I hustled home to check online for a Raymond Parkerworth Junior obituary. I couldn't find the obit for Wilson or a notice from Galliano, but that search led me to other newspapers in the region, including Baton Rouge and New Orleans. Starting with the big cities and consulting a map of Louisiana, I surfed around a pretty wide area and didn't find any mention of Ray Junior anywhere.

After that I ran out to the gun room. My memory was Joe didn't keep any handguns but I was still undecided about protection and thought I'd just check and see what my options were.

Joe and I lived at the east end of the house. At the west end a breezeway connected off the kitchen to a three-car garage. The gun room was inside the garage, next to the special laundry room with a washer and dryer only for rig clothes.

I hit the light switch.

The gun room was the size of a big walk-in closet. Joe hunted and fished – historically a sore subject between us – and owned all the toys for both activities. There was a rack of fishing rods, with bait boxes, hanging hooks, and shelves full of tackle, creels, and everything else. He also had a padlocked rack of rifles and shotguns. The guns were gone, though: the bar across the rack was open and the padlock was hanging off. Pushing the bar arm in, I pulled the keys out of the padlock and found the key to open the ammunition cupboard. There were no handguns in there.

I surprised Luz and Joe by entering the kitchen from the garage side. The kitchen was large and outdated, in the worst shades of brown, with hideous wallpaper and oak trim and a view of the bare backyard through glass doors.

I said, "I see you've had an epiphany, Señor Balch."

Luz was standing at the stove and stirring a pot. Joe was sitting on a tall chair at the center island with a drink in front of him, snacking on tortilla chips.

He deadpanned, "Don't use those two-dollar words with me, miss. I'm not too old to paddle your behind."

"Animals are celebrating from here to Alaska—all your guns are gone. You saw the light and gave them to the sheriffs for destruction."

Luz's head whipped around. Joe reached for his trifocals, put them on, and flicked a glance at me. He was wearing his usual jeans and cowboy shirt and boots and looked exhausted. He was probably keeping Emmet's hours at the lease, and Emmet never seemed to sleep.

"What's this now?"

"I was just in the gun room. The rack's empty—your rifles and shotguns are . . ." I trailed off as Luz exhaled, *"Dios mío,"* melodramatically and stared at Joe.

Two places had been set at the island. I climbed on the tall chair to Joe's left. Joe's drink was bourbon on the rocks. Reaching for his glass, he took a good swallow. He wasn't digging this development and neither was I.

He said, "What were you doing out there, pray tell? You were allergic to guns last time I checked. You have an epiphany?"

"Sort of. I was wondering if you kept any handguns."

Luz's eyes widened some more. I pulled my collars up around my throat to say without saying what I might want a handgun for. Luz couldn't be trusted with that much information and she gossiped in two languages. I continued to pray that my faith in Cathy wasn't a mistake.

I said, "It could just be random theft, Joe. We're right on the highway and the garages aren't locked or alarmed, and you always know who's home by what vehicles are out front."

There was a sudden smell of burning: Luz had neglected her pot. Turning back to the stove, she got busy stirring.

Joe said, "It chaps my behind, excuse the anatomy again, to lock this house up. My folks moved here after the war. We left the keys in the car and never locked our doors. With the drugs and the thieving anymore . . . my Lord. Here's gravel in your girdle."

Shaking his head, he toasted me and drank.

"Who knows you keep guns in the garage?"

"My friends — every old-timer from here to the county lines. Better question is — who doesn't know?"

"And you don't bother to hide the key?"

Joe's cell phone rang. It was lying beside his place mat, next to his cigarettes and lighter.

"Excuse me." Wiping his hands on his napkin, he picked up the cell phone and read the incoming number. "I have to answer this." He flipped the phone open. "I want good news, Emmet . . . Damn . . . Damn a second time . . . All right. I'll be out when you see me."

He closed the phone and, putting it down, reached up under his glasses to rub his eyes. He really did look tired.

I said, "Did we get kicked off?"

"No." He talked through his hands, then raked back his thin gray hair. "They're setting a mechanical plug now — trying to."

I didn't know what a mechanical plug was. Before I could ask, Luz was bringing our plates, warning us in Spanish they were hot. She removed her oven mitts and spooned salsa verde over Joe's enchiladas and did the same for mine. Joe didn't talk until he'd eaten the first enchilada and started on the second.

"I don't mind saying you've opened a can of worms."

There were two cans now — and I didn't want to discuss either of them with Luz in the room. When Joe didn't get a reaction, he flicked a glance over at me. I tilted my head at Luz; her back was to us at the sink. The faucet was running so I lowered my voice and chose the less controversial can of worms to start.

"One of my theories is that Mills hired on at the wildcat so that they — whoever *they* are, whoever the cabal involves — would have a scout actually on the rig, not just sitting one field over with binoculars."

"Ron sent Kenny out to Minerva."

"That's what Gerry said. To put it bluntly — you pay Bray's salary. Isn't he supposed to be on your side even if he's mad at you for

126

not buying him a triple? Same with Boots Mahin. I'm guessing he was driving his wife's truck that night. Why would he be caught anywhere near Dan Fox and Mark Bridges? He's supposed to be on your side too, and West Coast is a dang rival of yours."

"They're too big to be any rival of mine. I pump twenty-nine hundred barrels a day – they pump fifty thousand."

Joe was almost done with his food. I ate faster and waited for him to answer my questions. Ripping a tortilla, Joe mopped up the last of his beans and rice with it, and then swigged the last of his bourbon. He may have been contemplating. I got the sense he was evading.

Finally I said, "Richie and I followed Bridges to Bakersfield almost a week ago. Have you decided what you're going to do? I hope you haven't spoken to Mr. Mahin because –"

I stopped.

Luz was frankly eavesdropping. She'd turned off the faucet and was just fiddling with a crusty pan. Joe noticed her and also didn't like it. Sticking his phone in the flap pocket of his shirt, he scooped up his cigarettes and lighter, pushed back his chair, thanked Luz, and walked out of the kitchen, signaling me to come with him. He wasn't a guy who dawdled over meals in the Continental fashion anyway. I thanked Luz and hurried to catch up to Joe in the foyer.

He'd paused at a framed photograph hanging beside the den door. It was him, Mahin, and Bray on a hot, windy afternoon, standing in front of a pumpjack.

Everyone was in shirtsleeves and holding on to the hat in his hand. What little hair they had was blowing. Tan, with the slant in his back and a checked shirt, Joe was the old rancher. Mahin stood beside him, the executive – a large, pale, flabby, bald guy in polyester slacks and a big silver belt buckle. Like Joe, he looked country rich. Bray stood next to Mahin, bowlegged, in working denims – a small, fit guy who could still wrestle drillpipe if he had to. Mahin and Bray were in their sixties and looked, if not dynamic or sexy or brilliant or distinguished, at least suited to the setting and comfortable with a pumpjack. Nobody was smiling.

I said, "This was taken last year when you pumped the thirty millionth barrel of oil at Wilson Flats."

I tapped the glass over Mahin's feet. He was wearing cowboy boots in wild peacock colors. "Custom-made to mark the occasion and a milestone in bad taste."

Joe just nodded. Then he said, "Bastards," with feeling as he started down the hallway to his suite.

16

JOE HAD FIXED himself another bourbon and dozed off in a wingback chair by the glass doors, facing out at the rig. I didn't care that he did – although I never got to the question of Ray Parkerworth Junior – because he was so obviously dead tired. And he'd explained a lot before he fell asleep, enough for me to understand why he was ticked at his main guys and how that fight related to the scouting.

As head of acquisitions for West Coast Energy, Dan Fox had made multiple offers on Balch Oil. Each new offer had been higher and more extravagant than the previous one.

But Joe had nothing but contempt for the "corporate knuckleheads," as he called Fox and West Coast. Fox's latest offer, in his view, was plain foolish. They didn't just want Joe's twenty-nine hundred barrels a day. They were also after his proven reserves and unexploited mineral acreage, especially the mineral rights to the Minerva play. Minerva wasn't a single wildcat drilling operation. There would be Minerva no.2, no.3, and more, depending on what they found with the first well. Minerva no.1 was only part of a larger projected deep-gas play in an unexplored geological trend that covered thousands of underground acres.

That's where the fight had started – with West Coast's offer to buy all Joe's oil and gas holdings, from actual production to the wholly speculative and unproven Minerva play.

Joe said he'd never sell out to the knuckleheads, as if I didn't know it. He was proud to be an independent: he always had been independent and always would be. No individual or board could force him to sell either, because he was the majority stockholder in a private corporation. When I'd asked deadpan if that didn't make him corporate, he'd deadpanned me back.

Hilary Mahin, on the other hand, was desperate to sell Balch Oil. He was the financial mind behind the Balch companies' success and Joe had never *not* followed Mahin's advice on a major issue before.

Joe had started at the bottom with nothing and knew the Westside oil fields as well as anyone. But Mahin had taught him about money, broadening his business thinking and goals and saving his bacon during the 1980s bust. Now Mahin believed oil prices couldn't go much higher. A bust and recession were coming and if West Coast wanted to be foolish, that was their problem: Mahin thought Joe should cash out while the cashing was spectacular. For once Ron Bray agreed with Mahin. West Coast had no interest in Balch Drilling, and Bray thought he'd have more power and a bigger budget if Balch Oil was sold.

Mahin and Bray agreed on another thing: Joe should *not* be wildcatting for deep gas. They were against Minerva no.1 and the entire wildcat play.

Joe had started to describe the situation as a "goddamn clusterf–" and caught himself in time. But that's what it looked like to me too. I couldn't believe all this was combusting underneath the daily meetings at the house and Joe's gold-medal deadpan.

It was at that point that he'd drifted off. I'd asked why those guys would oppose Minerva. The answer was so long coming that I finally peeked around the chair and saw Joe had fallen asleep sitting up.

After easing the empty bourbon glass out of his hand, I slid the door shut that he'd opened to hear the rig.

As I left on tiptoe, I made a circuit of the room looking for anything related to Ray Parkerworth Junior. I thought maybe I'd missed a memento or photograph somehow. But Joe didn't keep personal photographs, except for one that had hung over his fireplace since I could remember.

It was a formal seated portrait of RAY J. PARKERWORTH SR. – as identified by a plaque on the frame. The portrait was black-and-white and taken in the 1960s. Ray Senior was an older, paunchy, coarse-looking man in a cheesy suit and string tie, with a tumbler of whiskey in one hand and a fat cigar in the other. He had dark bags under his eyes and the archetypal feel of the oil fields – a guy who'd spent his life cursing iron and rock, working hard and boozing harder. Difficult to believe that was Alice's father, but it was.

I closed Joe's door softly and ran up the hall to find Luz. She was in her room off the kitchen packing a suitcase. Luz loved drama, she luxuriated in drama, and she'd worked herself into a ripe panic over the missing guns. Usually she lived full-time with us but she'd been sleeping in less since Alice went traveling and Joe moved to the lease. Now she'd decided to go to her daughter's because she was afraid to stay overnight – never mind that the guns could've been stolen months ago. Joe hadn't been in the gun room since before his heart attack.

Logic was lost on Luz in her state. But she stopped folding clothes to listen to Joe's program as dictated to me.

He wanted Luz to ask her handyman cousin to come and put deadbolts on the gun room and connecting door to the breezeway. He'd authorized me to call the sheriffs and report the theft, and call an alarm company to wire the house "up the kazoo." He also told me the name of an electrician who'd install floodlights in the front and back; I was supposed to call him and the alarm people first thing in the morning. I'd suggested trimming the eucalyptus trees too. Joe told me to have at it.

The arrangements were dramatic enough to calm Luz down. She still insisted, though, on sleeping at her daughter's until the lights, locks, and alarms were functioning. I carried her suitcase outside for her and set it in the back of her battered little pickup dripping with rosary beads and Virgins of Guadalupe. She warned me to take care of myself and putt-putted off towards the interstate. I stood in the driveway watching her single taillight recede and asked myself how *I* felt about sleeping at the house.

I didn't believe Joe's guns had been stolen months ago. Me, I didn't believe in coincidence.

Touching my sore neck I suddenly wanted to jump in my truck, zoom down to L.A., crawl into Doug's bed, pull the covers over my head, and be safe. The desire was almost overpowering. Doug wanted to marry me and live with me. I had a key to his cottage in the hills. I'd left clothes there. I could easily do it, easily — right this second —

But nuh-uh.

I'd been here before too, the moment when the fear really hits and you have to beat it down. Laughing out loud, I reminded myself I'd seen bullets flying around me, been shot at close range, and almost bled to death in a culvert beside a freeway . . . and it wasn't *that* bad.

"Suck it up, little sister!"

Smiling, I turned and jogged back into the house.

I left Doug a message asking him the best way to research a death in Louisiana. I would've liked to go through Alice's suite for mentions of Ray Parkerworth Junior. She lived at the opposite end of the house, the kitchen end, so it was doable. But I didn't want to risk Joe catching me in her rooms. He'd told a story on himself, which I'd heard before, to explain why he was prepared for combat with his top men. A guy had told him once, "Joe, if I ordered a hundred sons of bitches and they only sent you, I'd be happy." He didn't like Alice but he respected the proprieties and if he caught me I'd be forced to explain the Kenny Mills/Ray Junior theory. It was premature yet to give Joe that kind of pain. *And* it was useless to suspect Alice based on no facts. There was only a suggestive sequence of events — Joe got sick, Ray Junior died, Kenny Mills died — with lots and lots of money at stake. I clenched a fist. I *had* to find out the circumstances of Ray Junior's death. *Dang!*

Checking the time, I ran down to my room to doctor my neck, grab a warm coat, and change into boots, looking in on Joe on my way back out. He was snoring quietly in his chair. I turned on the sound system and extra lights and ran around making sure the exterior doors were locked. I also made sure the front entrance was locked and lit. With three pickups in the drive, it looked like plenty of people were home. I was avoiding the back gate so I jogged west along the highway, looped through the dark fields, and came up behind Emmet's trailer, climbing through the barbwire and sneaking in through his end door.

The TV was on and the trailer smelled of cooking, but Emmet's hardhat and jean jacket were gone. One concern was the gin-rummy game that happened sometimes in the evening. Joe wouldn't be there but the mud logger might. Staying hidden in the storage room, I peeked at Emmet's desk. The deck of cards and score pad weren't out – just the perpetual can of 7Up, tin of chewing tobacco, and messy papers.

I took off my coat and sat down on the floor to wait.

Risk and expense, I thought, finishing the conversation with Joe. Those were two obvious reasons Mahin and Bray would oppose Minerva: risk and expense. Wildcatting was absolute, total, 100 percent risk – and Joe was spending a minimum of ten million dollars to drill this first well.

The fact that Joe's guys were fighting him added a special new dimension to things.

Normally the competition scouted your wildcat to find out what you were finding but for free. If they got news of a significant hydrocarbon show, they'd try to lease the minerals around your well and start drilling themselves, or they'd prevent you from stepping out, or both. That was the usual game. It wasn't the game here because Joe already had the play leased up. But Mahin and Bray might align with Dan Fox and the scouting plan just to track the progress of drilling. Joe personally owned the majority stake in Minerva – Balch Oil had only a minority stake. Minerva's success or lack of, though, would affect the market value of the company, which both Mahin and Bray wanted sold. I bet they'd love to unload Balch Oil right now. Statistically, nine out of ten holes were dry: the chances of a rank wildcat like Minerva coming in were minuscule.

But – but – buuut –

If Kenny Mills *had* been a scout, Mahin and Fox and those guys wouldn't kill their own man on the rig. What for? What would their reason be? Only a member of the pro-Balch party might potentially do that, *if* scouting was behind the murder. Unless Mills was expendable to his bosses – a sacrifice to the main plot and conspiracy. That thought, as outrageous as it was, unleashed a train of reasoning that led to a possibility so bold I almost couldn't believe it occurred to me.

I was examining the possibility from all angles when the middle door of the trailer slammed open and Emmet stomped in, shouting:

"Goddamn it to hell and back, Richard!"

I peeked around the filing cabinet. Emmet was really steamed – madder than I'd ever seen him. Richie appeared in the doorway, big, good-looking, and freckled, his face dirty and unreadable in full safety gear.

Emmet yelled, "Close the damn door! You's lettin the heat out!"

Stepping inside, Richie shut the door and pulled off his gloves and hardhat.

"I want to know what the hell happened to my goddamn hoses!"

Emmet grabbed a batch of invoices from a slot on his desk and snatched through them, pointing to one.

"Here's the damn ticket! Delivered and paid for three days ago!"

He stared at Richie aggressively. His face was beet red and I noted a new Eye for my catalog: the Burning Eyeball of Doom. It was bulging and bloodshot. It glittered with menace.

Emmet flung his arm in a wide arc to mean the lease.

"I got pump parts disappearin when I need 'em! My bit breaker walks off and hides behind the pits! I got oil leakin out my koomey! Drill-collar clamps is upside down when I distinctly seen 'em upside right not one hour before! Now my brand-new air hoses's got holes in 'em?! What in cryin hell is goin on around here, Teach?!"

Richie had no answer for him, and Emmet didn't expect one. He was almost panting as he shouted:

"I'll tell you what! I'll tell you what! Some damn sumbitch is screwin with this old man, is what!"

I thought that would blow the roof of the trailer right off. Emmet relieved his feelings by stomping up and down between the desk and the couch, shoving his chair under the desk to get by. It was only three steps both ways and sort of comical in the narrow space because of his size. The trailer shook and objects rattled and I could feel the floor vibrating underneath me. Richie just stood at the door blank-faced.

Holy cow, though. Oil leaking from the accumulator? That was bad: the koomey was command control for the blowout preventers. But it gave my wild idea more fuel.

After a minute Emmet stopped stomping and panting and caught his breath. Stripping off his hardhat and jean jacket, he threw them on the couch and moderated his tone.

"Get on back to work, son. No one's blamin you."

Richie nodded and went.

I watched Emmet reach for his chewing tobacco and decide he didn't want it. Muttering, "Sumbitch, sumbitch, sumbitch," he stomped to the kitchen, checked in the fridge, slammed the fridge shut, and opened and slammed the cupboard doors one by one. I waited behind the file cabinet for him to cool off.

The banging and crashing finally ended and he came out of the kitchen to sit down and call the supply house for more hoses. After he left a message and hung up, I knocked on the floor, scooched forward into the light, and smiled:

"Excuse your language?"

Emmet swiveled his chair and looked down, unsurprised. He rumbled, "I do not and I will not."

"Maybe it's that old joke. Lock a roughneck in a padded room with three steel balls. Come back later – one ball's broken, one ball's missing, and one ball's stolen."

That got me the granite treatment. Crossing my legs, I said more seriously, "I have a theory – new as of a few minutes ago."

"How you doin?"

Emmet lifted one hand at me and wiggled an index finger. Interpreting in context, I opened my collars and showed him my neck.

Two days later the injury was less livid but more multicolor and spread out. I'd laughed that afternoon, looking in the bathroom mirror. The blues, greens, pinks, and yellows, sprinkled with black dots, made me look like an Impressionist flower garden. My entire neck hurt, up past my jaw line and the ridge of my skull. The worst-looking place was under my right ear where dark blue bruising covered the flowers.

I said, "How long have you been in touch with Doug Lockwood?"

"After Christmas. That man's lookin out for you, little sister – somebody needs to."

Which was why I wasn't going to mention Joe's missing guns to Emmet. I wanted to break that news to Doug myself. Emmet would hear about it soon enough anyway.

"What if certain people want Joe to fail here? They want this wildcat to fail?" I closed my collars again and stood them up.

Emmet hooked his thumbs in his overalls and went to the squinty-eye – his speculating look.

"Joe and I had dinner tonight and he told me about the clustereff going on with Mahin and Bray. I'm sure you know more about it than I do. Those guys didn't want Joe to go wildcatting because it's risky and expensive, right?"

Emmet murmphed. It was a yes.

"How much of the ten million is Ozark's bill, if I'm allowed to know?"

"Day rate on this ole gal is forty thousand includin extras."

"Forty grand a *day?*"

"Them's boom prices. Rigs is in short supply."

"Yow, that's twelve–" I stopped to count the zeros. "That's a million-two every month! It'll be even more when I get my fifty-cent raise."

Granite.

Smiling at him, I continued.

"I can see why, if West Coast Energy wants to buy Balch Oil, and

Mahin and Bray want it sold, that they might get involved in the scouting even if it's treason. Have you got conclusive evidence that they *are* involved? My only evidence so far is circumstantial – Mahin caught at Dan Fox's house with Mark Bridges, and Bray sending Kenny Mills out to you."

Emmet murmphed and rocked his chair once. It was a no.

"All right, good – and I'm assuming Joe hasn't made the mistake of asking them straight out. Meanwhile, what if scouting isn't enough for those guys? What if they want Joe to fall on his face? They couldn't stop Minerva from being drilled. Maybe this is their way of stopping it period and, I don't know, demoralizing Joe so badly that he'd sell his oil company."

Emmet was shaking his head – a definite shake, not one of his invisible micro-shakes.

"But you said yourself somebody was screwing with you. I heard you. Ruined air hoses, leaking accumulator – it sounds like deliberate sabotage."

"It don't fail nothin in the long run though, see. Slows down drillin and rises costs, tries my delicate temper – but it's Mother Nature what decides in the end. We hit pay or got us a duster. It's no more simple than that."

"You've had to do a lot of repairs."

"Normal on a long, tough hole."

"Did the sabotage start before or after Kenny Mills was killed?"

Emmet pondered, and shook his head. "Cain't say for certain."

"On Christmas Day the OSHA woman said the rig could be red-tagged if Mills died because of safety violations." Here I went with my bold new idea. "Maybe his murder was part of a larger plan to shut Minerva down completely."

Emmet rocked his chair and turned to look out at the rig. I was on the floor below him with no view, so I listened to the rumble of the engines and the squeak-squeak of his springs.

After a silence, answer not coming, I said, "What's the story with our mud logger?"

Emmet didn't hear me. I stuck my leg out and nudged his chair, raising my voice. "What's the story with our mud logger?"

"Say what now? That's my deaf ear." Emmet turned his head.

"I thought you couldn't hear in both ears."

"Left's more worse than right."

"I was asking about the mud logger. Isn't it his fault we got lost? That's set drilling back at least a couple of weeks. When you count the cost of the rig, plus wasted drilling days, plus a new survey, setting a cement plug, setting the mechanical plug, plus new men and material for directional drilling, plus days trying to get kicked off, plus —"

"You's rubbin salt in the wound, little sister."

"I'm sorry. I was just trying to illustrate that getting lost has cost you time and money, and maybe that was sabotage too. Isn't the mud logger supposed to know approximately where you are?"

My father sometimes worked as a mud logger, known as a well-site geologist if you had a petroleum geology degree. Part of the job was to look at cuttings every ten feet to see what rock they were drilling and whether that matched the formations they thought they'd be in.

Emmet micro-shook his head.

"When you's wildcattin like this one here you got to go by your geologist's best guess — fancy seismic and computer modelin won't help you, not in the depths we's at. We was hittin our tops, hittin our tops, then come a day it just weren't feelin right no more. That ole bit is like a snake huntin water and it done lost the scent."

"You mean you stopped the drilling at seventeen thousand some-odd feet because something didn't *feel* right to you?"

Emmet didn't answer. He was cogitating, rocking his chair. Eventually he said:

"Worse that happens, we plug and abandon afore TD. But you jump through hoops of fire to show them insurance boys you cain't continue with the drillin and didn't make no mistakes gettin there. Them fellas'll turn the well over to another outfit and another till they find somebody to TD it for 'em, else they owe you a bunch of money they ain't wantin to pay."

"But if conditions got so difficult that Joe gave up before total depth, he'd just write off the loss, wouldn't he?"

I got a stony-eye for that, like the notion of giving up was heretical. Emmet said, "Lot worse has to happen to shut this booger in. You have no idea how bad these deals can get — nooo idea."

He shook his head again. "It's them drill-collar clamps's got me thinkin a plan's afoot. It's like the sumbitch is sendin a message."

"What do you mean? What kind of message?"

Emmet didn't want to say. He worked his false teeth in his mouth and didn't want to say.

I pressed. "Come on. What difference does it make if the drill-collar clamps are upside down?"

". . . It's a old superstition in the oil fields. You don't want 'em upside down — it's bad luck."

"And you believe that?"

"Little sister, I seen it come true too many times in my day." Emmet pointed out the window at the drilling rig.

"It's like as though the sumbitch is tellin me that there deal is jinxed."

17

T HE OFFICE OF the *Wilson Gusher* was located in an old stucco storefront on the main street of town, across from the Kwik Gas and around the corner from the sleazola Spud Inn.

I walked into the *Gusher* the next morning to see Audrey. She waved from her desk behind the counter.

"Ann! I heard you quit your job on Joe's wildcat and were asking around about Kenny Mills!"

Audrey was dumpy and energetic, about sixty, with a journalism degree from Stanford, and she always wore stylish suits because her role model was Rosalind Russell in *His Girl Friday*. Joe introduced us years ago and we'd hit it off instantly. I'd even asked her about a job when I moved to Wilson, not realizing she was the only paid person on staff: the paper ran six pages maximum and she wrote and edited most of it. I'd covered a few events for her then stopped because she rewrote everything I turned in. The *Gusher* was basically a booster sheet and I didn't boost very well.

Walking behind the counter, I lied to her face.

"I did quit – I couldn't take the work physically. I'm gathering material for a piece on the life and death of a rig hand, and Joe's asked me to consider writing a history of the Parkerworths and Balches."

Audrey said, "Warts and all?" with one eyebrow up and rich innuendo.

I gave her an eyebrow back. Audrey was hilarious.

"I thought I'd start with the late Ray Parkerworth Junior. I know practically nothing about the guy — I missed his memorial and I missed his obituary and couldn't find it online."

Audrey got up and went to a stack of papers, pulled an issue from November, opened it to an inside page, and pointed:

"I thought he merited a longer piece but I was vetoed by Alice."

I skimmed it. It was definitely a stingy announcement — no picture and a dry paragraph with Ray Junior's birth and death dates and next of kin. It didn't even bother with the stock phrase about his loved ones mourning the loss. I noted his mother's full name, Celeste Parkerworth Mancuso, of Balboa Beach and Palm Springs. Mancuso: that was the Italian name Cathy couldn't remember. Audrey hovered at my shoulder while I reread the notice more slowly, marveling at the human dramas it hid. Cathy had spared me no details. A few of them might even be true.

I said, "It doesn't mention how he died. I didn't want to bug Joe about it."

Taking the newspaper, Audrey folded it and slipped it back in the stack. "He worked as a welder on offshore platforms and apparently fell off a stairway and drowned in the Gulf of Mexico."

"Was he drunk and/or stoned at the time?"

Audrey started walking towards the rear of the office, gesturing for me to follow. She said, "A reasonable guess, but that's the extent of my knowledge and not thanks to Alice. I was obliged to call the funeral home in Louisiana. Her brother was a sore subject, apparently."

Scratch that chore off my to-do list. I was planning to poll funeral homes in Louisiana later today.

"Any evidence of foul play? Did you ask about a police report?"

Audrey stopped and turned, one eyebrow arched. "Hmmm. Why do you say *that?* I wonder, I wonder."

I kept walking, not answering, and she had to hurry to stay

ahead of me. She opened a door in the back and hit a light switch. Long overhead fluorescents blinked on and I was looking at a very large, very messy and musty storeroom. It had ceiling-high shelves, like a library's, stuffed with newspapers in ragged piles. There was a row of old-fashioned index files and, to my right, a table with a computer and a microfiche machine.

Audrey said, "You're welcome to the use of this but, be warned, we're still in the Miocene here. Every issue before 2002 is on microfiche—the rest are on computer, except for the ones from the past three months that haven't been scanned yet."

She walked inside to turn on the machine and I started in after her. She said, "Hold your horses, Annie Oakley. We need to discuss quid pro quo."

Going to the index file, she pulled out the *B* drawer and the *P* drawer. "Who murdered Ken Mills?"

"Find me a clear motive, Hildy, and I'll tell you." Hildy was the name of Rosalind Russell's character. "I'm beginning to think it was a trillion-to-one accident."

"People are saying it was because of crystal meth."

"Why kill him on a drilling rig in a tule fog? It's a lot of trouble when you could just drive over him at the Spud Inn."

Audrey conceded that point with a nod. "Some are saying you were fired because you know something Joe wants covered up."

"It's true." I stage-hissed, "He voted against Arnold Schwarzenegger in the recall election!" Audrey slapped my sleeve and I continued in a normal voice:

"That's ridiculous. Have you heard anything Stanford would let you print—one single undeniable piece of evidence or irrefutable fact from an unimpeachable source that would lead the objective observer to an unequivocal and inescapable conclusion?"

Audrey thought about that and shook her head. I said, "Me either. Why did Alice not like Ray Junior?"

"I don't know, although I could make several guesses. Why did you ask about foul play?"

The phone rang in the outer room. Audrey checked her watch. "Shoot, I had an appointment at ten. That's probably her."

She hurried out for the telephone and I set my things down. I hadn't used microfiche since Coalinga's Black Flood.

Audrey came back. "I have to dash. Stay as long as you like – if I'm not back when you leave just pull the street door shut." She waggled her finger at me. "We're not through with this negotiation, don't think we are."

"Can I have your cell phone number in case of something?"

She gave it to me, asked for mine, then snorted. "Life and death of a rig hand – Balch family history. My *foot*."

I gave her a sweet, innocent smile. Snorting again, she took off, and I got to work. There were two full drawers of indexed Parkerworth and Balch references.

I started with specifics: the bonehead Dogleg robbery.

Knowing Ray Junior's birth date, I could pinpoint the years he would've been in high school. A cross-reference in the *M*s for Mills and I hit it. I found the corresponding microfiche, set it on the glass, and read.

There wasn't any more to the story. Some fifteen-year-old idiots got drunk, stole a car, tried to rob the Dogleg, and got caught because it was still open. I checked forward in the index for news of a hearing or sentence. Nothing – probably because they were juveniles. So I flipped through the cards for every Ray Parkerworth Junior mention and pulled the corresponding microfiche. I got his 1967 birth notice, a few team wins as a kid, and glimpses of a teenage hood: arrests for underage drinking and fighting Taft High fans at a football game. There was one blurry picture of him – a sullen, pimple-faced beanpole standing with Joe and Manny at a Balch Oil barbecue.

When I couldn't find any references to Ray Junior after 1983, nothing more on Kenny Mills, and nothing of interest about Mark Bridges, I sighed and dug in.

I pulled the 1966 issue announcing the marriage of Raymond Parkerworth Senior, sixty-six, to Celeste Stephens, twenty. James Whitehead of Calgary, Canada, acted as best man, and Alice Parkerworth, eighteen, was the maid of honor in a pink Chanel ensemble from Bullock's Wilshire of Los Angeles. The picture of the wedding party was a trip. The men were so *old* and the women so *young*. Alice looked like a perfect cutout doll and gazed in adoration at my grandfather, who was famously handsome and sexy. He was also vain of his tailoring, according to one of my aunts. I compared his suit to the groom's: the contest wasn't even close.

The front page of every *Gusher* featured the going price of Midway-Sunset crude – the local heavy crude. As I read through dozens of issues, I watched the price fluctuate from $6.00 a barrel at the lowest, to $83.30 that month, January of 2008 – a record high.

And Lucy Boyd no.1 was mentioned over and over as Wilson's salvation.

It was also the salvation of Parkerworth Drilling, a dinky little contractor on the verge of bankruptcy when a young driller named Joe Balch convinced his boss to go wildcatting. With the Wilson Flats discovery, Joe jumped from driller to head of the new Parkerworth West Valley Oil Company. Later it was Joe who hired my grandfather – an engineer and reservoir specialist – to install his patented small-scale steamflood system in the Wilson Flats field, the first system of its kind in the world. Joe was really responsible for the success of the Parkerworth companies. He'd grown them until they became Wilson's largest locally based employer and given back to the town with numerous charities and improvement projects. It was a Balch Oil grant that had funded the petroleum studies program at Wilson High School.

The *Gusher* rarely mentioned Joe and Alice in the same issue – and never in the same sentence or paragraph, except for their wedding.

Alice Parkerworth became Alice Parkerworth Balch in 1967 at a modest ceremony in the home of the newlywed Mr. and Mrs. Ray Parkerworth Senior. The *Gusher* made *modest* sound chintzy, like Wilson had been cheated of a big bash. *Jean* was Alice's maid of honor – whoa! The two women certainly didn't speak now. I studied faces: Did Jean and Joe love each other even then? Emmet was Joe's best man and he looked fantastic in the picture – like someone let a woolly mammoth into the living room. The marriage happened right around Ray Junior's birth so of course I had to wonder if Alice married to get away from a stepmother who was only two years older and had just produced an heir.

Not long after Ray Junior was born, Ray Senior died. From that point the players scattered and I began remembering the history myself.

Joe's business affairs were covered religiously and he was mentioned or quoted in almost every *Gusher*. But by the early 1970s, Alice and Celeste Parkerworth had more or less disappeared. Both women were present at the christening of the Parkerworth Community Center. And both women showed up for annual Balch board meetings, as recorded in the society column. Wilson's first lady, Mrs. Hilary Mahin, always threw a tea party in conjunction with board meetings, which the widow Parkerworth, later Mrs. Mancuso, attended each year—but Alice never did. I read and read. Nothing gave me any bead on Ray Junior's relationship to his family or the Balch companies. I was looking for any kind of corroboration for what Cathy Rintoul had told me.

I'd started on Hilary Mahin, thinking about food, when the bell on the street door tinkled. Nobody'd been in all morning. I stuck my head out to look and it was Audrey.

She called, "How are you coming along?" as she dropped her purse and walked back to join me.

I said, "Do you want to get some lunch?"

Audrey's eyebrows flew up and she tapped her watch. "It's almost three o'clock!"

I slid the *M* drawer shut. No wonder I was hungry and thirsty. "What's the deal with Celeste Stephens Parkerworth Mancuso? When did she leave town?"

"Why do you want to know?"

"How long have you lived in Wilson, Audrey?"

She shot back, "Why?"

"Because I'd like your help and advice."

Audrey's mouth curled. "Don't fall in love and end up in this

145

hick burg—that's my advice." Then she grinned and rubbed her hands together.

"But I am *dying* to help. What can I do?"

Sitting at the bar in the Dogleg's back room, I wolfed a tri-tip sandwich and smiled about a bunch of things.

I smiled because Jan was away on a visit to her mother.

I smiled because I was a vegetarian before I moved to Wilson. I flashed on my favorite L.A. restaurants and what I wouldn't give right now for curried spinach or a bowl of Vietnamese soup. What I wouldn't give, even, for lettuce that wasn't iceberg. Luz's cooking was tasty but it relied a lot on beans and rice and shredded meat. On the other hand: you couldn't work twelve hours outside on a winter night with a leaf of arugula in your stomach.

I smiled because I was seeing so clearly how Alice was my grandmother's creation. She'd been born with no money or pedigree, like Evelyn, and it could only have been Evelyn who'd showed her the road to Bullock's Wilshire and Chanel.

I smiled thinking about Audrey.

She told me she'd dig into the Balches' estrangement. When and why the coldness started she didn't know and promised to find out. I was looking for anything that illuminated the question of inheritance but I didn't tell Audrey that. Because Mrs. Mancuso hadn't come to her son's memorial and hadn't sent excuses or flowers, she'd been talked about. Tramp. Rotten mother. Gold digger. Flake. A high-school dropout, she'd been waitressing in the Dogleg's front room when she met Ray Parkerworth. Her father drove a bulldozer in the oil fields and drink took him down early.

All that confirmed what Cathy said.

My warmest hope was that Audrey could get inside executive politics at the Balch companies. Joe had told me as much as he was going to, and that was under duress. I could sit and surveil Mahin and Bray, tail them around, watch who they met with, but how could I possibly overhear a private conversation? Audrey's husband was chief loan officer at Wilson Bank & Trust and would know local business gossip. Whether he'd repeat the juicy stuff was a different story, but Audrey also promised to fish in other ponds. I told her I was lucky to have a righteous legwoman, however quaint her use of the American idiom –

A bark of laughter snapped me out of my reverie. I lifted my head and looked around.

It was the afternoon lull and the Dogleg's back room was nearly empty. The jukebox was silent, the flat-screen on mute, the tables and chairs neatly arranged for the dinner rush. Nobody I knew was in when I came in – no Mark Bridges, no Oklahomans playing eight-ball. Now I saw Gerry not far off, propped against the bar, talking to a middle-aged man in a letter jacket standing between two stools.

Our mud logger.

Putting my sandwich down I scooted over and leaned, trying to hear. Gerry and he were mean-mouthing someone, some company man who took bribes from suppliers – but I couldn't catch names.

Gerry barked another laugh and I scooted back to my sandwich.

Audrey had confirmed that Gerry was like Jean – a loyal ally and friend to Joe. She'd said Gerry could gossip with the best of them but could also be silent as the grave. Joe's life, public and private, was sacred.

Gerry sent the mud logger off without food or drink, then came over to refill my Coke. *What I wouldn't give for an ice-cold shot of sparkling water. Not club soda – the fizzy European stuff.*

I covered my glass. "Thanks, I'm good . . . So nobody wanted Joe to drill Minerva. He's such a jerk – he never told me that."

Throwing his towel over his shoulder, Gerry propped himself on the bar again. He was way more relaxed with Jan gone, although his eyes were always roving, scoping the room, customers' needs, and the door to the street. He'd rolled up the sleeves of his cowboy shirt. The lumpy scar on his frozen left thumb ran past his wrist up his forearm.

"They surely didn't. Joe formed the LLC to buy up the play and drill Minerva himself because Boots fought him when he tried to put it on Balch Oil's schedule. Boots brought the board in on his

147

side against Joe. Joe could've pushed it through but he decided to save time and energy and just drill it himself. Boots thinks the best place to find oil is an oil field. He doesn't have the *huevos,* excuse my French, for that kind of risk. They also none of them know about the deep gas."

"Ron Bray had no power or say in the matter, right? Just an opinion?"

"That is correct. It isn't often you find Boots and Ron on the same side. Boots is a nervous Nellie — he's always planning for the next bust. Ron's a boom guy. If it was up to him, Balch Drilling would have twice as many rigs right now and jobs in every western state."

"Plus the triple on Minerva."

"That is correct."

"And yet Joe's been talking about drilling deep for a long time. The Minerva play can't have come as a surprise."

"Joe's always said, 'There's forty-five thousand feet of sediment in the San Joaquin Valley and two-thirds hasn't been explored vertically.' The money's there now and he's rolling the dice. Joe knows no fear, you know that. Never has."

Nodding, checking around the room, I said in a lower voice, "One theory I'm working on is that Mills's death, the scouting, West Coast's offer for Balch Oil, and what looks like sabotage on Minerva are all tied —"

Gerry started to nod before I was finished. He knew — he'd heard. Emmet must've talked to Joe.

"I see it and I don't. I do and I don't."

I waited for him to elaborate. Removing my plate, he wiped the bar top, then said:

"If Joe finds gas it's good for everybody in one way but it upsets the status quo. These big guys like West Coast aren't oil finders — they're what you call depletion experts. They own most of the production in this area but our fields are old and they pump less oil every day. West Coast's problem is how to slow the rate of decline — they don't wildcat as a rule. Now, they might in a bust when drilling contractors and service people are starving and they can drill a well for a buck ninety-eight. But if Joe makes a gas find, it's a new game out here. The big guys'll have to get off their butts and do something for a change or their stockholders will want to know why."

"Or not. The big guys just try and buy Joe out."

Gerry glanced to his left as a customer took a stool. Wiping his hands, he excused himself and went to serve the guy. I played with my drink glass, making designs in the wet spots on the bar. Emmet was right, I decided suddenly. My theory sounded good but what did it accomplish to make Minerva harder to drill? It was almost impossible to shut a well down, so why the sabotage? Whose agenda did it satisfy? And why spook Emmet with the drill-collar clamps?

When Gerry came back, I tilted my head up the bar. "That was our mud logger you were talking to."

"You mean Bud?"

"What's Bud's story? I know he's Balch Oil's geologist."

"He's been Joe's rock hound going back years and years. He's really the guy responsible for the Minerva play. He fell in with some foothills geologists from Calgary and got a wild hare up his—" Gerry stopped, and started again. "Convinced Joe that under our flat country here are tricky, dipsy-doodle formations like the ones up against the Rockies that produce so much oil and gas for Alberta."

Gerry stretched his towel across the bar and sketched dipsy-doodles beside it with his finger. I felt a lecture coming on.

"The towel is north–south, see this. The theory is the same tectonic factors that pushed the Rockies up are at work in our section of the fault zone, only—"

I had to interrupt.

"Sorry, Gerry, but I take it everybody trusts Bud the rock hound. You and Emmet and Joe have known him forever, right? If Minerva was his idea too, he'd have no motive for sabotage or for shopping Joe to his opponents."

Emmet and Joe hadn't taken home *all* the medals in deadpan: Gerry'd won a few himself. But I would've sworn, looking into his tough old weathered face, that my remark had startled him. He covered it by grabbing his towel and going to check on the customer down the bar.

When he came back there was an awkward pause before I decided to change the subject.

"Is Ron Bray actively devoted to Emmet's destruction?"

"Funny you should say it. That very question is being discussed—" Gerry broke off and looked past my shoulder as I got bumped hard from behind.

I twisted around and there was Richie, lurching clumsily onto the stool beside me when almost every stool at the bar was open. He knocked into me again and didn't seem to notice. He stank of liquor, not beer, and I realized he was blotto—out-of-his-gourd drunk.

Thumping the bar with his fist, he shouted, "Tequila!"

I said, "Richie! You're on tour tonight!"

Richie turned in my direction, swaying and glassy-eyed. It took him a second to focus, then:

"Pup!"

He lunged for me and planted a sloppy booze-kiss on my mouth. I tried to wrench free but he was too strong and I only managed to pitch backwards off the stool, pulling him down on top of me. We hit the floor in a pile and his weight crushed the breath out of my lungs. Winded, sure that he'd cracked a rib, I struggled and pushed, trying to suck in air and get him off me—

And abruptly he was. Gerry had rushed around the bar, grabbed Richie by the collar, and jerked him away. Released, I rolled over gasping. Richie knelt on the floor, suspended by his collar, weaving and dazed. Then Gerry let go and gave him a shove and he toppled over and lay still.

I lay still too, letting my breath come back and feeling my rib cage for breaks. Reaching over the bar, Gerry grabbed a pitcher of ice water and dumped it on Richie's head.

Richie slurred, "What the hell!" and turned his face the other way. Gerry kicked him with the instep of his boot.

"You should be ashamed of yourself, boy. Apologize to the lady."

I watched as he hauled Richie roughly to his feet, kicking his legs to prod him upright. Richie slurred, "Sorry, Pup." He was much bigger but Gerry handled him with no effort.

I said from the floor, "Help me up too, please. I'll drive him back to Jean's."

Gerry pushed Richie onto a barstool and extended a hand to pull me to my feet. He said, "Careful of the ice."

I straightened up slowly, pressing my right ribs. Gerry seemed to look concerned so I smiled at him and got a thin stretch of a smile back. Richie, dripping with water, was tipping to one side and starting to slide off the stool. Gerry grabbed his arm, yanked him to standing, and dragged him stumbling to the street door.

I put money for lunch on the bar and followed them slowly outside. Gerry knew my pickup. I beeped the remote unlock and he marched Richie to the passenger side, shoved him into the front seat, kicked his legs inside, and slammed the door against him. Richie's head thunked the window but his eyes didn't flutter or open — he didn't even flinch.

Gerry said, "You all right alone with him?"

I was still catching my breath. "That wasn't personal, believe me. I don't know what it was. Please don't tell Emmet — he'd have a fit."

Gerry nodded, escorting me around to the driver's side and pulling the door open. As I climbed in I said, "I need to know about the famous break-in where Kenny Mills, Ray Parkerworth Junior, and Mark Bridges tried —"

Gerry cut me off. "It isn't true."

"They didn't get drunk and break into your place?"

"No, that happened, the worthless little bast —" He caught himself.

I smiled. "Imagine I'm a worm on Joe's wildcat, Gerry. You should go ahead and say *b-a-s-t-a-r-d-s*." I spelled the word out to be funny. "I already realize those guys won't be remembered for their moral character."

But Gerry just couldn't. He said instead:

"There's rumors in town Junior was killed because he was coming back to claim his inheritance, and they're saying Kenny was killed because he knew about it. It's a load of BS, excuse my French. People have nothing better to do than jawbone over their back fence."

"Who's supposed to have killed them or had them killed?"

Gerry shook his head, disgusted. "Alice, Boots, Joe's brothers, me, you, Mrs. O'Leary's cow — anyone the town thinks is in line for the companies. Joe — Joe did it. They say he hated Junior because he stole the companies from him."

"And it's not true."

"Not worth the spit to say it." Shutting the truck door, he stepped up onto the boardwalk and headed back inside.

I rolled my window down and called, "Do you have an address for the O'Learys' barn?"

Gerry just flapped his towel at me without turning around.

18

NIGHT WAS FALLING and Kyle and Lynn were standing at the bottom of Jean's driveway in work clothes, coolers at their feet.

As I pulled in they rushed the truck to ask if I'd seen Richie. He was supposed to drive them to the rig and he was late. When I pointed at my passenger slumped against the door, out cold, the guys cursed in stereo. I climbed down, explaining where I'd come from as they galloped around the truck – big blond Kyle in the lead, dark shaggy Lynn right behind. They obviously had experience with this kind of emergency because they wrestled Richie out of the passenger seat and had him standing, propped under each arm, in no time.

They lift-dragged Richie across the driveway. Kyle coached him up the front steps while Lynn, staggering sometimes, filled me in. He said Richie's wife called that morning to say she wanted a divorce and Richie'd hit the bottle and had been drinking ever since. Lynn called it twisting off, a binge like that. I had to ask him to clarify. The term came from drilling, he said. If you put too much torque on the drillpipe it stripped the threads that screwed the pipe together and the drillstring came apart in the hole. Twisting off was a real mess which, seeing Richie in that condition, I could imagine perfectly.

I threw open Jean's front door so they could shuffle through sideways.

Kyle coached Richie across the living room and up the half flight of stairs to the upper level—a narrow squeeze for three moose. They were staggering down to Richie's room when Richie suddenly groaned and made a blech-y heaving noise. As if choreographed, Lynn ducked from under Richie's right arm and Kyle ducked from under his left and they slung Richie into the bathroom just as he started to hurl. Kyle leaped in after him and I heard scuffling, thumps like knees hitting tile, then the sound of Richie puking his guts out.

Lynn grinned down at me. He stood blocking the bathroom doorway—I'd stayed at the foot of the stairs. I said, "Grab Richie's keys. You guys have to go." I fished for my keys as Lynn relayed the message.

"Bale! Get his keys, buddy!"

I took the ignition key off my key ring. "Take my truck to the Dogleg—it belongs to Joe Balch so try not to crash it. Richie's truck is out front there. You can leave my key with Gerry."

We heard more thumps and a muttered word. There was a hiatus in the puking, then Lynn stepped back and Kyle appeared jingling Richie's keys, checking the time on his phone.

I said, "You guys go. I'll take care of Richie."

Kyle gave Lynn a push and they catapulted down the stairs. Jumping out of their way, I tossed Lynn my key as they thundered out of Jean's, slamming the front door with a china-rattling bang. I heard puking resume above me and ran into the kitchen to call Emmet. I was going to tell him Richie caught a stomach bug but I was too late. Gerry'd already called: Emmet knew his best driller had twisted off. I said Kyle and Lynn were coming and tried to tell him the latest from Richie's wife in Sayre to explain Richie's drunk. Emmet warned me not to pester him. He was two hands short that tour and they were running in the hole to try to set a different plug. I offered to take Richie's place on the brake. Emmet said, "Next year, little sister—when you's all growed."

Jean got home from work about the time I was making Richie

comfortable on the bathroom floor. After tugging and tugging I'd realized I couldn't put him to bed myself, not while he was unconscious.

Hearing Jean in the kitchen, I called out hello. She came upstairs, murmuring, "Oh my – the poor boy." when she saw Richie sprawled between the bathtub and sink, a rolled towel under his head for a pillow. She was wearing a skirt and school heels but I asked her to help me get Richie to his room. We each took a foot and dragged him out and down the hall – then had to leave him on the floor because we couldn't engineer him into bed. Jean said it was like trying to coordinate a sack of potatoes and apologized for being too old.

Walking back downstairs she invited me to stay for dinner. I told her I'd eaten a late lunch, so she offered me coffee and dessert. I got the distinct feeling there was something on her mind. She wouldn't let me help in the kitchen but I did anyway. As I was getting forks and knives and she was pulling food from the fridge, she said:

"What exactly is happening over at the house, Ann?"

Of course Joe wasn't going to tell Jean about the stolen guns. He'd specifically forbidden me to mention it. But he didn't say I couldn't ramp up suspense or excite amorphous fear in order to pry information out of Jean.

I said, "Haven't you talked to Joe?"

"I have." She hesitated. "I've also spoken to Luz . . ."

Luz: the queen of vague terrors.

She didn't know one-tenth – one-*one-hundredth* – of what we knew, but she was totally freaked. I'd left her that morning racing around, bossing her cousin, bossing the electrician, bossing the alarm guys, to fortify the house as fast and securely as possible. Joe had had to eject her from the foyer when the sheriffs came to take a report about the guns. Answering the front door, Luz had wailed to the deputies that we were all going to die murdered to death.

Jean repeated quietly, "Please tell me what's happening. Luz does tend to exaggerate and one can't always believe what she says."

Standing by the coffeemaker, Jean had a knife poised over a pan of homemade brownies. I could only think what a nice woman she'd always been. And what a nice woman she was in her old-fashioned green-and-purple kitchen and her schoolteacher's sweater set—billeting a bunch of strange roughnecks and not even minorly upset when she finds one of them passed out in her bathroom, reeking of vomit. I'd been prepared to harrow and manipulate her, but suddenly I just wasn't.

I said simply, "Joe doesn't want to worry you."

Jean nodded, not happy, and started to cut the brownie into squares. I leaned on the counter beside her.

"I wish I could reassure you but I can't. We don't have a handle on Kenny Mills yet at all, and with Joe's guns missing we have to assume he's personally in danger, some kind of target of the conspiracy—"

The front door of the house opened. There was the bang of the screen and footsteps.

"You there, Jeannie?"

Turning, Jean brightened at the voice. Joe called, "Did I miss a free meal?"

"No—come in, Joe. We were just getting started."

She set the cake knife down and wiped her hands on her apron as Joe walked in. Seeing me standing there, he crooked a finger. I pushed off the counter and followed him into the living room.

He said low, "Remember this number—seven-seven-five-eight. Don't write it down, remember it."

I whispered, "What is it?"

"Pass code for the alarm at the house."

"Seven-seven-five-eight. I'll remember—it's the date Lucy Boyd came in." I indicated the kitchen. "Luz spilled the beans."

"That's the reason I'm here."

"Then why are we whispering in the living room?"

"Because you're leaving."

"Can I take a brownie first?"

Joe clapped me on the shoulder and raised his voice. "On your

156

way out get in the front seat of my truck. Emmet sent you some pepper spray and you'll find a manual for the alarm. You'll be tested tomorrow."

"What are you doing about *your* protection, Joe?"

He deadpanned, "I'm relying on your enterprise and daring, young lady."

"You shouldn't—"

I stopped because I realized he was kidding. He also didn't want to discuss his own safety.

Joe winked at me. I winked back and went to get my brownie and say goodbye. As I was leaving I bet myself Joe had a weapon of some sort in his truck. I grabbed the pepper spray and alarm booklet, then checked under the front seats, in the glove compartment and console, and the back seat.

I found a brand-new shotgun on the floor, underneath a blanket, where the driver could reach it fast. I didn't check to see if it was loaded because of course it was.

Gerry was holding my ignition key, and between customers he told me the latest news. Hilary and Caroline Mahin had just publicly disowned Suzette, and Suzette had been spotted that evening hanging around her parents' house. Gerry also got me the unlisted number for Mike Garcia—Manuel Garcia the Second, Jean's oldest son, a hotshot lawyer in Bakersfield. It was time to try Mike, I'd decided.

The Mahins lived in the same neighborhood as Jean, only a few blocks away. Typically the best neighborhoods had names ending with Hills or Heights or some species of tree. But there were no native trees or high ground in Wilson and this was just called the southwest part of town. Nothing about Wilson was fancy or pretty, either, and people with money didn't blow it on pretentious housing. The Mahin homestead was a large, plain ranch with a landscaped lawn surrounded by a wrought-iron fence. Lights were on outside and in-, but as I cruised by, I couldn't see any action.

It was impossible to hide in that flat, open setting. I just blessed the anonymity of a white truck and parked in a less-lit patch between two houses down the way.

Keeping one eye on the street, I grabbed my phone.

I located a Donald A. Mancuso in Palm Springs that cross-checked with a Donald A. Mancuso in Balboa Beach. The desert place didn't answer but down the coast I spoke to a snooty secretary with a British accent who wouldn't tell me where Mrs. Mancuso was or when she might be due. I told him it was urgent and concerned her son. The secretary asked which son, so I said. I left my name and number, told the secretary to tell Mrs. Mancuso I was friends with Joe Balch, and stressed again it was urgent.

One end of the Mahin house went dark. Somebody had turned off the driveway lights.

Squinting at Gerry's scribbled number, I dialed Mike Garcia. I hadn't seen Mike in a few years but I knew his voice the minute he answered.

I said without preamble, "Want to take me to the diner for a Coke?"

Mike started laughing. He looked and sounded exactly like his father and was the same kind of good man. I had a major crush on him when I was in high school and he was in law school, and that was a line I'd used as a teenage femme fatale. It became a joke between us.

"Ann Whitehead – what a pleasure! I heard you were living with Joe. Mom says you're roughnecking on the wildcat."

"Wuffnecking, actually, and it's a blast. Do you have time for a top-secret and confidential talk, Mike?"

"For you I do. Let me close this door – wait."

He put the phone down and I scoped the street and the Mahin house another time.

He came back on the line. "Go ahead."

"I didn't know you were practically raised with the late, unlamented Ray Parkerworth Junior. Your aunt Cathy told me Celeste Parkerworth dumped the baby on Luz and Joe, but he was trouble

158

by the time he could ride a tricycle. The only person he'd listen to was Manny, so he moved to your house and stayed until he was fifteen, then got sent to juvie for breaking into the Dogleg with Kenny Mills."

Mike was quiet. Finally I had to say, "Mike?"

"I'm here . . . I've heard the gossip from Aunt Cathy and Tía Luz. I hope you're not acting on Aunt Cathy's belief that Kenny was murdered because of some mystery or ambiguity relative to the disposition of Joe's estate."

Mike had taken a more serious, lawyerly tone. I said, "Which belief are you questioning – murder or the motive?"

"Until Tía told me about Joe's guns I didn't believe it was murder. I'm questioning Aunt Cathy's proposed motive.

"Be aware that when Junior turned twenty-one he assumed control of his inherited stock and immediately made a deal to sell the entire block back to Joe. As part of the deal, Junior voluntarily renounced his seat on the board of Balch Corporation and all future claim to the companies. Joe had intended to groom Junior as his heir and successor – it was Ray Senior's last wish and what everyone expected. Junior never did appreciate his luck. He had a decent amount of brains but he was lazy and undisciplined. His ideas always ran to the easy score. He'd rather rob a saloon for cash in hand than own a successful business. This is a matter of public knowledge, Ann. I can put you in touch with reliable people who'll attest –"

A dark figure moved on the gravel path in the Mahins' front yard.

I leaned forward in my seat. I hadn't seen where it came from, the street or a hedge.

The figure moved out of the shadows. I said, "Mike, I have to go. I'll call you back." And dropped the phone.

It was a skinny woman with straggly, electric hair, who bent down, scooped up gravel from the path, and threw it with a jerky motion at the front door of the house. The glass in the door rattled and clinked. I heard it clearly in the night silence. Bending again, she scooped up another handful and threw it – and scooped up another handful and threw it. The light over the door shattered and the falling glass made loud breaking noises.

The front door opened and Caroline Mahin called in a trembling voice, "We'll phone the police, Suzette! Go away!",

Sliding out the passenger side of the truck, I crept up and flattened myself against the fender.

A man's voice came from the large picture window. He was backlit and I recognized, through the sheer curtains, Hilary Mahin's pear-shaped silhouette. He boomed in an awesome patriarchal voice:

"The police have been summoned! They will be here in one minute!"

Suzette stooped for gravel, threw one last handful at the house, and took off. Hurdling the low iron fence, she raced up the sidewalk straight at me. "Death on a cracker" about covered it. She looked thirty going on ninety and high as a kite.

I stepped out, blocking the sidewalk, and grabbed her as she tried to dodge past. "Suzette! I need to talk to you!"

She stopped dead. Panting hoarsely, she looked at me with shimmery, pinwheel eyes.

"Who killed your boyfriend, Kenny? Who are you afraid of?"

"*Him!*"

Shrieking, Suzette stuck one arm out rigid and jabbed a finger at her father's silhouette in the window. Then she ripped out of my grasp and ran. I wasn't going to chase her. She zigzagged up the sidewalk like a crazy person, whipped around the corner at the end of the block, and vanished.

19

OUR MUD LOGGER drove off the lease every morning at six. I'd seen him do it regularly the weeks I was on tour and assumed he was going to breakfast. I also assumed he was going to the Kern Diner because they served the best breakfast in town – not that there was a whole lot of choice. I wanted to make sure, though, so I called Emmet at 6:05 A.M. Thursday. He picked up the phone with a grunt, sounding ragged out and preoccupied. I wished him a cheerful good morning and got:

"No time for socializin, little sister."

"Ah ain't socializin – Ah is detectivizin. Where does Bud eat breakfast?"

"What you wantin Bud for now?"

"The diner?"

Emmet murmphed and hung up. It was yes.

The diner was yet another not-fancy, not-pretty Wilson building. Its chrome shell was ancient, updated and enlarged by a wraparound stucco addition painted the usual desert tan. The exterior also featured a folk-art rendition of the history of the Westside oil fields, complete with mule teams, wooden derricks, and California's greatest gusher, Lakeview no.1, from 1910.

Early on a weekday morning the diner was packed. Cars and trucks filled the parking lot and people were standing outside in the cold waiting to be seated. As I cruised by on Kern Street I spotted Bud's pickup in the lot. It was an ordinary white Ford but I recognized it by a dent in the tailgate. I saw Mark Bridges's jacked-up red clown truck — it was hard to miss. Ron Bray's Balch Drilling pickup was there. I also spotted Richie's pickup, charcoal gray with Oklahoma plates. Kyle and Lynn were inside. They must've come directly from the rig.

Circling the block, I set up in the alley behind the diner to wait. Doug had agreed this was a slim chance. But he also agreed, based on my account, that Gerry hinked when I'd said Bud had no reason to shop Minerva and Joe to the opposition.

The hink turned out to be real. Bud was a gambler.

After he ate a leisurely breakfast, I followed him to a casino almost three hours north and east of Wilson in the foothills of the Sierras. Late morning on a winter's day, the huge lot was still fairly empty. Bud parked in the row closest to the front entrance and walked inside. I stayed down on the winding approach road to give him a few minutes and to check the casino's website, then drove up and found a spot by a fenced area in the far corner — a maintenance yard where other white trucks were parked.

Settling down to watch I called Emmet again, hoping to catch him in a better frame of mind. He resisted at first but I told him where I was and pried the Bud story out of him.

"Thrill jockey."

That's how Emmet described our mud logger: a thrill jockey. Bud lived for high risk and high stakes — things like stud poker and wildcatting. It was hilarious because you'd never know it to look at him. He was the most dull, prosaic, middle-aged geek, with thick glasses, a comb-over, and a belly hanging out of his perennial jeans and letter jacket. The few times I'd seen him up close he was wearing the same old Beatles T-shirt.

But I was reminded of something my father often said: you pay your engineer to be right nine times out of ten, and your geologist to be wrong nine times out of ten. Geologists searched for oil and gas reservoirs. They're the ones who told the company or investors, Drill here. It was a science. It was also an art and a vibe, and geologists were traditionally the mystics and dreamers of the oil fields. They made educated guesses with which the earth mostly didn't cooperate.

My guess was that Bud had lost control. His love of the gamble had tipped over into compulsion, and Emmet and Gerry were concerned he'd become a liability on Minerva . . . maybe even a rat.

I swept the parking lot and casino front for the umpteenth time. The casino was big, with one- and two-story sections done log-cabiny to look rustic, and easy on exterior neon to spare the town's view or the wildlife. Cars had started rolling in steadily. The second parking row had filled up, and the third, so that all I could see now of Bud's truck was the white roof of the cab.

The afternoon was also getting dark and darker. The sky had turned a slate color like it might snow. Inside the truck I was definitely feeling the cold. I made a deal with myself: I'd go for coffee in an hour if Bud's truck didn't move. There was only one road into the casino and I could watch it from the fast-food joint at the bottom, where the road intersected with the highway.

Meanwhile I had projects to keep me warm.

I e-mailed Jean to enlist her help with my revenge plan for Kyle: the plan had come to me in a flash as I tailed Bud up I-5. There was an e-mail from her inviting me to a potluck tomorrow night.

Grabbing the pepper spray Emmet sent, I read the instructions and practiced pulling the canister out of my pocket and arming it for use. It was no match for a gun but it would incapacitate any human who got near enough. After the pepper spray felt natural, I took the alarm manual and studied the keypads, how to turn the system off and on, and the different levels of protection. Joe had bought a deluxe model with glass-break and motion sensors – all sorts of bling. I was memorizing command codes when my phone rang, and I picked it up automatically without checking to see who it was.

"Ann?"

Damn: *Alice.* Too late to hang up – I'd already said hello.

I took a deep breath. "Alice, what's happening?"

"Your grandmother and I are in Beverly Hills. I've heard you quit your job. Is it true?"

"Who told you that?"

"It isn't important who told me. I want to know if it's true or not."

I tuned her out as my mind raced forward. Alice would admit if Joe or Luz had told her, which I couldn't imagine anyway. As far as I knew she talked to no one in Wilson because there was no one worth talking to, in her opinion. She'd told me that more than once. How did she hear I'd quit?

"If it's true—"

An idea popped out of my subconscious. I interrupted her. "Hey, Alice?"

"Yes. What is it?"

"You're on Balch Corporation's board of directors."

"Of course I am. You know very well I am. Balch Oil and Balch Drilling are my father's companies—Parkerworth Oil and Parkerworth Drilling. Of course I'm on the board. I'm also an important stockholder. Why do you ask?"

I smiled—I'd seen a likely source. Alice knew Hilary Mahin better than just nodding to him at the house. And Mahin might be keeping tabs on me.

"Ann?"

"Alice?"

"You are in danger."

"Excuse me?" I cupped my hand over my non-phone ear. Suddenly I was paying verrry close attention to Alice Balch. "I'm in *danger?* Is that what you said? Danger?"

Alice backpedaled smoothly. "I meant, *Are* you in danger? I was asking a question. What is going on up there?"

I looked out at the sky. "I think it's about to snow."

"Don't be flippant—I'm not in the mood for it. Some hand is killed on my husband's well and you are injured seriously enough to quit. Today I'm given a pass code and told a burglar alarm has been installed at the house. Joe was raised in the country—that house has never been locked. Something is going on up there and I insist upon knowing what it is—"

The first few flakes were starting to fall. They melted on my windshield, backlit by the neon reds and yellows of the casino entrance, standing out now in the early twilight. Bud's truck was still parked in the same spot. A bunch more vehicles separated it in the front row from me at the back, but the white roof of his cab hadn't moved. I decided I could be more productive elsewhere. Switching the phone over to my left ear, I reached for the ignition while Alice continued to talk.

Bud's trailer was identical to Joe's and Emmet's — last in the line up the west side of the lease, on the far side of the steel hut where the crews changed their clothes.

I trekked through the dark fields and, ducking between the barbwire, tiptoed along the end of his trailer. Peeking around the corner edge I could see Richie's pickup and Trey's junker car and, past them, Emmet's pickup and two more white pickups. I looked up at the rig: they were coming out of the hole. Kyle was in the derrick unlatching a stand of pipe; all the hands would be on the floor. Sliding around to Bud's end door, opened it, climbed into his storage room, and—

I almost gasped.

There was Bud. He was seated at the desk under the window. Emmet was standing over his left shoulder, not even a yard from me.

I froze in a crouch, conscious of how loud the diesels were. Easing the door shut softly I held my breath and waited. Nobody'd heard me. I was on Emmet's deafer side and both guys were concentrating. Bud had a pencil and a stacked computer printout. Emmet was frowning at the printout, his hands in the pockets of his overalls.

Holding one sheet up, Bud pointed with his pencil. "Shallow hole was a piece of cake. The tops ran true — San Joaquin, Etchegoin."

Those were the names of geological formations. Bud had that

165

local twang–I'd never heard his voice before. Emmet just murmphed.

Bud hit two points along the margin, folded that sheet of paper, and picked up the next lower one. He consulted something lying flat on his desk like he was comparing it to the printout.

"Reef Ridge–top was four hundred feet off." He tapped a point. "It starts to get interesting right about here."

He folded pages back and picked up new ones in sequence. He tapped. "Antelope. We thought we'd find it at ninety-eight hundred and twelve-five. We find it at ninety-six hundred and not again since."

Pulling a hand out of one pocket, Emmet reached to point at the flat sheet on the desk. "Never yet found none of these boogers."

Bud pointed at the printout. "Little taste of the Monterey here we didn't expect. I don't know where the rest of them went." He consulted back and forth, tap-tapped and folded pages, moving towards the bottom of the stack.

"McDonald, McLure. McDonald again at twelve-eight. We didn't expect them that shallow. I thought we'd find the Temblor at fifteen-five–at seventeen-two we were still looking for it."

Putting the pencil down, Bud felt for a highball glass sitting beside him. He bumped it with his knuckles and almost spilled it. Still not looking, he got a firm hold on the glass and took a slug of the clear liquid inside it. Vodka? I wondered. Ice water?

Emmet leaned forward to unfold some pages and lay them out in a column. He pointed. "Oil shows."

He pointed some more. "Lost circulation. Swellin clay. Gas–just enough to scare you to death."

Bud nodded. "The oil might pay for this well and then some. Don't hold me to it, though." He pointed to a couple of places.

"I don't like these overpressured zones. I've never seen them before and can't explain them."

"Get in line behind me, sir. Like I been sayin, I hate our stinkin drillin program. To my mind it weren't conservative enough. Closest producin well's at twenty-one hundred so records is no damn use and I ain't never seen nothin like the rock around here for screwin with honorable men. Should of drilled us a bigger top hole and went from there."

They both studied the printout. Bud folded it slowly back to the beginning. "We'll know where we are when we drill out the window. If we're in the McLure, we're found, old-timer."

"Let us hope." Emmet clapped him on the back. "See you shortly. Gird yourself for a severe whuppin."

Emmet tromped out, slamming the door. Bud sat and guzzled the rest of his drink, then stood to neaten the desk and put the well log away. He kept his trailer more like a field office than Emmet's fuggy home-away-from-home.

A low hiss: "Little sister!"

I flinched and turned. Emmet had opened the end door. He crooked his finger at me and pointed at the ground. Crawling to the sill, I jumped down into the yard and followed him around the end corner.

"What the hell you doin?!"

"I called but you weren't in your trailer—"

"You was out of range—I tried to warn you. Here Joe wants a meetin all in a lather—"

We both shut up. We'd heard the trailer door slam and footsteps on the metal grating of the stoop. Bud's trailer was level with the diesel engines and the acoustics were different—you could hear better and not shout. Emmet stuck his head around the corner to eyeball the yard, checking up at the rig before he pulled back.

I said, "What's my crew doing tonight?"

"We's comin out to pick up that whipstock and run it in so's we can kick off and get back to drillin this hole."

"How's Richie? He must have an epic hangover."

"Don't know. Cain't find Teach."

"Can't find—"

Emmet cut in, "Not the moment, little sister—they's waitin on me for gin rummy. What you want in Bud's bunkhouse?"

I deadpanned, "I was planning to steal the logs, sell them to the highest bidder, and retire to a South Sea island with the money."

That got the slitty-eye.

I said, "I'm looking for evidence Bud's gambling habit has compromised Minerva. I assume that's what you and Gerry are worried about, that Bud's thrown in with the bastards."

I didn't say I was also looking for Joe's stolen shotguns and/or rifles.

Emmet worked his false teeth, squinting, then stuck his head out again to check activity in the yard. He moved, so I followed. Pulling open the end door he said, "Be quick now—I is standin guard."

He gave me a boost and shut the door behind me. Bud had left his lights on and the blinds down: perfect.

I hurried.

The storage room was empty. I ran into the kitchenette and sped through the cupboards and drawers. Empty, all empty, except for drink glasses and the plastic utensils that came with takeout food. In the fridge I found ice cubes and vodka. I checked the tiny bathroom, then ran into the bedroom. The bedroom had fake paneling, a linoleum floor, and cheap blinds like the rest of the place, and was almost bare. Bud was sleeping on a mattress on the floor. There was a metal chair beside the mattress with a flashlight and a deck of cards on it, but no other furniture, no clothes and no nothing else in the closet.

Racing back to the main room, I tried the desk.

I checked the drawer where I'd seen Bud put the computer printout. Copies of all the logs were in there and in the drawer below. They were thick batches of paper with HALLIBURTON and SCHLUMBERGER stamped on top—hundreds of pages of numbers and plotted graphs, super-scientific, super-secret, unreadable and uninterpretable by someone like me. I also found Bud's handdrawn log, a stack of folded graph paper detailing the various formations we'd drilled, with geologic symbols and hash marks for footage.

In the top left drawer I found a pile of invoices billing Bud's services to Balch-Min LLC. Poker items were kept in the bottom left drawer – slim books on strategy, stray chips, and two more decks of cards.

Bud was a neatnik. The drawers were very orderly and I made sure I left everything the way I found it.

Opposite the desk, where Emmet had his napping couch, Bud had a worktable with machines and gadgets I used to know the names of. There was a microscope and porcelain dishes, droppers, bottled chemicals – a thing that looked like a toaster oven. There was a metal box that spit out a ticker-tape reading of gas in the drilling mud. There were clean rock cuttings in separate piles and different-colored pens, pencils, and drawing tools. There was a computer and technical books on California geology. One book was sitting out: *Diagenesis, Deformation, and Fluid Flow in the Miocene Monterey Formation.*

The book had an envelope stuck between the pages and I could read the return address: a collection agency in Bakersfield. I slipped out the envelope. It was business size and addressed to Bud on a street in Wilson. The flap had been ripped open so I grabbed the letter and read. It was short.

Bud owed a Bakersfield casino an enormous sum of money.

No wonder he'd driven three hours to gamble when there was a casino much closer. I skimmed the letter again. The tone was surprisingly reasonable and the letter offered Bud a choice of ways to repay the debt and time frames to pay it in. Gambling debts gave you the image of mobsters with baseball bats breaking kneecaps, but it wasn't like that at all. There were no threats, overt or implied –

Emmet hissed, "Time, little sister!"

I slipped the letter back into the envelope, closed the book, and ran. Emmet moved aside to let me jump down. Grabbing his jean jacket I pulled him around into the shadows.

"*I hate you!*"

"Do what now?" Emmet cocked his better ear at me.

"I spend hours finding out what you and Gerry already know!

169

Our mud logger's in debt to a Bakersfield casino for – I'll make it a round number – two hundred and fifty-three *thousand* dollars!"

The muscles of Emmet's face did work when he was deeply shocked, which was what he was. He even went pale around the mouth.

After a pause to absorb it, he rumbled, "Mercy sakes alive."

"You mean you didn't know?"

"I know he likes his stud poker and ain't been winnin here lately. He's into me for a goodly amount – Gerry same."

"What about Mahin or Bray? Would he borrow money from them?"

Emmet murmphed. "Could be maybe."

"Joe?"

"We's makin sure Joe ain't heard a whisper of this." Emmet held up one finger, then pointed towards the rig. "That deal there's causin trouble enough."

"Did you tell him about the drill-collar clamps?"

"I most certainly did not."

Emmet started to walk away but I stopped him. "Is there anything else I should know about the trustworthies on the lease? How about Tommy at the gate? Is he supporting a secret second family?"

"Not that I'm aware of. He has eight grandkids."

"What if he has sixteen and they all need braces? Orthodontia is expensive."

I immediately felt bad about the joke. Emmet was too upset to give it the granite treatment it deserved. He stuck his fists in his overall pockets and stepped into the yard, heading down to his trailer without another word. He didn't even check up at the rig.

20

I SAT IN THE Dogleg the next afternoon trying very hard not to doze off. I'd drunk two large Cokes and two coffees and my stomach felt acid, and all I wanted was to lay my head down on the table and shut my eyes.

Gerry commented on the caffeine intake and I told him about my screwed-up, patchy sleep. He thought I was complaining about morning tour. He said that was the trouble when the oil business never slept. Every working rig on the planet, of which there were several thousand at any given moment, drilled around the clock, nonstop. You could always tell an oil town, he said, because the wheezers were out at four A.M. looking for a place to eat breakfast. I knew Joe kept odd hours and Emmet didn't seem to sleep at all: he catnapped. Gerry said he was up at four A.M. every day. He couldn't break the habit and he wasn't the only old guy waiting at the doors when the Kern Diner opened at five.

Coincidentally I'd received a call from Greece at four that morning. I'd been sitting by the fire in my room speculating about Alice and Bud when my cell phone rang and I nearly jumped out of my skin thinking someone had tripped the new burglar alarm.

The reception was terrible. Between garble and delay, it took me a minute to realize it was the gold-digging tramp, bad mother, and flake Celeste Parkerworth Mancuso. She was on a cruise in the Greek islands and had just received the message I'd left at her house. I'd eliminated the theory that Kenny Mills's death related to inheritance of the Balch companies—but I was looking at Alice again as involved somewhere somehow, so I was happy to talk to Mrs. Mancuso. Communication was a pain, though, and we had to shout and repeat ourselves constantly. She'd known my grandfather and asked after my grandmother and wanted news of Joe's health. Before I could ask my own questions, we were cut off. Caller ID had shown a number with a U.S. area code, but when I tried calling her back, I only got some strange static.

I'd phoned Mrs. Mancuso again when I woke up, with no luck. I'd called her Balboa house for a direct number, which the snooty secretary wouldn't give out. Anyway, people were sleeping on the yachts in Greece by that time.

My head started to nod. I caught it and made myself sit up straight and review the day.

I'd spent a few useless hours watching Bud's house and casing his block. He lived in the same neighborhood as Jean and the Mahins, in a smallish brick ranch that looked new.

I'd learned there was a Mrs. Bud who drove a Buick sedan and unloaded groceries from the carport into a side door. I'd learned they were having furnace problems—and had plenty of time to realize how I lost Bud at the casino. I shouldn't have been satisfied with watching a white roof rows away. There were too many white pickups in this part of the world and I hadn't paid attention every minute. I should've cruised the lot periodically to make sure I still had the one with the dented tailgate.

I'd also realized I had to start distinguishing makes and models. Mark Bridges's red clown truck was easy—it was telling one white pickup from another I needed to learn. Richie knew a Ford from a Chevrolet in the dark just by the headlights and could recite the stock features and performance rating of any American-built pickup. But Richie was a gearhead too. I'd seen him disassemble and repair things when Emmet had the parts and didn't want to wait for a mechanic.

I felt a jab in my ribs and jerked up straight as Gerry whispered, "There he is, just coming in."

Gerry nodded at the street door. I turned and saw Mark Bridges. Gerry whispered:

"He still doesn't know we know he's scouting. Joe doesn't want West Coast to replace him with a smarter guy. Dumb as the proverbial box of rocks, Mark is – and that's insulting the rocks."

Busing my empty glasses, Gerry wiped the tabletop and kept moving. It was Friday and the back room was filling up with the after-work crowd. Bridges headed for the bar, climbed onto a stool, and twirled his Dodgers cap backwards like he always did to drink. He had on a gray sweatshirt and I sat watching his broad back, thinking he looked like he'd played high-school football – a thick, short guy on defensive line – but the years and the beers were catching up and he'd be fat soon. Already he overlapped the barstool pretty good.

I'd reviewed my options and realized any approach on Bridges had its problem. But I could work off "dumb as a box of rocks," plus the fact that, in theory, I didn't know who Bridges was and Bridges didn't know who I was. I'd wing it and see what happened.

Grabbing my sunglasses and jacket, I walked over to the bar and took the stool on Bridges's right.

He didn't notice me because he was telling the waitress the punch line of a dirty joke. She pretended to laugh while I caught Gerry's attention and signed for a beer. When Gerry brought it, Bridges turned, knocking his knee into mine. I slid over for more room. His face was puffy and moist like he already had a few beers down him.

I nodded hey, roughneck style.

Bridges saw who it was. His expression changed as the mental wheels started turning. Looking away, he hoisted his glass and chugged, then looked back with an aggressive sneer.

"Who do you think you are, huh?"

Caught by surprise, I just said, "Me?"

"Yeah – sticking your nose in other people's business. You're not from here – you don't belong here. You think your grandfather makes you somebody, huh? Knowing that bastard Joe Balch makes you somebody, you can just come in here and stick your nose in people's business?"

Bridges had his pudgy hands wrapped around his beer glass, squeezing and releasing it. I thought of my hurt neck as he glanced down the bar at Gerry loading drinks onto a tray.

"Balch is a bastard but people think the sun shines out his ass –"

Breaking off, Bridges half turned at a commotion behind us. Two sets of strong hands clamped my arms and forcibly pulled me off the stool. I'd draped my jacket over one leg and had to grab it before it fell.

"Pup, we're headed to the Oasis! You come with us too!"

It was Kyle. Carrot Bobby was with him, and the Oasis invitation made no sense because Kyle was on tour tonight.

I tried to say, *"Let go –"*

Kyle had my right arm and Bobby had my left. Suddenly I stopped resisting: I knew why they were abducting me, of course. People jumped out of the way as I was hustled across the room, my feet barely touching the floor. I twisted around to see what Bridges was doing. He'd turned back to the bar and sat hunched over his beer. Gerry, though, had seen it all and flapped his towel goodbye.

Out on the sidewalk I said, "I was talking to Bridges because –"

I didn't think goofball Kyle could look so grim. He released my arm, saying, "Get in the truck." Bobby shoved me, the jerk.

I climbed into JD's pickup, sandwiched between Bobby driving and Kyle riding shotgun. We kept silent the whole way out to the lease. Something had changed if Kyle and Bobby were speaking again. The melodrama back in Sayre must've gotten resolved.

Tommy waved us through the barrier gate. Bobby parked in front of Emmet's trailer and pushed me to get out Kyle's side. They escorted me up the metal stairs between them and Kyle pounded on the door, then pulled it open. The trailer was warm and smelled like roast beef. Emmet sat perusing a worn manual with his sock feet on the desk. Seeing us, seeing our faces, he put the book down, leaned back, and hooked his thumbs in the bib of his overalls.

"How can I help y'all?"

Kyle said, "We caught her talking to the scout —"

" — at the Dogleg." Bobby pushed me.

I turned on him, one hand in a claw. "Push me again and you'll get the curse of the stick lizard!"

I curled my fingers like fangs, heard Kyle stifle a snort, and turned back around. One look at Emmet's face and I knew instinctively how he was going to play this.

He took off his reading glasses and fixed a hard eye on me. "That right what Bale says, little sister?"

I nodded.

"Got any excuse for your sorry quislin self?"

I shrugged. "I only told Bridges what I knew. We found the Antelope at ninety-six hundred and the McDonald at twelve-eight, although you didn't expect it that shallow, and you hadn't found the Temblor as of seventeen-two. You're hoping to be in the McLure when you drill out the window, you don't like overpressured zones, and you wish you could've drilled a bigger top hole. I think that's it. No, wait — I told him we've had oil shows and enough gas to scare you to death, but I didn't know how much at what depth. I told him I'd find out."

I checked over my shoulder. The looks on Kyle's and Bobby's faces were priceless: they were gaping. It was all I could do not to laugh, but Emmet was Emmet, every inch stone.

"I'll call over to the Dogleg right now." He fake-leaned for his desk phone. "Tell that lazy good-for-nothin myself."

Covering a smile, I went and sat on the armrest of the couch. Emmet leaned back and rocked in his chair.

Kyle grinned. "Sorry, Pup." Bobby mumbled, "Sorry," and opened the trailer door to leave.

Emmet said, "Nope, you boys done good — stay a minute. Me and her's got us a small project. This is for your ears alone, hear?"

Bobby shut the door and they both nodded as Emmet tapped me on the leg. "Show 'em your neck."

Kyle said, "Teach told us she quit. Didn't she quit?"

Folding my collars down, I unbuttoned my top buttons and

turned my head. It was almost a week later and my neck was still stiff and sore to touch. But the imprint of the chainlink was less clear, the bruises were fading, and the flower garden had spread out into pastel blobs.

Emmet said, "Some bastard tried to put a end to our little sister."

"Or just scare me off." Then I added, because the Oklahomans were inside the circle of trust, "Bridges being one of the candidates."

Kyle and Bobby looked at my neck, then looked me square on, which Bobby hadn't done since we met. They were both impressed.

Closing my collars, I looked back at Bobby. "I'm working on Kenny Mills's murder. How about the idea that someone was gunning for Richie and killed the wrong guy in the fog?"

I'd dismissed that theory Christmas Day after reviewing the logic but I wanted to torture Bobby a little.

"Like you, Bobby, for instance."

Bobby was a big ox but he had a redhead's fair skin and a fresh country face, and when he flushed he turned bright red like a kid. He stared at me, then at Kyle, then at me, then at Emmet.

Emmet said gently, "Answer the woman, Carrot."

"No, sir. No, sir – I did no such thing, Emmet, sir."

"Teach and you was scufflin in the yard afore it happened."

Bobby immediately glared at me. Emmet said, "Don't be blamin her. I seen the split lip on Teach."

"I swear to God I did not! I will swear it on the Bible!" Bobby put his left hand up and his right hand over his heart.

"I know you didn't, son." Emmet nodded at the trailer door. "You boys go on – Bale's late for safety meetin. Not a word of this, all right?"

Bobby dropped his hands and stood looking dazed so that Kyle had to nudge him. Reaching for the door, Kyle said, "Carrot's driving Pup."

Emmet said, "Wait on her outside."

They left, slamming the door and clattering down the metal stairs, Kyle slapping Emmet's window as he passed.

176

I said, "Richie must've told those guys what I was doing. They didn't even blink about Mills being murdered."

"Teach ain't a talker – you got to figure my boys know a lot without bein told in so many words. Seen that pretty new pickup out front of the changin hut?"

I stood up and looked left out Emmet's window, pressing my cheek against the glass. Richie's pickup was parked closest and, past it, almost dwarfing it, was a white pickup I'd never seen before. The lease lights bouncing off made it glow in the dark.

"Trey come to work in that tonight." Emmet said it like it was portentous, but I didn't see what it portended.

"He washes up from Wyomin in a ole beater and here he's drivin that little darlin? Where I come from, a F-150 dualie, four-by-four, bells and whistles, stickers up around sixty – probly more in California. You tell me how he affords it."

"Maybe it belongs to Steve."

"Who is Steve now?"

"Trey has the name Steve stitched on his coverall."

Emmet pulled his sock feet off the desk and bent over for his boots. "I's gettin you his address in Bako. He bears watchin, Trey does. He bears watchin."

21

BOBBY HAD DROPPED me on the street and gone on inside
the Dogleg before I discovered my truck had been vandalized.
The blades on the windshield wipers had disappeared and
the arms were bent up at an angle, with the help of pliers it looked
like. It was a pissy thing to do and I assumed Mark Bridges had
done it. I didn't see the clown truck anywhere or else he would've
gotten his own medicine back: pepper spray in his air vents
would've been nice.

Standing up on the running board, one knee on the hood, I tried
to bend the arms in, but I was afraid to snap the hinges and I was
also already late for Jean's potluck. Luz was bringing the contribution from our household. All I had to do was race home, shower
and change, then swing by the liquor store on Kern for Joe's favorite bourbon. I knew Richie had drunk the bottle Jean kept around.
According to Kyle, Richie drank every drop of booze in the house
before he went missing.

It was the usual big, noisy scene at Jean's: a bunch of cars and
trucks parked out front and her living room jammed with people,
most of whom I knew or recognized. Luz waved at me and I waved
back. The frilly couch and matching chairs were full, and guests
had pulled in dining chairs and folding chairs and sat in clumps
and circles – talking, smoking, drinking, balancing dessert plates

on their laps. Kids chased from room to room and up and down the stairs. More kids were playing under the dining table. I took in the chaos with a general "Hey, everybody," and dodged on through to the kitchen.

"Ann!" It was Audrey.

"Ann!" It was Cathy Rintoul, out of uniform.

I lifted the bottle of bourbon at them. Cathy was scraping plates and handing them to Audrey who was loading the dishwasher. A slim man with jet-black hair stood at the sink with his shirtsleeves rolled up, washing more dishes. Mike Garcia.

I heard, "We're glad you could make it," at my elbow and looked down.

It was Jean sitting at her place at the kitchen table. Joe was on her left, in his place, his back to the wall. They were both smoking. I handed Joe the bourbon, saying, "Sorry I'm so late," to Jean. "I was abducted by aliens. Did you get my e-mail? Are we on for Sunday night?"

"We are." Jean nodded, smiling broadly. "I have everything you asked for." Joe said, "Bless you, my child."

"It's for the house, mister. Promise you'll share."

Jean stood up to pour Joe a drink and I went to tell Mike hello. I tapped him on the shoulder and he turned, a pleasant, pie-faced man in his forties. The only signs of the hotshot lawyer were tailored slacks and a blue button-down shirt. Mike pulled one hand out of the soapy water and offered to shake. I called his bluff and shook it, which made him crack a smile exactly like his father's. Wiping my hand on my jeans I said quietly, "You were a big help the other night about Ray Junior. Sorry I haven't called you back to thank you."

"I thought of something else after we —"

"Let me dry, Michael." Jean intervened, passing me a clean plate and taking a dripping bowl from her son. "The spinach enchiladas are still on the dining table, Ann. They were a big hit."

Joe snorted, "Spinach?" He knew very well that the spinach enchiladas were the result of a struggle. Luz thought if it didn't involve meat, it wasn't food.

I leaned down to him. "I need to ask you something about Mark Bridges, Joe—"

"Let's don't spoil the party with that turd."

He was right—it could wait. I just hoped he wouldn't see his windshield wipers before I explained. I walked into the dining room and Audrey followed, whispering juicily, "I have so much news!"

The general noise level was high but, stepping around two little girls with princess dolls, I kept my voice down:

"I'm listening, Hildy."

Audrey stuck beside me as I served myself enchiladas. She said, "Boots was invited tonight but they called and canceled."

"Do we know why?" I got bumped by a running kid and fumbled my plate. "Who *is* that fiend?"

Audrey told me while I started to eat. All these people were Garcias and Garcia relatives because January 11 was Manny's birthday and Jean had continued to throw the traditional party. Guests also included friends, neighbors, Jean's colleagues at the high school, and Balch employees past and present. Audrey pointed out a retired science teacher and an overnight oil millionaire from Taft, two men who, she thought, would've liked to marry Jean if there were no Joe. Audrey's banker husband was also present. He looked like a male Audrey, rotund and sly.

The running kid bumped me again. He seemed to be doing laps. Audrey said, "Jean has someone staying in the playroom—the children are usually up there."

I pulled her over to stand against the wall. "Why did Mahin cancel tonight?"

"There's big trouble brewing, apparently, in the Balch ranks." Audrey leaned in, getting confidential. "Ron Bray was also supposed to be here but he canceled. They met with Joe today and, apparently, the fur flew."

"What's the trouble about?" As if I couldn't guess.

"Well, *apparently*—"

I stopped her. "Audrey, that's three *apparently*s. When you say *apparently,* are you reporting true fact or just digging on suspected drama?"

"This is as true as true can be. I heard some of it from Joe himself and the rest from my husband."

"Okay, then."

I nodded and kept eating. Audrey went on, "Apparently there are several bones of contention. You know Joe fought his own men over the Minerva play."

"I do know. I also heard Mahin brought the board in against Joe. Do we know whose side Alice was on?"

"Alice?" Audrey arched one eyebrow. "Say more. I am intri-i-i-gued."

"There is no more—just a thought. Those guys fought Joe because wildcatting for deep gas is risky and expensive, right?"

Audrey shook her head. "It's worse than that. Wildcatting at all is considered unnecessary, a wasteful extravagance—"

Cathy walked into the dining room to clear the remains of the buffet. Reaching, I snared a last enchilada as she held out the dish for me. Audrey knew Cathy's reputation as a bigmouth and waited until she'd left to continue.

"Everyone out here is making money with the price of oil rising every day. Even if you do nothing, you're still making more money and so there's no reason to take risks. You have to understand the Westside mentality, Ann. These independent producers are a hardscrabble bunch. They mistrust booms—they still remember the eighties when heavy crude fell to six dollars and it didn't pay the electricity to run their pumps. A lot of people went broke."

"I remember."

The enchiladas were tasty. Luz had had her revenge with salt and pork fat to drown the flavor of spinach.

"Mind you, and as no doubt you know, Joe hasn't put all his eggs in the Minerva basket either. He's being conservative, doing what everyone is doing—drilling in-fill, opening up abandoned wells, working over his producing wells. He's also saving for hard times, I'm sure. Oil men out here save their money."

Swallowing, I nodded. "Have you ever seen a German luxury sedan on the streets of Wilson? Alice's Jaguars are the closest thing."

Cathy came in again to clear more dishes. Her antennae were twitching and I could tell she was dying to know what Audrey and I were talking about.

When she went back into the kitchen, I said, "That's one bone of contention. What are the others?"

Audrey's focus had shifted to her husband in the living room. He'd gotten up from his chair and was shaking hands with Cathy's husband.

Audrey checked her watch. "Shoot, Sam wants to go home. I wish you'd come earlier."

I said, "Other bones of contention – quickly."

"The sale of Balch Oil is one. Emmet's power is one. Joe's retirement is one, apparently. Who'll run the companies when Joe decides . . . shoot!"

Her husband had started across the living room towards us.

I said, "Emmet's *power?*"

"I'll write you the details." Audrey waved at her husband. "I'm coming, Sam! Say our goodbyes and thank Jean, will you?"

The husband veered into the kitchen. Audrey pinched my arm and whispered:

"None of them appreciates how important Minerva is to Joe. *I* think it's his last hurrah and he knows it. It's Lucy Boyd all over again – wildcatting brings back his youth. It means he isn't just sitting on his duff counting his money until his heart gives out. I hope that doesn't sound cold because I don't mean it that way. I love Joe dearly."

Pinching my arm again, Audrey took off. I called, "E-mail me!" at her retreating back.

I walked into the kitchen to leave my plate and look for Cathy. The women were all gone and the kitchen was filled with men. Some stood; some had brought chairs in from the living room and ringed Joe at the table. They were smoking cigars, drinking the bourbon I'd brought, and talking oil. Hot coffee was on but it was being ignored. Snagging a cookie, I squeezed over to Mike. He was leaning against the fridge sipping bourbon and listening to the discussion about how long it would be before oil prices collapsed.

I said low, "Can you finish your sentence now?"

"These guys, doom and gloom – they never enjoy their good fortune." Mike made a circle with his drink glass, shaking his head. "Except Joe – look at him. He's in heaven with that wildcat of his. I admire his guts."

I looked at Joe. He wore his standard deadpan as he listened to some guy's opinion of New York traders and snot-nosed stock analysts.

I pressed, "What was the something else you thought of?"

Mike took my arm attorney-fashion and turned our backs to the kitchen table. "It doesn't change anything for your purposes, it is just an illustration of Junior's character. I've received letters from him over the years asking for loans – Mom has too, as has Tía Luz. It was always the same sad song and dance – the world's done Junior wrong – and we've had to assume he blew the money Joe paid him for his interest in the companies –"

"Daddy!"

"That sounds like mine." Mike smiled and turned as a pink projectile latched on to his pants leg, demanding a ride. "I was through anyhow."

The daughter squealed as she clung to his leg and he shuffled her into the living room. I followed them, glancing around for Cathy. Jean sat on the couch, squished in a row of Garcias with a grandkid on her lap. I waved to catch her eye and called, "Have you seen Cathy?" Luz pointed at the front porch, signing that Cathy had stepped out for fresh air. I'd be glad for some fresh air myself. The house had gotten exponentially hotter and stuffier since I arrived. Walking outside, I found Cathy leaning on the porch rail, wrapped in her saggy cardigan and smoking a cigarette. The night was cold but the cold felt good.

"What happened to Joe's windshield wipers?" Cathy bent her arms up parallel. "They look like goalposts."

I perched on the railing upwind of her with my back to the street.

"I spoke to Mike, Cathy. He killed your theory stone dead. He says that when Ray Junior turned twenty-one he sold his stock back to Joe and renounced his seat on the board of directors and any future claim to the companies."

Cathy shrugged. "I know he did. The whole town knows that."

"But" – I almost laughed, she said it so blithely – "Cathy! Then your theory was crap! How could Ray Junior's death be related to Kenny Mills's death if Junior had no more stake in the Balch oil empire and therefore nothing for anybody to steal from him?!"

Cathy pointed her cigarette. "Never mind Junior. Look."

Sighing, I twisted around.

A Wilson police car with flashing cherry lights was pulling up in front of Jean's. It double-parked, blocking the street, and a young cop got out the driver's side to open the back doors. As we watched, Richie climbed out one side and Carrot Bobby climbed out the other. They were both in handcuffs and looking disheveled. That made me smile. The cop opened the front passenger door. A pair of legs swung out, and a pair of cuffed hands grabbed the roof of the car for leverage. A guy appeared and my smile turned to an O –

Doug!

I slid off the railing and turned for a full-on view.

Doug! Doug! Doug!

The cop herded his prisoners between cars towards Jean's front walk. Richie and Bobby hung back to let Doug go first. His nose was dripping blood and his zippered turtleneck was torn at a seam. Everybody's face was blank but I knew Doug so I could tell he was pleased. He also looked so much more mature than Richie and Bobby – harder, thinner, a grownup among the big, corn-fed farm boys.

Grabbing Cathy, I whispered, "Run inside and warn them!"

Cathy was agog. She stubbed out her cigarette and hurried into the house shouting, "Police! Police!" for the whole neighborhood to hear. Party-buzz died down instantly, except for the kids, who had to be shushed.

I held the screen door wide and watched the group file up the stairs.

Doug passed not looking at me, and Richie and Bobby passed staring straight ahead. Richie was sallow from his marathon twist-off, and I smelled beer but the guys seemed sober. They were also humming with suppressed excitement – I could feel it as they went by. Bobby's hair was stiff with dried sweat, and a monster gouge on his chin was bleeding. Richie had an eye starting to puff and red marks on his exposed skin. Everybody was jacketless; shirts were ripped and missing buttons. Richie was limping because he was short one boot.

The cop took the screen door and I ducked inside. Joe had stuck his head out of the kitchen and men crowded him from behind. Putting the grandkid off her knee, Jean stood up. The whole room was riveted.

"Evening, Mrs. Garcia." The cop touched his cap. "You know these individuals?"

"I do, Tyler. They're staying with me."

Cathy piped up, pointing at Bobby, "He's billeted with us."

The cop got his keys and uncuffed the guys, who automatically rubbed their wrists. They wouldn't look at one another or at anybody else.

The cop said, "We've had more calls out to the Dogleg since Mr. Balch spudded that well. The Okie boys love to brawl."

I saw Richie open his mouth to object to *Okie*. Doug stepped on his foot and Richie shut his mouth.

Joe said, "Watch it, Tyler, my lad. I'm right here."

The cop touched his cap again. He hadn't noticed Joe but he wasn't apologetic.

"With all due respect, Mr. Balch, Gerry's going to want to speak to you this time. They did some damage."

Clasping her hands, Jean said, "Well, thank you for bringing them home in one piece. I'm sure it won't happen again."

Bobby rolled his eyes at that but the cop didn't see. He said, "The only reason they aren't in jail is this man here." He indicated Doug, who was wiping his nose with a napkin someone had given him.

"This man understands that when the police arrive, the fight is

185

over." The cop turned to leave. Jean said, "Would you like to stay for coffee, Tyler?"

"Thank you, Mrs. Garcia. We're not through mopping up yet."

He walked out jingling the handcuffs. I thought the Oklahomans would spontaneously combust but Doug gave a sharp headshake and went to make sure the front door was shut. Putting his finger to his lips, he stepped over to the picture window and looked out. The room was silent – everybody was watching him. The reflection of the cherry lights had been swirling and bouncing off the living-room walls. The lights moved and went away.

Doug said, "He's gone," and Richie and Bobby ex-*ploded*.

They burst out in raucous whoops, pounding each other on the back and talking all at once. The room erupted with them. People started talking and laughing and the kids squealed and leaped around. I kept my eyes on Doug. He walked back to Bobby and Richie and shook their hands.

He said, "It was a pleasure working with you. That was an education from true masters."

Bobby thanked him with a solemn face. Richie clasped Doug's hand in both of his, and I saw that Richie's knuckles were raw. He said, "A privilege and an honor, sir. I hope we can do it again."

Doug nodded. "Thanks, man."

Then the Oklahomans were mobbed by Joe and other guests wanting a blow-by-blow. Doug slipped out of the living room as Jean clapped like a schoolteacher.

"Please, everyone! Everyone! Let the boys get cleaned up! They can tell us all about it afterward!"

I walked into the kitchen, looking for Doug. Jean bustled in behind me and opened a cupboard. She pulled out a first-aid kit and went to the fridge for cold beer and an ice pack.

Handing the things to me, she said, "He's in the apartment over the garage. Joe wanted him at the house but Doug thought it would be better to stay here until he saw what was what."

"Is he LAPD or not?"

"Talk to him."

Jean shunted me towards the back door, pulling it open herself because my hands were full. I trotted down the back stairs, around to the side yard where Jean had a detached garage. As I started up the stairs I heard Doug laughing his head off.

On the landing I nudged the door open with my knee and went in.

It wasn't an apartment. It was more of a studio – one big room with a bathroom in the corner. Doug's overnight bag sat on the bottom bunk of a kid's bunk bed and the whole place had been converted to Kid. It had cartoon-print curtains and painted kid-sized furniture. Letters of the alphabet were taped to the walls, and the shelves were crammed with toys and all sorts of board games, books, stuff for art, and sports stuff.

Doug stood at the bathroom sink in his bare feet, naked from the waist up and bent over laughing. He'd splashed water on himself and he was dripping water on the floor. The laughter made him gasp in pain. He had marks and scrapes everywhere – even a half-moon that looked like teeth marks below the old bullet wound on his side.

"Why didn't you tell me you were in Wilson?"

Doug slapped the sink. "Holy shit, that was *fun!* Ow! Ouch! Come here and kiss me!"

I set the first-aid kit, ice pack, and beer on a kid's table and went in to kiss him. I said, "You're soaking wet."

"Careful of the ribs. I think I was kicked."

I'd started to put my arms around his waist. Pulling them back, I reached up to touch his neck. He held me close and murmured against my mouth, "I haven't been in a righteous bar fight since I worked patrol at Wilshire."

"What started the fight?"

"I believe someone called someone else a dumb Okie."

"That'll do it." I stroked the teeth marks on his side. "You've been bitten and for once it wasn't by me."

Leaning back and lifting his arm, Doug looked down and burst out laughing again.

"Ou-ouch! Shit, that hurts!" He lowered his arm to press his ribs and wince.

I kissed him one last time and let go. "Jean sent you first aid." I showed him what I'd brought. Holding his side, he grabbed the beer and the kit and I went and sat in a kid's rocking chair, drying my face with my sleeve.

Doug said, "The judge declared a mistrial this afternoon. We caught that juror we had under surveillance sleeping with one of the defense team. I had vacation time coming—"

Suddenly I couldn't keep my eyes open.

Relief hit like a tidal wave, and my head was swimming suddenly and my hands and feet were going numb. Lying back, I felt like I was being sucked down and down into that wonderful warm place where sleep happens. I'd been running on nerves and caffeine for too long . . .

But I tried to rouse myself.

. . . I had to tell Doug the latest news about Mark Bridges. Bridges hated Joe and seemed to hate me too, because of my grandfather—

Doug said, "Gold cigarette case?"

His voice sounded like it was bubbling up from deep underwater. No, I thought, not a cigarette case. Bridges hated my grandfather—

"Pumping, pumping, pumping? What are you talking about, Ann? What's pumping?"

Not pumping, Doug. *Hate*—

I felt myself being lifted from the rocking chair and stretched out on something soft. My boots were removed, my jeans loosened. Doug's voice came from the way far distance:

"You're exhausted, baby—you go to sleep. The big, strong policemen will do some work for a change."

Rolling over, I pulled the blanket up and told him how glad I was to see him—how relieved and happy he'd come . . .

. . . so happy he came . . .

22

I T'S AMAZING WHAT I don't know almost three weeks after Mills's death. Amazing and pathetic."

I spread my arms to show the amount of paper lying around – and I'd only just gotten started.

I'd slept straight through until Sunday evening and had woken up incredibly lucid. When Doug walked into Jean's playroom, I was sitting on the floor surrounded by large sheets of kids' drawing paper, mapping out the conspiracies. I had a sheet in my hand with KENNY MILLS MURDER printed in red crayon at the top.

Doug dropped his keys and, peeling off his coat, sat down cross-legged on the floor beside me.

Looking over the sheets of paper, he shifted some that overlapped so he could see and read them all. He picked out a sheet labeled PEOPLE TO TALK TO / KM. It was color-coded in red crayon to match my Kenny Mills speculations. I'd listed everyone on the lease at the time Mills died and a bunch of people who were elsewhere, including the unknown X – someone among the anonymous multitudes who could've snuck up to the rig floor in the dense fog.

"I'm liking Trey right about now, though, with that snazzy new truck." I pointed to a sheet of paper I'd laid longways and drawn a double arrow on. Along the bottom I'd printed in purple:

Doug barely glanced at where I was pointing. He said, "You're reasoning ahead of the facts."

"A tendency of mine."

"That's run you into a ditch more than once." I bumped his shoulder as he tapped his finger down my list. "All these people are suspects – *all* of them, until they're definitely eliminated. That's what we've been working on while you were asleep."

"Who's 'we'?"

"Kern sheriffs and I and Wilson PD. You found the guns missing on Tuesday – but Joe and Emmet didn't want the disruption and it took until Friday to convince them we needed to pull the cops back in on this. As of yesterday, sheriffs reclassified Mills from accident to criminal homicide."

I had a separate piece of paper marked JOE'S ARSENAL – ??? It only had a heading, nothing else, and I'd used a black crayon to represent guns.

"Did the homicide guys admit they weren't completely satisfied with the autopsy report on Mills?"

Doug nodded.

"Did you tell them I got attacked?"

Nodding, Doug laid the PEOPLE TO TALK TO / KM paper down between us so we could study the list together.

I'd printed in red:

On Minerva Lease Christmas Eve

1. Tommy – guard at barrier gate
2. Bud – mud logger/well-site geologist with gambling debt
3. Three Schlumberger loggers (one on floor found Mills's body)
4. Trey – floor hand – origin Wyoming – bio unknown

Down the right side of the paper, inside a wavy red line I'd doubled in pink crayon, was my Circle of Trust:

1. Me
2. Emmet

3. Richie "Teach" — driller
4. Kyle "Bale" — derrickman
5. Bobby "Carrot" — motorman

Note: The theory that Bobby killed Mills by mistake, incited by Richie's adulterous liaison with Bobby's sister, Arielle, has been disproved.

Pointing at *Circle of Trust,* Doug said, "This isn't the way to run a murder investigation."

"I'm not wrong about the Oklahomans."

"It's too late now." Doug nudged my shoulder with his.

I leaned to pull out another page of my Kenny Mills reasoning: PEOPLE TO TALK TO / KM / 2. Handing it to Doug, I said, "I'm *so* glad you're here!"

Doug was concentrating. He just patted my leg and laid the new page on top of the previous one. I'd written in red:

Off Minerva Lease Christmas Eve

1. Suzette Mahin — crystal-meth addict — Mills's girlfriend — non compos mentis — daughter of Hilary "Boots" Mahin (see SCOUTING MINERVA NO.1 and BALCH COMPANY POLITICS)
2. Local hands on Emmet's three other crews
3. Local people working for subcontractors and suppliers used at the lease — Halliburton (cement + logs), equipment rentals, bit companies, casing crews, mechanics, truckers, etc., etc.
4. X — assorted unknown townies or crankheads — anybody anywhere who knows a lease and drilling rigs well enough to get around in a tule fog

Note: Emmet won't like his crews being questioned.

I said, "This is all so stupidly amorphous without a motive." I tapped my crayon on the blank sheet where I'd written KENNY MILLS MURDER — MOTIVE???

I amended, "Or too many possible motives."

Doug didn't react. He was frowning at number three. I said, "I

191

didn't think of these guys until tonight. You probably did –"

Doug made a small gesture that meant shut up. Shutting up, I watched him review the off-lease list again.

The floor of the playroom was linoleum. Doug slid back to get his legs under him and sit up on his knees. He started arranging my papers into rows. First row, closest to us, was the Kenny Mills stuff. In the second row he put SCOUTING MINERVA NO.1 and BALCH COMPANY POLITICS and my double-arrowed MURDER LINKED TO SCOUTING MINERVA – ???

In the top row he put my two blank pages headed JOE'S ARSE-NAL – ??? and ALICE BALCH – ???

He had a pyramid when he was done. Looking around, he reached for some sheets of blank paper.

"Pass me the crayons, would you?"

I pushed the box over to him. Doug checked the pyramid to see which colors I'd already used. Choosing a magenta crayon from the box, he rested his elbows on the floor and block-printed:

RAY PARKERWORTH JUNIOR – ???

I said, "Ray Junior? I thought we'd shelved him. I told you what Mike Garcia said."

Doug shook his head. "I've suggested the sheriffs take an official look into the circumstances of his death. What do we know about it? Only what Mrs. Balch has said and what a funeral home told your friend Audrey."

Grabbing another sheet of paper, Doug picked a lime-green crayon out of the box and printed:

JIM AND EVELYN WHITEHEAD – ???

Doug's thought was that the attack on me might not be related to Kenny Mills: it might be related to ancient Whitehead history. But I couldn't hang around hashing it out with him because tonight was the night for Kyle's payback. I needed to move Doug's Jeep out of sight and make final arrangements with my henchwoman, Jean.

I found her in her kitchen wearing a puffy down jacket and grading school papers at the table. As part of the gag we'd turned off the heat in the house.

I said, "You're being a great sport."

Jean stopped reading to look up. Her nose was red from the cold.

"Here you are, empty house, all peaceful and quiet, and I'm freezing you out and planning to destroy your bathroom."

Smiling in her kind way, she shrugged. "The house has been quiet for too long—I didn't realize it until the boys came. I'm enjoying the company immensely . . . See what I found? I think they'll make a better snake."

Jean pointed at the kitchen counter where we'd laid out our props. There were green garbage bags with leg holes cut in them, a couple of bandannas, rubber gloves, a shovel and a spade, and a pair of those dark, giant wraparound glasses that block out sunlight. I'd brought my own sunglasses with me. Jean was indicating some brownish-gray wool leotards.

"They're a better color than the others—more lifelike."

She'd arranged the leotards in a coil and I stood back, thinking they'd look fantastic through the frosted glass of the shower door. We'd already hung my plastic twig dinosaur from the ceiling of the shower stall. I'd pierced a hole in the dorsal fin and Jean supplied elastic to thread through it, to make the dinosaur bounce and swing. The tricky part had been getting the front claws latched just right over the top of the stall door so that pulling the door open released the dinosaur.

"Should I call Gerry?" Jean was reaching behind her for the telephone.

"Let me get set up first." I grabbed the leotards, then tapped the coffeepot. "What's your vote? Venom or no venom?"

I thought it would be more entertaining if my mythical rattlesnake had sprayed deadly venom at Jean. The venom was just going to be a splash of coffee on the inside of the shower door.

Jean hesitated. "Mightn't it be a little . . . too much, perhaps?"

"You're right—we don't want to overplay it."

I left, first to check the main floor and upper floor, making sure Jean had all the lights on. Two terrorized women would turn all the lights on. Then I took the half flight of stairs to the lower level,

193

where Kyle and Lynn slept. Their bathroom was down a hallway. I went into the bathroom and, squatting, coiled the leotards around the drain on the floor of the shower. I shut the door to see the effect through glass: fantastic. Standing on tiptoe, I grabbed my dinosaur, tested the twig in his jaws, and latched his front feet over the metal strip on the shower door. I opened the door experimentally one more time. The dinosaur's feet released and he bounced and swung inside the stall above my head. That would be Kyle's eye level, or close enough.

As I shut the shower door and relatched the dinosaur's feet, I called, "You can try the Dogleg now!"

Flipping off the bathroom light, I ran up the hall, hit that switch off, took the stairs in two jumps, and ran into the kitchen to throw on my deadly-reptile combat gear. Jean had found Gerry. She was explaining what we had planned, and judging by her side of the conversation, I got that Gerry was enchanted. Meanwhile I was stepping into a large garbage bag like it was pants and tucking the open end into the waist of my jeans. I knotted a bandanna around my neck, stuck my sunglasses on my head, put on the rubber gloves, and picked up the spade.

Jean's closing words to Gerry were "Kyle, or Kyle and Lynn . . . We don't want a mob —"

I interjected, "Man, I'd love an audience, though!"

Jean smiled at me. "Whatever you think best, Gerry, but Ann needs Kyle . . . We'll tell you how it goes, yes, for sure . . . Bye-bye."

She hung up and stood up. Her job was to watch the alley from the kitchen door. Mine was to watch the street in front. Doug's job was to lie low even if he heard yelling. Why would we send for the Oklahomans if there was already a man close by to save us?

I said, "Remember — frozen with terror."

Jean nodded. "Frozen with terror."

I ran into the living room and stationed myself beside the picture window. If Kyle rushed, which he would, he'd be here in nine minutes. Seeing my reflection in the glass, I wanted to hoot: I looked ridiculous. Hooting wasn't good, though, because I was supposed to be scared out of my mind. So I used the wait time imagining scary things to work myself into the appropriate fright.

Eleven minutes later Richie's truck came barreling around the corner. I called, "Here he is, Jean!"

Jean hurried in from the kitchen carrying a broom like a weapon. Removing her slippers, she stepped up onto her frilly couch and stood there on the cushions, rigid. We hadn't rehearsed the broom. She was an ace.

Gerry had done his job too. I watched the truck screech into the driveway and brake hard. Kyle leaped out the driver's side, Lynn leaped out the passenger side, and they both raced for the front stairs. I ran to the door as Kyle snatched the screen open and he and Lynn piled inside. Their faces – Kyle's hayseed goof and Lynn's shaggy moon – were identically serious and determined. It was all I could do not to laugh.

I had the spade in one hand. Grabbing Kyle's jacket with my other, I pulled him towards the kitchen and started talking fast in a strained voice:

"Jean found it in you guys' shower."

I pointed to where Jean stood, frozen with terror, on her own couch. She was using the broom for balance.

"I read about it online. It's called a southern Pacific spittler, the only rattlesnake indigenous to this part of California. It's coiled but I'm guessing it's about four feet long, three to four feet –"

I shuddered and glanced at Jean for confirmation. Frozen with terror, she could just barely whisper, "Awful!"

"Normally they hibernate during the winter. It was probably under the house and got in somehow, looking for warmth or water. The guy at the poison center said that happens. I called."

Kyle and Lynn had almost stopped breathing. We were in the kitchen now. I passed a garbage bag to Kyle, making sure my hand shook. As derrickman he was senior to Lynn so naturally he would kill the snake.

"Put this on – like me."

Kyle took the garbage bag and stepped his legs into the holes I'd cut in the bottom.

"A spittler spits its venom. It doesn't strike out and bite like a rattlesnake – it sits up and spits. You don't want the venom to touch your skin, or your clothes. It'll soak through fabric."

Kyle tucked the garbage bag into his jeans. Propping my spade against the cupboard, I stood on tiptoe to tie the bandanna around his neck. He put the dorky sunglasses on his head, pulled on the rubber gloves, and I handed him the shovel. I grabbed my spade again and headed back out of the kitchen.

"It aims one of two places – either directly ahead, that's why the garbage bag, or at the shiniest part of its victim, the eyes."

The eye detail came from the spitting cobras of India. As I said it, I put on my sunglasses. I stopped at the top stair leading to the basement, which was ominously dark. Jean still stood rigid on the couch. My hands were shaking worse and I felt my throat drying up –

"I'll go, Pup." Lynn reached for the spade.

I'd been waiting for him to offer. "No, Lynn. If something happens, we'll have to get to Bakersfield and Richie wouldn't want me driving his pickup. That's the closest place for the antivenom –"

Kyle blurted, "Two hours from here?!"

"Shhh!" I put a finger to my lips. "Did you hear it rattle?"

Lynn froze and Kyle leaned, listening, down the stairs. I smiled what I hoped was a ghastly but brave smile. "We're not going to die, you guys. The poison is slow acting and I turned off the lights and heat so the snake will be sluggish."

My voice started to tremble: nerves.

"Here's my idea. It's on the floor of the shower. Lynn stays at the bottom of the stairs, I run ahead into the bathroom. When I say *now,* Lynn and I hit the lights, I open the stall door, and Kyle has two hands free to kill it with the shovel. Ideal would be a shotgun but obviously we can't."

Jean made a strangled *eep* sound. Not rehearsed.

"You have to *kill* the snake, Kyle. If you just injure it, it'll go nuts and we're really in trouble." I pulled the bandanna up over my nose. "Okay?"

Kyle and Lynn had nothing to add. They were looking like the last two white men at the Alamo. Kyle put on the dark glasses, snugged the bandanna over his nose and chin, and adjusted his grip on the shovel. At his nod I took off –

– down the stairs, down the hall – distance memorized, running on tiptoe, laughter rising, garbage bag rustling – into the bathroom. I found the light switch with my spade hand and the shower door with my left, and when Kyle crossed the threshold I shouted, *"Now!"*

The bathroom lit up. I yanked on the shower door and let out an earsplitting shriek.

Kyle yelled and swung his shovel down at the coiled leotards as the dinosaur bapped him in the forehead. Kyle thought the snake had hit him with spit. Yelling, ducking, twisting, he swung at the dinosaur, smacking it into the wall. I shrieked as Kyle bent to kill the deadly reptile. The shovel clanged on the tile floor, clanged and clanged, and I couldn't control it anymore. My shriek turned to a howl and I ripped off the bandanna, howling with breathless, maniac laughter.

The shovel stopped in midswing. Kyle looked down at the limp leotards, up at the bouncing dinosaur –

I pointed. *"Oklahoma stick lizaaard!"* and, dropping the spade, took off at a sprint. Kyle yelled:

"Grab her, Lynnie!"

As I launched for the middle stair, Lynn stuck his foot out and tripped me. I went sprawling into the living room and Lynn had me pinned on the carpet before I could roll away.

That's where Doug found us.

I was screaming with laughter, wiggling to get loose from Lynn, who was sitting on my legs, tickling me with the twig and the dinosaur – and from Kyle, who was rubbing the leotards in my face.

Doug said, "I'm sorry to have to break this up."

He stood in the kitchen doorway. We all heard the serious note in his voice and stopped where we were.

"Emmet called. There's been shooting at the lease."

Lynn said, "It's part of the joke." He poked me with the twig.

"Is anyone hurt?"

That was Jean from the region of the couch. I couldn't see her from the floor – Kyle was blocking my view.

Doug said, "No, no one's hurt, but I want Ann to come with me and I need you men to stay with Jean."

Realizing it wasn't a joke, Lynn jumped off my legs and stood up. Kyle jumped up too, offering a hand to help me. I bent my knees and put both arms out. Kyle took one and Lynn took the other.

As they lifted me to my feet, Lynn said, "That was good, Pup. You got us good."

Kyle grinned. "Real good."

23

WE WERE PASSING Joe's house headed out to the rig when Doug braked, hit his turn signal, and cranked a sudden left into the circle drive. He'd noticed what I hadn't because I was reliving my triumph and paying no attention: all the new floodlights were off, and the yard and house were pitch-black.

Grabbing the dashboard, I sat forward as we pulled around the circle.

The headlights of the Jeep swept the front of the house. Nobody was home. The only vehicle in the drive was the Balch Drilling pickup, parked where it was always parked. But the front door was standing wide open. A cheesy painting of wooden derricks and mounted cowboys that normally hung in the front hall had been sliced up and tossed into the driveway. And windows at both ends of the house had been smashed, including one in my room.

Doug said, "There's no alarm."

Pulling out my phone, I switched it on. "I have reception. Who do you want me to call?"

"We'll leave it and come back." Doug punched the gas and accelerated around the drive, turning left at the highway.

"I expected something to pop – sheriffs started a new round of interviews this morning and I've been making myself visible."

He booted it to the lease. Tommy waved us through the gate like he and Doug were already old friends. The extra Baker Hughes trucks were gone from the yard and, looking up at the rig, I saw the kelly turning in the derrick: we were finally kicked off and drilling ahead. That was good news at any rate. Doug parked and we jumped out. I ran up Emmet's stairs first, knocking on his window to warn him before I pulled open the trailer door, and Doug followed me inside. Warm, smoky air washed over us, scented by whatever Emmet had fixed for dinner.

Emmet said, "Evenin, y'all."

He was looking disgruntled. He had a three-day beard and dirt stains on the knees of his overalls. The 12-gauge was leaning against the desk beside him. Joe stood in the kitchen smoking a cigarette. His new shotgun was propped against the fridge and his jeans were dirty too.

Doug said, "Joe — would you get Chief Clark out of bed for me, please? Someone's broken into your house and I need it watched until we're through here."

Joe deadpanned, "When it rains, it pours," as he stubbed out his cigarette, then moved for the phone on Emmet's desk. I stepped back to let him pass and he winked at me.

Clark ran Wilson PD. I was guessing Doug wanted an instant favor because the Balch house was in sheriffs' territory and, like the antivenom, the sheriffs were two hours away.

Joe waited through a bunch of rings then said, "Jack, it's Joe . . . Sun's up in Yokohama . . . I have Doug Lockwood with me. He'll explain the situation . . ."

Doug took the receiver Joe passed to him. "Chief Clark? I apologize for disturbing you —"

While Doug talked and listened, Joe sat down on the napping couch and I caught Emmet's eye. Pointing up the line of trailers, I whispered, "Where's Bud?"

Emmet mimed shuffling a deck of cards. I whispered, "When did you see him last?"

"This mornin. Spoke to him when we went to drillin here a while ago —"

200

Doug interrupted, putting the phone down. "All right, now—what happened exactly?"

The way they told it, it was a little after eleven P.M. They'd been going over costs when they heard ping-ping-ping-ping in the west wall of Emmet's trailer. They dived for the floor, recognizing the ping, s holes sprout over their heads as the bullets passed through that wall and out the east wall. They gave it a few minutes, waiting for more shots, then got up and ran outside. They couldn't see anything in the open field on the west side of the lease. But they found bullet holes high on Joe's trailer, and discovered that one bullet hit a stud in the east wall of Emmet's because there were only three exit holes. Emmet had dug out the slug and he showed it to us. Joe pointed to the small crater in the wall over the desk. Full metal jacket, he said.

Doug stopped them to ask if the changing hut or Bud's trailer had been hit. They'd checked—the answer was no.

They'd grabbed their shotguns and jumped in Emmet's pickup in the hopeless hope of finding the guy, or evidence of the guy, in a huge, dark, empty cotton field. They'd driven into the field in a straight line west of the trailers, looking for tire tracks, foot tracks, and/or spent shell casings. They didn't find anything but they'd tripped and fallen in the loose dirt and finally gave up. Coming back to the lease, that's when Emmet called Doug.

Joe had another cigarette lit. He puffed on it and coughed. Doug said, "Did either of you notice if the Balches' house was dark?"

Emmet said, "I seen it was dark drivin off location—didn't think nothin of it."

Nodding, Doug checked his watch. "Someone's spreading rumors, trying to cause trouble between your Oklahoma and California hands. That's what started the Dogleg fight."

He pointed in the direction of the top doghouse. "You flying the Oklahoma flag is a sore issue. The local guys also think the Oklahoma guys are getting better pay. They heard about the per diem—"

Joe said, "Nothing wrong with that. Emmet's boys are living away from home—a per diem is standard."

201

Emmet put in, "There now, Joe, you know the per deem's out-blown. Ozark bribed them boys not to go out to eastern Oklahoma."

"It's a competitive marketplace—you pay top dollar for experienced hands in this kind of boom."

Emmet grumbled, "Payin top dollar for some worthless damn bums."

Doug said, "Still, someone's spreading trouble with your local hands. This shooting could be related—it's a possibility to consider along with the others. We'll have to report it to the sheriff."

Joe almost always smoked with the cigarette between two knuckles of his fist. He put his fist and his flat palm together in prayer position and looked up at the ceiling. "I just want to drill this well in peace, dear God."

He paused, then deadpanned, "Ten million cubic feet a day of dry gas would be welcome too."

"At least ten." Emmet micro-bowed his head. "Amen."

I was leaning against the trailer door keeping an eye on the yard. A white pickup rolled by and I said:

"Bud is here."

Emmet craned to see out his window. Doug said, "Let's take a look at your house, Joe."

Joe stood up to get his shotgun and Balch Oil jacket as Doug bent to talk to Emmet. Emmet listened, listened some more, and murmphed.

Joe took off ahead of us. On the short trip, Doug told me what he'd discussed with Emmet—and I joked about Doug's own Circle of Trust—before we braked to a stop at home. Lights had been turned on and two Wilson PD cars were sitting in the drive. One uniform cop stood guard at the front door watching Joe inspect the vandalized painting. Joe was nudging it with the toe of his cowboy boot.

Doug called, "Please don't touch anything!" as he went to talk to the guard. It was Tyler, the young cop who'd brought everyone home from the Dogleg in handcuffs. He recognized Doug.

"Dispatch said . . . *You're* the LAPD detective?"

I said, "Can I go inside?"

Doug repeated, "Don't touch anything."

I ran into the house. Except for the painting, the foyer and living room were undisturbed. I stuck my head in Joe's den: also undisturbed. There was more damage down the right hallway. Whoever it was had gone along knocking the vintage oil-field photographs off their hooks. I ran to my rooms. The bedroom was fine but my sitting room had been lightly trashed. Stuff had been swept off tables, and furniture bumped out of place. The worst was the smashed window. The guy had picked up a chair and thrown it at the window –

"Jesus Christ – son of a bitch!"

Joe was swearing across the hall. I ran over to see what the matter was.

His sitting room was helter-skelter – everything was everywhere. Books and papers on the floor, desk drawers ransacked. The computer monitors had been pushed over, the couch tipped on its back, and a basket of firewood dumped on the carpet. The portrait of Ray Parkerworth Senior had been knocked slantways. One sliding glass door had been shattered and the cold was blowing in. Joe stood by the door looking at the fireplace, then at the backyard. I saw the bare spot on the hearth and realized the guy must've taken the Lucy Boyd drill bit and thrown it through the glass.

"I'll check the rest of the house." I ran.

Doug was walking down the hall towards me. I said, "Joe's suite," pointed, and kept going.

The other end of the house looked fine: dining room untouched, kitchen and Luz's room untouched. Who knew where Luz was. The door to Alice's suite was ajar. I thumped it wider and walked inside.

Her rooms were totally her. She'd redone them in pale colors in her old-money taste, with antique furniture and needlepoint rugs and lots of other elegant, expensive objects I didn't know the names of or reasons for. I did know an escritoire, though, and the antique French writing desk had been disturbed. The envelopes in the pigeonholes weren't arranged in descending order of size, and one of the narrow drawers was open.

I ran over for a closer look. The drawer contained a checkbook and other neatly stacked banking items from Wilson Trust. There were also business letters lying on the desktop – a couple addressed to Joe and postmarked last month.

Doug came up behind me. "Anything?"

"The vandal was either an art critic or interior designer. Look, Alice's museum stuff untouched but that oil painting from the foyer cut to shreds."

"Be serious, baby." Doug glanced around the sitting room.

"The desk." I almost tapped the escritoire and caught myself. "Luz comes in to clean but she'd never leave disorder like this – Alice would have a cow. And Alice has been opening Joe's mail. Look, here's a letter from his lawyer from last month."

"How long has she been away?"

I counted backwards. "Five weeks or so. She went down to L.A. the middle of December, then to Hawaii for Christmas. Now she's back in L.A."

"With your grandmother."

"With my evil grandmother."

Joe appeared at the hallway door. He hovered, clearly not wanting to enter Alice's domain. I said, "I'll go check the gun room."

Doug said, turning, "We should notify Mrs. Balch."

"It's not bad in here." Joe flicked a glance at Doug and deadpanned, "Do we have to?"

I grabbed a glass of water and made myself comfortable in the living room watching Doug as he worked with the sheriffs' deputies and print team.

He'd told me the cops blew off ordinary vandalism: the sheriffs would've sent a deputy to take a report for insurance purposes and that would've been it. But this wasn't ordinary vandalism, not with everything else going on – the shooting at the lease, and the damage to Joe's rooms in particular with nothing of value stolen. Also, whoever'd done it had the code to the burglar alarm. They'd broken in through the utility room by the breezeway but were able to turn off the alarm. That's why the sheriffs sent out a print team and why the detectives working Kenny Mills were coming later.

"Ann, you okay?" Doug detoured through the living room, telling a print person he'd catch up with her.

I said, "I just realized something. I dig the detecting part of crime but not the police and legal part. I love bombing around finding stuff out but I don't like rules. Does that make sense?"

Doug smiled. "It does, sure."

I flapped a hand to mean the invaded house and assorted cops. "You're in your element."

"One of my elements." Squeezing my shoulder, he took off.

I got up for more water and found Joe at the kitchen island. He was looking completely wiped. He'd poured himself a bourbon and was eating spinach enchiladas with one hand and holding his cell phone to his ear with the other.

"Out of the frying pan into the sloughing shale. Hooray . . . Get some rest, old-timer . . . Good God, is it that late – early? . . . I'll try."

He pressed a button and put the phone down. I said, "I hope the McLure is a sloughing shale."

"You have big ears. Yes, the McLure's a shale."

"So you're found . . . we're found."

He nodded.

"Joe, why does Mark –"

A deputy stuck his head into the kitchen. "They need to speak to you in the garage, sir."

Setting his fork down, Joe wiped his mouth. He said, "That spinach'll kill you," and walked out.

Luz showed up at six A.M. and flipped her wig when she realized she might've been home during the break-in. Luckily Doug had experience with hysteria and upset, and a real sympathy for people, which I admired. He talked her off the ledge to the point where

she was almost purring as he escorted her to find a print techni-
cian. The homicide team arrived from Bakersfield soon after. Doug
set us up in Joe's den so I could tell them firsthand about the attack at the back gate. I wished I could've given them something
useful but the fading marks of chainlink didn't supply any more
facts about who'd slammed my neck into the fence or why. Beyond
that, I reviewed almost every last thing I'd seen, done, heard, and
thought since Kenny Mills was found dead. The detectives were
not thrilled with me.

When Alice stalked into the foyer around nine, Luz was fixing
breakfast for the Bakersfield crowd and Doug, Joe, and I were sitting in the living room drinking coffee.

Alice looked cool and cold. Every hair and necklace was in place
and she wore a nubby, multicolor Chanel jacket. Removing her
sunglasses, she frowned at the cowboy-derrick painting someone
had propped against the wall. The canvas was in ribbons, and the
frame was dusted with fingerprint powder.

"Is this why I was called here so urgently, Joseph?"

Joe didn't want to deal with her. He flicked a look at Doug,
prompting Doug to set his coffee mug down and stand up. "Mrs.
Balch—"

"Who are you?"

Alice had never met Doug. I'd never wanted to introduce them.

I butted in with a smile. "This is Doug Lockwood, Alice. He's a
good friend of mine and he's also with LAPD. I—"

"LAPD?" Alice gave Doug a glacial stare. "How is LAPD involved? Are you the person who sent the Beverly Hills police to my
home?"

Doug wasn't liking her or her attitude. I saw his expression click
over from softball diplomacy to the stone cop mask.

"Kern sheriffs made the call at my request. We were concerned
when your husband couldn't reach you—"

Alice interrupted Doug again. "You woke up—"

Joe snapped, "For God's sake, listen to the man, Alice! And do
what he says!"

I was trying to figure out what was wrong with her. Something was going on. She was cold and she was angry but I'd seen her at both those temperatures. This was something else. She stood in the foyer stiffly, in the same spot she'd stopped, almost like she was . . . afraid?

Doug said, "Come with me, Mrs. Balch." He indicated her end of the house. "The sheriffs need to know if anything is missing from your rooms and they'll need your fingerprints."

As if on cue, all the cops came filing out of the kitchen, relaxed and chatting among themselves. I won't say Alice froze when she saw them – her normal state was already close to frozen. She stepped back, put her hand on her necklaces, and frowned at the one detective picking his teeth, like he was too tacky to live. I watched Doug assess her reaction as he signaled for a deputy and the print team to come with him.

Doug said, "Mrs. Balch – please, if you would?"

Alice moved reluctantly. That group disappeared down the left hall while the rest of the cops thanked Joe for breakfast and walked out to their cars.

"I'm too damn old." Joe yawned and reached under his glasses to scrub his eyes. "I'm going to lay down in the den."

I said, "Can I ask about Mark Bridges before you do?"

"Ask me later. Not now."

He had difficulty pushing himself off the couch but waved me away as I started to jump up to help him. Walking slowly out of the living room, shoulders drooping, he rubbed the base of his spine, the place low down where it slanted at a permanent angle. In that moment Joe did look old – and unwell.

I'd been trying since Friday night to find out why Mark Bridges hated him and had to wonder why he kept putting me off. I also had to wonder again about Alice. She plugged into the conspiracy – or conspiracies – from too many possible angles. As I sat wondering, I heard her cold, shrill voice from the kitchen:

"You gave my alarm code to some Mexicans!"

Luz came back with a hot denial.

"There was five hundred dollars in my desk! Who stole that money – you?!"

Their voices spiked. Glass broke with a loud smash, and the noise escalated to a sustained scream.

Leaping up, I ran.

They were struggling in the space between the island and the kitchen sink. Alice had Luz by the apron, shouting accusations. Luz had dropped some dishes and was trying to pull loose, screaming insults at the top of her lungs. I jumped in between, trying to separate them, slipping on glass and getting elbowed in the process. Doug and the sheriffs' deputy raced in from the far door. The deputy grabbed Alice, who ordered him not to touch her. Doug ran around the island to get Luz. Luz stopped screaming and ducked behind Doug. Alice let go of Luz's apron as the deputy found leverage, I pushed her and he pulled and —

A strange woman appeared out of nowhere.

She was a luscious brunette with laughing hazel eyes that took in the scene. Broken dishes all over the floor. Doug, braced on the counters to protect Luz. Me, catching my breath at the sink. Alice, frozen still, restrained by the big deputy. Luz straightening her apron, hidden behind Doug.

Dimpling, the brunette said, "Have I come at a bad time?"

Alice glared at her, made a very un-Alice-like noise, and stamped her Chanel flat twice.

Luz squealed, *"¡Querida!"*

24

THE LUSCIOUS BRUNETTE was Celeste Parkerworth Mancuso — tramp, rotten mother, gold digger, and flake.

Our phone conversation had worried her, she said. She'd cut short her Greek cruise and hurried up to Wilson unannounced. Joe invited her to stay. Alice tried to object but Joe overruled her, asking me to give up the guest suite and move into the spare room next door. I was thrilled to do it, just glad he wasn't kicking me over to Jean's. Alice was coming unglued and this deal was busting wide open and I didn't want to miss a single minute.

Someone knocked on the hall door as I was pulling clothes out of my closet. I called that I was back in the back.

I hoped it was Doug because we needed to discuss our agenda for the day. But Alice walked into the bedroom. She'd fixed her hair and perfume and had regained her coolest cool.

She said, "Don't change rooms, Ann. I will not have you sleeping on a foldaway sofa and sharing a bathroom with Luz. How could I face your grandmother?"

In one split second I decided the truth might be as good a strategy as any to unglue Alice more. Anyway, this was something I'd wanted to say to her for years.

"Alice, I get the idea you're ashamed of Wilson and your Parkerworth roots." I dropped some shirts on the bed and looked at her.

"I bet Evelyn's never told you her parents ran a roadside diner and she was waitressing when she met my grandfather. Granpap's father was a well shooter, very working class, like the crews who do completions now. Granpap had his first paying job at sixteen, with Standard Oil for two dollars a day. You and Evelyn act like the Whiteheads are Rockefellers – but that's probably as close as we ever got, Granpap's Standard Oil paycheck."

Alice sat down in the easy chair, arranging her necklaces. Her face was tight and blank.

"Furthermore, John D. Rockefeller grew up poor. His father, if I remember the story, was a traveling medical fake and a bigamist. *Further* furthermore, Edward Doheny was a miner on the skids when he and his partner hand-dug the discovery well on the Los Angeles field in 1892. The oil business is full of stories like that – guys who came from nothing and made a few bucks, like Granpap and your father and Joe."

I went to the closet and, grabbing a suitcase, laid it on the bed and unzipped it. It was Alice's turn to talk.

After a silence she said, "Evelyn was born with class. She has exquisite taste in her genes."

Alice straightened her spine a smidge as she crossed her legs. I went to the dresser and started emptying drawers, laying loose armfuls of clothes in the suitcase.

"Ann . . ."

I stopped packing and looked at her.

"Do you know who that woman is?"

"Sure. She's your father's second wife and the mother of the late Ray Junior."

Alice fiddled with her necklaces, silent. I continued to look at her.

"*She* is the reason I . . ."

Trailing off, Alice glanced at the bedroom door. I reached with my foot and pushed it shut.

"I do not like discussing my private affairs and you'll promise me not to mention any of this to Evelyn. She has no idea about any of it."

"Promise." I crossed my heart.

"You're wrong. I'm not ashamed of Wilson or the Parkerworths. On the contrary, I love this town. I love the oil business and I'm proud of the contribution the Parkerworths have made to the Westside, economically and in other ways. I even love our desert—it has an austere beauty, I feel. It's one subject on which Evelyn and I disagree. She thinks this is the world before God invented green."

Alice smiled without humor or warmth. "That's your grandfather's line. Jim was a brilliantly witty man. He didn't intend it as criticism."

I sat down on the bed, nodding. I was bursting with questions but I waited.

"Celeste—" Alice had a tough time even saying the name. "Celeste poisoned Wilson for me. I keep rooms in this house for the sake of appearances but she blighted my life here. *She* is the reason I live in Los Angeles and alone. She stole the Parkerworth companies from me when she seduced my aging father. She stole my husband and the hope of a family—to this day I believe Ray Junior was Joe's son. After Senior died, Celeste found the baby inconvenient. She asked Joe to raise him on the condition that I leave this house. That was almost forty years ago."

Holy crap, I thought. Cathy's tales had prepared me but I hadn't expected anything quite so harsh. All I could say was "Holy crap."

"Ann, your language."

But I also wasn't ready to feel sorry for Alice: I needed proof before that happened. I just sat looking at her.

"Has anyone told you where the name Minerva comes from? Do you know its significance?"

I nodded. "It's Jean Garcia's middle name."

"You see? Jean Taylor and I were best friends growing up and she is Joe's latest mistress. My husband has named his most im-

211

portant well after his girlfriend and, believe me, the town is aware of it. Celeste turned Wilson against me. With this I have become an outright laughingstock. *I,* Alice Parkerworth."

She was showing no emotion as she started to pinch along the crease in the leg of her slacks.

I said, "What are you going to do?"

"Unfortunately, or perhaps ironically, I still love my husband and very much regret our separation." She stopped pinching. "Joe has always been susceptible to women. He was not faithful in the brief time we lived together – Celeste was only one of many. Now Joe is ill and I will not leave him unprotected with that woman. There's no telling what she might convince him to do."

"Despite the danger?"

Alice tightened between the eyebrows. A question.

"You know, *danger.* You asked if I was in danger when you heard I quit the rig, because of the roughneck who died and the new burglar alarm."

"That is precisely why you are coming to L.A. with me. I have to run down now and make the arrangements for a longer stay here. We can leave as soon as you've finished packing."

Alice smoothed the crease of her slacks and stood up. She wasn't getting my point – which I found interesting.

"If I'm in danger, Alice, then so are you. Look what just happened to the house."

"Oh no, he –" She broke off. I let the words hang for a breath then said, "He?"

Alice was to*hoh*tally cool. "Naturally I assume it was a he. Luz's Mexican friend, the man to whom she gave the alarm code."

A lame and also illogical catch but I pretended to buy it. I tossed a pair of rig socks into the suitcase. Alice said, "This works out well. You can keep your grandmother company while I'm up here."

"Alice?"

She'd started for the door. I said, "Did Evelyn or Granpap make any enemies when Granpap was working in Wilson back in the 1960s?"

"Enemies? Most certainly not. Hurry up with your packing."

She indicated a stack of clean Balch coveralls on the floor of the closet. "Leave the rig clothes here."

Smoothing her necklaces, she opened the bedroom door and was gone.

A little later, Luz told me Doug went to the lease with the cops.

She couldn't say what time they went – she was too discombobulated, still freaked from the screaming match with Alice and the mess to clean up. She asked if I'd take the cowboy-derrick painting out to the trash. The painting was awkward and heavy but I managed to drag it across to the bins by the garage. The guy who'd broken in, I was thinking, must be some kind of strong to pick up that drill bit and throw it through a glass door. I might've said two guys did it because I'd seen my crew carrying wooden bit boxes on and off the rig floor: it took two guys. But now I had Alice on record with a single *he*.

That was only one of the things I was dying to talk to Doug about.

Alice's Jaguar was gone from the circle drive. In a second conversation, I'd said *no* to L.A. enough times that she finally heard *no* and left in a state of frigid displeasure.

Mrs. Mancuso's Escalade was also gone. But there was a metallic blue pickup parked behind Joe's truck. Luz said it was mine. My pickup was getting the windshield wipers fixed and this was a loaner, dropped off by a couple of Jean's *guapos*. From the way Luz described the handsome boys, it sounded like Richie and Kyle. I asked where Mrs. Mancuso was. Luz said she and Joe had gone out to lunch. I made a note of that: Joe hadn't slept all night, and the last time I'd seen him, he was dead tired. I told Luz the guest suite was ready for Mrs. Mancuso and took off for the lease on foot. I didn't mind the back gate or eucalyptus trees on a sunny day.

I found Emmet in his trailer consulting a pile of paper and doing pencil calculations on a notepad. The bullet holes had been covered with duct tape. He'd shaved since the previous night and he was wearing his reading glasses. When I walked in he didn't look over but my Oklahoma stick lizard was sitting at the far end of his desk, next to his can of 7Up and the television playing rodeo.

Pointing at the lizard, I said, "Hey!"

Emmet glanced up, then went back to his figuring. "The boys's brung him here for safekeepin — named him McGraw."

"Why does McGraw need to be kept safe?" Unbuttoning my jacket, I perched one hip on the near end of his desk.

"'Cause Bale don't never know when he's beat. I told him joke's over, you two is quits, but I's keepin McGraw with me to remove temptation."

"You should've seen Kyle killing the deadly spittler. It was classic."

Emmet slit-eyed me sideways. I smiled and leaned in to see what he was doing. His notepad was covered with numbers and math.

I said, "I hope I'm not one of the worthless bums you're paying top dollar for."

"Cain't recall. You ain't been to work since —"

I preempted him. "I know, the Black Flood. But thanks to the layoff my neck's almost well — you'll see me on tour Sunday. Where's Doug, do you know? Have you talked to Bud about —"

"Hush a minute."

I hushed. Suddenly I could hear the rig engines and the squalling of the brake. The trailer smelled good, as usual; something was stewing on the stove. Emmet multiplied two numbers and drew a box around the total.

Flipping to a clean page, he said, "Pay attention, little sister, you'll learn somethin."

I stood up to look over his shoulder. With his pencil he drew a vertical line down the middle of the page. "Our first hole, only it ain't straight like this in life — it's more like a corkscrew in the ground."

He wrote *17,213 ft.* at the bottom of the line. I said, "Where you realized we were lost."

Non-nodding, Emmet drew hash marks up the vertical line, noted where plugs had been set, wrote more footage depths, then drew a swooping line to the right. The hole now looked like an up-side-down Y.

He tapped his pencil point on the branch of the Y. "Got kicked off here and we's on our redrill, off in this direction." He indicated the right-swooping line.

I quoted Joe: "'Out of the frying pan into the sloughing shale.'"

Emmet just murmphed.

"Drillin ain't nothin but volumes and pressure. We's drillin this well overbalanced—meanin I got more weight in my mud than the formations what're pushin back at me. Not much more, just so's I stay on top of pressure downhole and the bad fracturin and faultin you run across in these parts. Drillin for oil is what I call plain-Jane. Drillin for gas is a whole different deal. You drill a gas well extry-careful—deep gas extry-extry-careful, even when you's in a proven field which we ain't."

He waved his pencil out the window at the three mud pits on the far side of the rig. The high, long, open tanks sat end to end, full of drilling mud at different stages of being cleaned for reuse.

"Them mud pumps's like your heart and that there mud's like the blood in your body. If it don't circulate and do its job keepin the hole open and the formations off, you's in some trouble. These young engineers don't believe it, but I has me a theory how the same pressure you find in your shale is the same pressure you's goin to find in this gas zone you's fixin to drill below it. Follow me?"

I followed him, roughly. Somehow the presence of a pressured shale announced the presence of natural gas, and both could be controlled with the same mud weight.

"But my rule though is—and I tell these young toolpushers and young engineers and company men—my rule is, drill *every* well like it were a wildcat. Drill cautious—don't cut corners—you won't never get caught with your britches down that way. You do not want to be lookin down that hole and have that booger be lookin back at you. That is a starin contest you might very well lose."

Emmet set his pencil aside and, taking off his glasses, swiveled his chair. I stepped around to face him.

"Don't know where Doug was headed from here. Bud was on the road comin back from the casino, he says, when them shots was fired. You had a chance to see about Trey for me?"

"Not yet. That's why I'm chasing Doug—he and I need to discuss a plan of action. Do you think Trey murdered Kenny Mills?"

I thought the abruptness of the question might rattle or shake the granite mountain. It didn't.

"Somethin ain't right there, little sister, is all—ain't only that new pickup. He brings a tabby kitten to work last week. First tour I seen it I asks him not to in my polite way—sumbitch looks at me like *Who you think you are, old man?*"

"You should fire him."

"Cain't afford to." Emmet paused to cogitate. "He's a good hand, Trey, but I ain't never took to him."

On an impulse I put my arms around Emmet and squeezed. He leaned away and hunched his shoulders. "What you huggin my neck for?!"

Wachuhugginmahnekfer?!

I laughed and let go. Reaching over, I tore off the sheet of paper with the drawing of Minerva and walked out, sticking it in my pocket.

25

DOUG HAD LEFT a message on my voice mail telling me he was headed north to check on Bud's story with the casino. When I tried to reach him I got a recorded message saying the wireless subscriber was out of range.

So I made my own agenda.

I filled the loaner truck with gas, hit I-5 headed south, and tried Jean. She'd also left a message asking if I'd come to the lease the following morning to talk to her honor students. I didn't get her in person but said yes to the class talk and thanked her profusely for her help with the rattlesnake. If it weren't for her and her in-spired acting, Kyle and Lynn wouldn't have fallen for the gag as hard as they did. But the subjects I actually wanted to talk to Jean about I couldn't possibly bring up: The forty-year-old melodrama as described by Alice. Mrs. Mancuso's alleged theft of the Park-erworth companies. Joe's married-bachelor life. His relationship with Jean. Jean's relationship with Alice. Were two such different women ever *friends?* But all, all impossible to mention.

However . . .

I called Audrey and caught her at the *Gusher* office. She'd heard about the vandalism and was dying for the scoop but she was in the middle of something. She said she'd call back in two shakes of a lamb's tail. I asked if she'd learned to talk like that at Stanford.

217

Next try: Cathy Rintoul.

Cathy couldn't exactly be trusted, but her big mouth might point me in a helpful direction. My interest in the melodrama and romance wasn't prurient . . . okay, it was partly prurient. Mostly I wanted to find out if that history had anything to do with the main conspiracies: murder, spying, and/or sabotage.

When Cathy answered her cell phone, I said, "Cathy, it's—"

She hissed, *"Ann! What's this we hear about a burglar at Joe's? Were you there? What happened? I've been trying the house but nobody answers. Where's Luz? Was she hurt? I'm stuck in McKittrick and the whole town—"*

"Cathy!"

"What?"

"Why are you hissing?"

There was silence. I heard a door shut, then the wind and a squeaky pumpjack at her end. I checked my mirrors and up the freeway.

Cathy came back on in her more usual busybody voice. "My patient was asleep."

I said, "Someone broke in and did some damage. Nobody was home, nobody was hurt, money was stolen, the sheriffs are investigating. How could Jean and Alice ever have been friends and how long have Jean and Joe been in love?"

"Is it true Celeste is up?"

"No way. I answered your questions, now you have to answer mine."

There was another longish gap. I heard Cathy lighting a cigarette and the pumpjack again in the background. I could picture her on the sun-bleached swing in front of the old guy's doublewide trailer.

Sensing her reluctance, I said, "If you don't want to gossip about your sister, how about Joe? I'm still under oath. He was never faithful to Alice, I heard, and Celeste Parkerworth stole him from her, whether before or after Ray Senior died, I don't know. I also heard he's sleeping with Jean, which I've never—"

Cathy exhaled explosively. "Who on *earth* told you they were

218

sleeping together? That is a deep, dark *secret!* Who *told* you? *Celeste?*"

"Holy cow!" I started smiling. "But I'm glad for Joe. Do they really sleep together? Jean's so careful about her reputation and Manny's memory. They must go somewhere else, right?"

"There's never been anything wrong between them, Ann – get that straight. I don't know when Joe fell for Jeannie or when Jeannie fell for him. I only know Joe didn't declare himself until well after Manny's death, *well* after. Even then, Jeannie was reluctant because Joe *is* married on paper."

"He shouldn't have gone so public, naming his play Minerva." I checked my mirrors again and out the side windows. It was a bright day but the valley was filled with a yellow-brown haze and I couldn't see the hills to the west and south or the Sierras to the east.

I heard the puff of a cigarette – several puffs – then:

"It's a real tribute to Jeannie because everybody tried to stop him from drilling wildcat. She's the only one who believed in him and the deep gas."

"That's not true – Emmet believes. Bud believes. Gerry told me Bud did the geology on the play based on some theory of some Alberta foothills geologists."

Cathy exhaled and hm-hm'd "Yes" at the same time.

"Emmet wasn't here, though. He was back in Oklahoma, and Bud's always full of crazy schemes. Jeannie's the reason Joe listened to this one. She says the U.S. has enough natural gas in the ground to be energy independent. Or close to it, anyway – she'd tell you the figures. She's a brain, my big sister, unlike me."

Cathy boomed a *"Ha!"* that hurt my ear.

"Jeannie showed Joe, convinced him that natural gas was the only alternative to oil that could work now – not like these alternatives the greens are so hot on because they hate the oil companies. Joe's a practical man. He sees the changes coming. He knows natural gas is a cleaner-burning fuel, and he's a Californian through and through. Most of our natural gas is pipelined in from other places, Canada and other places. Jeannie thinks – we all think – wouldn't it be wonderful if gas were found here in the San Joaquin, right under our own feet?"

A vegetable truck was poking along in the fast lane. I moved over into the slow lane before saying, "I can't believe Jean was ever friends with Alice. She was maid of honor at her and Joe's wedding."

"Pity. You know how Jean is – it was pity. Everybody hated Alice in school and Jean felt sorry for her. That's the whole story."

"What happened to the friendship?"

Cathy snorted. "They haven't spoken since Jean started dating Manny back in college. Alice is a terrible bigot."

"So you probably aren't aware of how she as a director of Balch Corporation voted on the Minerva issue."

"Alice would oppose anything Joe wanted to do."

"Because?"

"Ann, oh, come on – she *hates* him! Honestly, don't say you don't know it. Alice is the *b-i-t-c-h* from *h-e-l-l*." Cathy spelled the words out. "*You* don't like her, do you? I've never met anyone who liked Alice – maybe people in L.A. –"

Cathy snorted again. This time it was repressed laughter, not contempt.

I said, "But Jean hung out with Alice at one point. Doesn't she ever talk about her? Was it Jean who told you Alice trapped Joe into marriage?"

A tanker went screaming past and I realized I hadn't been watching the road or the speedometer. I also had to watch for exit signs. Trey lived on the north side of Bakersfield so I wasn't going as far as I was used to.

"Bless her heart, my sister is a sweet woman. She lives by the motto 'If you can't say anything nice, don't say anything at all.'"

"You called her a Pollyanna because she wouldn't believe Kenny Mills was murdered."

"She believes it now. Do you think this burglary is connected too?"

"My interest at the moment is Alice, and things related to things that happened forty years ago when dinosaurs roamed the earth and oil was still forming in Kern County."

"If I asked why, you wouldn't tell me, would you?"

I did an Emmet murmph.

Cathy inhaled on her cigarette and exhaled. "Jeannie's older than I am, Ann. I was nine when she went off to college and I don't remember Alice as a child. There are plenty of rumors, though – gossip we've all heard that goes back to when Ray Senior was alive and Joe and Alice were first married. The whole town will tell you Joe is Ray Junior's real father. Jeannie's good friends with Celeste but even *I* never had the nerve to ask if the story's true. My sister would *die*."

There it was: the exit I wanted.

Thanking Cathy for the help, I paid her back with "Mrs. Mancuso arrived this morning – I had to move out of the guest suite" and hung up to concentrate on the ramp and my directions.

Trey lived in a middle-class area on a bluff overlooking the Kern River oil field. I approached his place up a winding road from below and couldn't believe the panorama. It was sort of an industrial nightmare and also sort of wild, like cinematic wild. Pumpjacks, workover rigs, and drilling rigs; huge storage tanks, small tank batteries, and injection wells; steam pipes, steam co-generators, solar panels; clusters of buildings; parked and moving vehicles; a network of dirt roads; poles carrying electric and phone lines; and more, and more, and more, as far as you could see.

Taking off my Balch Oil cap, I cruised Trey's address.

Emmet must have gotten it wrong because this didn't look like a place for Trey – a family-sized home with neat hedges bordering the lawn. The garage was down a driveway at the rear, a driveway barely wide enough to accommodate the back end of an F-150 dualie with its two sets of two tires. There was no Ford pickup in sight, but a swank Harley tricked out in chrome was propped in front of the garage, and a tabby cat was sitting on the porch on top of a cat crate ...

Maybe it *was* Trey.

I turned around in a driveway farther down, made another slow pass of the house, and parked at a bend in the street half hidden by a giant banana plant. Sliding over to the passenger seat, I slumped low and considered my options.

This wasn't the kind of neighborhood where you could park in a metallic blue pickup and be inconspicuous for long. I checked the time: 4:03 P.M. I'd never had a conversation with Trey. I didn't know how, or if, he adjusted his awake schedule on weeks off from the rig. Getting out of the truck would be risky. But – I was sure he'd never recognize me in civilian clothes. On tour I was zipped to the chin in coveralls; I wore safety glasses and a hardhat, and I'd also started wearing a headband for warmth, despite my pinchy hardhat. I bet Trey didn't even know I was brunette, although who knew what he saw or didn't see with the thousand-yard stare.

I had to find out if that was his house.

There was a middle school somewhere close by because kids that age were trailing home on both sides of the street, looking grumpy and weighed down by backpacks. Staying low, I watched them walk past. When a group of girls stopped in front of the house this side of Trey's, I decided to take my chance.

Jumping out of the truck, I hurried down the sidewalk. The girls were crowded around one girl with an iPhone, reading the screen and giggling. Most of them looked up as I apologized for the interruption.

"Someone told me the guy next door has kittens for sale but he doesn't seem to be home. Do you girls know anything about it?"

A tall girl pointed at the house we were standing in front of. "My mom'll know."

I thanked her and went up the walk to ring the bell. A woman about my age answered the door. She had a smear of purple jelly on her shirt, a kid on her hip holding a jelly sandwich, and she looked like she could use a diversion in the worst way. Smiling, I took off my sunglasses and said the same thing to her I'd said to the girls. She didn't know about kittens for sale, but I made a joke about the grape-jelly face and kept her talking and pretty soon the story came out.

It was definitely Trey.

That house was a rental, which already the homeowners didn't like. Trey had moved in about the time he started at the rig and had since become the bane of the neighborhood. He was dealing drugs, the woman was sure: he had too much money for a regular roughneck. I asked which drugs, looking for a crystal-meth link, but she didn't know. He also rescued cats and dogs. They'd had to call his landlord because he wasn't mowing the lawn, and they'd had to call the cops because he chained a pit bull in the back-yard and the dog barked all night. Cats were the latest problem. The cats were multiplying, and he'd trashed the front porch with crates and food dishes. Nobody wanted their kids near the guy. As she said it she checked on her daughter, still giggling in her circle of friends.

I could think of more questions but they'd sound suspicious coming from a kitten buyer, so I asked if she knew when Trey might be home. She didn't: when he wasn't working he was unpre-dictable.

Safely back in the truck, I called Doug again and this time got his voice mail. I talked until it beeped me off, then redialed and talked some more. I told him about Alice, her blighted life, and the *he* who didn't pose a threat to her. I told him what Cathy had said to contradict Alice. I told him where I was and why, and what I'd learned from Trey's neighbor. I also told him I was being prudent and super-careful.

I'd just hung up from Doug when a white Ford dualie material-ized down the street.

Hunkering lower, I strained to see in the falling dusk.

Shadows interfered so I didn't know it was Trey until he pulled into his drive, parked, and climbed out of the cab. I saw the next-door neighbor stick her head out and call her daughter inside, which scattered the clump of girls. Trey was oblivious to all that. He opened the tailgate and started unloading fifty-pound sacks of pet food like they weighed fifty feathers. A sack on each shoulder, he walked up the drive towards the garage. I heard barking behind his house, and cats appeared from bushes and other yards to follow him.

On his nth trip with sacks, Trey stopped suddenly to look up the street in my direction. I checked my right-side mirror –

Yikes!

I slid onto the floor, hunched, and covered up as Mark Bridges rolled by in his red clown truck. *Saved by the blue loaner* – which was Bridges's own fault since he wrecked the wipers on Joe's truck.

Chances of having been spotted were low, but I stayed down a good five minutes before raising my head. Those guys might be cunning enough to stand outside and wait for me to appear. Holding my breath, I listened. I raised my head a little more and checked out the windows: no one. I had the pepper spray in my pocket. Putting one hand on it, I put my other hand on the seat, levered myself up from crunch position, and peeked over the dashboard. Bridges's truck was parked in front of Trey's house and neither guy was visible.

At 6:26 P.M. by my cell phone, Trey and Bridges came out of the house, crossed the porch, got into Trey's pickup, and took off. It was winter dark.

Following them to East Bakersfield, I decided as I drove that Trey's pickup with its wowed-out rear end was at least as cartoony as the Bridge-mobile.

They parked and went into a place called Noriega's that had a plain white façade and a door flanked by glass bricks. I'd eaten lunch there with Joe and it was a total scene – a famous Basque bar and restaurant that served meals family style at long tables in the back room. The main Bakersfield action had moved west since Noriega's opened in 1893. The street was badly lit, and the surrounding blocks seemed like an old warehouse or wholesale district associated with the old, closed train station. But there was another hopping Basque bar down from Noriega's and a third one around the block.

I parked in a dark spot – out of the green-orange glare of the restaurant signs – to settle in and watch Noriega's front entrance.

Fifteen minutes later I went "Whoa!" and sat up tall.

Our mud logger was going into Noriega's with Ron Bray. First
Trey together with Mark Bridges, now those two.

I leaned forward, wishing there were some way to get inside
the restaurant and look around. But Noriega's was in the middle
of a city block. It had a front and back door only, and it was just a
couple of open rooms, no partitions or aisles –

Suddenly Trey was outside.

On reflex, I tipped sideways to peer over the dash.

He came out the front door alone, headed up the street at a fast
walk, then broke into a run. I watched until he angled off into the
parking lot up the block. Switching on my engine, I put the truck
in gear and rolled forward. By the time I was level with the parking
lot, Trey's taillights were receding down the side street. A pudgy
figure came barreling up the alley from behind Noriega's. The figure ran under a floodlight: Bridges. He stopped at the side street,
looked right, looked left, saw Trey's taillights, and ran, waving his
arms over his head. Coasting forward, I made the left. Trey's taillights brightened as he hit his brakes. The passenger door flew
open. Bridges raced for it and jumped in, and Trey blasted out of
there before the door was shut.

I was just speeding up to catch them when my phone rang.
Glancing down, I saw Doug's name on the display. I braked, pulled
over, and answered:

"Hooray – but I can't talk! I'm tailing Trey and Mark Bridges
around Bakersfield! Trey and Bridges *together!*"

"Where are they? Where are you?"

At the intersection straight ahead, Trey had blasted through a
red light, moving fast.

"They're in Trey's truck up the street! I'm a block behind! I'm
hanging up – I don't want to lose them!"

Doug snapped, "No, Ann!" in his sternest official voice. "You're
coming home! You can't be doing errands of that nature, certainly
not alone. I'm headed to Jean's now – meet me there."

"I've also got our guy Bud in Noriega's with Ron Bray on a dinner or drinks date. Shouldn't I at least—"

"Come *home*."

"But—"

"I'll see you in two hours. You can 'but' me then."

He hung up and I hung up. Figuring I could do one last teeny-weeny errand, I threw the pickup in reverse and backed back up the street. I checked down the alley and, at the intersection, braked and checked down towards the restaurant. I didn't see Bud or Bray outside looking for anyone or seeming like they'd given up the chase.

26

STOPPED BY THE house on my way to meet Doug because I was early, and also because Mrs. Mancuso's Escalade was parked in the circle drive while Alice's Jaguar was not.

I found Luz in the kitchen slumped on a high chair at the island. She had an almost-gone margarita in front of her and looked so unhappy that I said:

"Luz, what's wrong? *¿Qué te pasa?*" I walked around the island to sit down next to her.

She glanced over without answering. Her eyes were bloodshot and heavy, her plump face was mooshed, and I realized she was drunk. Luz wasn't a drinker but I'd seen her like that before, after one of her Saturday dances. This was Monday and she hadn't been out because she wore her work costume – stretchy pants and a baggy man's shirt. But her ribbon was coming loose and her bun had slipped.

"*¿Qué pasó, compañera?*" I patted her arm. "Did something happen? Where is everybody? Where's Mrs. Mancuso?"

The mention of Mrs. Mancuso had an instant effect. Staring at her drink, Luz started talking very slowly in Spanish. The last time she was drunk she only spoke Spanish. She was addressing the margarita and slurring her words so it was tough to catch a lot.

What I got first were two names: Celestay and Hunior. I guessed Celestay was Mrs. Mancuso. Hunior I realized must be Ray Parkerworth Junior.

"Le partió el corazón a Señor Joe. Le partió el corazón a su mamá. Me partió el corazón."

"I don't understand, Luz. Can you say it in English?"

Luz broke off, blinking slowly and tipping the last of the margarita into her mouth. It looked like she wouldn't continue but she did.

"Celestay good woman, wonderful woman – she friend to me. She too young for being mother. She no know how. I love Celestay – I no do good job with her baby. Hunior bad boy – *niño malo* – hard boy. He no listen to me. He listen to Manuel only. He leave his family – die alone far away. He break Señor Joe's heart. He break the heart of his mother. He break my heart.

"Le partió el corazón a Señor Joe. Le partió el corazón a su mamá. Me partió el corazón."

I patted Luz's arm again, searching for something to say but mostly feeling like she ought to be jolted out of this mood.

"Hey, Luz? Were Alice and Joe ever happy together?"

I also wanted information and, cynically, thought this might be the right moment to get it.

"Were they?"

Luz broke off in mid-*corazón* to turn her head and look at me. I said, "What's the story with Alice? Does she love Joe – does she hate him?"

I didn't think Luz was going to respond. She sat slumped, just staring at me with bleary eyes.

"I heard why she married Joe. Why did Joe marry her?"

Luz changed as a fierce, fighting look slowly came over her face. Her gaze sharpened and, slurring her words less, she cut loose.

"Señor Joe young and stupid – we warn him. Celestay she warn him. Everybody they warn him. He no believe. La señora, she no like José. She no like José since I come here work forty years. Señora Alice bad woman. She here now because is . . . mmm . . . *zopilotes.*"

228

Taking one hand off her glass, Luz mimed pecking and bobbed with her nose like a bird picking meat off a carcass.

I said, "Buzzard? Vulture?"

Luz nodded slowly, pointing up with her finger. "Vulture in desert. She circle in air, circle, circle, waiting Señor Joe to die. *Ella quiere todo el dinero.*"

Because Alice wanted all the money.

Luz slipped off her stool unsteadily and repeated, *"Quiere todo el dinero – todo, todo,"* as she went to pour herself more green stuff out of the blender –

"You've had enough for tonight, Luz, darling."

Mrs. Mancuso walked into the kitchen. Luz turned unsteadily. Mrs. Mancuso removed the drink glass from her hand and set it on the counter.

"You go on to bed. It's been a long day for everyone."

Luz slurred, *"Querida."* Putting her arm around Mrs. Mancuso, she dropped her head on Mrs. Mancuso's shoulder, who said, "Time for beddy-bye, dear."

Dimpling at me, she added:

"I need to talk to you, Ann. Don't run away."

She walked Luz out the far door and turned down the hall.

I checked the clock and checked to see if Doug had called. I was having a hard time reconciling the things I'd heard about Mrs. Mancuso with what I was seeing. Tramp, rotten mother, gold digger, flake: that was according to Cathy and general gossip. Alice said she'd poisoned Wilson against her – stolen her husband and the Parkerworth companies. But Mrs. Mancuso was Jean's good friend, and Luz loved her, and so did Joe in his deadpan style. Joe had no tolerance for bad or bullshit character, as he defined them – although if he and she had been intimate back in dinosaur days –

"Well, there now!" Mrs. Mancuso walked into the kitchen fluffing her hair with her fingers.

Whatever else she might be, she was definitely a kick.

She and Alice were about the same age but otherwise nothing alike – like hot was different from cold, and va-va-voom was different from postnasal drip. I'd only met her that morning but she seemed to bubble with perpetual fun. Even with Alice's insults, she bubbled. And I would've called her style supercharged Southwest. The brunette was dye, she liked lots of makeup, her lips and nails were *red*, and she was very tan from the cruise. In skintight jeans, she was as flashy and curvy as Alice was slim and classic in Chanel. She wore silver and turquoise and a big belt buckle – and also had the biggest diamond I'd ever seen in her wedding ring.

"Who were you two talking about? Who wants all what money? I bet I know – I bet I can guess."

Mrs. Mancuso took the chair Luz had vacated and, smiling, put her hand over mine and squeezed.

"Does the maharajah know that's missing from the palace?" I pointed at her wedding ring.

Mrs. Mancuso dimpled. Holding the ring up to the light, she tilted it to make the diamond sparkle.

"My husband is such a darling, funny man. He says if you can't see it in a satellite photo, it isn't big enough."

"So you're getting India for your anniversary?"

Mrs. Mancuso bubbled off into a laugh. Pulling both hands out of her reach, I tucked them under my legs and wondered: Was it a bad mother and flake who could laugh like that a few months after her son's death? Or was it a gift? It had taken me more than a few months to get over my sister's death last year.

I said, "What did you want to talk about, Mrs. Mancuso? I have somewhere I need to be."

She caught her breath and smiled. "Call me Celeste, dear – please. Mrs. Mancuso is my mother-in-law and it makes me feel old and decrepit."

I just nodded. From the first minute we spoke on the phone, she'd treated me like family because of the Whiteheads. But I was going to be cautious until I knew what she actually was and whose side she was on. That was why I'd stopped by in the first place: to start figuring out where she fit.

"Joe told me what's been happening here." Mrs. Mancuso patted the island where my hand used to be. "I'm worried about him. I don't think he's recovered from the heart attack, do you?"

230

I shook my head. "And he's under a huge amount of stress. What did he tell you exactly?"

"Well, he said . . ." She bit her lush bottom lip. "It all seems . . . is it true? It must be, because Joe doesn't lie. One of the roughnecks murdered and —"

She talked and I listened, sitting on my hands.

Basically Joe had told her everything he knew. Everything — starting with Kenny Mills, the scouting, the sabotage, the attack on me, the missing guns, right down to that day with the shooting at the lease and the vandalized house. Luckily everything Joe knew wasn't everything to know. He didn't speculate about suspects or motives. And I noticed he omitted Hilary Mahin and Ron Bray from the narrative — as possibly involved in the spying, and as opponents in the fight over the sale of Balch Oil. For the rest, Joe held nothing back. It was the strongest possible proof that Mrs. Mancuso was inside his Circle of Trust.

When she got done, I just shrugged. "That's the situation, more or less."

"But . . . it isn't right . . . who would do such terrible things? Someone here in Wilson? I can't believe it. Not to Joe . . ."

She chewed her lip, and her hazel eyes were serious as she searched my face for an answer. I shrugged again.

Releasing her lip she said simply, "How can I help?"

"You won't tell anybody what you just told me, first off."

"Now, Ann, don't let all this paint and plastic surgery fool you." Wagging a finger, she did a hilarious girlie imitation of Emmet. "I tell new friends it's the three Ps — paint, plastic, and more paint. I'm not as dumb as I look, thank you very much."

I had to smile at that. "You're on the board of directors of Balch Corporation, right?"

She nodded.

"Then second, you can help by telling me how everyone voted when Hilary Mahin brought the board in to fight Joe on the Minerva play."

Mrs. Mancuso opened her eyes wide.

• • •

I was sorry I'd hurried my talk with her when Doug called as I was racing to meet him at Jean's.

He'd been held up in conference with the sheriffs and Wilson PD. The cops had done a batch of interviews and were going over them, sifting the testimony for leads, discrepancies, suspicious gaps, and anything else they could find. Doug wanted me to know they'd found Colt .45 shell casings in the field west of the lease, and that Bud's story had checked with the casino up north. He'd left the poker table about an hour before the shooting: he would've been on the road home. Bud's time was also accounted for on the evening I was attacked. Which didn't mean he wasn't selling well secrets to pay his gambling debt. But added to what I'd seen at Noriega's – that Trey and Bridges ran from him and Ron Bray – progress was being made. If the known spy, Bridges, was avoiding two suspected spies, it meant possibly that Bud and Bray weren't part of the scouting scheme.

Putting Bridges together with Trey, though, was more than progress: it might be our first real break. Doug said it was making the cops very happy – and he acknowledged that it came as a result of unauthorized action on my part. I didn't rub it in. I gave Emmet the credit and accused Doug of trying to sideline me.

I was also still breathless from Mrs. Mancuso's revelations and started to summarize, calling Alice a "liar, liar, pants on fire," even though I didn't know for sure yet who was lying or whether it mattered –

Doug said to save the revelations for later. He told me where Jean hid the extra key to his apartment and said to go on up and wait for him inside. If I wanted to, he added, I should pull the mattresses off the bunk beds and make a big bed on the floor so we could have a comfortable night. We hadn't slept together since he arrived in Wilson . . . partly because, like the previous night, we hadn't slept period.

There were no lights at Jean's house. Her car was gone from the driveway and, when I pulled around back, I saw that Richie's truck wasn't in its usual spot in the alley.

I parked at the garage and reached for the flashlight in the glove

232

compartment before I remembered I wasn't driving Joe's pickup. I checked anyway in case the loaner had a flashlight, but the glove compartment was empty except for the owner's manual and a road map.

Jumping down from the truck, I turned to close the door and heard running footsteps –

Someone rushed out of the dark behind me. He snarled, "Get out of my town, you rich bitch!"

Mark Bridges.

I tried to run –

He grabbed my collar and shoved me into the truck door, slamming it shut. I struggled as something swished through the air. On instinct I ducked right. A metal object crunched against the pickup – a beer can. Beer sloshed up the glass and soaked my face. I dipped left and went for the pepper spray in my pocket. A swish – I ducked the wrong way. The can caught me on the head and crushed my nose into the window. Grunting from pain, I fumbled to arm the spray as Bridges shoved me down into the gravel and tried to kick me and missed.

"Last warning, bitch! Get *out!*"

I rolled under the truck, tangled in my jacket, struggling to free the pepper spray to use it. I saw his boot swipe by and kicked at it. Bending, he chucked the beer can at me and took off. I squirmed to avoid flying beer, and the pepper spray sprayed in my pocket. The gas hit my eyes, nose, and throat simultaneously. I rolled out fast from under the truck, coughing, trying to look for Bridges in the dark with eyes that were stinging and filling with tears.

Leaping up and ripping off my jacket, I threw it down the alley and ran stumbling up Doug's stairs to get away from the stink of chemical.

Up on the landing I dabbed my eyes and blinked them, coughing. I heard an engine start not far off and looked but couldn't see if it was Bridges.

He'd been watching Doug's place from the neighbor's yard.

And he wasn't the guy who strangled me at the back gate. When Bridges grabbed my collar, I'd felt his fist on my bare neck. His hand was hot and fleshy, and he didn't have the strength of the guy with the cold, iron grip.

But he was strong enough. Through blurry vision I could see blood pouring from my nose onto my shirt.

Stanching it with my sleeve, coughing, I started back down the stairs. I had to get my clothes off and needed Doug's key to get in.

27

"YOUR TEACHER MRS. Garcia told you what Sheik Yamani once said."

The morning was sunny and bright. Joe was standing in the yard in front of his trailer talking to fifteen of Jean's students. Everyone wore a new Balch Oil hardhat except him. He had on aviator sunglasses, a blue Balch Oil windbreaker, and his Stetson. Jean was standing to his side in khaki pants and steel-toed boots, looking very cute with her hair mashed down by a hardhat. The kids were grouped in a tight semicircle around them so they could hear over the diesel engines.

One kid's hand shot up. Jean said, "Robert?"

"Sheik Ahmed Zaki Yamani was Saudi Arabia's oil minister from 1962 to 1986. He's famous for saying 'The Stone Age came to an end not for a lack of stones.'"

Jean nodded. "Very good, Robert." Some of the kids rolled their eyes at the teacher's pet.

Emmet and I were standing at the back of the semicircle. The sun was making my injuries throb, my bruised head and cut nose, so I moved around to stand in Emmet's shadow. I'd already tried to take off my pinchy hardhat but he wouldn't let me. Good news was the cops now had an opening to request electronic surveillance on one of our suspects. Bridges had provided the wedge. They wouldn't arrest him for assault because they needed him running around loose using his cell phone. Man, did Doug howl when he heard the story: me attacked with a can of beer, getting myself with pepper spray. I could still feel a mild sting.

Joe said, "Yamani hit the target in my view. Technology will change before we run out of oil. Maybe the greatest oil mind of our time, Zaki Yamani. I'd buy him a drink if his religion wasn't against it."

The kids tittered as Joe cracked a minor smile. I saw Jean glance at him and hold the glance. Joe was pale and drawn – slanting more than normal, like he couldn't make the effort to straighten up. He really didn't seem good.

I used the pause to stand on tiptoe and whisper loud to Emmet, "You were right! Something *isn't* right with Trey!"

Emmet had his fists shoved in his pockets and was squinting at the derrick. He nodded without looking at me, a micro-non-nod.

A girl raised her hand and Jean said, "Yes, Martha?"

"Mr. Balch, sir, do you think they'll reopen the outer continental shelf for drilling?"

Joe turned in her direction. "There was a time I thought yes. I thought security of supply would override the environment. The scales have tipped with this global-warming hoopla."

Martha spoke up again. "Do you hate the greens, Mr. Balch?"

A ripple went through the group like Martha had done a daring thing. Joe managed another smile.

"I'll say this, young lady. There are crooks, sons of bitches, and knuckleheads on both sides of that fight."

The kids tittered again at "sons of bitches." A girl with braces next to Martha put her hand up. "But what do you say when someone says Big Oil is bad? We read it all the time."

Joe pulled his sunglasses down his nose and eyed her over top of them. Everyone got the sarcasm and laughed. Even Jean smiled. Joe said:

"Oil comes in all sizes as we Westsiders know. The bad guys in this business to me are the moneymen at the publicly traded companies. That sorry bunch dances to Wall Street's tune. There isn't enough profit in God's wide world for those greedy New York bastards and they have us by the short—"

Jean interrupted smoothly. "Mr. Balch—"

It wasn't just the imminent vulgarity; she'd seen something was wrong. Joe was suddenly having trouble catching his breath.

Jean started, "On behalf of—"

Another kid stuck his hand up. Jean said, "Make it brief, please, Steven."

"Would you go into the oil business today if you were us?"

Joe stretched one corner of his mouth. He was in pain. I looked at Emmet. Emmet was frowning—he was seeing it too.

Joe said:

"Son, I don't know what to tell you. I've spent fifty-five years on a rig floor. My work was my play and my play was my work. I enjoyed the hell out of every minute." He stopped for breath.

"I know young people nowadays don't want to go into this business. They think it's a dirty, sunset industry. My advice is, do the best you can and enjoy the hell out of it."

Joe's knees were folding. He looked like he wanted to sit down except there was nothing to sit on close by. He reached for Jean as Jean reached to prop him up and said calmly, "Emmet, would you show the students around the lease?"

Emmet rumbled, "This way, children," and began to move.

The kids began to move. I cut through them, not rushing, and took hold of Joe's arm. He was *pale* pale and panting in rapid breaths.

Jean whispered, "I'll call the ambulance, Joe."

"No, Jeannie—no ambulance. Take me home."

Mrs. Mancuso had delegated me to guard Joe's door. She'd locked it from the inside after Jean and I brought him home and the doctor had come. My orders were to only let Luz in, and Cathy when she found another nurse to watch her old guy in McKittrick.

The concern was Alice. She was due from L.A. around noon and I had the job of keeping her out of Joe's rooms when she showed up. Joe had told me to tell Alice, from him, to go back to Los Angeles or go to hell. He had enough breath to say that. As he'd turned his back, Jean shook her head to rescind the hell part. Mrs. Mancuso — who heard it too — just dimpled.

Doug had gone to Bakersfield with the homicide detectives to work on the application for electronic surveillance on Mark Bridges. The application was a huge, arduous deal: sheriffs would describe Bridges's attack as attempted murder and lay out their entire case. They were also going to subpoena Bridges's cell phone records back to Minerva no.1's spud last September. While one detective wrote out the application, the other was continuing interviews. The cops were slogging their way through the same list of names it took me three large pages to write in red crayon . . . and Kern sheriffs did *not* have a wavy pink Circle of Trust.

Doug had been very upset last night to find a pile of my clothes in Jean's yard and me bleeding in his shower trying to soap off the smell of pepper spray.

His first impulse, purely male, was to rush out and put some hurt on Bridges. His second impulse was more professional. Bridges had made a serious strategic error by jumping me: Bridges was going down. I'd made Doug howl over the beer-versus-pepper-spray-rolling-under-truck farce. But when he'd asked me to explain "liar, liar, pants on fire," he stopped laughing and listened carefully.

As I iced my nose I'd told him that what I'd heard from Mrs. Mancuso was the exact opposite of what Alice had told me.

According to Mrs. Mancuso, Alice despised Wilson and despised the oil business and always had. Ray Senior willed the Parkerworth companies to Joe because without Joe, there would've been no companies, and Ray Senior knew it. Senior also made sure Alice didn't have any stock or say in the business because she'd told her father — Mrs. Mancuso was witness — that she'd sell the companies if she ever owned them. Mrs. Mancuso denied having an affair with Joe and that Ray Junior's father was anyone but Ray Senior. She denied forcing Alice out of the house too. She said it was Alice who refused to live with Ray Junior or raise him. She'd chosen to move to L.A. instead.

Mrs. Mancuso also said Alice opposed Minerva from the start. She'd been squarely on Mahin's side, along with most of the Balch board.

Doug had been suspicious of Mrs. Mancuso's candor. So was I. Even given my Whitehead credentials—so was I. At this stage, I'd told him, it was still a matter of she-said / she-said. I saw no reason yet to trust Mrs. Mancuso's account any more than I trusted Luz's or Cathy's, who both hated Alice. I knew who I was inclined to believe but that was prejudice too.

The front doorbell rang.

Tensing, I sat forward, until I remembered Alice wouldn't ring the bell and relaxed back against the door. There were masculine voices in the foyer and the sound of heavy feet hurrying down the hall.

I scrambled up as two men appeared—Hilary Mahin and Ron Bray. Mahin, pasty and pear-shaped, had on chartreuse cowboy boots and was walking ahead of Bray. Bray wore his workingman's denim and would've looked tan and fit compared to most people and looked especially tan and fit compared to Mahin. They both had that down-home Westside style. Unless you recognized the style, you'd never guess they had big jobs or money in the bank. You'd probably just think they were hicks.

I said, "Mr. Mahin. Mr. Bray. What can I do for you?"

Mahin ignored me, forcing me to step aside as he walked up to Joe's door and knocked.

"Joe? It's Boots. Can I come in?"

Bray stayed back, ignoring me too. He'd taken off his Balch Drilling jacket in the warm house. Mahin knocked again, then jiggled the doorknob and found it locked.

He called, "Joe?," at the door louder. "It's Boots!"

Mahin realized he was going to have to speak to me. He semi-turned, not making eye contact. "What do you know about this?"

"Joe had some kind of spell at the lease. The doctor's with him now."

"How serious is it?"

"I don't know."

"Is he conscious?" Mahin was putting his questions abruptly and rudely.

"Last time I saw he was."

I was focused on Mahin and didn't hear Alice come down the hall. Suddenly she was right there in a fur-lined coat, pulling off leather driving gloves.

"Boots, Ron — good morning. Is there a problem, Boots? Why is Dr. Foreman's car here?"

She didn't see me, then she did. "Ann, what's going on?"

"Joe's inside with the doctor."

Putting her gloves away Alice walked briskly to the door, necklaces jingling, perfume wafting. Mahin had to step back to let her through. She said, "Is it his heart?" as she turned the knob. The knob caught. She tried to twist it again and realized the door was locked.

"Why is this door locked?" She looked at me. "Who's with Joe? Is *that woman* with him?"

"Jean and Mrs. Mancuso are inside."

Alice's face went tight and tighter at the names. I said, "Joe was talking to Jean's class when —"

Raising her voice, Alice rapped on the door. "Joseph, dear? It's Alice. Let me in." She grasped the doorknob and shook it.

I said, "We aren't supposed to disturb —"

Alice broke in coldly, "I am his *wife!*"

Mahin backed up to stand against the opposite wall with Bray. Bray hadn't said a word so far or changed his expression.

"I have a right to see my husband!" Alice rattled the doorknob again, calling, "Joseph! It's Alice!" She waited, listening, ear close to the door.

"I'll go around to the back."

She took off up the hall, walking rapidly. I saw Mahin and Bray exchange a look before Mahin moved and Bray followed him. They weren't rushing to catch Alice but I wouldn't take any chances. Once they were out of sight I knocked my special knock on Joe's door. The lock clicked, the door opened a crack, and Jean's face appeared.

I said low and fast, "Did you hear?"

Jean nodded.

"Alice is coming around outside. Mahin and Bray may or may not be with her. Lock the sliding doors and close the curtains. Hope they don't bring a screwdriver for the plywood."

All the broken windows had been covered with plywood until replacement glass came.

Jean shut the door and clicked the lock. I sat down on the carpet, betting Alice would be back but more relaxed about it now. A couple of minutes later swift footsteps came down the hall, almost running, and Alice reappeared alone.

Practically stepping on me, she grabbed the doorknob, shook it, and gritted through her teeth:

"He can't do this. It isn't legal. I'll call Dex. Better yet, I'll see Dex right now."

She turned and went rushing back up the hall. I leaped up and ran after her, calling, "Alice! Calm down! Calm down, Alice!"

In the foyer she brushed past Luz, who'd come out of the kitchen to see what the noise was about.

Unperturbed, Luz said, "*¿Cuál es su problema ahora?*" She looked fine after her margarita melancholy of the night before – no traces at all.

Alice kept going down to her suite and we heard the door slam with violence. I glanced around for Mahin and Bray.

"Where'd those two guys go, Luz, and who is Dex?"

The doorbell rang.

"*Sí*, they go." Luz wiped her hands on her apron and went to answer it. "Señor Dex *abogado* of Señor Joe long time."

"Oh, right – Dex."

At the door was a deliveryman from a medical-supply company. He had a white deal that looked like a small fax machine that he said was a portable EKG. Watching for Alice, I covered the rear as Luz walked him and machine down to Joe's rooms and knocked

241

her special knock. Mrs. Mancuso cracked the door, then swung it wide and pointed to the bedroom. I guarded the open door, watching up the hall. The lights were on in the sitting room – the closed curtains and boarded glass door cut out all the sun.

I said, "How's Joe?"

Mrs. Mancuso dimpled. "Stubborn and just plain ornery. The doctor's calling it arrhythmia but Joe refuses to go to the hospital for more tests. They're in there arguing. Dr. Foreman won't win that one, you can be sure."

I lowered my voice. "Alice is headed to Bakersfield to speak to Dex about her legal rights as Mrs. Balch."

"Dex?"

Checking behind her, Mrs. Mancuso stepped closer, also lowering her voice as she said, "Then this will get messy. Joe's finally going to file for divorce – and hallelujah, we all might add. Joe and I drove over yesterday to talk to Dex."

I said, "Why file now –"

"Celeste? Ann?" Jean appeared in the open doorway. "Would you come help us move the bed around, please? Joe wants to face the rig."

Jean went back in. Taking hold of my arm, Mrs. Mancuso pulled me into the sitting room. I shut and locked the door as she whispered, "Jean doesn't like to be in the house while Alice is home –"

Joe came walking out of the bedroom in pajamas and his ratty flannel robe. His color was close to normal again.

"Why are you two whispering? This isn't a damn funeral parlor."

I gave him a loose salute and Mrs. Mancuso dimpled at him. She played those dimples like a virtuoso – sometimes the right one, sometimes the left, sometimes both together, everywhere on the scale from shallow to deep.

Moving the bed didn't take long with everybody's help. Joe had sliding glass doors in his bedroom. Jean opened the curtains and he had a big view of the south side of the lease, only slightly obstructed by the eucalyptus trees along the back fence. They'd been trimmed up and thinned at my request and it gave him a much better view than before.

242

When Mrs. Mancuso and I walked out, Joe was standing at his desk reading the day's oil news off his new computer. The vandal had wrecked the other computers beyond repair. I stopped and called: "I'm going to whisper," which got me a vintage deadpan. The doctor's voice came from the bedroom. "I need you in here, Joe."

Joe tightened the belt of his robe and obeyed grudgingly.

Pulling Mrs. Mancuso into a huddle, I whispered, "Why's he filing for divorce now?"

"It's Jeannie." Mrs. Mancuso was whispering too. "Jeannie's taken the brake off because of his health."

I nodded because it made sense. Otherwise I might suspect Mrs. Mancuso of being the mastermind.

"I have to run some errands. When is Cathy due, or does she know yet? Will you be okay without me watching the door?"

Mrs. Mancuso shook her head and then nodded it. I whispered, "You have my cell phone number and Doug's cell phone—"

Mrs. Mancuso interrupted, dimpling. "Isn't he just too handsome? Is Doug your fella?"

"He is. Call the lawyer also and warn him that Alice—"

"Ann!"

Startled, I stopped. Mrs. Mancuso whispered, "I am *not* as dumb as I look, you young thing!"

"Sorry." I poked a finger in each cheek, smiling to make dents beside my mouth. "It isn't the paint and plastic—it's the dimples."

Mrs. Mancuso was still laughing as she locked the hall door behind me.

28

AUDREY WAS EATING lunch at her desk in the *Gusher* office. I walked in from the street and before I could say hello she started bombarding me with rumors and questions about the rumors. I waited for her to finish, then used her own trick of answering a question with a question:

"What do you know about Alice Balch's relationship with Celeste Parkerworth Mancuso – and vice versa?"

"Celeste is in town, I heard. Is that right?"

I took my sunglasses off and perched one hip on the edge of her desk. Audrey was so predictable.

"It's absolutely right. Is she or isn't she a tramp, rotten mother, gold digger, and flake? Did she or didn't she ruin Alice's life by stealing her husband and her father's companies, and by forcing her into lonely exile by making her departure a condition of leaving Ray Junior for Luz and Joe to raise?"

Audrey's eyebrows went higher and higher as I reeled off Mrs. Mancuso's alleged domestic crimes. Pushing aside her sandwich and Diet Pepsi, she leaned forward, excited.

"Heavens to Murgatroyd! Why do you want to know? Does it have anything to do with Ken Mills –"

I held up a flat palm. "No questions, Hildy. Answers."

"It's not fair! Isn't a lovely and talented legwoman allowed to know one single, solitary *thing*?" She faked a puckish pout and tapped her computer keyboard. "Just this morning I sent you an e-mail about the Balch companies, what's going on with Boots and so forth. Where's my quid pro quo?"

I was pulling out my phone to check e-mails, then stopped, realizing she had a valid point. "You're right—"

"A-*ha!*" Audrey plumped back in her chair and crossed her arms triumphantly.

"—but the sheriffs are involved now, with the Wilson cops and my friend Doug, the LAPD detective. So I can only confirm that your rumors are true for once. That's how my nose got cut—a guy jumped me in Jean's alley last night. Pressure is being applied and people are starting to crack. When you can know the whole story, I'll tell you, I promise."

Audrey's face had gone sober partway through my speech. Uncrossing her arms she sat forward, all business. "I'll print out the e-mail for you. And Joe?"

"He's home in his robe—he seems fine."

As Audrey hit keys, checking to make sure the printer was on, she said:

"About Alice and Celeste there are rumors galore. I won't repeat them, which is the reason I haven't gotten back to you about what originally caused the estrangement between Alice and Joe. I'll tell you what I *do* know as a fact. Celeste missed Ray Junior's memorial service because she hadn't been notified. Alice never called her although she told everyone she had. Jean spoke to Celeste afterward to ask why she hadn't made an appearance, and it came out."

"You got it from Jean?"

Nodding, Audrey hit a key and looked at me with arched eyebrows as the printer started to print.

"Under duress and not for publication. *Entre nous,* Ann—a person who is capable of that is capable of almost anything."

"You mean Alice."

"I mean Alice."

Audrey waited for three sheets of paper to drop into the paper tray and, grabbing them, handed them over.

"I have my own take on Celeste, whom I like very much. I'm aware of what's said about her, but I've gotten to know her over the years and I've come to the conclusion that Celeste is nature's child. She always leads with her heart – and it's a good heart. The mistakes of her youth, of which there were apparently legion, came from being impulsive. There isn't a malicious or calculating bone in that woman's body."

"Is she a liar at all?"

"Celeste?" Audrey snorted. "Celeste only lies to spare people's feelings. Every year she comes to tea at Caroline Mahin's after the big Balch board meeting, and *every* dad-blamed *year* she says how wonderful Caroline's homemade scones are when they taste like stale cow patties. Caroline's scones are a local legend."

Smiling, I glanced down at the papers in my hand. Audrey had written a lot. I said, "Do you mind if I sit here while I read this?"

"Be my guest. I'll just be tippy-typing away."

Audrey tippy-typed and I read.

The first paragraph was mostly old news about West Coast Energy's offer on Balch Oil and the frictions it had caused. I didn't know, though, that Mahin wanted Joe to sell Balch Oil *and* Balch Drilling at the top of the market so both men could retire. The sale of Balch Drilling might also put Ron Bray out of a job, something Mahin wouldn't mind one bit. There was no love lost there.

The e-mail moved on to the question of Emmet's power.

General opinion was Emmet had too much of it. Joe was operating Minerva no.1 lean and mean, his typical style. He was acting as his own company man and virtually letting Emmet drill the well. Mahin et al. argued there was too much money at stake: it wasn't the proper way to drill a challenging and expensive wildcat. In today's oil business you had layers and layers of executives, geologists, and engineers on that kind of well – the toolpush ran the rig and crews, period. Joe, they said, also had no experience with deep gas. Joe argued that experts designed the well, and few people were more qualified to drill it than Emmet, given his California knowledge and success in Oklahoma finding deep gas.

I said, "What do these jerks care how Joe drills Minerva? They were against it in the first place."

"Read on, cowgirl." Audrey didn't look up from typing.

Mahin, Bray, and unnamed board members of Balch Corporation had opposed the Minerva play. But now that Minerva no.1 was actually being drilled, Mahin and Bray wanted back in. Their opposition had hurt their relationship with Joe, which had hurt their chances of getting heard on the issue of the sale. Mahin wanted to see Minerva's accounting and wanted Balch Oil's engineer to consult. Bray wanted to boss Emmet, although Emmet was employed by Ozark Drilling U.S.A. Inc. So he was sniping from the sidelines and hoarding his seasoned hands even when a Balch rig was out of rotation for maintenance. He wanted to make Emmet look incompetent. His plan had backfired in one respect: Joe had reamed him for sending Kenny Mills out to work.

I saw the rationale for spying here – I'd seen it for a while – but not for sabotage or murder.

"This is great stuff, Audrey. It can't all be pillow talk."

"There's been a sinister development since I wrote that." Audrey stopped typing and looked at me. "Apparently –"

"Apparently?" I smiled.

"*Apparently* Boots has threatened to sue Joe for control of Minerva. It's a legal technicality, as I understand it. When they voted whether to drill the well for Balch Oil, apparently Joe should have recused himself. He didn't and now technically he's taken advantage of a corporate opportunity and violated his fiduciary responsibility. I believe that's the language. It's a lever Boots can use apparently, but it's really just a maneuver. What he wants is to pressure Joe into selling Balch Oil."

"Who'll run the companies when Joe dies, do we know?"

Audrey poked my knee, arching one eyebrow. "More to the point, my fine feathered friend – who will *own* the companies when Joe passes from here?"

She waited for her question to sink in. Thinking about it, I watched the traffic go by on Kern Street.

Audrey said, "Joe runs the companies but he also owns eighty percent of the stock in Balch Corporation, the parent. The way it's set up, only a relative by blood or marriage can own stock, and normally when a husband dies, the wife inherits everything. Alice is notorious for hating the oil business. All of Wilson knows she vowed never to step foot on a rig floor as long as she lives."

"She told me she loved the oil business."

"Alice loves the *money*. When she gets her hands on Balch Corp. she'll sell the whole shooting match faster than –"

Audrey snapped her fingers.

First Mrs. Mancuso and now Audrey. Added to Luz and Cathy Rintoul, a consensus was building and it looked like Alice was the liar, pants on fire.

Audrey said, "Did you read my PS?"

Glancing down the third page, I shook my head.

"I just had to get that off my chest. Wilson people, the older generation especially, think if Minerva comes in and Joe finds his gas field it'll save the town, like Lucy Boyd did in the fifties. To put it bluntly, nobody and nothing can save Wilson. People simply don't want to live here anymore. I can't print that in the *Gusher,* however, or say it at the Fourth of July picnic – and I'll thank you not to repeat it either."

She gave me a mock-stern look. I nodded, although my mind was still on our previous subject.

Alice loves the money. *Ella quiere todo el dinero.*

Luz had made me see a new possibility. I didn't know where it fit – or *if* it fit – but Alice was definitely up to something. I should've seen it before. All that phony "Joseph, dear" garbage and "I'm his wife – he's my husband" crap. Hanging around Wilson since Joe's heart attack, worrying about what he ate and smoked, hiding his truck keys so he wouldn't work too hard. I put it together with the lawyer's letter addressed to Joe I'd found open on her escritoire.

California was a community-property state. In a divorce, each partner was entitled to half the common assets unless other arrangements had been made. If one partner died, the survivor got half the common assets, by law, and usually the other half too, because married people left their stuff to each other. But I knew Joe. He wouldn't leave his half of a stale cow patty to Alice. The only way Alice would get everything – as opposed to just half of everything – was if Joe died without a will. He had a will, though, and a living trust, and he'd do anything to protect his beloved companies. He often joked that he hadn't made a will because he wasn't ready to die. I remember distinctly him saying it in the hospital one night, and . . . Jesus! *Alice had been there.* Alice, who wouldn't know a joke if it yanked on her necklace.

Was that her game?

Did it have anything to do with Ray Junior's premature death, what was happening at the lease, or the *he* that had vandalized the house?

Or maybe it was just another inheritance grab incubating for the future. The world was full of those too.

Did I not tell Audrey that people were starting to crack?

I'd pulled in to park in front of Emmet's trailer when his door flew open and I heard:

"*Rrroowweeuurrgh!* Get the *fuck* out my *bunkhouse,* you *bastards!!*"

Emmet appeared holding two guys by their jackets and fighting furious mad. Roaring, he shoved them out of his trailer backwards onto the small metal stoop. He was so massive and strong that he had them flapping like two bags of rags. One guy was Boots Mahin. The young guy with Mahin, I didn't recognize.

Red in the face, spraying spit with every word, Emmet was profane like I'd never heard him profane.

"*Y'all got no business in here! Readin my depths! Nosin through my tickets! You got no damn fuckin business!*"

He bent Mahin back over the top of the railing. Mahin went limp, looking scared to death. Emmet was rougher with him than with the young guy. The young guy struggled to loosen Emmet's giant fist from his collar. Emmet let go and stiff-armed him backwards down the stairs.

Stumbling in the gravel and holding his throat, the young guy squeaked, "But Mr. Balch—"

"*Mr. Balch nothin! You is a sacrificial lamb, my son! Joe and me don't want you and don't need you and this sumbitch here knows it!*" He shook Mahin, who looked, besides scared, extremely uncomfortable bent back like that.

"*You all is trespassin on private property! Get your sorry damn asses off this lease afore I call my boys to eject you off!*"

Jerking Mahin upright, Emmet shoved him down the steps. Mahin tripped and collided with the young guy, who grabbed him to stop him from falling.

Emmet turned and pointed at the Balch Oil pickup parked in front of Joe's trailer.

"That goes for you, Bray, you connivin bastard! You done been warned! This ain't Boots' well and it sure as shit ain't your rig!"

I'd seen the pickup as I was driving on, but hadn't noticed Ron Bray at the wheel. Mahin and the young guy stood frozen a couple of yards from me. They looked too rattled to move.

Emmet yelled, "God*damn* it, get yourselves gone! I don't mean *now!* I mean *right* now!"

Breathing hard, he clenched his fists as he started down the stoop—major Burning Eyeball of Doom.

The young guy took off, dragging Mahin with him. Emmet followed behind. They thought he was coming after them. The young guy let go of Mahin and broke into a run. Checking over his shoulder, Mahin sped up. I heard Bray start the truck. The young guy snatched the passenger door open and dived into the back seat. Emmet closed in but stopped as Mahin reached the truck and climbed up, and Bray hit reverse and then spurted forward in a spray of gravel. The arm of the barrier gate was already raised, Tommy no doubt having seen the trouble. Bray flew underneath the gate and down the lease road, throwing up dust and gravel, fishtailing on the washboard surface.

Emmet tramped down to the lease entrance and motioned Tommy to drop the barrier. Shoving his fists in his overalls, he stood there, planted on wide legs, watching what I was watching: Bray turn left at the blacktop, slow down, make the right where the blacktop ended at the cotton field, and disappear behind the eucalyptus trees as he headed for the highway.

When they were gone, Emmet turned and tramped back and I climbed out of the pickup. He signed for me to precede him into the trailer. I went in and sat down on the couch, noticing he'd put McGraw on the TV set. Walking into the kitchen, Emmet got in the fridge and held up a can of 7Up.

"Sodee pop?"

I shook my head. He poured himself a glass and came and sat in his chair. I said, "Are you okay?"

"Boots." Emmet was disgusted. "His asshole jumped up grabbed his neck, cut off the blood supply to his brain."

I had to smile at that very vivid picture.

"Don't be tellin Joe what you seen now."

"Who's the young guy?"

"Joe's engineer over there. I's more than willin to tutor him on the gas but I won't have him spy down my hole for that bunch of no-goods." Sipping his 7Up, Emmet muttered, "All gone plumb crazy with the price of oil."

I had come for corroboration of Audrey's scoop. After that scene, I knew her stuff was accurate. And Mahin and Bray were starting to crack too. Switching subjects, I said:

"I read in the *Gusher* you were best man at Alice and Joe's wedding in 1967. Did you warn him not to marry her?"

"Ain't commentin on that."

"No comment is a comment. You must've known my grandfather since you go back that far with Joe."

Emmet murmphed. It was a yes.

"So I'm looking for a thing Granpap might've done, serious enough that someone in Wilson thinks I should pay for it today." I tapped my neck.

Emmet hooked his thumbs in his bib and rocked his chair, gazing out at the rig. It hit me suddenly that Emmet had never mentioned my grandfather, which was probably significant –

The desk phone rang. Emmet unhooked one thumb and reached for it. "Yep . . . Ain't seen hide nor hair of the bastards, Joe. How you doin?"

The pretty lie in action, I thought.

"We got some tight spots – I's back up the hole wipin . . . Little sister's settin right here. I'll send it on with her . . . Yep."

Emmet put the receiver down, leaned for a piece of paper, and passed it over. It said *Drilling Report* at the top and was filled out in pencil.

"Bring this to Joe for me."

Skimming, I saw they'd been on Minerva a hundred and twenty days. "Is tonight soon enough? I have to turn in my loaner truck before the mechanic closes and meet Doug at the Dogleg."

Emmet blinked for okay.

"I've been meaning to ask, too, if you've had any sabotage lately. Are your drill-collar clamps right side up?"

"Not so's you notice. Keepin a eye on them clamps."

"We've been lucky about the tule fog. I've seen it sock in solid for months – you too, I bet."

"Knock on wood when you say *tule fog*."

I knocked on the fake wood of the trailer wall. Deadpan, Emmet knocked on his own head and took another drink of 7Up. Finally I had to say something.

"You must be the only teetotaler in the oil fields."

Rocking back in his chair, Emmet pointed at the rig through his window. "Was a time in my life, little sister, I only cared about two things – drinkin and drillin. 'Tweren't all that long ago neither."

"Can I ask why you stopped?"

"Come home knee-walkin drunk one night and the wife says, 'Big boy, it's me or that whiskey bottle – you choose.' Quit cold turkey. Keep the last fifth I ever bought in the toolbox of my truck as reminder. I believe I shortened that woman's life with neglect. I believe I did."

He rocked his chair. After the neck-hug incident I knew better than to offer any sympathy.

"You weren't a fan of Granpap, were you?"

Looking out at the rig, Emmet made a murmph noise.

I just nodded. Emmet was getting super-easy to read. This murmph was a no – and I shouldn't bug him for more because that's all he was going to say about Jim Whitehead now or ever.

29

GAIN, I RUSHED to make an appointment with Doug, and again, I got a voice mail saying he'd been held up on official business and would meet me at the Dogleg when he could.

I hoped that meant the cops were making more progress. I wasn't sure if I was or not.

At six P.M. on a Tuesday the back room wasn't crowded. There were scattered dinner customers, a few people at the bar, and my crew – Richie, Kyle, and Lynn – drinking beer and playing eight-ball with Dean, the guy who worked derrick on daylights opposite us. Gerry saw me come in and flapped his towel. I didn't see Jan anywhere and prayed she was still out of town.

My guys waved their cues. I waved back as I crossed the room and climbed on a stool. Gerry came down to serve me. Looking right and left, he said first thing, "How's Joe?" in a low voice. He didn't have to shout with the place not full.

I said, "He was fine at noon but you should call the house if you want the latest report."

"I tried a while ago and couldn't get around Alice. Can't get through to Joe's cell – reception's for squat over there."

"Try the house number now." I checked the time. "In theory Al-ice was going to Bakersfield."

Gerry went to the end of the bar to use the phone. I studied the dinner specials on the chalkboard until he came back.

"Cathy says he's stubborn as a mule, won't lay down and rest. Sounds like Joe." Gerry took his towel and wiped the bar top. "What can I get you?"

"I'd like to talk about my grandfather if you have a minute."

"There's something you want to see." Throwing the towel over his shoulder Gerry motioned me to follow him.

He ducked under the bar and led me across the room, around the empty pool tables, to the side wall. That wall was like the other Dogleg walls – rough timber and covered with pictures and objects in oil-field and western themes. The only light came from the stained-glass Budweiser lamps hanging over the pool tables, so Gerry lifted a framed photograph off its nail, stepped to the end pool table, and held the picture under the light.

He said, "I forgot it was here until the boys knocked it off in the brawl Friday night."

The colors of the photograph had faded with age. Three men were standing with a piece of machinery, surrounded by the Westside desert. I recognized a jowly, coarse-looking Ray Parkerworth Senior – and a young Joe in cowboy shirt and jeans. Gerry put his finger on the third man. It was Granpap, looking glamorous as usual in an expensively tailored overcoat. He had a fat cigar in one hand and his dress Stetson in the other.

I said, "When was this taken?"

Turning the picture over, Gerry showed the date. December of 1965. He said, like I didn't know:

"Joe, Ray, and Jim were thick as thieves. Jim designed the first small-scale steamflood for Wilson Flats. Boosted their recovery rate to fifty percent."

"Can I have this to look at?"

Gerry handed me the picture. "Have it to keep with my compliments, dear. Now if you'll excuse me . . ."

A group had walked in from the street. Gerry headed back to the bar, signaling the waitress to seat the new people. I hurried back with him.

"Did Granpap make any enemies while he was working in Wilson?"

Gerry eyed me enigmatically as he ducked under the bar. He wasn't a moose like the Oklahoma guys and I'd gotten a straight, level look I couldn't interpret except that it wasn't an instant negative. Sliding onto a stool, I leaned the picture against the chrome thing that held ketchup and salt.

I said, "Mark Bridges hates Joe. He also hates *me* and it seems to be on account of Granpap. Last night he called me a rich bitch and told me to leave town and I want to know why."

The waitress arrived with a big drink order and Gerry got busy filling it. Watching him work, I laughed on the inside about *rich*. I'd thought about asking someone for a per diem to cover the cost of Kenny Mills's murder investigation. It wasn't cheap to run a pickup truck, and my rig savings were draining away fast.

Gerry came back wiping his hands. "Mark's a . . ." Gerry searched for a word and couldn't find one, probably because he wanted to keep it clean.

"Emmet says he's a bone-lazy good-for-nothin like his daddy."

"That would be correct." Gerry smiled without teeth. "Mark hates Joe because his dad hated Joe. Mark's dad hated Joe because they broke out in the oil fields together then Joe drilled Lucy Boyd for Ray and the rest is history."

I got it. "And Granpap made Joe even richer with small-scale steamflood so Bridges's father hated Granpap too."

Gerry shook his head. "More than that. Without Jim there'd be no Balch Oil today."

"What? What about Wilson Flats? I thought Parkerworth Oil owned that production."

"It does—it did. But Ray was negotiating to sell Wilson Flats to Shell because output was already dipping and the new steamflood was designed for the big fields like Midway-Sunset and Kern River, where increased production would pay for the upgrade to steam—pipes, injection wells, generators—"

Gerry had cranked into lecture mode.

Half listening, I zoned out the engineering and geologic arcana and added what Gerry said to what I already knew.

Most of the county's crude oil was heavy, which meant it was harder to get out of the ground than lighter-weight crudes. When initial production peaked in terms of barrels per day, you might've produced 10 percent of the oil in the reservoir, and the rate was downhill from there. In the 1960s, Joe, running Parkerworth Oil at the time, heard about Granpap's work with secondary recovery in the older oil fields south of L.A. Granpap had been involved in experiments with water- and fireflood, then steamflood, and Joe invited him to Wilson to discuss a feasible steamflood method for Wilson Flats.

Gerry was saying, "Steamflood isn't an exact science. Steam's injected underground to heat and move the oil, but steam doesn't know where lease boundaries start and end. Jim told Joe right off the bat, Let the big guys steam the west extension of Wilson Flats that borders North Belridge —"

Gerry reminded me of Richie on tour. Richie would overexplain technical stuff when I had a job to do and only wanted the bottom line, like, Is it safe to spray soap on this dealybob?

I broke into the monologue.

"Sorry to interrupt, but it sounds like Granpap may've stepped on a few toes if small producers were selling to Tidewater and Shell not knowing that neighboring leases would benefit from steamflood. Or if people were jealous of Joe's initiative and charismatic Tex-Canadian consultant."

"Jim wasn't a diplomat, I'll tell you that for free. He was a plain-talking engineer with no patience for fools. Old-style oil-field Jim was — they don't make them like that anymore."

Smiling, I quoted from a book about the history of the Alberta oil and gas industry. "'Whitehead was a master of the colourful and inventive maledictions of the oil fields and relished their boisterous use.'"

Gerry nodded. "He cut a wide swath in Wilson. To answer your question, Jim did step on toes. Excuse me again —"

The waitress had called for help as more dinner customers rolled in. Rapping his knuckles on the bar, Gerry walked away.

I tilted the photograph to study Granpap. He died the year I was born but I'd grown up with his sacred memory and a million stories about him.

My father's stories always focused on Granpap's oil knowledge and favorite dicta: "As Pap used to say . . ." The picture of the Spindletop gusher that hung in Father's office had belonged to Granpap. When I was five I asked what the picture was and got my first lesson in the oil business. My father said, "*This* is the real beginning of the oil industry right here. It wasn't Drake's well, Titusville, Pennsylvania, in 1859. It was Spindletop – 1901, Beaumont, Texas. Pap used to say, 'Every schoolchild should know the name Spindletop. It's as important to the history of the United States as the Declaration of Independence and Appomattox.'"

My grandmother didn't have a clue what Granpap did as far as I could tell. Her stories were always about power, money, fame, and her reflected glory. The Great Jim Whitehead: Man of Myth and Legend.

From Evelyn I'd heard about Granpap catching malaria in a Venezuelan jungle, buying the Colt .41 revolvers because of Bonnie and Clyde, and getting up in Winston Churchill's face over oil for the war effort. When I moved to L.A. for my newspaper job, she told me about a dinner party at the home of the Jimmy Stewarts. That's the kind of thing Evelyn said: "the home of the Jimmy Stewarts." She remembered exactly what the wives had on and the bland compliment Stewart paid her. I'd asked what year it was because I wondered what movie he was filming; I'd thought it would be cool if it was *Vertigo*. My grandmother couldn't pinpoint the year – 1965 or '66, she thought, based on the outfit she wore. She said the men didn't talk about the picture business anyway. They talked about oil.

I scooped some ice out of my water glass and pressed it on my nose.

When my love for the oil business flipped over to hate, it wasn't just because of the aborted rigpig attempt. It was also based on ambivalence about Granpap. He was supposed to be so great but in private he was violent, tyrannical, and alcoholic, secrets hidden by the family that I eventually figured out from various hints and from my father's domestic style. Granpap was also a misogynist – a fact no one hid – and his contempt for women was exemplified by Evelyn, a silly snob half his age whose classic complaint was they never found oil near decent department stores, the only exceptions being Dallas and L.A.

I smiled and took one finger to tickle Granpap under the chin. He really was glamorous, even in his sixties. He made Joe and Ray Senior look like a couple of rubes.

Doug tended to think that if anyone had made dangerous enemies in Wilson, it was Granpap, not Evelyn. I agreed with him. He'd suggested I call Evelyn to ask about Granpap's possible enemies. I told him Evelyn couldn't be counted on to tell the truth. Proof: she'd said Joe was nothing before my grandfather made him rich. Her job was keeper of the flame. Alice same. She'd instantly dismissed the idea that Granpap might have enemies up here.

Now Gerry was saying Granpap made too many enemies to count and I had to wonder what'd happened with Emmet. Had my grandfather been undiplomatic or boisterously maledictive? Did he step on Emmet's granite toes?

It was *something*, because I didn't see Emmet disliking a competent or foul-mouthed oil man for no good reason.

30

'D MOVED TO a high table for a view of the room. I'd eaten dinner and gotten aspirin from Gerry for my sore nose – and I was
back mulling the problem of Granpap when I heard a shout from
the pool tables.

Doug had walked in the street door and the Oklahomans had
spotted him.

Walking over to shake hands, he got introduced to a second table
of Oklahomans – guys who'd come off daylight tour at six. Then he
took Richie, Kyle, and Lynn aside for a talk. I saw Richie stick his
arm up like a periscope and point in my direction. Doug turned
his head and I waved. The huddle went on and seemed serious,
judging by Kyle's concentrated frown and glances Richie was darting around the room. At one point all three guys craned for a hard
look at me. After Doug finished, he passed through the crowd to
talk to Gerry. They had a longer conversation than buying a beer
or dinner required, and Gerry was nodding in a more than casual
way. Doug did finally get a beer, though, and threaded through the
people and low tables to come sit with me.

I said, "What was that all about?"

"Here's the face I fell in love with." He set his beer down and
touched the cut on my nose while I helped him off with his coat.

"What were you telling my crew? Did sheriffs get permission to wiretap?"

Loud moans came from the Oklahomans as someone sank a shot. Doug shook his head. "He's still doing the paperwork. The DA will review it tomorrow and they'll submit it to a judge."

"What about Bridges's cell phone rec—"

Doug interrupted, "I'm fried, baby—it's been a tough day. Let me drink this and eat something first."

He tipped the beer into his mouth and took a swallow. I moved the photograph of Granpap so Doug could see it and pointed down the line.

"Ray Parkerworth Senior. Joe. Jim Whitehead."

Doug shifted the picture to catch the light as his cell phone rang. "I'll probably have to get this." He fished in his jacket for the phone and, after checking the display, put the phone to his ear.

"Emmet, sir?"

Doug checked his watch. "Do you have the address? . . . Roger that . . . I'm at the Dogleg. I'll send one of your boys if that's all right with you . . . Very good. Keep me posted."

Punching the phone off, Doug put it down. "Mrs. Balch invited Bud to dinner at the Petroleum Club in Taft."

"Yow!"

"Hang on a second." Doug got up and went to talk to the pool players, specifically Lynn. I watched Richie pass Lynn the keys to his truck and Lynn rack his cue, grab his jacket, and head for the exit. Going to Taft, I imagined, to stake out Bud and Alice. Kyle detained Doug and I could tell from gestures that the guys wanted him to take Lynn's place at eight-ball. The waitress arrived with Doug's meal, blocking my view of the discussion. I asked her for hot coffee and another beer and she went away. Doug came back and sat down again.

I said, "My crew acts like you're their hero."

Doug reached for his napkin and fork, speared some salad, and ate. "Yeah, Richie's a friend for life. I told him to verify that the woman who claimed to be pregnant was actually pregnant. That's the oldest trick in the book – 'Marry me, I'm going to have a baby.' It turns out she was lying. If Richie'd thought of it sooner he could've denied the affair completely."

I squeezed Doug's arm. "I didn't know you were so cynical." Doug just shrugged, chewing.

"I can't believe how much the band o' bros likes you, though. You made an impression at that fight. Which reminds me – was Trey there?"

"He never comes to the Dogleg. The guys say he drinks over in Bakersfield and keeps to himself. Why?"

"Because I remembered something. Christmas Eve when Trey and I pulled Bobby and Richie apart, Trey said, 'Stupid fucking Okies.' Maybe he's the one agitating the crews, with Mark Bridges's help maybe. Was Bridges there Friday night?"

Doug nodded.

"Okay, see? Also, if Trey's neighbor thinks he's dealing, we have to consider a link to Kenny Mills and crystal meth."

Doug was agreeing as the waitress came with his beer and my coffee. I wrapped both hands around the mug and took a sip. *What I wouldn't give for a righteous big-city cappuccino.*

Doug said, "I like your Oklahomans too. When I was twenty I was the same guy as them."

"You? I don't believe it."

"Have I never told you why I joined LAPD?"

I shook my head, sipping coffee. Doug scooted his stool around so he could watch the street door while he talked and ate.

"You know that my bible when I was young was *Endless Summer*. My buddies and I dreamed of that life. Our only ambition was to travel the world looking for the perfect wave."

I remembered Doug and I discussing surf movies – *Endless Summer* being the mother of them all. He'd grown up near Huntington Beach, one of the towns in California called Surf City U.S.A.

Doug said, "Winter of our senior year at UCLA, my buddies and I got into a war. The offshore storms were sending in waves like nobody'd ever seen on our stretch of coast – ten- and twelve-foot waves, sets that wouldn't quit. Word got around and pretty soon outside guys were showing up from as far away as Santa Cruz. We had a shack at the beach that belonged to parents of one of the guys we used as a crash pad in the summers. We took turns ditching class and sleeping there nights, rolling out at sunrise to protect our territory. My buddies even stopped smoking dope – that's how serious the situation was."

On *dope,* I raised my eyebrows facetiously. Doug claimed he'd never smoked marijuana.

"A few weeks of this and things were hostile. Guys were messing with each other's rides, their cars, their dogs. Someone slashed my wetsuit I left hanging out. Boards went missing – my girlfriend gave another girl a black eye."

"I thought surfing was all groovy and laid-back and mystical, dude."

"Sure, yeah, that's the official line, and you can certainly get into some mind-bending shit with the ocean if you're open to it. But the water's no different from land. You'll find angry guys out there, and lost souls – idiots – ego, bad character. Immature kids like myself at that age – think you know everything."

Doug reached for his beer and took a drink. He'd managed to keep eating between sentences.

"It isn't easy to stage a crash – you're dealing with a number of variables and you don't want to get hurt yourself. These were also bigger waves than most of us were used to, *heavy* waves. This one guy, though, a real thug from up north, didn't turn turtle when he should have. I saw the whole thing and still can't say if he did it on purpose or not. His board kicked up and clipped my buddy, knocked him off his board, and he hit the water wrong."

Doug slapped one palm on the table. "A wave just crushed him. He's in a wheelchair, paralyzed from the waist down."

"Holy cow." I winced. "You've never mentioned this friend."

"Yeah, I have. Dave."

"The real estate agent in Long Beach with the five hundred kids and surf trips to Australia?"

Doug nodded. "Dave was always happy-go-lucky – he's a great guy. But his crash was the end of paradise for me. I went kind of crazy for a while. We all went kind of crazy. One of our buddies gave up surfing and became a Mormon. Out of the blue I decided I was going to be a cop – not a cop, a homicide investigator."

"Why that as opposed to Mormonism or some other extreme life choice?"

Nudging me with his knee, Doug smiled.

"It took me years to figure out why, yeah. I think now it's because I seriously wanted to kill the guy who hurt Dave and it shocked me, like I didn't know who I was anymore. The law and the uniform felt like protection against chaos. A lot of guys go into police work for that reason. I also wanted a job that demanded everything I have in the way of brainpower and guts and muscle, like surfing. I didn't know then how tough the work would be on the emotions. But I found out reading water trains you to observe closely out to the horizon, back to the shore, down to the ripples under your board. Waiting for the right moment on the right wave teaches patience and to make up your mind in a split second. You sit, you sit, you sit, you sit, then paddle like hell –"

A loud chant started up from the pool tables. Doug stopped talking as we both looked over. Something had set the Oklahomans off and they were chanting in a chorus:

"'I don't say *fear* the gas! I say *respect* the gas!'"

They pounded their cues on the floor, toasted the ceiling, each guzzled a mouthful of beer, and chanted louder:

"'*I don't say* fear *the gas! I say* respect *the gas!*'"

Gerry called from behind the bar, "Boys, that's enough!" He was amused, though.

Richie pounded his cue and toasted Gerry, shouting, *"To Emmet!"* The Oklahomans shouted behind him, *"Old Iron Ass!"*

They drank their beer, wiped their mouths, and cracked up laughing. Doug smiled and started to finish his thought. Then the laughing stopped abruptly and we both sat straighter to see why.

Mark Bridges had walked in from the Dogleg's rear entrance.

The room didn't freeze exactly – there were more people in it besides us and the Oklahoma guys. But the pool tables went quiet and I could suddenly hear the song on the jukebox and the hum of other conversations.

Richie flashed a look across at Doug. The light was just good enough to make that possible and we were sitting up high. Doug acknowledged his look, turned, and flashed a look over to Gerry. Gerry nodded. The signals were as clear as semaphore if you were paying attention. Bridges wasn't. He was in tunnel vision, probably desperate for a drink. Beelining for the bar, he climbed on a stool and switched his baseball cap around backwards.

Richie gave his pool cue to Kyle and walked away. He could've been headed to the washrooms, which were in the rear by the exit. But I knew he wasn't.

I whispered, "Richie's going for Bridges's truck."

Pushing his plate aside Doug leaned into me, whispering, "I'm looking for Joe's guns and the Colt that shot up the trailers." He kept his eyes on Bridges's fat back.

I watched Gerry wipe a clean glass, pour Bridges his usual draft beer, and set the glass in front of him with a toweled hand. It was subtle – Gerry hadn't touched the glass himself. I looked at Doug, thinking, *Fingerprints.*

Doug whispered, "Fingerprints. Bridges has no record, and sheriffs are trying to match unidentified prints from the Balches'. Tell me about your day –"

"Here's Richie already."

As he crossed the room, Richie caught Doug's eye and shook his head, mouthing, *Locked.* Doug held up two fingers and nodded. Richie continued to the pool tables and grabbed his cue, saying something behind his hand to Kyle.

Doug said, "The cab and toolbox are locked. They'll go to plan B at my signal."

"Don't get the guys in trouble, Detective."

Doug nudged me with his knee and refocused on Bridges. "I want to hear about your day."

I launched in and covered what'd happened since noon, emphasizing the information I thought might be important.

I told him about Alice and *todo el dinero* and he remarked, "So

265

far we aren't finding any record of Parkerworth Junior's death in the Galliano area."

"What about the funeral home?"

"Yeah, they can't tell us a great deal. The problem is Port Fourchon's in the neighborhood, and don't correct my French. It's a hub for servicing the offshore platforms — lot of activity, big transient population. The large companies keep good records on a jobsite death — small ones not so good, and we don't want to ask Mrs. Balch where her brother worked as a welder. We don't want her to know we're looking into him. It's also rural Louisiana. Communication with local law enforcement from here is tough. Sheriffs may have to send a man."

Bridges tilted his head way back to drink the last drop of his beer. He set the glass down and Gerry whisked it away with a toweled hand, then reached under the bar for another glass to pour Bridges a fresh beer. Gerry made it all look natural and Doug nodded with satisfaction. Glancing over at the pool tables, I saw Richie looking to Doug for the sign. Doug shook his head at him.

I whispered, "What are you waiting for?"

"Insurance. Two glasses with fingerprints, not just one. Go on."

I finished my recitation with Audrey's stuff, small-scale steamflood, Granpap's colorful mouth and numerous potential enemies, including Emmet. When Doug did nothing but frown I asked him about their progress that day.

Besides initiating steps for a wiretap on Bridges, sheriffs had eliminated the three Schlumberger loggers as suspects for my attack. Meanwhile Wilson PD had tracked Suzette Mahin down in Antelope Acres. They'd attempted an interview but she was babbling and they sent her to Bakersfield on a seventy-two-hour psychiatric hold. She did maintain that her father murdered Kenny Mills so, reluctantly, the cops talked to Hilary Mahin. Mahin could account for his whereabouts during the time frame of Mills's death: he'd had a late night wrapping presents and decorating a tree. Still, the cops thought Suzette's accusation might indirectly be true if her father was involved in some conspiracy at Minerva.

Richie looked over for the umpteenth time. Doug caught his eye and nodded *go*.

Backhanding Kyle with his knuckles, Richie racked his cue and waited for Kyle to rack his. That left Dean alone at the pool table, but Dean knew something was up and just bent to make a shot. Richie and Kyle walked to the bar. We had them in profile as they cut through the people. With customers on both sides of Bridges there wasn't a lot of room for a confrontation. Richie took Bridges's left shoulder and tapped it as Kyle set up on Bridges's right. Bridges twirled around on his seat. Seeing who'd tapped him, seeing Richie's face, Bridges lost his friendly two-beers smile.

Gerry came down the bar to make a triangle of standing men while Richie started to talk. I saw Gerry glance at me and realized suddenly there was more to this than strong-arming Bridges for his keys.

"No!"

I lunged off my stool. Doug reached out and pulled me back, wincing at the wrench to his injured ribs.

I whispered, "You told those guys Bridges jumped me!" I tried to pull out of Doug's grip. "You're going to get them in trouble!"

Hanging on to my sleeve, Doug said quietly, "Listen, Ann. Bridges may be stupid but he knows who I am and even *he's* wondering why the cops haven't knocked on his door after last night."

Richie stepped back, making motions for Bridges to get up. Bridges wouldn't; he stayed glued to his stool. Looking around for help, he saw Gerry. But Gerry wore one of his tough-old-dude expressions and Bridges realized there'd be no help there.

Doug said, "I want Bridges to think we didn't go to the cops, that this is your revenge, the guys on your crew. Whoever he's working for or with, they're bound to be smarter than he is. He might not have, but if he did tell them he jacked you up outside my place and nothing happened, they might add two and two—"

Suddenly Richie grabbed Bridges by his sweatshirt and hauled him to his feet.

Bridges didn't resist although he could have—he was shorter

but he weighed about what Richie did. Richie held him in two fists as Gerry said something, dipping his head towards the rear. Richie jerked roughly and Bridges began to move. They disappeared through the doorway by the bar that led to the washrooms and back entrance, followed by Kyle.

I sat down again. Doug let go of me and whispered, "We have to do this, baby. I'm only sorry it can't be me. Besides, the guys wanted to do it – I gave them the choice and they volunteered. You understand."

I just shrugged because I did understand.

We waited and watched, not taking our eyes off the doorway. I sipped lukewarm coffee, Doug played with his beer glass, and Gerry kept tabs on traffic past the bar. Inside ten minutes, Richie and Kyle were back.

They were alone and looked the same as when they left except Richie's shirt was untucked in front. I didn't know what I was expecting – blood probably – and felt relieved. Blank-faced, the guys made their way across to our table, Kyle waving to get Gerry's attention. Gerry threw his towel over his shoulder and ducked under the bar to join us.

As he walked up, Richie let his disgust show. "Chickenshit wouldn't fight me. Sat his coward ass on the ground and wouldn't raise his hands to defend himself."

"I thought he was going to cry." Kyle grinned and gave me a light punch on the arm. "I guess ambushing a *girl* is all he can handle."

I gave Kyle a curse-of-the-stick-lizard claw. Doug said, "Where is he?"

Richie said, "Took off out of here in that pitiful truck." He lifted his shirt, pulled out a windshield-wiper blade he'd stuck down his jeans, and laid it on the table.

"No sign of firearms. We looked everywhere there was to look. Frisked him too, to make sure it'd be a fair fight. He wasn't packing."

I said, "Did he ask what you were looking for?"

Kyle said, "We didn't tell him." Richie said, "Asshole's none too bright."

Doug nodded. "Good work, men – excellent work. Thank you."
The guys nodded as Doug said to Gerry, "I'm buying a round for
the pool players."

"Keep your money, son. The Dogleg's buying."

Gerry slapped Richie and Kyle on the back and herded them
away. Doug slid the wiper blade over to me without comment.

31

THE DOOR TO Joe's suite was standing ajar. Security measures had been relaxed because Alice wasn't home.

I stopped in the hall as I heard Mrs. Mancuso laugh and say, "Tell the one about Red Adair. I love that joke."

If Joe responded, I couldn't hear it. I was pretty sure by now that Mrs. Mancuso was bona fide, but maybe I could be absolutely sure. I moved closer to the open door to eavesdrop.

Mrs. Mancuso said, "You do too remember, you old fuddy-dud! A Texas oil man dies and goes to heaven."

Cautiously, I peeked in.

They were sitting in the main room with the lights off, all the curtains open, in front of the glass door that wasn't boarded. As my eyes adjusted to the dark I could see the silhouette of Joe's wing-back chair, and the chair from the couch pushed up next to it with the outline of Mrs. Mancuso's poofy hair. The two of them were looking out at the rig. I could dimly see the lights of the derrick from where I stood.

Joe said, "Texas oil man dies and goes to heaven –"

Laughing, Mrs. Mancuso cut in, "Remember you used to say that wasn't the funny part?"

"Are you going to let me finish?"

A hand came up to pat the wing of his wingback chair. The diamond flashed in the light from the hall.

Joe said, "Texas oil man goes to heaven and God meets him at the Pearly Gates. Oil man says, 'Why, there's gates bigger than this in Texas.' God walks him inside and shows him the vast infinity of heaven. Oil man looks around and says, 'There's ranches bigger than this in Texas.' God gets a little impatient. He points down to the fires of hell and says, 'Anything bigger than *that* in Texas?' Oil man says, 'Nope—but we got an ole boy in Houston who'll put it out for you.'"

Joe's accent was perfect and Mrs. Mancuso went off into peals of bubbly laughter. The silhouette of her hair swayed and I smiled too, although I heard that joke in nursery school. I even met Red Adair once as a kid, at the Petroleum Club in Calgary during Stampede. When the laughter died down I knocked and called:

"It's Ann, Joe! I brought the drilling report!"

Mrs. Mancuso called, "Come in, Ann!" and I saw her stand up to turn on a light. Joe poked his head around his chair and deadpanned, "You get abducted by aliens between here and the lease?"

"If you weren't so old-fashioned Emmet could just e-mail it to you." Stepping inside, I closed and locked the hall door.

Joe said, "Put it on the desk."

I dropped the report on his desk as Mrs. Mancuso checked her watch, a gaudy silver bracelet.

"It's time for your pill, Joe, and I want you to get some rest. Jean's due here in a bit."

Joe grumped but he got up and, tightening the belt on his robe, moved for the bedroom more docile than I thought he'd be.

He said, "Have Luz put coffee on."

"It's all taken care of, darling—you go in and rest." Mrs. Mancuso shooed him through the pocket doors. "Don't forget your pill."

Sliding the doors shut, she dimpled at me. I said, "Alice may also be home soon. We should batten down for that."

I walked over to the glass doors and pulled the curtains shut, noticing Joe's new shotgun propped beside his chair. He seemed safe here with all the people but he wasn't taking any chances, I guessed.

Mrs. Mancuso said quietly, "We don't need to worry about Alice," as she pushed the other chair back to its place by the couch.

"Why not?"

Plumping cushions, she switched on another lamp.

"Alice knows about the divorce. They had a conference call with Dex this afternoon and Joe read her the riot act. You should've seen the way she behaved after you left. Poor Jeannie — Alice said *terrible* insulting things to her. She was horrified, and I couldn't believe it myself, even of Alice. She was intercepting Joe's calls and visitors. She intercepted his mail, look —"

Mrs. Mancuso pointed at Joe's desk, where there were some business letters with the flaps slit open.

"She bullied Luz too, forcing her way in here using Luz's knock, and tried to make Jeannie and I leave. Cathy swears she's trying to kill Joe with the stress."

I made a mental note of that idea. It wasn't inconceivable, given what I suspected about Alice's greed for every last Balch dime. I also now put Alice with Mark Bridges, Hilary Mahin, and Ron Bray in the column headed People Starting to Crack.

"Joe's asked her move out — take her furniture and everything and go, as soon as she can get organized. Until then she's confined to her end of the house under threat of a restraining order —"

Four soft knocks came from the glass doors, spaced to make two longs and two shorts.

Mrs. Mancuso put her finger to her lips. "It's Jeannie. She's early."

Glancing at Joe's bedroom, she tiptoed over to the glass doors and pushed the curtain aside to unlock the latch. Jean walked in with a cold blast of air, dressed for the cold and carrying a briefcase bulging with papers. If Jean was sneaking in the back way, I thought, we weren't completely unconcerned about Alice.

Mrs. Mancuso kissed Jean's cheek and then slid the door shut and locked it, putting her finger to her lips again and motioning towards the bedroom. She whispered, "Joe's resting."

I waved at Jean. She smiled at me as Mrs. Mancuso helped her with her coat, saying, "Coffee, Jean, dear?"

Jean shook her head. Perching on the arm of the chair, I said, "I have some questions for you both—"

Mrs. Mancuso shushed me, flapping one hand. "Lower your voice, lower your voice! Joe hasn't slept all day!"

Jean brought her briefcase and sat down on the couch. It looked like she was going to grade papers. I dimpled at Mrs. Mancuso by making cheek dents with my fingers and lowered my voice:

"Emmet hates Jim Whitehead and I want to know why."

Time stood still.

I'd hoped to get a reaction but hadn't expected anything so dramatic. I looked at Jean—I looked at Mrs. Mancuso. They weren't breathing.

Seconds ticked by . . . then time slooowly started to roll again.

Jean twisted around to look at Mrs. Mancuso. Mrs. Mancuso looked back at Jean. They knew something—that much I could tell. And whatever it was, it wasn't good. Biting her lip, Mrs. Mancuso came over and sat down beside Jean. She wanted to talk but didn't know where to start.

"It's . . . well . . . family isn't always . . ."

Jean's kind face went wrinkly with dismay. "Don't, Celeste."

I said, "It has nothing to do with heavy oil or small-scale steamflood, does it? Emmet and my grandfather?"

"Come sit by me, Ann."

Mrs. Mancuso patted the couch on her right side. Jean looked resigned as I got up to go over and sit. Sighing, she started to pull papers out of her briefcase then realized that was silly: this unpleasantness couldn't be avoided. She pulled out her cigarettes instead. Mrs. Mancuso took my hand and held it.

"Honey, you have to know that Jim was a movie star. When I was nineteen he was the sexiest man I'd ever met and he was old enough to be *my* grandfather."

She dimpled. "Oops, so was Ray Senior," and glanced at Jean.

"Today they have medical names for men like Jim but back then

273

we called them sex maniacs. If it was female and had a pulse, Jim made a play for it."

Jean blurted unexpectedly, "*Young* and female."

"*Young* and female, what else?" Mrs. Mancuso patted Jean on the leg. I was connecting the dots fast – zap, zap, zap.

"Emmet and Betty were just married and she and I were waitressing at the Dogleg. Jim made a play for Betty, and Emmet caught him with his hands all over her. She and Ray and I had to pull Emmet off him – it took the three of us *and* some customers. Back in those days Emmet was two hundred pounds of bouncing oil-field hell. He would've broken Jim's neck, let me tell you."

I wondered if this was what Gerry also meant when he said Granpap cut a wide swath in Wilson.

Mrs. Mancuso dimpled again, her eyes laughing. "Now, me – I didn't resist Jim. Neither did Alice, did she, Jeannie? It happened on the trip to Los Angeles, isn't that right? When you two were in high school? I've always wanted to ask."

Jean sat, looking unhappy, holding her pack of cigarettes like she wished desperately she could smoke.

Seeing that Jean wasn't going to answer, Mrs. Mancuso continued:

"Alice fawned over Evelyn on one of Jim's business trips here and they took her to Beverly Hills – her first trip ever down south. Remember how she'd changed when she came back, Jeannie? All her grown-up talk about the Polo Lounge and Chanel, parroting Evelyn, who was always so snippy to us poor country mice. I bet Jim seduced her right under Evelyn's nose and Alice was dumb enough to think she'd be the next Mrs. James Whitehead, or mercenary enough –"

Jean cleared her throat. "She was young, Celeste . . ."

"She never loved Joe. She never even liked him, not even this much." Mrs. Mancuso held up her pinkie and touched the tip of her red fingernail with her thumb. "She chased him and married him when she realized Jim would never divorce Evelyn."

Jean shook her head but it wasn't a no. It was her being sad for people.

Patting my hand, Mrs. Mancuso worked both dimples contritely. "I'm sorry if I've shocked you, Ann. Forgive me, but you asked."

I just shrugged. I wasn't shocked—or even surprised. My only thought was it didn't reduce the list of people who might've tried to strangle me on a chainlink fence.

There were running thumps out in the hall and a sudden frantic pounding at Joe's door.

"Celestay! Celestay! La señora come! ¡Viene ya!"

Luz was panting and only a heartbeat ahead of Alice, who said, "You're fired, Luz! Get out of the way!"

We heard a clunk-thump and all of us jumped up. Mrs. Mancuso started for the door. I leaped ahead of her and planted my back against the door to block it.

Knocking sharply, Alice called, "Joseph, we need to talk!" in a tone she was attempting to make sweet.

The pocket doors slid open and Joe appeared, putting on his trifocals. He looked muzzy, like he'd woken up from a sound sleep. With another sharp knock, Alice dropped the sweet and commanded, *"Let me in this instant!"*

Walking to the door, Joe signaled me to move aside. As I moved he snapped, "For Christ's sake, Alice, get a hold of yourself!"

"Don't curse at me like I'm well gang, Joseph Balch!" She rattled the knob. "Open this door!"

Joe thought about it, then twisted the lock and flung the door wide. Alice stalked in, face cold, smoothing her necklaces. She ignored Mrs. Mancuso but stopped at the sight of Jean, who stiffened for a verbal assault.

Joe said, "I should've divorced you a long time ago. I was too damn lazy—I regret it now."

Alice's face tightened. Coldly, she stared at him and her tone was chilling. "I will fight a divorce to my last breath."

"Dex told you the rules." Joe jerked his thumb up the hall. "Out."

Alice hesitated and Mrs. Mancuso moved closer to Jean as if to protect her. Joe jerked his thumb again.

Not looking at me, Alice said, "I want to speak to Ann," and turned on her heel and left.

I shrugged at everybody and followed her. Joe slammed the door behind us as Alice stalked up the hall and stopped outside my room. I came up and she took one step closer to keep the conversation between us.

"Ann, I need you to do something. It's very important."

"I will if I can. What is it?"

Alice was too refined to point a finger. She indicated Joe's suite with a lifted hand.

"You see now what I am forced to put up with. My husband, entertaining his mistresses in my home. Now that trashy woman has convinced him to divorce me. Joe has no desire to divorce me. I call Celeste trash, Ann, because she is trash, and do you know she made my brother trash? You've perhaps wondered why I rarely speak of Ray Junior and didn't waken you for his memorial service. It is because he rejected myself and the family and went away twenty-five years ago. He died in poverty and filth under a false name—he'd stolen another man's identity. Needless to say, I can hardly be proud of that."

I was nodding, making a sympathetic face, even if some of the story was twisted off the truth. She'd explained, though, why the cops weren't finding any record of Ray Junior's death in Louisiana. But I didn't ask for the name he died under: strategic mistake.

"As you know, I think of the Whiteheads as family. I think of you as the daughter I didn't have because *that* woman"—Alice glanced down the hall—"ruined my life. I've left Evelyn on her own in Los Angeles with my maid. What I want you to do is join her and keep her company while I straighten out the situation here."

Jesus, was I dense!

Alice was trying too hard to get me out of Wilson—*way* too hard. The Bridges incident wasn't public knowledge yet. But last week she'd said I was in danger. *She knew who attacked me under the trees.*

"I don't—"

Alice cut me off. "I'm aware that you go to work Sunday evening. I will have this settled much sooner."

How did she know my schedule at the rig? We'd never discussed it.

"It's not about work, Alice. There's the roughneck who died on my tour and I'm helping the cops—"

"Yes, yes, I've heard. You cannot tell me that is more important than your grandmother."

Out in the foyer the front door beeped. The alarm was set to beep if an exterior door opened: someone had come in from the driveway. Hearing voices, I looked up the hall.

Cathy Rintoul appeared in her nurse's uniform and carrying a pile of bedding. She smiled when she saw me—then saw Alice and gave her a neutral nod as she went on down and knocked her knock on Joe's door.

Next came Doug with our mud logger. Rain or shine, fog or heat, Bud wore his letter jacket and looked like a science geek, not a compulsive thrill jockey. Moving to give them room, I watched Alice for a reaction since she and Bud were just together for dinner. Alice had no reaction: her face stayed cold and tight. Bud was off in the clouds, not seeming to notice us, looking at the vintage oil-field photographs on the opposite wall.

As Doug passed he nodded at Alice, then tilted his head and eyes at me. He wanted me to come see him when I was done.

Waiting until the two men disappeared into Joe's suite, Alice said, "Who is that man?"

"Doug? I introduced you to Doug yesterday—"

"The other man, Ann. Who is he?"

Holy cow, I thought. *Whoa!*

Abruptly Alice took off, walking quickly up the hall towards the foyer. I took off after her.

"What's the matter, Alice?"

She threw "I forgot something" over her shoulder and walked even quicker. I followed to see where she'd go. She continued across the foyer and down the hall to her rooms. I heard the door slam, turned, and raced back to Joe's.

Mrs. Mancuso opened up at my special knock. Cathy had

dumped the bedding and was on her knees making a fire with Jean's help. The pocket doors to the bedroom stood open and Doug was behind the desk scanning oil news on the computer screen.

Going over to him I whispered, "What's up?"

Doug spoke into my ear. "Mrs. Balch offered to pay Bud's gambling debt in exchange for the logs on the wildcat. He's in there telling Joe about it."

"Two hundred and fifty-three thousand bucks?!" I was still whispering. "She pretended to me she didn't know who Bud was."

Doug lifted his eyebrows — his stone-cop-face equivalent of *Whoa!*

"If Bud's telling Joe, I guess it means he isn't part of the spy plot."

Doug made an ambiguous *huh-uh* noise. "Yeah, Bud barely knows Mrs. Balch. When she called him about dinner he wondered why and went to Emmet. Emmet told him to find out what she wanted."

"Emmet's the man." I nudged Doug. "Circle – of – Trust."

There was a knock at the hall door and Luz called, "Coffee!"

Mrs. Mancuso went to answer as I whispered, "Meanwhile, I think Alice knows who tried to strangle me, and Ray Parkerworth Junior died under a false identity."

Balancing a tray with coffeepot and cups, Luz came in and crossed to set it on the table.

"False identity?" Doug frowned.

Bud appeared in the bedroom door. He turned to say something to Joe, who was still inside.

"The drilling break's due soon and —" Bud broke off. "Joe?"

We heard a bang and a crash and a scary groan. Shouting, "Joe!" Bud darted into the back.

Luz screamed and everyone dived for the bedroom, jostling one another, bumping into furniture. Running around the desk, Doug barked, "Everybody, calm! Stay back! Let Cathy through!"

His arms out, he cleared a path for Cathy. I grabbed the desk telephone and started dialing 911.

From the bedroom Mrs. Mancuso cried, *"Oh, Joe, darling!"*

32

THE PARAMEDICS RUSHED Joe to Bakersfield unconscious. Alice insisted on riding in the ambulance with him and that was only a whiff of the nuttiness to come.

Everybody jumped in a vehicle and caravanned over at top speed – Celeste, Jean, and Luz in Celeste's truck – me, Cathy, and Bud separately. By the time we arrived at the emergency room they'd taken Joe somewhere else, but nobody would tell us where. Cathy tried to pry information out of the staff using her nurse credentials while I prowled the corridors for a glimpse of Alice. It occurred to Jean to call her son Mike to see if he knew someone who could get news for us. Around midnight we learned that Joe'd had a massive stroke and he was up in the intensive care unit – and it didn't look good.

The ICU was down a long hall and locked so it wasn't open and public like other parts of the hospital. I stayed downstairs to call Doug with the latest, then went up. As I stepped off the elevator, I saw Celeste, Jean, and Mike in a huddle outside the ICU. Bud and Cathy were sitting in the tiny waiting room off the hall – Luz wasn't in evidence. I walked down to the huddle and Mike reached for my arm to pull me in.

"We have a problem, Ann."

Through the glass windows of the unit, I could see Alice with a doctor. Inside, the ICU was a maze of glass so the nurses could monitor patients visually from a central area. There were maybe ten beds.

Mike was talking in a lawyer hush.

"Alice has no authority here. Mom is Joe's medical power of attorney. We can't reach Dex, and Alice won't let me in to explain the legal situation to her and the people in charge. We think, however, she'll allow you in."

Celeste and Jean were standing close together and looking so upset it was upsetting.

I stuck my hand out and waved to catch Alice's attention. I said, "Mike, I think Alice thinks Joe hasn't made a will and that she's going to get *todo el* Balch *dinero* —"

Celeste gasped, *"What?"*

"You know how Joe jokes about it — I think she's operating under that assumption. Is it a good moment to tell her she's wrong?"

Alice had spotted me waving. I pointed at my own chest and mouthed slowly, *I — want — to — see — Joe*. I pointed inside where she was.

Jean breathed a faint "No."

"I agree. In my judgment also, not a good moment." Mike shook his head. "Let's deal with first things first."

The automatic doors of the ICU slid open and an orderly in blue scrubs said, "Miss Whitehead? Mrs. Balch has asked you to come in."

Pocketing my phone, I followed him inside. It was loud in there. I'd imagined a funereal quiet but the machines were loud, the constant announcements over the PA were loud, and medical personnel were hustling and bustling everywhere.

The orderly led me past Alice down to where they had Joe. I wanted to cry when I saw him. The room was crammed with machines beeping and displaying — red lights and ghostly green lines in the semi-dark. Joe was in a big bed hooked up to the machines and to IV drips and catheters. His eyes were closed and his mouth slightly open and he looked shrunken, almost dead already. I put my hand on the sheet and felt my throat close up and tears start to fall.

Alice walked in, smoothing her necklaces. "They've done one CAT scan thus far. The damage to his brain was severe."

She was speaking in a brisk tone.

"They'll do another CAT scan in twelve hours to see if his brain has deteriorated further." Alice tapped the metal frame of the bed. "Already at this stage, the doctor says, even if he regains consciousness he'll be a vegetable the rest of his life."

I cleared my throat. "Could you be *any* more brutal about it, Alice? I mean, *Jesus.*"

"Those are the facts. We must get used to them."

"All right, since we love facts —" I crooked a finger at her. "Who's looking after Joe?"

Drying my eyes, I walked out of the room checking around for somebody official. Alice hurried after me. I spotted the tall white coat she'd been talking to earlier. He was leaning on the nurses' station reading a chart and I went over and butted in without introducing myself.

"Doctor? Mrs. Balch has no authority with Mr. Balch —"

"It's not true!"

"The woman outside in the hall, Jean Garcia, is Mr. Balch's medical power of attorney —"

"It's not true! I'm his wife!"

Alice was trying to insert herself between me and the doctor. I evaded her, stepping back and to the side. "The man with Mrs. Garcia is a lawyer and —"

"He isn't *my* lawyer! He isn't my husband's lawyer!"

The doctor was recoiling, his expression neutral, not wanting to get involved or pick sides. The nurses and aides had paused to spectate.

The doctor said, "If that's the case the hospital will need proper legal —"

Alice shrilled, *"She's a liar! I am Mrs. Balch!"*

Turning, I headed for the entrance doors. They opened for me automatically. Celeste, Jean, and Mike were waiting in an anxious knot. They'd seen enough through the windows to guess how successful my mission had been.

I said, "You're going to have to get Dex. Alice won't be dislodged and the hospital can't do it without proper legal something."

"What did they say about Joe?" Jean was whispering.

I reached out to tug on her wrist. As I looked at her and Celeste and Mike, my eyes filled with tears.

Wednesday it was semi-anarchy until Dex arrived. He'd gone down to L.A. for meetings and couldn't get back to Bakersfield until early afternoon.

Alice had slept on a cot in Joe's room. She'd tried to send Luz to Wilson for her cosmetics and nightwear, and Luz had cursed her. Bud and Mike went home, but Celeste, Jean, Luz, and Cathy stayed and opted not to go to a hotel. The ICU waiting room had just a few uncomfortable chairs so they fanned out through the floor finding couches to sleep on. I was delegated to keep watch because I didn't sleep at night, and because everybody still thought I had power with Alice. They were mistaken: Alice was now my enemy. And I was hers. I amused myself for part of the night thinking of ways to frame her for Kenny Mills's murder.

Visitors started showing up at eight in the morning. Jean and everybody, looking ragged, had gone out for breakfast and I was alone to greet the first group, a contingent of Balch Drilling hands with flowers and cards led by a Latino toolpush who read a speech about how much they liked Joe as a man and a boss. I soft-pedaled Joe's condition while Alice watched from inside the ICU. She frowned at the working class and was afraid, I thought, to come out in case I tried to prevent her physically from going back in . . . a legitimate fear.

Emmet and Hilary Mahin stepped out of separate elevators as the Balch guys were leaving. Emmet had shaved and come from the rig in his overalls, and Mahin was wearing black boots. He looked past me, wanting to ignore me, and obviously not speaking

282

to Emmet after yesterday's violence. I spread my arms wide to stop them in the hall together.

Emmet rumbled, "How's he doin, little sister?"

"Boots!"

I looked over my shoulder. Alice had emerged from the ICU far enough to stand on the threshold between the open glass doors.

"I must speak with you!" It was an order.

Not budging, arms still spread, I said, "Jean is Joe's medical power of attorney but Alice took over last night and she's running amok. We're waiting for Dex to come slap her down."

Alice called, "My husband is here!"

Mahin said to me, "Is he awake?"

"I don't know. Alice won't let us in and the staff won't answer questions. We have no standing."

"Well, I'd better go then. I'll find out."

Mahin made a move and I let him pass and head on up the hall. The elevator doors opened and Celeste and Jean got off. Spotting Emmet, they rushed over with worried smiles.

Celeste put her arm partway around his huge middle and hugged him. "It's bad, dear. Very bad."

Jean nodded. Emmet got the granite-eye and Celeste hugged him harder. I handed Jean the speech the Balch toolpusher had written. As Jean read it tears started falling and she dabbed at them with a tissue.

Boots Mahin rejoined us almost immediately. He had a funny look on his face – funny for him because he was always so businesslike and bland. In someone else I would've called it shocked disbelief.

He said, "Alice just told me to accept West Coast's offer on Balch Oil and find a buyer for Balch Drilling while I was at it."

"Emmet, come here! I need to speak to you!"

Alice had reemerged to stand on the threshold. Emmet made a big show of turning his back, shifting on his feet like an elephant. He took up half the hallway.

Mahin said, "She told me I'm in charge of Minerva no.1. I'm

283

supposed to tell you" – Mahin glanced at Emmet – "I'd be sending out a full-time company man. He'd use Joe's trailer and have unrestricted access to the accounting and logs, and final say in decisions."

I looked at Emmet, thinking, *That's what Mahin wanted – that's why Emmet threw him off the lease yesterday.* Emmet understood my look and held up one finger.

"Little sister – we is all on the same side now."

Mahin said, "Has she lost her mind?" in a dazed voice.

Gerry, Jan, and more Wilson people stepped out of the elevator as we heard the clatter of wheels and the swish of uniforms, soft-soled shoes, and sheets. Two aides were wheeling Joe towards us on a gurney. Breaking apart, we flattened against the walls to let them through. Alice was hurrying behind the gurney. When she saw Jean reach out to touch Joe, she commanded:

"Don't you dare, Jean Taylor! Don't you dare!"

I wouldn't have thought Emmet could move so fast. He stepped in front of Alice to block her path, saying, "You girls go on. I got her."

Celeste and Jean took off, crowding the gurney for a look at Joe. Alice tried to push Emmet, saw it was futile, and retreated back into the ICU. Joe was taken to the far end of the hall through a wide door with warning strips and an orange sign, AUTHORIZED PERSONNEL ONLY, and he disappeared.

He came back – but we didn't learn until early afternoon that he'd been taken for a second CAT scan and his condition had gone from bad to worse.

Loads of people had stopped by. Alice had picked and chosen who would see Joe and tried to have the hall cleared, which made Gerry almost punch her. But Dex finally arrived with the magic papers. We heard Joe's CAT scan results and Alice was removed, threatening to sue as she left the floor. And visitors kept coming. Balch employees. Joe's colleagues and business associates. Hunting and drinking cronies. Relatives. Guys from Taft and L.A. and farther south. Jean stayed inside with Joe while Celeste greeted people in the hall, advising Joe's close friends not to go in. He wouldn't want to be seen or remembered like that: it wasn't him anymore.

Late Wednesday Doug came to take me for a meal. Time and space had lost their shape and I didn't care that a judge had authorized the wiretap and the sheriffs would go up on Bridges's cell phone Thursday morning. I didn't care they weren't tapping Bridges's landline – I didn't care who they'd interviewed since yesterday – I'd forgotten who Kenny Mills was. I had to care about one piece of news, though. I'd been summoned to court Thursday to testify in the case of the Kwik Gas armed robber. The trial had been postponed twice and I was finally needed. I told Doug I refused to go; I'd pretend I didn't get the message. Doug went stone cop on me and said attendance wasn't optional.

I rushed back from court Thursday afternoon and Joe's condition had worsened to grim. Jean had withdrawn life support and she was ushering friends in to say their farewells.

When it came my turn, Jean stepped outside to leave me alone with Joe. I stood beside the bed, resting my hand on his shoulder, seeing him how he'd been in the past. There were too many memories going back too far – so much to say that there was nothing to say. I knew how he felt about me and he knew how I felt about him although we'd never, ever talked about it. He'd die if he knew I was standing there crying my eyes out. The thought made me smile, and I realized I did want to promise we'd bring Minerva in for him. I started to bend down, then stopped. No, that wasn't what I wanted at the very last.

Leaning down close, I whispered in his ear:

"Joe, me wuffneck."

Friday went by in a blur.

The terms of Joe's living trust became known and it blew everyone away except Jean, who already knew.

Joe had created a foundation for energy education and research. He'd made Jean head trustee, and Emmet and Celeste co-trustees. I'd been put in charge of field operations at such a generous salary I was stunned. I'd never expected anything from Joe – it never even occurred to me. He'd put everything he owned in the foundation: Balch Oil, Balch Drilling, his Balch stock, and his cut of the community property. When Alice turned twenty-one, she'd signed a post-marital agreement that put the businesses out of community bounds. She'd persuaded herself the agreement wouldn't stand if Joe died intestate. But he hadn't, and instead of hundreds of millions of dollars she was looking at maybe twenty-five or thirty. Joe had also inserted a no-contest clause in the trust. If Alice sued and lost, she'd lose everything.

Alice went bananas when she heard. It took all of us to contain her while everything else was going on at the house. Phones were ringing; people were dropping by with food and drink; out-of-towners were wanting a place to stay until the service; relatives were trolling for expensive mementos. Typical of Joe, he'd asked for no fuss. He wanted to be cremated as quickly as possible and his ashes poured down Minerva's drillpipe. Alice flipped over that stipulation. She didn't want a tacky rig-floor memorial – *especially* not on Minerva. Just to have some peace, Jean agreed to negotiate the point. The concession outraged us but we didn't argue. Jean was holding up bravely, but we were all a breath away from total hysteria. One more problem and we would've started screaming and never stopped.

Our pain and upset worked perfectly for the cops, though. The Kenny Mills case was busting wide open.

Doug was running back and forth between Wilson and the sheriffs' wire room in Bakersfield. Stupefied from lack of sleep and exhausted from emotion, I still registered what he told me even if I couldn't feel any excitement.

They'd started surveillance on Mark Bridges Thursday morning. Immediately they captured calls to two people significant for our purpose: Dan Fox at West Coast Energy and Alice. The Alice call allowed the sheriffs to apply for wiretaps on her, which were in place by Friday morning. They were surveilling her landline in Wilson and her L.A. numbers, cell and home. I hadn't known the strict rules around wiretapping. Captured calls were privileged communication and Doug wasn't allowed to be specific about what the sheriffs were getting. By Saturday, however, they were getting enough that they needed me to identify a voice and explain certain references if I could.

It was Doug's idea to take me over to Bakersfield late instead of early Saturday. I'd finally fallen asleep and I thought he'd just wanted to let me sleep, until we got to sheriffs' headquarters in an outlying area by railroad tracks and grain elevators.

Walking in the lobby, Doug showed his LAPD credentials to the uniform cop behind the glass.

"Evening, Deputy. Detective Zelkovic or Ramirez still here?"

"They're gone for the night, sir. They said you'd be coming. They left a list."

The deputy buzzed us in. Thanking him, Doug walked me through an underlit maze of desks, offices, and corridors in a practically empty building.

He stopped at an unmarked door in an anonymous hallway, punched a code, pushed the door open, and checked inside. The room was dark.

A weirdness in his manner prompted me to say, "Why are you being furtive?"

"Because I'm about to do something unethical."

I was too surprised to react. Pulling me into the room, Doug hit the lights, making sure the door shut behind us. The room was windowless, white, and institutional. It had two curving tables with stations for computer monitors and a lounge area with vending machines and a flat-screen TV.

Doug went to the nearest station and turned on the computer. There was a piece of paper beside the keyboard and a pair of earphones hanging over the screen. He signaled me to come put the earphones on.

"You worked this case harder than anyone – you deserve to hear a little of this. Sit down."

Taking the chair, he switched it around and made me sit with my back to the screen. He pulled a second chair over for himself.

"There are civil penalties if an unauthorized person hears a captured call. It won't affect the criminal prosecution but sheriffs are concerned about the kind of attorneys Mrs. Balch can afford. First I'm going to play you two snippets, okay?"

"Authorized?"

"Authorized, yeah – for the good of the case."

I nodded, settling the earphones more comfortably. Doug was consulting the list of cues the sheriffs had left and hitting keys. He said, "This came in this morning."

Suddenly a familiar voice hit my ear:

"Meet me at Narducci's at two . . ."

Doug said, "Who's speaking?"

"That's Trey."

"Are you sure? I can play you other snippets."

"Sure – it's Trey. He doesn't talk much on tour but that's definitely him. He must like the Basque bars."

I turned my head and saw Doug nodding.

"He's our guy then. His cell phone is listed under another name in care of a mail drop. Sheriffs sent a man to photograph the Narducci's meet – they needed to put the voice with the face. Now this."

"Wait, Doug. What do you mean, our guy?"

But another familiar voice was already in my ear. Mark Bridges:

". . . steal samples off the shale shakers and smuggle them out . . ."

I said, "That's Bridges. Is he talking to Trey?"

"He's talking to an individual named Gregory Woodward – Greg. Do you know who that is?"

"Probably a local hand on the daylight crew opposite mine. There's a Greg who hangs around the Dogleg and we've seen Bridges approach him. Is he spying? Samples are cuttings coming out of the hole in the mud – rock cuttings."

Doug pulled out a pen and scribbled a note. "It looks like the scouting is just between Fox and Bridges. Joe's men, Mahin and Bray, haven't been referred to."

I said, "Is it unethical to tell me that?"

"Yes, it is, yeah. And there's more." Doug set his pen aside and glanced at the door. "Mrs. Balch hired Trey back in the fall to shut Minerva down."

My jaw dropped. "Alice?! *Alice* did?!"

"Yeah, she's been paying him to sabotage and steal at the lease – to create any kind of trouble he can. He's been inciting anti-Oklahoma feeling among the hands."

"And Kenny Mills?"

"It appears that Mills had an attack of paranoia in the fog and came at Trey with a hammer. But we have no confession, no direct testimony. We have Bridges calling it self-defense."

"That's not reliable – he got it from Trey." I realized I was still wearing the earphones and took them off.

"No, it isn't, but no other motive has been offered. Trey's been blackmailing Mrs. Balch since the murder – that's for money on top of what she's paying him. As long as she doesn't report what she knows, she's complicit."

My mind was clicking into gear and I found my excitement rising as I saw the picture crystallize.

"Why doesn't Alice call his bluff? Why doesn't she dare him to go to the sheriffs? *He's* the killer . . . Then it was Trey who shot up the trailers . . . Did he jump me at the back gate? It must be. I was right – Alice knew!"

"According to the wiretap, Mrs. Balch didn't instigate or approve that incident. She did give Trey the alarm code to your house. Part of his mandate was to put pressure on Joe in his weakened health. Nobody has said Mrs. Balch wanted Joe dead. It has been implied, however."

"*Why aren't these assholes in jail? Why isn't Trey in the gas chamber?*" Sitting forward, I grabbed Doug and shook him. "Does LAPD have an unsolved murder you can frame Alice for? They shortened Joe's life, sure as hell! I *hate* them!"

"Calm down, baby, calm down. I know."

Doug pressed me gently back into the chair. "Arrest warrants have been prepared for Mrs. Balch and Bridges. But sheriffs can't make a case solely on the testimony of coconspirators and they have nothing substantive from Trey on tape. If they make arrests now, Trey will do a flit, and it's Trey we want."

I said, "How did the triangle form? How did Alice recruit Trey, and Trey hook up with Bridges, and Bridges hook up with Alice?"

"They'll start rolling over on each other once they're in custody." Doug scooted closer to the table and hit keys on the keyboard.

I said, "Does Trey have a criminal record?"

"They'll run him through the databases now." Doug hit more keys. "Sheriffs are expecting a break any time. Because of the terms of Joe's trust, Mrs. Balch has realized the game's over and she's attempting to fire Trey. He's rejected the figure she offered and jacked his price up. Look at the screen for me quickly, Ann. These are all calls from today."

I turned around and watched Doug run his finger down a column of Call To and Call From telephone numbers. It was mostly two numbers going back and forth. One of them was the 323 area code – Alice's cell.

Doug said, "Mrs. Balch is using Bridges to negotiate the deal. Put your earphones on. Trey's talking to Bridges."

I put the earphones on.

". . . tell that cheap bitch a million bucks. A million in cash and I walk away. She has it – the old bastard's croaked –"

Snatching off the earphones, I leaped up, wanting to strangle Trey and leave *him* for dead under the trees. Calling Joe an old bastard, that murdering lowlife.

33

I T WAS MY FIRST tour on in three weeks.

I'd missed the rig and was glad to be back at work Sunday evening. I probably hadn't missed the cold, hunger, or thirst – the
sweaty, smelly damp – or the cramp I was about to get from the
scrub brush. And I *knew* I hadn't missed my pinchy hardhat. But
I looked forward to the distraction and felt almost happy as I
changed clothes in the lean-to then crunched across the gravel towards the rig stairs, remembering just how loud the diesel engines
were. Kyle caught me at the bottom of the stairs and twanged,
"Back in the saddle again!" I bumped him with my cooler as he
joke-elbowed me aside to beat me up to safety meeting.

Richie, Lynn, and Trey were already in the doghouse. There was
also an extra guy – a directional hand stationed permanently to
watch a computer graph that tracked the path of the drill bit. He
was reading a Bible and the crew ignored him, so I did too. I set
my stuff on the bench and, grabbing my safety gear, went to stand
between Kyle and Lynn, opposite Trey. The cops were searching
Trey's house that very moment. They'd held off until Emmet confirmed his arrival at the lease.

Richie's instructions were brief.

"We're running in the hole. We'll break at eight thirty – Trey and
Pup'll clean the floor for Mr. Balch's service at nine. Questions?"

Richie always asked and there were never any questions. We stuck our earplugs in. Richie adjusted his safety gloves – Kyle and Lynn each put a chew of tobacco in his cheek. Trey started to zip his coverall and a peeved *meow!* came from somewhere.

Richie snapped, "Get rid of the cat! Emmet's told you!"

I looked across the circle, keeping my gaze at chest level. Inside his dirty orange coverall, under the *Steve,* Trey had sewn a pocket to carry a kitten. I could see its tabby head sticking out.

Trey gave Richie the thousand-yard stare and left the doghouse without a word. Richie did his ritual check of the top-secret computer screen as Kyle nudged me:

"Seriously, Pup – we're sorry for your loss."

The other guys nodded. I smiled at them and nodded back.

Sliding the steel door open, bracing for the cold, Kyle and Lynn walked out. Through the window I watched Kyle climb into his harness and start up the derrick, and Lynn head to the pipe rack. My first job that tour was to search Trey's clothes while the guys were tripping pipe.

Trey reappeared out on the floor.

He stuck an unlit cigarette in his mouth and pulled on his safety gloves as he walked over to where Lynn stood. Richie hit the throttle and they both looked into the derrick. I zoomed out of the doghouse, down the stairs, and across the yard to the changing hut.

Slipping inside, I hit the light switch and heard the kitten meow. Trey had made a bed for it on his coat but the kitten was shivering. I grabbed Richie's coat, scrunched it on the bench, and tucked the kitten between two folds.

Trey's coat was an old camouflage hunting jacket: I proceeded to search the pockets. The crew kept their valuables on them so I didn't expect to find a wallet. I did find an interior pouch especially sewn to carry a small animal. It was covered with cat fur. The lining of every other pocket was stiff and black with dried oil, and the pockets were bagged out of shape, as though Trey had carried heavy objects in them.

The door of the changing hut creaked.

I spun around, my heart thumping. It was Emmet. I hissed, "Don't sneak up like that, dang!"

Emmet stepped inside, scaring the kitten. It jumped off Richie's coat and skittered out the open door. Emmet bent stiffly and swiped at it with one hand, but too late.

"It'll find itself a heatin duct. What you got, little sister?"

I showed him Trey's jacket, pointing at a pocket I'd turned inside out. "All his pockets are greasy like this."

Emmet micro-frowned. "My small parts's gone missin that way – bet they's drivin off the lease."

Nodding, I put the jacket back on the bench the way Trey'd had it. Emmet rapped a knuckle on the locker with the cleaning supplies.

"Need the elevator, front stairs, and top doghouse spick-'n'-span for the service."

"I'm so glad Jean stood up to Alice in the end."

"Way I hear it, Alice backed off."

"Really?" I shrugged. "I must've slept through that twist."

Pushing on the door, Emmet stepped back outside. I stuck my head out behind him to ask, "Do you know what the plan is? Has Doug told you?"

"He's comin in plenty of time for Joe's service, with or without the sheriffs. Depends on where they's at with the search and warrants and such. Cain't arrest Alice afore we bury Joe – bad as she is, it wouldn't be right."

Slanting a glance up at the rig, Emmet rumbled, "Damn sorry bastard."

I thought he meant Doug until I looked up too. Trey was clearly visible in the doghouse window.

I said, "I better hurry."

Emmet tromped off. Getting my mop, bucket, and scrub brush, and the rubber gloves for dishpan hands, I carried everything across the yard and dumped it beside the powerwasher. I flipped the on switch, grabbed the wand, and dragged the hose over the accumulator lines to the front set of stairs. The stairs up to the floor were steep and narrow, slick white steel and open tread. I was halfway up, pulling the hose to the top, when Trey appeared on the landing outside the doghouse and started down.

I kept going towards him. He paused a few stairs above me and said, "You kiss that old Okie's ass pretty hard!"

I whipped the wand sideways, clanging it across the handrails to block his descent and shouting to make sure I was heard over the engines.

"Fuck you, Trey! I let your kitten out of the changing hut by accident and Emmet's trying to find it!"

My tone and the swearword startled him. For the first time since we'd worked together, Trey seemed to wake up to the reality of my existence. He lost the thousand-yard stare and aimed his gaze directly down at me.

Doing a Joe deadpan, I looked him straight back. Then I lowered the wand, shoved past him, and continued up the stairs pulling the hose.

People started showing up around seven o'clock. Things were in such disarray that nobody'd made a formal guest list, and at first, Tommy was barring everyone at the guard gate. He didn't know who, other than family and the obvious friends, he was supposed to let pass. People who wanted on stood around by his little trailer, some of them carrying hardhats. Other people were parking their cars and trucks in the open fields outside the barbwire on all four sides of the lease. With the wind walls and doghouses you couldn't see the rig floor from the ground. But people parked, sat, and stood everywhere they had an unobstructed view of the rig.

Celeste and Luz came at seven thirty to set up a VIP lounge in Joe's trailer. I saw Celeste have trouble squeezing her Escalade through the groups at the gate. Jan and Gerry followed behind in a Dogleg pickup and unloaded food and drink into the trailer with Luz's help.

The lease road wasn't built for two-way traffic. Gerry had to drive in the ditch to get around the line of waiting cars—and the jam got worse when Celeste took control at the entrance. She sent

Tommy out to turn cars around, organize parking, and screen vehicles trying to come up the road. I had a great view from the doghouse landing and caught parts of the drama as Celeste – who knew *everybody* – sifted through the crowd saying yes and no to people. It was mostly no for safety reasons, and that caused trouble. At one point she went to a tiered system where Joe's intimates were let into his trailer and B-list people were allowed to stand outside. Or sit – if they found an empty pallet or were smart and had brought folding chairs.

I didn't catch all the action because I was rushing around madly scrubbing. Emmet had just wanted certain areas clean, but Joe's friends might want to inspect his wildcat drilling operation and I thought things should be immaculate.

By eight o'clock there were problems closer to the rig.

The crowd kept growing and people started climbing through the barbwire, and there was no one to stop them except Emmet, Bud, and Gerry.

Since we weren't drilling, the directional hand was sleeping in his truck. He refused to get involved, though, when Emmet asked him to guard the back stairs. The rig floor had two sets of stairs. The back set was at the opposite corner from the front, between the offside doghouse and the drawworks. I was on my knees scrubbing the bottom stair when a guy, a stranger, appeared suddenly. It was a loud zone for the diesels so I didn't bother yelling. I jumped up and chased him along the mud pits with spritzes of soapy water. He ran smack into Emmet, who was trying to be everywhere. Emmet collared the guy and pointed to the nearest fence.

Watching the guy go, Emmet shoved his fists in his overalls. "I got a bad feelin about this here deal!"

"Don't be gloomy!"

Joe's death had hit Emmet hard: when I'd seen him at the house, I'd tried to be brave and cheerful for both of us. Now I waved my brush at the catwalk where we were standing. "I miss one tour and your rig's a disgrace!"

Emmet darted me an eye. "She's a proud ole gal! Make her shine for the visitors!"

"I'm done until I have to clean the floor! Is there anything I can do to stop the invasion?!"

"Run tell people I'll tap my air horn, let 'em know service's startin – tap it again when it's over!"

He headed off to check the east fence. I ran back to the stairs, grabbed my accouterments, and ran them and the hose down to the powerwasher. Going through the engine house, I found Bud patrolling the north fence. I told him what Emmet told me, asked him to pass the information along, then cut across the yard in between the racked drill collars and Bud's trailer.

The west side of the lease was popular – it and the south side had the best views. Outside the barbwire there were a couple hundred people bundled up for the cold, standing against the fence, sitting in lawn chairs or on the hoods of their cars or the tailgates of their trucks. I saw whole families and a big Latino contingent – and I saw a number of jackets and caps with the Balch logo. The old coots who'd told me the Okie jokes must've come early because they were sitting in the first row at the fence, wrapped in blankets and sharing a thermos.

Like most of the crowd they were respectfully quiet. I ran up to tell them about the air horn, asking them to pass it along. I asked the people nearby to do the same and, as I turned to run, saw Gerry talking to Doug behind Emmet's trailer down the fence. Waving, I jogged towards them, but they didn't recognize me in my filthy rig gear and hardhat.

I had to remove the safety glasses and get close before Doug's face changed. He and Gerry were finishing a conversation. Doug said something and Gerry replied, "I'll get on it," and took off.

I said, "What's Gerry doing? What happened with the search?"

We could talk freely because nobody was at the fence right there: Emmet's trailer blocked the view. Doug wore a ski jacket and Balch Oil hardhat. He was in high-serious cop mode and I knew there'd be no extraneous chitchat. He said:

"We found Joe's shotguns and rifles, several pounds of marijuana, an unregistered handgun, some crank. I left before sheriffs were done – I don't know if they found anything tying Trey to

Mills. They'll be here after the service to arrest him on an open charge – and arrest Alice. Wilson PD's on the way also. They have a tail on Bridges. We'll get him last."

Doug indicated the scene outside the barbwire. "I like this setup. Trey will think the police presence is for crowd control. I have Gerry organizing men to patrol the perimeter and guard access to the rig. Your guys are on Trey."

Gerry stuck his head around the trailer and signaled Doug he was needed. Squeezing my arm, Doug said, not smiling, "This is the white-knuckle portion of our flight."

He went off and I went to finish spreading the word about the air horn. I only got as far as the south fence. I ran into Gerry there again and he said he'd spread the word for me.

I checked the derrick.

Kyle was hanging out from the monkeyboard, latching the elevators on to another stand: they were still making up pipe. I ran to Joe's trailer. Alice and I hadn't spoken since the hospital but I was sure Evelyn would be up and I wanted to get the meeting over with. We hadn't been able to reach my father about coming. When he disappeared like that, he was usually twisted off.

Threading through the B-list, digging out my earplugs, I leaped onto the stoop and pulled the door open. Inside the trailer it was smoky, semi-crowded, and broiling hot. People were talking in low voices. I pulled off my hardhat and looked around, getting some strange stares. The trailer wasn't swank, in keeping with Joe's no-frills aesthetic, and the design was different from Emmet's. It had an open living room where Emmet had his office and storage room.

I didn't see my grandmother. Jean, in a black dress but wearing steel-toed boots, was deep in conference with Hilary Mahin. As head of Joe's foundation, she was running Balch Oil and Balch Drilling now. Ron Bray hovered close by, trying to eavesdrop on the conference. Audrey was there with her husband, and Cathy with hers, and more people I knew or had just met. Food had been laid out on the desk and Luz was in the tiny kitchen a yard from me, mixing drinks and serving coffee.

I said, "Where's Celestay?"

Luz ducked her head in the direction of the bedroom. She was all in black and her bun ribbon was black, and she hadn't been able to talk without crying since Tuesday night.

I walked back to the bedroom, excusing myself and trying not to brush people with my dirty coverall. A twin bed had been pushed against the wall to make space — it was piled with winter coats and hardhats. Celeste was talking to Caroline Mahin and Jan. Jan spotted me in the doorway and scowled, which made Celeste turn her head. Hugging both women, she walked over to me. Trey's tabby kitten was riding on her shoulder, claws dug into the fabric of her dress.

I said, "Sorry to interrupt but I was looking for Evelyn."

Celeste's eyes lit up at seeing me in roughneck gear but she could only manage one sad dimple. The last few days had been tough on her, between Joe and holding the line against Alice. She looked gorgeous anyway in swirly black silk — and rig boots — and hadn't neglected her makeup.

"Ann. You didn't actually think Evelyn would be here, did you? Joe was much too blue-collar for her, *much* too much. She was only polite to him while Jim was alive."

Reaching out to pull my sleeve, Celeste added, "You make a cute lease hand, darling."

I just dimpled at her. "Do we know why Alice agreed to have the memorial here? Where *is* Alice, by the way? Is she even coming? Didn't she swear she'd never set foot on a drilling rig?"

Celeste pointed to the trailer's south wall. "She's at the house writing Joe's eulogy. She intends to read it, she's informed us through Dex."

"She doesn't give up. Damn."

"I think she agreed because she thought the riffraff, as she calls them, of the county would come and turn it into a circus."

"Well, you should see it out there. There are hundreds of people and it's like a church only colder, with diesel engines."

Tears welled suddenly in Celeste's eyes. I pulled off a glove to pat her. Putting a black handkerchief to her nose, she said in a muffled voice, "Alice has to come – she has the ashes. She took them when we weren't looking."

As if feeling her distress, the kitten mewed. I started to lift it off her shoulder. "This belongs to one of the crew. I'll –"

"No, don't. I love carrying the little thing." Celeste scratched the kitten's head and it leaned into her fingers, purring.

I said, "Like the guy it belongs to. He's got pockets everywhere to carry animals."

"That reminds me of Junior." Celeste sniffed and dabbed her nose, attempting another dimple. "He was such a sweet boy. His pockets were always full of creatures. When Luz taught him to sew he made pouches himself in his –"

I went very still.

Trey was Ray Parkerworth Junior. Ray Parkerworth Junior was Trey.

Celeste may've been talking but I turned right around and left as the images flashed through my mind.

Alice opening the letter from Louisiana addressed to Joe. Alice destroying the letter from Louisiana. Alice flying to New Orleans herself and taking weeks to settle things. Trey not wanting to trip pipe beside Joe the night he killed Kenny Mills. Trey sleeping with his face covered in the doghouse. Trey hiding between trailers the morning OSHA questioned us and Joe was present. Trey living in Bakersfield, never drinking with the crew at the Dogleg. The cops not finding a trace of Ray Junior's death. Alice saying he died under a false name. Alice knowing Trey. Trey knowing Mark Bridges, Ray Junior's boozer-stoner-loser buddy.

Trey calling Joe "the old bastard."

I had to tell Doug!

Rushing out of the trailer, I vaulted the railing of the stoop and, dodging B-listers, started across the yard looking everywhere for Doug –

"Pup!"

Richie was crossing the yard towards me. "Where'd you go to?! Time to clean the floor! Put your hardhat on!"

"Find Doug for me, Richie! It's important! I need to speak to him now!"

Putting my hardhat on, I ran for the powerwasher. Someone had already pulled the hose up the back stairs.

I ran up to the rig floor and found Trey hosing. I grabbed the big broom and started pushing muddy water across to the pipe ramp.

The years and the oil fields had done a harsh number on Ray Parkerworth Junior. Not that he didn't deserve it. I'd only seen the one picture of him in the *Gusher* – a sullen, pimple-faced beanpole. The sullenness was still there and the people who knew him might've recognized that, or his voice, or signature stare. They certainly would've recognized the kitten-in-a-pouch motif. But I couldn't see teenage Ray Junior anywhere in the surly biker dude spraying soapy water in an orange coverall, with his prematurely lined face, beer gut, gray ponytail, and snake tattoos. His bulky muscles were disguising too, and most people wouldn't look past the beard and silver tooth. Was the tooth even real?

Steve. Had the orange coverall belonged to a Steve? Maybe that was Junior's name in Louisiana as a welder on offshore platforms. Or was he Steve in Wyoming, his supposed previous stop?

That letter from Louisiana: Was it Junior writing for a loan? He'd written other people for loans. He might've written Joe.

Wait a minute. Audrey said she called a funeral home in Louisiana for details of Ray Junior's death. So did the cops. How'd that work? Did Alice bribe them to lie?

I caught movement in the top doghouse. Kyle and Lynn, finishing sandwiches, were getting up to listen to Emmet as Richie joined them.

It hit me:

Kenny Mills died because he recognized Trey as Ray Junior.

Christmas Eve, Mills's first tour on, he said something and Trey/Ray bashed him with a hammer. I didn't believe for a minute it was self-defense. He and Mills were high-school buddies – they'd tried to rob the Dogleg together and done time as juveniles for it. Mills would've blown the whole plan: you couldn't trust a crankhead to keep that kind of secret.

But Mark Bridges was also Ray Junior's high-school buddy. Why was Bridges still alive? Was Trey squeamish about a second murder? Or were Trey and Bridges united in hating Joe, wanting to screw with his wildcat and getting paid to do it?

Trying to be cool, I looked around frantically.

Where was Doug?

34

THE DOOR OF THE top doghouse slid open and Richie stepped onto the floor and shouted, "Speed it up! They're coming!"

To Trey he said, "Crew's going down to get out of the way!" To me he said, "You're on the flow line!"

"Me?!"

"Emmet says you're family! Flow line!"

Stepping up close, I whispered in Richie's ear, "Find Doug!"

"Not now, Pup!"

He clanged the door shut and Trey and I mopped, spread the Floor-Dry, and broomed it off in record time. Going into the offside doghouse, I checked out the window down at the shale shakers: that's where the flow line dumped the drilling mud coming out of the hole. With the drillpipe in the slips, the pump was idling and no mud flowed.

Guests started arriving four at a time via the open-cage elevator. I watched them as they walked onto the floor. Everyone wore a hardhat and steel-toed boots, and they arranged themselves in a circle on the rubber safety mat around the rotary table. I'd double-scrubbed that mat with no discernible result: it was hopelessly stained with mud and oil. I counted forty people at least with Gerry and Jan, Audrey, Luz, Bud, Cathy, Mahin, Bray, their spouses, and more, including Joe's brothers, their wives, and adult kids.

I realized that with the rows of people I wouldn't be able to see the actual ceremony from where I was. Grabbing a short ladder, I set it up in the doorway of the doghouse and climbed onto the middle step. The view was perfect.

Last to appear were Celeste, Jean, Emmet, and Alice. Alice wore ostentatious widow's weeds in a Chanel cut, complete with black veil, and leaned theatrically on the arm of the lawyer, Dex. Dex looked like an actor anyway, tall and dignified, in a dark overcoat and hardhat. Alice had refused to wear a hardhat – probably rig boots too. I couldn't see her feet from my perch across the floor.

Something must've just happened.

The crowd opened to let the principals through and Celeste was looking furious, Jean in shock, and the lawyer appalled.

The veil hid Alice's face but she was clutching a sheet of paper and an old cowboy boot that belonged to Joe. Emmet, in the rear, stopped to tap a short blast on the air horn. Celeste used the diversion to suddenly snatch the cowboy boot away from Alice. Celeste was my new hero. Everyone saw her do it – there was a collective gasp, which I didn't hear because of the diesels. Alice lunged for the boot and Dex restrained her as Celeste gave the boot to Emmet. Gripping Alice's arm, the lawyer spoke into her ear. Alice stopped struggling but her angry breath puffed the veil in and out.

Over the engine noise, Celeste shouted, "Jeannie would like Emmet to say a few words!"

Faces went immediately solemn. Emmet passed through the crowd with the cowboy boot. Stepping up to the drillpipe he said in his quiet-loud rig voice:

"We will now pray."

He bowed his head and shut his eyes. Everyone except Alice bowed with him. I bowed my head but kept my eyes open to watch Alice.

There was no movement in the crowd and no sound the roar of the engines didn't drown out. The rig floor was bright under the lights, and holding still like that, you could really smell the cold winter air, the cold steel and cold grease. After a minute Emmet opened his eyes and glanced around, waiting for everyone to finish praying and look at him.

With his left hand he opened the valve that was screwed into the top of the tool joint. With his right, he tilted Joe's cowboy boot and slowly poured a stream of ashes down the pipe. When the ashes ran out, he twisted the valve shut and looked past the derrick into the night.

"Joe Balch," he said. "Oil man."

The guys in the crowd were stony-faced—most of the women were crying. I was all cried out, but I'd misted up the inside of my safety glasses.

Looking down again, Emmet tapped the drillpipe. "Safe trip, old friend. See you over there."

Celeste sobbed once and clung to Jean. Jean was blowing her nose into a handkerchief. I wiped my eyes under the glasses and remembered the flow line. Jumping off the ladder I ran into the doghouse to check out the window—

Holy shit!

Mud was spewing out with such force it was gushing horizontally, straight over the shakers and over the pits!

No panic: I knew not to panic. This is what blowout preventers were for. But I could feel my heart beating faster.

Quickly I walked back to the ladder, stepped up, and waved to get Emmet's attention. He saw me over the heads. Pointing at the flow line, I mouthed, *We're taking a kick! A kick!* I showed him how bad a kick by shooting one arm out straight.

Granite calm, Emmet blinked me a nod and said, "I need everybody off the floor now!"

People turned and started to move for the elevator, but Alice must've seen me wave. Throwing her veil up, she shrieked, *"The well is kicking! Run for your lives!"*

Panic broke right out.

The crowd, knowing rigs, switched directions and rushed for the front stairs. But the steel floor was slick and someone slipped, and someone else fell over him, and suddenly there was no order as people tried to help people up or tried to get around people who

304

were down. Emmet waded through the pandemonium, trying to reach the driller's console to call the hands. I saw Gerry get to the air horn first and blast the signal for a BOP drill.

Realizing what I could do, I leaped off the ladder and ran across the floor, calling, "Stay calm! It's under control! There are back stairs!"

I grabbed the two closest people, dragged them by their coats past the drawworks, and pushed them. I ran, grabbed somebody else, and pushed him at the back stairs. A bottleneck developed by the top doghouse as people piled for the front stairs. I grabbed two more people and twirled them around, saying, "Stay calm! There are back stairs! Past the drawworks! Back stairs!"

Meanwhile Gerry had plowed into the bottleneck, wedging a passage for Emmet, who was elbowing and shoving without mercy.

"Out the way! I need the remote!"

The machine that worked the accumulator by remote control sat on the landing outside the top doghouse.

Repeating, "Stay calm! It's under control!" I pulled people out of Emmet's way, spun them around, and pushed them towards the back stairs. Someone, Hilary Mahin, slipped on the mat by the rotary table. His wife helped him get up again and they both trotted for the back stairs.

I grabbed Luz and somebody and pushed them across the floor. "Back stairs! Be careful, it's —"

I stopped, holding my breath, hearing something through the noise. Pops — one-two-three-four-five-six — that sounded like gunshots.

And I was starting to smell gas.

Emmet shouted, "No pressure in the remote! Sumbitch cut my hoses!"

The bottleneck on the landing had miraculously cleared. Emmet looked over the railing into the yard and bellowed:

"Where's my motorman at? Where's Lynn? No one on the koomey! Teach!!"

I'd seen BOP drills. Without a thought, I sprinted to the landing and ran headlong down the front stairs, three at a time, sliding down the handrails with my gloves. In a blur, around the edges of the lease, I could sense action and emotion, people running, cars moving. But my heart was pounding in my ears and all I could see clearly was the bright red accumulator ahead of me.

Suddenly the koomey's warning light started to spin and an alarm went off with a high-pitched squeal. I raced to throw the levers, bam, bam, bam, bam, to close the rams on the BOPs, and looked at the gauges, already knowing it was too late. The koomey had no pressure too.

Emmet came lumbering down the front stairs. *"Get away from here, little sister! Bastard cooked us!"*

The smell of gas was getting stronger and stronger. Something twitched on the ground behind the koomey — a knee, a leg in a raspberry coverall. I ran around to see. Kyle lay in a spreading pool of hydraulic oil. I could see holes, surgical holes, *bullet holes,* in some of the koomey lines. Oil was pouring out, pumped out under pressure since I'd thrown the levers.

Kyle was trying to roll over. I squatted down to help him, panting, "Come on, Kyle, we have to go!"

In pain, Kyle lifted one hand and pointed across the yard at the mud logger's trailer. I twisted around and saw Bud fly out the door, do a flip over the railing, and land in the gravel in a heap.

"I got you, son!"

Emmet lifted Kyle as I jumped up and raced over to Bud, told him to run, and kept running. Leaping onto his stoop, I burst in the open door. The place was a shambles, desk drawers flung out, geology stuff all over, and Trey and Alice were wrestling for Minerva's logs.

Alice screamed, *"I want them! They're mine!"*

Trey yanked the logs out of her grip, turned, and saw me in the doorway. Like lightning, he whipped a hand inside his coverall and pulled out a gun and aimed it straight at me.

35

M Y MIND STOPPED. My breath stopped. I got completely calm and the whole world got very, very silent.

Slowly I raised my hands to show Trey they were empty. Alice was frozen, a blond black crone, watching us. And then –

The lights went out all over the lease.

The trailer, the derrick, the yard: suddenly pitch-dark. Bud's heater and fridge died. We stood there motionless and heard the diesel engines whine down . . . cough . . . and stop.

No lights, no engines. That was eerie. They'd turned everything off to prevent a spark.

Now the silence was real . . . except for the faint noise of splashing mud and a fainter noise of voices on the wind.

Sounding weird in the quiet, I said, "Whatever you do, Trey, don't shoot. There's gas."

We could all smell it.

My eyes were adjusting and moonlight was enough to see Trey start to lower the gun –

"Those logs are mine!"

Alice sprang for Trey, Trey charged at me, and the gun went off. The bullet zinged past my head and out the trailer door.

A split second later an explosion knocked us sprawling.

A ball of fire came hurtling towards the trailer, melting heat like a blast furnace. I dropped to the floor, scared shitless, sure I was about to incinerate. Suddenly the ball of fire sucked backwards in a huge gust of hot wind, sucked down under the rig, and shot straight up through the floor and derrick in a spectacular, volcanic pillar of flame. The sudden roaring and pounding was like a million freight trains and the light was blindingly bright.

I lay on the floor blocking the doorway. My hearing was wonky, like muffled, and I felt heavy, like the air was pressing me down.

Turning my head away from the light, I felt the heat singe my hair and shoulders. The skin of my face already felt burned. I'd lost my hardhat. But inches from my hand was the gun.

I could see Alice. She was under Bud's worktable, moaning, smashed against the wall in an unnatural position.

Trey I could not see. He was behind me somewhere.

Stretching out my fingers I could just touch the gun's barrel. A boot stepped on my wrist and pinned it. I looked up. Trey was standing above me, still holding the stack of well logs. He bent down, grabbed the gun, stepped over me, and walked out. Raising up partway, I swiped at his ankle to try and stop him –

"Where you think you's goin?!"

Emmet – right outside the trailer.

Gravel crunched and something hit the trailer wall with a thud. I heard metal clang, a thud, a grunt, another thud, and gravel. It sounded like a happy ending. Raising all the way up, I crawled on hands and knees out to the stoop. The heat was so intense I was instantly drenched in sweat.

Doug and half the county's law enforcement were ringed around, gazing down at Trey.

He was lying in the yard unconscious. His mouth was bloody and Emmet was kneading his fist, wiping it on his overalls. The gun had been flung out a ways and a deputy stood guarding it. Bud got down to gather up the logs as I shouted over the burning well:

"Ray Parkerworth Junior!"

I saw Doug nod.

"Don't give a good goddamn it's Lazarus hisself raised from the dead!"

Emmet hauled off and gave Trey a stiff kick. The cops didn't move a muscle to stop him.

Grasping the door frame, I pulled myself up to standing. My head felt woozy and my legs were shaking badly. It felt like I'd soaked two layers of clothes with fear sweat. Doug jumped on the stoop to come prop me up.

"Are you hurt?!"

I shook my head.

"You wild woman! Second to last off the floor!"

I just gave him a shaky smile. "Did Bud tell you Alice is in there?! She was trying to steal the logs! She *is* hurt!"

Turning to a sheriffs' detective, Doug shouted, "Scott! Mrs. Balch is inside the trailer!"

The detective trotted up and we squeezed over to let him get past us and go inside.

Emmet said, "Better get on out of here! Heat'll melt them rubber seals and that fuel tank'll go!"

He pointed at the blue metal tank that held the diesel fuel. It sat across from Bud's, close to the rig.

From inside the trailer came Alice's outraged voice. "You are *not* arresting me! I am returning to Los Angeles! I have a houseguest!"

Three cops bent down and grabbed Trey's shoulders and boots to pick him up and carry him off. He was out cold.

Doug wrapped his arm around my waist and steered us down the steps. I was actually okay but I liked being helped. The roaring, blazing well was a jillion times louder than the diesel engines ever were. It was a percussive beating in the earth and the air and everywhere in your body.

I looked around the lease.

The fireball had blistered paint on the rig, the row of steel houses, the mud pits, the trailers, and the parked trucks, including Trey's brand-new one. The ground in places was scorched black and the derrick's white was turning black.

I remembered discussing the sabotage with Emmet and him saying, "It's Mother Nature what decides in the end." Nobody could predict a kick or make one happen. But Trey took full advantage of this one. I bet he'd already cut the hoses on the remote, then when he heard the air horn and saw people evacuating the floor, he shot the koomey lines.

I said, "Is everyone okay? Where are Celeste and Jean and Luz? Do they know who Trey is?"

Doug had steered us around behind Bud's trailer, up to the west fence. He held two strands of barbwire wide for me to climb through and climbed through himself. Indicating the field south of the lease he said, "Everyone's shaken up but they're fine. We haven't told them about Trey – they've had enough for right now."

"How did you find out?"

"Sheriffs' search turned up identification in his name. I'd suspected it for a while."

The flames lit the sky and sent our shadows jerking across the dirt field. It was so bright out there you could see like daytime. Looking west, I saw there were a lot a *lot* of people. They hadn't gone home. They'd moved their cars and trucks and themselves waaay back into the field and were standing, some covering their ears, watching the unholy column of fire.

I suddenly realized I didn't know what'd happened to the rest of the crew.

Checking around, I saw Emmet behind us in the field, walking off by himself. I told Doug, "I need to speak to my toolpusher."

Emmet stopped and turned to face the rig.

I jogged over to where he stood. He'd taken off his jean jacket and had his fists jammed in the pockets of his overalls. I noticed that his cheeks were shiny wet and I thought he was sweating. We were all sweating from the heat, even at that distance from the rig. It wasn't sweat on Emmet, though. He was crying. He hadn't cried when Joe died, and now tears were streaming down his face.

He said, looking at the rig, "Not no more – but was a time we had a manual close on them BOPs."

His voice was its normal rumble – he wasn't choked up. I stuck my hands in my coveralls and watched the rig with him.

"Quick thinkin there. You done good." He dipped his head forward a bare inch.

310

"No thinking involved—it was reflex. Did the guys get out, Richie and Lynn? Are they all right?"

Emmet nodded a non-nod.

"Have you called for help?"

I got another non-nod as I racked my brain for some way to comfort him.

"The good news is we found Joe's gas!"

Emmet squinted up at the flames. They were shooting high above the crown of the derrick. The steel was already starting to soften and the derrick was starting to sag.

He didn't answer, but the roaring was loud and I was on his deafer side. I raised my voice. *We found Joe's—*"

"Ain't ours, little sister—we's thousands of feet from TD."

Emmet thought about it, and then murmphed.

"Might could be maybe though. Too soon to say."